FOR *the* RECORD

Christine,
I give you
the stars!

KA Lunde

Also by K.A. Linde

FOR *the* RECORD

RECORD SERIES BOOK 3

K.A. LINDE

Montlake
Romance

Text copyright © 2014 K.A. Linde
All rights reserved.

Published by Montlake Romance, Seattle

www.apub.com

Amazon, the Amazon logo, and Montlake Romance are trademarks of Amazon.com, Inc., or its affiliates.

ISBN-13: 9781477825907
ISBN-10: 1477825908

Cover Design: Laura Klynstra

Cover Image: MaeIDesign

Library of Congress Control Number: 2014908877

Printed in the United States of America

To the Campaign.
For the hardest and best times.

Chapter 1

JUST THE BEGINNING

Time stood still as Liz Dougherty stared out at the crowd of reporters visible through the backstage curtain. It was hard to believe that just a year and a half ago she had stood on the other side of the stage for the first time. Brady Maxwell had been announcing his run for Congress and she was covering the event for her paper, and now she was standing with him as he was about to announce their relationship to the world only months before her college graduation date.

His fingers laced with hers and he squeezed gently, giving her the reminder and reassurance that his presence already brought to her. Liz looked up into his handsome face, admiring the strong jawline, the confident dark brown eyes, the perfectly put together hair, and the full lips that drove her crazy. She loved this man.

"We'll get through this," he whispered.

"I know." She sent him a soft smile.

We'll get through this wasn't exactly the comfort she had been looking for, but she knew *everything will be okay* was a lie. Brady didn't make promises that he couldn't keep, and neither of them knew if everything really would be okay.

The workers backstage gave them a wide berth as they went about their business. She and Brady had been briefed and rebriefed until Liz had gotten a headache from it all. She took it in stride, though. She knew how to address reporters, considering she was one.

To everyone else, Brady probably looked completely in control. He always was. But she knew that he was worried. Not necessarily about himself or what this would do to his career at the moment. He was more confident now that he had taken control of the situation and was handling it in the way he knew how. But his brown eyes betrayed that he was nervous about how Liz would take it.

Only time would tell what would happen, just like time was what they had needed to find their way back to each other. The only thing Liz knew for certain was that she wanted to make this work.

"Heather will introduce me. I'll give a speech. No questions. Just a short statement, and then I'll be back with you," he told her in that confidently casual manner only he could manage.

"Brady, I know. Heather and Elliott have drilled it into my head," Liz said. Brady's press secretary and lawyer didn't exactly see eye to eye with Liz on everything, but she trusted them enough to get her through one press conference. "I'm not even the one speaking. Worry about yourself."

"Nothing to worry about. I do this every day."

"And I've been on the other side dozens of times. I can handle standing backstage for one press conference." She gave him another small smile. She didn't need people to keep telling her what was going to happen. She was nervous enough without the reminder meant to placate her. She took a deep breath and tugged on the necklace dangling around her neck. Brady had given it to her when they had first been together, and it felt comforting to have it hanging there now. She hadn't worn it since he had been elected to office.

"I know you can. I just want you to be prepared for the reactions," Brady said, running his thumb up and down her hand. "People aren't going to be kind about our situation."

Liz sighed softly. "Do you think we could be alone for a minute?" she asked, giving him a pointed stare. *Alone. Hint. Hint.*

"I have to be onstage," he reminded her.

"Soon. Heather hasn't even made her announcement. I just need a minute."

"I'd say I generally need more than a minute, Liz," he said, his signature smirk crossing his face.

Liz couldn't help but chuckle. "Maybe more than a minute. That's a way to make the headlines. 'Congressman Maxwell's Affair Confirmed, Caught Having Sex in Backstage Bathroom.'"

"Don't tempt me," he said. His eyes were already darting around the room as he calculated how much time they had.

Liz ducked her head down and looked up at him through her thick black lashes. "Please, Brady."

"Oh, you know how much I like when you beg." Brady immediately started walking toward a small back room. Not a bathroom, at least. That was a relief.

There were a few people in the room crowding around a computer monitor and talking among themselves. Brady's appearance made them jump out of their seats. "How can we help you, Congressman Maxwell?" the first guy asked.

"I require the use of this room prior to my speech." He gave them an easy smile, but he might as well have threatened them, the way they jumped to leave. It was a bit strange to watch this side of Brady compared to the way he was with her when they were alone.

He still had an air of authority that never left, but they were equals in their love. This was all power.

And she found power immensely attractive.

As soon as the door was closed and locked, Brady had her back pressed into the wall, and his lips moved from her mouth to her ear down her neck. God, she couldn't get enough of him and he was only kissing her. It was intoxicating. She had no idea how she had lived in that interminable purgatory without him.

It had been less than twenty-four hours since they had officially come out to Calleigh Hollingsworth, the reporter at the *Charlotte Times* who had broken the story along with Liz's ex-boyfriend, Hayden Lane, yet they couldn't keep their hands off of each other. Liz certainly felt as if they had a lot of time to make up for, and the way Brady's hands were traveling down her dress made it seem he had the same idea.

Reckless or not, Liz wanted Brady . . . and she wanted him right now.

"God, baby, I missed you," Brady groaned.

"You've been with me all morning," she teased.

"Not the way I wanted." He pulled her back from the wall and walked her toward a chair that he kicked out from under the table. His eyes were full of mischief as he started undoing his pants. "We don't have much time."

"You're serious?" she asked, a bit surprised that he wanted to go through with this right here, right now. But Brady wasn't someone to deny himself what he wanted. And there wasn't any *real* danger of them getting caught. At least . . . not by a reporter, which was all that mattered.

Plus . . . she had never been good at turning him down, and her body was already aching for him.

Brady smirked at her. "Baby, I never joke about wanting you." His loosed himself from his boxer briefs and took a seat facing her.

She took a step toward him and his hands moved to the hem of her modest knee-length skirt. Pushing it up around her waist, he tugged her thong off and moved her so that she straddled him.

Her heart was already racing. It hadn't been long since they had been together at Brady's lake house, but already she couldn't get enough of him. Every time she was with him it was a new unbelievable experience. Every time was better than the last. Every time reminded her that it was worth it to be with him. In the end, he was what made her happy.

Brady moved her hips so that she was hovering over him and she leaned forward so her hands rested on his shoulders. She wanted to grab on to his hair and use it for leverage, but thought that might be a dead giveaway when they left.

Her head tilted back when she felt him enter her. A moan got caught in her throat as he pushed her body the rest of the way onto his dick. "Oh, God," she murmured.

His thumb trailed along her bottom lip and her tongue flicked out and licked it. Fire lit up his eyes. He shifted his pelvis up and she groaned again. His hand covered her mouth. "Not a word, baby."

And he then proceeded to make that practically impossible. He gripped her hips in his hands and started moving her up and down on him. The quick, rough rhythm he started coupled with the uncertainty of how long they had before someone came looking for them pushed her to the edge. She bit down on her lip hard to keep back the moans and screams that she wanted to let loose. As Brady hit the right spot over and over again, she couldn't hold back anymore, and so she covered her mouth with his.

Their lips moved in time. It was a frenzy of heated bodies and scorching kisses and passion that nothing else rivaled. Liz felt her climax hit and she gasped against his lips as she throbbed with pleasure. Brady finished after her and they sat there for a minute, reveling in their stolen moment.

And then they heard the knock at the door.

Liz scrambled backward off of him and lunged for her underwear. Brady stood casually, adjusted himself, and righted his suit. He didn't look like anything had happened at all, aside from the lazy smile that crossed his face. As she rushed to put her underwear back on, Brady snatched them out of her hand and stuffed them into his pocket.

"What are you doing?" she hissed.

"Go without them."

"Brady," she groaned.

"I want to be onstage imagining you ready and waiting for me again."

"You're going to get yourself all turned on while onstage," she pointed out, snaking her hand down his arm and trying to get to his pocket.

He yanked her close again. "It's worth it."

She stared up at him intently. Blue meeting brown with an unparalleled intensity. "You're worth this," she whispered.

Worth coming out about their relationship. Worth dealing with the reporters. Worth giving up her privacy. He was worth everything. A soft smile crossed his lips as he seemed to understand what exactly she was saying, and then he dropped a sensual kiss on her lips.

A promise. He'd make sure she was right.

"Brady!" they heard Heather call from the other side of the wall.

He smirked at Liz before unlocking and opening the door. "Heather, we were just coming to see you," he said casually.

"Brady," she groaned, shaking her head. She assessed him top to bottom. "You can't do this already. You're going to drive me batshit crazy."

"This is different than normal?" he joked.

Her voice lowered and she glared at both of them. "I don't even want to know what was going on in here. I can only imagine. Can't you at *least* wait until we get back . . . or something?"

"Don't know what you mean, Heather," Brady said, crossing his arms. "Don't I have a speech to give?" He grabbed Liz's hand and started walking out of the back room.

Heather dropped in easily at his side and started going over the speech as if nothing had happened. Liz suspected that meant they would be getting shit later for going off like that. Checking out her cell phone, she realized they had been cutting it close. She dropped her phone back into her purse, and her eyes darted around the room for a bathroom.

But Heather grabbed Liz's attention again. "Please stand right here and *do not* move again."

"I'm not a child, Heather," Liz snapped.

"Then perhaps you should take this more seriously," she snapped right back. "You're a liability, and sneaking off and doing . . . whatever you were doing is not helping anything."

"Heather," Brady said, his voice dangerously low.

Heather straightened considerably and seemed to realize that Brady was right there. Oh, this was going to be fun.

"Just getting everything in order," she said coolly. Yeah, Heather was not happy. She was probably worried that her perfect candidate was now involved in a scandal with a college political reporter who had written negative articles about him. Not to mention that she and Brady had been *caught* and their names smeared across the front headline of newspapers all weekend.

Heather's job was partly damage control. And Liz was the damage. Liz understood why Heather would act like this, but it didn't mean she had to stand for it. Heather took one last look at Liz before walking over to Elliott.

"She's such a bitch," Liz grumbled.

"She means well, but yeah . . . it's kind of her job," Brady said. "She just has to get used to us being together. I think she thinks this is a ploy."

"If she thinks that, then others will too."

"I intend to quell those responses before they get off the ground. You're here to stay."

His voice was so commanding that Liz had no room to doubt him. He didn't have to keep her around. After she had left him at his primary victory to ensure that he won the election, she had spent the next year with Hayden. She had never gotten over Brady, and their time apart had been sprinkled with sexually charged meetings and soul-crushing departures. The fact that they were here at all was a testament to their dedication to each other.

A minute later, Heather walked primly out onstage. She was tall, blond, and beautiful, with self-assurance that skyrocketed when she was onstage. Liz remembered being jealous of her trim figure. Not that Liz was big, but she was a bit more athletically built, with a large chest.

"Thank you so much for attending this last-minute press conference," Heather trilled. "I'm Heather Ferrington, Representative Maxwell's press secretary. No questions will follow the Congressman's announcement."

The crowd erupted into outrage. Liz didn't really blame them. She was sure Brady was going to get bombarded whether he wanted questions or not. That's what she would have done. Liz had suggested that Brady take a few questions to keep the reporters from revolting, but Heather would hear none of it. She wanted to control the message that got out. Apparently it was bad enough that Liz had already spoken to Calleigh when confronted about being the elusive Sandy Carmichael, Liz's pseudonym.

Heather sent them a scathing look. "No questions," she repeated. "The Congressman will be out in a minute. Thank you for your patience."

She walked back toward Liz and Brady stiffly. Liz was glad that she wasn't the one dealing with the brunt of that backlash right now. Though . . . she knew she would have to eventually.

Heather blew out a slow breath when she got back to Brady. "Just stick to the script." He nodded. His face grim for a second before returning to the neutral campaign mask Liz was used to seeing on his face. "And, Brady . . . good luck."

He gripped her arm softly. They had been working together since his career began and had a bond that came with spending an exorbitant amount of time with each other. After he dropped his hand, he turned back to face Liz. No one could see them backstage, but it still sent a nervous thrill through her system when his eyes were set solely on her.

"Still worth it?" he asked.

Liz nodded. "Always will be."

Brady leaned down and kissed her once more tenderly on the lips. Then he was striding across the small stage and to the podium as if he owned it. And he did. He always did. Brady was more comfortable on a stage in front of a crowd of rabid reporters foaming at the mouth than most people were in their daily lives. He kept that confident smile plastered on his face, swagger in his step, and gave off the air of a born-and-bred politician.

He adjusted the blue tie at his neck. It was his unspoken cue that he was ready to begin. Liz held her breath, and silence lingered heavily in the room as reporters leaned forward, anxious for what was to come.

"Thank you all for being here on such short notice. I'm sure you're curious about the recent allegations against my character.

And I'm here today to set the record straight." Brady paused, and Liz watched all the hungry expressions on the reporters' faces. "Politicians in the public eye are frequently held to a higher standard. We're expected to be impenetrable. We're expected to be superhuman. Every fault, every stumble, every hurdle we have to cross is open and accessible to the public. It is the life we chose, *I* chose, when I was sworn into office. It is a life I would trade for nothing, because it gives me the opportunity to work for the people I care about, to work for the citizens of this great nation."

Brady, easing into his speech, now smiled charismatically. Liz hadn't realized the knot of nerves that had gnarled up between them was so intense until it started to unravel.

"As you can imagine that life, this life, comes with limitations. And limitations are the last things politicians tend to talk about. But after the news that hit headlines this weekend, I feel as if it is my place to address one of these limitations. One of these, well, to be frank, ladies and gentlemen, have you ever considered how difficult it must be to *date* while helping to run the country?"

Brady leveled an amused look at them. The crowd chuckled at his statement, feeding into his speech. Good.

"An article ran in the *Charlotte Times* newspaper on Friday claiming that I had an affair with a university reporter, Sandy Carmichael, who I have since confirmed is Liz Dougherty. As a bachelor, I find it hard to reconcile myself with the word *affair*. While what happened between Ms. Dougherty and myself *was* kept from the public, it hardly constitutes an affair. It was my attempt to keep one aspect of my life private. I still *strongly* believe that what happened between us should remain between us, but I also understand the delicate position I find myself in. I did not come out about my relationship with Ms. Dougherty for any other reason than privacy concerns."

Liz sucked in the air she hadn't realized she had been without. That was the hardest part . . . hearing him discuss privacy as if they would ever be afforded it again.

"Privacy issues seem no longer to be a concern, though, and the very last thing I would want to see happen is for Ms. Dougherty's name to be smeared for being associated with me. After speaking with Ms. Dougherty," Brady said, his eyes darting to Liz briefly, "we have agreed that it no longer makes sense to hide our relationship. The article was only false in that it did not address the fact that Liz Dougherty and I are currently together."

Oh God . . . it was really happening. Liz felt tears well in her eyes. She had been the one to confess to Calleigh about their relationship, but hearing Brady say it to a room of reporters somehow made it all seem so much more real.

"It might have begun in secret, but from this day forward, we would like to make it clear that is no longer the case. Thank you so much for your time. I look forward to seeing many of you again."

Brady gave the reporters a warm smile and a curt nod before turning to go. And then the room exploded. Reporters pushed forward against the small stage, demanding to ask questions.

"But what of the age discrepancy?"

"What will your opponents think of the negative articles she wrote about you, Congressman Maxwell?"

"Representative Maxwell, just one question!"

"Congressman, can you comment on the use of a fake name to hide Ms. Dougherty's identity?"

"What else are you hiding?"

"Is this all a stunt from the campaign to cover up your sexual exploits?"

And on and on.

Liz had been expecting it. Even if Heather hadn't prepared her for the onslaught of questions, she would have guessed this would happen. She had been preparing long enough to be a reporter that she knew firsthand what that was like. She even knew which questions she would have asked. But none of that made it any easier. Her stomach flipped and she felt queasy as the reporters added insult to injury.

She turned away and tried to tune out the madness. She breathed in and out slowly and imagined herself back at Brady's lake house in the peace and quiet. The only thing they'd had was each other's company.

Brady wrapped an arm around her waist when he reached backstage and started walking her away from the stage without a word. He was trying to protect her. This was just the beginning, and he knew it as much as she did.

Chapter 2

BACKLASH

Perfectly done," Heather said, complimenting Brady as they walked toward the rear exit.

"I'm not sure that stymied any of their concerns," Brady said casually, as if none of this affected him. But of course, Liz knew that it did.

There was still much to figure out. Now that their relationship had gone public it hardly meant their problems were over.

"You didn't expect them to," Elliott, Brady's lawyer, cut in. "It's out there now. We go from here."

"Alex is back on board and wants to discuss strategy at noon," Heather said, talking about Brady's campaign manager. "Then we'll get the speech writer working on something for when you have to talk publicly. We want to keep the whole thing on message. We'll need to brief the staff. I don't want anyone talking to the press. I want them aware that if they do, it will come at the expense of their job."

Liz swallowed at that comment. She didn't want anyone risking their job. Though most political staff should know when to speak and when not to. It was just surreal being on the other side and having someone tell her when *not* to speak to the press, instead of Liz looking for opportunities to get people to talk.

"I think we can clear all of that up by this afternoon and then get you back in D.C. by nightfall. Your secretary informed me that there's an important vote coming up this week on education and you need to be in committee despite what is happening in your personal life," Heather droned on.

"Wait!" Liz spoke up, finally hearing exactly what Heather had just said. "You're going back to D.C. *tonight?*"

She knew that his job, his life as a member of Congress was split between Chapel Hill and D.C. It wasn't split equally, though. If she had to guess, from what she knew it was a seventy-thirty split, with more time in D.C. than at home. Still, she didn't think he would leave her that *same* day.

"He has to go back tonight," Heather said, not even looking up from the papers in her hands.

Brady turned to face Liz. She had put up with a lot since this had all exploded in her face, and she had known from the start they would have less time together. But she had broken up with her boyfriend, started dating Brady again, and had now officially announced their relationship to a sea of reporters. She damn well deserved a little more time with him before she was fed to the wolves.

"You're not reconsidering, are you?" he asked in a tone that made it clear that that was an unacceptable option.

"No, I'm not reconsidering. I'm wondering why in the midst of this madness I'm going to be left all alone to deal." Her voice was calm and controlled. She didn't want to sound whiny. She knew what she was getting into, but she had thought one more night wasn't too much to ask.

"You won't be alone, and you won't be dealing alone. Even if I'm not here, I'm still available to you."

"You make it sound like a business arrangement."

Brady's eyes turned molten. "You're the last person who would think it was."

Liz took a deep breath to try to calm herself down. She was working herself up and it wasn't going to help anything. "I know. I'm sorry. I just . . . we haven't had much time together."

"Sorry to interrupt," Heather said. She looked as if she was anything but sorry. "We have to get you out to the car now. We're expecting a bit of a holdup."

"We'll discuss this in the car," Brady said, squeezing her waist and then releasing her.

Liz wondered what exactly "a bit of a holdup" looked like.

It seemed that Heather's definition and Liz's were drastically different. A large number of the reporters had come around to the back entrance, where it was clear Brady was going to be leaving, and had swarmed the area to ask questions. Liz stared at the onslaught with her eyes wide.

Brady draped an arm protectively around her shoulders as soon as the door opened. "Stick close to me," he whispered against her hair.

She didn't need to be told twice. Actually she probably didn't need to be told once. Heather and Elliott cleared some space for them to walk through and then she and Brady were outside. It was a bleak February afternoon, completely overcast as they pushed through a sea of reporters to get to the waiting car beyond.

Liz heard the questions thrown at them, similar to the ones she had heard in the conference room. Cameras flashed overhead, people called out her name, microphones were thrust in her face. Liz did everything she could just to keep her head down and follow Brady's lead.

Elliott held the door open and Liz slunk into the backseat of the dark tinted town car. She heard Brady address the crowd briefly before following her inside. The door shut and then they were moving.

"What about Heather and Elliott?" Liz asked softly.

"I told them to take the next car."

Liz was glad. It meant they had a few minutes of peace without Heather interrupting every conversation. It was just the two of them. Liz's hands shook in her lap and she hadn't even realized it. "That was . . . intense," she whispered.

"Are you all right?" Brady asked, reaching for her.

She slipped under his arm and leaned into his shoulder. "Yeah. I should have expected it."

"It'll get easier with time."

She kind of hoped it would never get easier and everything would just disappear. She had never wanted to be in the spotlight. Newspaper journalism had been her chosen field in part because it ensured that she would never have to be in front of a camera. Didn't look like she was going to get off so easy.

Brady chuckled at her expression. "My reporter afraid of some camera time?"

It was like he had read her mind. "I'm not a fan."

"Well, hopefully you won't spend much time dealing with it."

"Agreed," she said softly. "So, do you really have to leave tonight?"

"Under the circumstances it would probably look better for me to continue about my business as if nothing were wrong. I wouldn't want to look like I needed to take time off."

"Well, that makes sense . . . but considering the circumstances, being your new girlfriend who you hadn't seen in over a year apart from this weekend and one night in October, I thought you could make an exception."

"You're my exception, Liz," he said, trailing his hand down her jaw.

Her eyes fluttered closed, all thoughts of what had just occurred flying out of her head. One simple touch and she was lost to him. It had been like that since the beginning. She hadn't been able to get enough, hardly been able to say no, found it impossible to stay away. Even when she had forced herself to walk out of his life, she had still thought about him all the time.

She tilted her head up to him and their lips met. It was like a dose of medicine for her system. His hand slid up her thigh, reminding her of their earlier exploits and the fact that she was still without underwear.

"How do you do that to me?" she whispered.

"What?"

"Make me forget all sense."

"Are you saying we don't make sense?" he asked, trailing circles into her inner thigh and slowly spreading her legs.

"We make perfect sense," she said. "Aside from all the reporters trying to prove us wrong."

"Someone is always trying to prove something." His hand brushed up against her sex and her grip on him tightened. "Like I'm trying to prove that I actually can keep you quiet for a few minutes."

"I think you did that earlier," Liz said with a smirk of her own. His finger swirled around her clit and she gasped at how sensitive she was. She tried to remain silent as he worked on her on the drive.

Dark-tinted glass separated them from the driver, but she still felt vaguely as if they were being watched. It should have kept her from getting completely turned on all over again, but it didn't. She was coming undone at the expertise of his fingers in the backseat of the town car.

When she felt like she might explode, he finally obliged her and delved two fingers inside her. He pumped into her a few times and it took every ounce of willpower not to cry out as he brought her to the point of ecstasy and then she tipped over the edge. She bit down on her lips and breathed heavily in and out as she came down from her orgasm. Her head was tilted back and her eyes closed.

Brady removed his hand from her. "Look, you can follow directions."

"Just barely," she whispered.

He kissed her again softly just as the car began to slow, signaling they were almost to their destination.

"Brady," Liz murmured. "Does that mean you'll stay?"

He laughed lightly and nodded when she looked at him. "Yes, baby. I'll move some things around."

—⊶—

Liz ducked her head. Unsurprisingly, Heather didn't like to hear that plans were changed. She had been a bitch to Liz ninety-five percent of the time Liz had known her, but the stress of the scandal was really pushing her over the edge. At one point, Brady even had Liz leave the room so they could talk. She could hear him and Heather arguing all the way down the hall.

They were at Brady's campaign headquarters in Raleigh. Liz wandered from the conference room where they were still arguing and down to his office. She closed the door and sat back in the over-size chair. With the computer booted up, Liz pulled up Google and steeled herself for what she was about to do. She typed in her name and then pressed Enter.

The top of the screen filled with a news tracker that updated as articles came in about her relationship with Brady. She clicked on one at random and skimmed the article. Words jumped out at her—affair, college student, reporter, scandal. She moved to the next article and the one after that and the one after that. After reading a handful of the same material she returned to the homepage and was surprised to see that a Wikipedia page came up under the search. She opened it and saw that someone had already added their relationship to the personal section of Brady's page. Great.

She was jolted from her search when the door opened. "Hey, you," Brady said with the same captivating smile. "What are you up to in here?"

"Torturing myself." He arched an eyebrow. "Just looking up news articles."

"That is never a good idea."

Liz tore her eyes away from Brady to stare at one of the last articles she had up on the screen. Someone had managed to get a relatively good picture of them together when they had fled the press conference.

Brady was at her side before she knew it. "Let me help you with that," he said, reaching over her shoulder, covering the mouse in her hand, and exiting out of all of the articles. "There, that's better."

"This was my life," she whispered. "I used to wake up and read news articles before going to class. I followed my favorites, legends in their fields, religiously. The time I wasn't reading articles, I was writing them. I lived at the newspaper. I took extra electives in the Journalism Department. Now I can't even open up the Internet."

"You can use the Internet, but Google searches of your name might not be the smartest idea right now."

"Yeah," she said with a shrug.

"It'll blow over. It won't always be like this," he said in a surprisingly reassuring voice. "Come here."

Liz stood up and then when Brady took her seat, he folded her into his lap. She kicked off her heels and tucked her legs underneath her.

"You can't do this."

"What?" Liz asked.

"Wallow."

"I'm not wallowing," she told him.

He raised his eyebrows. "You sure?"

She released a quick breath and then shrugged. "I guess."

"You know you're stronger than that."

"I survived life without you."

He smiled and kissed her forehead. "And you won't have to do that anymore. What's a few reporters after that?"

Liz nodded reluctantly. "You're right." She straightened and tried to put her fears behind her. There was really nothing she could do at this point. She had chosen Brady, and this was what came with that life. If she had to do it all over again, she would do the same damn thing.

"I usually am," he said, nuzzling her neck.

"Also incredibly modest."

"Oh, no, baby, I'd never claim that. You can reserve that for lesser men."

"I don't think I'm going to be seeing *any* other men. I like the egotistical one I already have."

"Egotistical, hmm?" He nipped at her neck and she felt her anxiety disappearing.

"Yep. Egotistical, arrogant, cocky . . ."

Brady gripped her hand and ran it along his dick. "You're right about one of those."

Liz giggled and stood. "You're insatiable, aren't you?"

His pupils dilated at the sight of her standing before him in the dress she had worn to the press conference. "I'm the only one, obviously."

"Oh, obviously," she joked, leaning forward and pressing their lips together. "How long before I can get you out of here?"

"Unfortunately it will still be a few hours."

"See? I have time to get to the newspaper," she told him. They had decided it might be best for her not to go to school the day of the press conference. But she couldn't stay away for much longer, since she was so close to graduating and needed the credits. She wasn't sure what was going on at the paper. She wanted to call Massey, who had been covering for Liz as editor while she had been sick last week after the poor way Hayden had taken the news about Brady, and find out what was going on. But she was a little worried about what she would find. The only people she had spoken to since all of this had hit the newspapers had been her parents and her best friend, Victoria.

The conversation with Victoria had been much more enjoyable than the one with her parents. They reminded Liz of all the fears she'd had when she had first agreed to going public. *What about your career? Will you finish school? How will this look going forward? Are you happy? Are you sure you want this?* Liz shut out the questions for now.

"I think you should give yourself more time. I'm not keeping you from the newspaper, Liz, but just imagine what it probably looks like right now," he said, giving her a knowing look.

Chaos. Gossips. Judgmental stares. She knew what was facing her, but the paper felt like home. It had always been her escape.

"I know what it will be like." Like the press conference but worse, because it was her peers, her coworkers, her friends. "I can't avoid it forever, though."

"No one would ever expect you to."

"I could have Victoria pick me up and get back there in an hour or so," Liz said stubbornly.

"I believe you would do it," he said. He crossed his arms over his chest and she read him like a book. He was daring her to do it and see how he would react. He had once thrown her over his shoulder without any hesitation because she wouldn't get in his car. That would be a hysterical headline: "Congressman Brady Maxwell Keeps New Girlfriend in Line Caveman Style." Oh, the backlash.

Liz sighed and cuddled back into Brady's lap. No use arguing right now. "How long will I have with you before you have to take me home?"

"Baby, you're mine now. I'm not letting you go home tonight." Brady turned her face up to him and she read what he was saying in his eyes.

"But I thought with the reporters hounding us . . ."

"They can hound us all they want, but if we're 'out' in public, you're staying with me," he said, kissing her lips lightly. "You still have the key. I've always belonged to you."

"I've always belonged to you too," she whispered.

Chapter 3
HEADLINES

Brady dropped Liz back off at her place the next morning before she had to be at the newspaper. He wasn't planning to leave North Carolina until late that night and promised to see her again before he left. She didn't like the fact that they would be separated so soon, but what else could she do? She had already delayed him an entire day. She just had to get used to their new relationship—only officially being together for three days and already out to the public while also dealing with long distance. All the best things in life rolled into one package.

Victoria was sitting on the couch with her boyfriend, Daniel, who Liz lovingly referred to as Duke Fan. "Hey," Liz said, closing the door and waving at the pair.

"Hey yourself," Victoria said. She jumped up off of the couch and rushed to Liz's side. "So how was it? What happened? Are you and Brady officially out of the closet now?"

Liz laughed and shook her head. "Have you not seen the news about it?" she asked incredulously.

Victoria just shrugged. "Psh! I don't watch or read the news. You know that."

"Ah. How could I forget? We went to a press conference yesterday and Brady told the whole world we were dating. We were basically mobbed on our way out of the place. It's kind of surreal."

"Oh my God, it's like you're a celebrity or something," Victoria said. "And dating a politician. I'm so jealous." Duke Fan huffed on the couch, causing Victoria to giggle and swish her hips. "So what happens now?"

"I think I try to go back to my life?" Liz said uncertainly.

"What? Somehow I thought this would come with more perks. Like you two eloping and moving to D.C. and going to a million fabulous parties *Great Gatsby* style."

Eloping! Where the hell did she come up with this stuff? They had just gotten together—marriage could wait.

"Pulling literary references out of your ass, Vickie."

"Ugh! Now that Hayden is gone can we drop the nickname?" she pleaded.

Liz dropped her smile almost immediately. Hayden. She hadn't had much time to think about him since he had attempted to apologize for ratting out her relationship with Brady and Liz had sent him packing. There had been too many other things going on, like Brady and the press and what the hell she was going to do with her life now that she was a political journalist dating a politician.

"Oh, sorry," she whispered.

"It's fine," Liz said. She didn't really want to talk about Hayden. Everything was too fresh after the breakup. A whole-year-long relationship down the drain for nothing.

"Well, don't feel guilty about what happened. He was the jackass who wrote the article. You didn't force his hand."

"I know. I know," Liz said, cutting her off. "I'm just going to get ready for class."

"All right. You sure you don't want to talk about it?"

"Very sure."

"Well, Daniel said he'd drop us off so we don't have to walk. Right?" Victoria asked. She turned toward her boyfriend with a smile.

"Sure thing, Vickie."

Victoria groaned and gave him a death glare. "Not you too!"

Liz couldn't keep from laughing. What a pair.

After changing into a loose, blue striped button-up tucked into a pair of skinny jeans, with dark heels, Liz tied her hair up into a messy bun and then followed Victoria and Daniel out to the car. They arrived on campus just in time for Liz to get to the newspaper before her class. Liz made plans with Victoria to walk home together, and then she crossed the busy street and in through the back door of the Union. She took the stairs up to the second floor and then rounded the corner to the newspaper office.

She stared at the office with a contented sigh. The newspaper was her sanctuary. She couldn't even count the number of times that she had walked through these double doors. It was like coming home when she walked into the office.

The paper had already gone out for the day and there were fewer students in the building as a result. That did not, however, mean that it was empty. Students milled around the desks looking over articles, rehashing articles from the morning, drinking coffee, some even frantically working on homework. She even caught a glimpse of Tristan, one of her coworkers in the campaign division last year, diligently laboring on what was likely another incredible piece.

Liz smiled at the familiarity of it all and walked through the bustling room to her office. She heard whispers all around her as more and more people glanced at her. She tried to shrug it off and keep walking.

Just when she made it across the room to her office, Massey stepped in front of her. "Liz!" she said with her normal bubbly personality. Massey was dressed in tight ripped jeans, a plaid button-down, and a North Face vest that she had monogrammed with her initials, like the majority of her other clothes. Liz glanced up and met her eyes.

"Hey, Massey."

She nodded toward the office. "Can we talk?"

"Sure," Liz said. Massey entered first and then Liz closed the door behind them.

Massey's smile dropped as soon as they were in the confines of the office. "What were you thinking? I didn't want to just go off in front of like everyone, but *Brady Maxwell*?" Her eyes widened. "I really thought you were the last person to sneak around on Hayden. I mean, y'all dated for like a year or whatever. He's a good guy. A little uptight, but you seemed to work well together. When I heard, I thought it was a joke, but then after the press conference yesterday, I finally had to accept facts. You cheated on Hayden. Still shocked!"

"Massey, no," Liz said uncomfortably. "You have the facts wrong."

"Um . . . I think Brady Maxwell told everyone exactly what happened."

"No. He said we were together and that we're together now. We were not together while I was dating Hayden," Liz said and then immediately felt shitty for the lie of omission. She swallowed the guilt that lodged in her throat.

"Wait, so you guys like broke up or something?"

Liz bit her lip. She hated what she was about to ask, but knew it was a necessity. "Is this conversation . . . off the record?" she whispered.

"Oh!" Massey said, looking guilty. "Yeah, sure."

So, she had been interested in making this some kind of interview. Great. Liz wasn't sure how much Massey would have actually written about, but she wanted to err on the side of caution.

"So . . . what happened then?"

Liz took a small breath. "I don't know what you've heard, but Brady and I had a relationship two summers ago. I left because I thought that I wanted more than he did. Well, it turned out that I wasn't the only one. After I told Hayden about what had happened, we broke up and Brady and I ended up getting back together. It's been a long week."

"How did you end up getting back together . . . and get him to go public about it?" Massey asked. "I mean if you wanted more before . . ."

"That was actually his idea. It was already out that we'd been together. He wanted to keep us together, and the only way that would happen was to . . . I don't know . . . claim me." Liz tried to put on a strong face for Massey. "Plus, I really wanted this. I've never been happier."

"But it was all in secret," Massey pointed out. "How do you even know it's going to work out now that it's out in the open?"

That was the right question, wasn't it? The only thing Liz could go on was past precedent. She loved Brady. She hadn't been able to get over him. She wasn't going to get over him. "I don't, I guess. I just know how I feel about him and I know how I feel without him. It's worth it to at least try."

"But if it fails . . . then it will be all over the news again."

"True," Liz said with a shrug. "I'm telling you I can't imagine my life without him. I'd rather risk a public scandal every day than to look back and wonder what would have happened."

"But . . ."

"Can we go without the buts, Massey? I've kind of had a stressful weekend. I'd like to get back to some semblance of normal in my life."

"But . . . do you think you'll ever get back to normal?"

Well, that depended on the definition of normal. Maybe the change with Brady would become her new normal. She could live with that.

"I don't even know what normal is," she finally admitted. She hadn't thought it was normal to be dating someone and always thinking of someone else. She hadn't thought it was normal to hide her relationship or her feelings. She hadn't thought it was normal to be miserable to give up someone she cared for. If those were normal, it would be better to try something out of the ordinary.

"Well, in case you weren't aware," Massey said, her voice still skeptical and cautious, "dating a congressman as a rising political journalist is *not* normal."

Liz laughed, hoping to lighten the mood. "*That* I did know."

"No, seriously."

"I know," Liz said, sobering. "I know there's a fine line. But everything negative I wrote about Brady was before we started dating. And I'm not going to write about him now. I can just supervise."

"Liz . . ." Massey said awkwardly, staring at the floor.

"What?" she asked.

"Um . . . about that."

"About what?"

"I'm really sorry. I hate to do this. I know you're so dedicated to the newspaper."

Liz's heart pounded. "Do what?"

"I think you should leave the paper," she blurted out.

"What?" Liz gasped. She felt the blood drain out of her face. This was her world.

"It looks bad for us to have our editor in the news. It puts a stain on the newspaper as a whole. You have to understand."

"You're kicking me out?"

"No, well, I can't do that," Massey said sheepishly. "I just . . . I mean, we hope that you'll step down without us having to speak with anyone. I mean we only have two months to graduation. It would just be a temporary leave of absence."

"A temporary leave of absence," Liz said hollowly. "Temporary in that in a couple months I'm graduating and never coming back to the paper."

"It's best for everyone."

Everyone but Liz. She was sure of that. How could it be better for her *not* to be at the newspaper?

"You can't be serious." But Massey sure looked serious.

"It wasn't an easy decision."

"An easy decision for who?" Liz snapped, her anger bubbling up. "As far as I'm concerned this is only a simple decision for you. Get rid of the problem and, let me guess—you become editor?"

"It wasn't like that," Massey said defensively.

"I'm sure, but you didn't answer my question."

"You left me in charge as editor while you were sick. It's an easy transition for me to just continue to do the work."

"That *would* make sense, Massey, if I hadn't slaved for years here to be the editor! You want to come in and take all of that away from me?"

"I'm not taking all of that away from you," Massey said. "I'm telling you that it's not feasible for you to continue to work for the paper when this is on the front page." She grabbed a newspaper off of the desk and slapped it into Liz's hands.

Liz glanced down and swallowed hard. A picture of her was on the front page. The headline read, "Congressman Maxwell Affair with UNC Reporter Confirmed." Liz tried to steady herself as she read through the article. It was pretty cut-and-dried—straight out of the information Hayden and Calleigh had written as well as from the press conference. Still, seeing it like that on the cover made her feel nauseated. She had gotten herself worked up about the other papers last night, but this was so much worse. This was *her* paper.

Her eyes drifted to the byline. Massey Davis.

"*You* wrote this?"

Liz knew somewhere in her logical subconscious that if things were reversed she would have done the same thing. She would have written the article and published it. She would have done it without blinking. But it still hurt knowing that her friend had done it to her.

"I'm sorry," Massey said softly. She actually did sound sincere. "Someone had to write it. No one really wanted to. We like you, Liz. We all liked you as editor. But we *couldn't* ignore this. The paper would have looked like it was biased, trying to protect its own and all that."

"Yeah, because that's really so bad."

"You know what I mean. We're supposed to be objective. You were news. And on campus, you're kind of big news," Massey told her.

Liz tossed the paper back onto the desk without finishing reading. "I guess I am now."

"You would have done the same thing."

"Irrelevant," Liz said, crossing her arms. "You're kicking me off of the paper, Massey. This is my life. This is everything I've worked for."

"I know," Massey said helplessly. "If things calm down maybe you can still come back."

Liz knew she was lying. The media haze around her relationship with Brady would lighten, but she would still be with him. There was no way the paper would take her back.

She contemplated asking Massey about the chances of her staying on if Administration got in the mix, but she knew that she didn't want to actually include the university in the decision. The paper was technically a separate entity from the school to keep its anonymity. It gave the staff freer rein to discuss matters the school itself might prefer that they not talk about.

Liz was sure that Administration would either defer to the judgment of the paper or somehow her taking it to a higher-up would end up in the paper anyway. Neither option was optimal. Likely both would leave her without a position at the newspaper.

All she knew at this point was that she needed to get the hell out of here. This had been her safe place and now she wasn't even welcome.

"Just temporary. Right," Liz said softly. She hoisted her purse higher on her shoulder. "Well, I guess that's my cue, huh?"

Massey sighed and looked as if she wanted to say something, but she didn't.

Liz grabbed the door handle to her, now, old office and wrenched it open. She glanced at Massey once more before walking out.

Liz didn't even give Massey any last parting words.

Chapter 4
SPIN

Liz stalked across the quad on the way to her first class of the day. She was mostly looking forward to her last class with her mentor, Professor Mires. Liz had started working for her as an assistant. After they'd successfully put together a political journalism colloquium, Professor Mires had helped Liz get an internship working with the *New York Times*, which landed her a job at the paper postgraduation. Liz would much rather think about that than what had just happened at the newspaper.

She had two months before she was supposed to be in New York City, and that seemed much more important than what she was doing right now. She wouldn't mind fast-forwarding through the difficult months.

Trying to shake off her conversation with Massey, Liz walked into the journalism building and found a seat in her advanced editing class. It ate at her that this would affect their friendship. She and Massey weren't close like Liz was with Victoria, but they had worked together the past two years. Liz didn't know what to do about it, and worse, she thought there might not be anything she *could* do about it. She wasn't about to go apologize for what she had said, and she knew Massey wasn't likely to either.

Facts were facts. Liz wasn't on the paper anymore. Massey was taking over her position. That was going to cause strain no matter what they said or did.

Liz had known that her relationship with Brady would affect her career, since it did call into question her objectivity. She just hadn't thought all of that would happen so quickly, or that it would mess up her friendships.

With a sigh, she pulled out her MacBook to take notes.

She felt stares all throughout class. That she *had* been prepared for, so she just tried to ignore them. People had the paper out on their desks, and some were giggling or whispering among themselves. That was fine. They could say whatever they wanted. It didn't matter.

When class ended, Liz took her time putting her things back into her bag. She was a little behind, since she'd missed part of last week. She wanted to check with the professor about makeup assignments, but she didn't want to do it with anyone else around.

"Hello, Professor," Liz said amicably. "I just wanted to ask you when I could come by to make up missed assignments while I was out last week."

"Do you have a doctor's note?" the professor asked, staring down at the legal pad in his hand.

"Oh . . . no, sir. I didn't end up going to the doctor, but I wasn't feeling well."

"Are you sure you weren't out with your boyfriend?"

"Excuse me?" Liz asked. She couldn't believe the professor had the audacity to say that to her.

"Just seems convenient is all, Miss Dougherty. I'll need a doctor's note or the assignment can't be made up," he said indifferently.

"Beg your pardon. This is the second class I've had of yours, and I've never missed before. I'm not sure how you could consider it convenient." Liz was struggling for control. She had been out sick last week because after she had told Hayden about Brady he had made her feel guilty about the whole thing and then forced her to have sex with him. She had been nauseated, depressed, and unable to function. A doctor wouldn't have done shit for her!

"I understand that, but that is my policy. It's written in the syllabus."

"You didn't say it was a problem when I emailed you last week," Liz cried in frustration.

"After reviewing the syllabus, you'll see that a doctor's note is required. I wasn't aware last week when you emailed me that you wouldn't have one when you returned. I'm sorry, Miss Dougherty. That is my policy. Is there anything else?" he said dismissively.

Liz's jaw slackened. Since when was she an untrustworthy student? She had always made it a point to get to the professors, go to their office hours, and overall show that she worked very hard for her grades. This just seemed . . . out of the realm of possibility.

"No, thank you," she finally answered. *Polite to a fault.*

She walked out of the classroom feeling heavier than she had before entering. She couldn't even fathom the effect zeros would have on her grade for this class. She had kept her 4.0 GPA for four years straight; she couldn't lose it her last semester!

Liz had a lunch break between editing and the advanced political journalism class with Dr. Mires. She walked out of the journalism building and started toward the Pit to eat before thinking better of it. Maybe being at the heart of campus surrounded by people reading about her wasn't in her best interest.

She turned around and started walking toward Franklin Street to pick something quick up when she was stopped suddenly by a flash. She staggered back a step.

"Miss Dougherty, do you have a minute to speak with me?" a woman asked.

"Sorry. I'm in a hurry," Liz said, trying to scurry past her.

"I'm Cynthia Redd with *Raleigh News*. I'd just like a minute of your time."

Liz shook her head. It was her instinct to want to talk to the reporter, find out more about her, find out what the article was on, but she knew what this was about. This woman wanted information about Brady. Liz couldn't provide that. "No comment," Liz said.

Another flash followed and Liz noticed that Cynthia wasn't alone. There were three other reporters waiting for her. "Miss Dougherty, Carl North with the *Herald-Sun*," one said, talking about the Durham newspaper. "We'd love to talk to you about your affair with Congressman Maxwell."

Liz didn't stick around to see who else was there. She just shook her head and repeated herself. "No comment. I have no comment about anything."

Then she turned and fled. The worst part was that she could hear the reporters following her. They probably thought that by tagging behind they could corner her and get her to speak. It gave Liz an entirely different perspective on the career that she loved so much.

Her name was called behind her and her stomach twisted. How could this be happening? She was in a relationship with a politician. That didn't mean she needed to be tracked down at school!

Since it was the end of a class change, there were still enough people milling around that Liz could veer through them to try to evade her tail, but it also had the problem of making her look entirely ridiculous. If people didn't already know who they were, having a swarm of press show up on campus and follow her around wasn't helping anything. Without a second thought, she darted into the nearest building, wove around the bottom floor until she found a women's restroom, and then closed and locked the stall door.

Her breath was coming out ragged and her hands were shaking. Holy shit! Her world had officially flipped on its head. Since when was she the person running *away* from reporters?

Liz fumbled in her purse for her cell phone and dialed Brady's number without thinking. He answered on the third ring.

"Hey, baby," he said pleasantly. "Do you think I could call you back? I'm on the line with D.C."

"Reporters," she gasped out. "Reporters on campus. Everywhere."

"What?" he growled, his voice fierce.

She ran a trembling hand back through her hair and took a shuddering breath. "I had reporters waiting for me after my first class. *Raleigh News, Herald-Sun*, and at least two or three other papers that I didn't get the names of."

"Shit! I'll get Heather on it now. She should have already handled this." Liz was sure Heather was not going to like being on the end of Brady's anger. "Where are you now? Did you say anything to them?"

"Of course not. I, of all people, should know how to handle reporters," she said, as if she hadn't frozen when she'd seen that they were tracking her. "I'm holed up in a bathroom on north campus. I just had to get away."

Liz heard his deep inhalation. "I'm sending a car now. I'll have the driver message you where to meet."

"Brady, I still have class," she said weakly, though she was suddenly in no mood to attend it.

"I think you should contact the professor and let him know that you won't be able to make it. Staying on campus isn't a good idea. We don't know if other reporters intend to show up," he told her. "Plus, I miss you."

Liz smiled. The first good thing to happen to her today. His statement brought unexpected tears to her eyes and she blinked them away. She hadn't realized quite how much stress she was carrying around with her until that statement.

"I miss you too. Sorry I'm keeping you from D.C."

Brady chuckled lightly. She could almost see him shaking his head at her. "This is much more important than what I was dealing with. You are more important. I don't want reporters showing up at school. You don't need to deal with that on top of classes and the paper and everything else."

"Well . . . I guess I don't have to deal with the paper anymore," she said, choking on the words. "They requested I take a temporary leave of absence after I showed up on the front page."

"Liz, I'm sorry," he said gently.

He had to know that she was sacrificing all of this for him. It was why she had been hesitant about going public after Hayden and Calleigh's article broke. She knew how much this would affect her life. She just hadn't quite foreseen how bad it would be.

"They're losing a great asset to their team. I truly believe it is a misguided decision on their part. But remember that they are just college students."

"I'm just a college student," Liz said defensively.

"You are so much more than that. You always have been. They might not see the error in letting you go now, but they will. In the long run, it's probably better for you anyway. You don't need anyone holding you back."

"And here I thought reporters were the only ones with spin," Liz said, attempting a joke to deflect his compliments.

"Politicians don't have spin. We have facts," he told her, deadpan.

Liz let his good mood seep into her. "Politicians and facts. Now you're a comedian."

"There's that beautiful laugh," he said softly. "That's what I wanted."

They disconnected shortly afterward. She checked herself out in the mirror to make sure she didn't look as frazzled as she felt, and then ducked out of the deserted bathroom. There were no reporters in sight, and she wanted to keep it that way.

Once she received a pickup location from Brady's driver, she briskly walked across campus with her head down. As soon as she spotted the black town car, she slid easily into the backseat. She felt covert as the car drove her away from campus.

She had assumed that they would be driving to Brady's office in Raleigh, but when the driver pulled off of Highway 40 early, Liz sat up a little straighter in her seat. They were headed into the Durham suburbs, and Liz could only guess that they were headed to Brady's parents' house. Why would he have her dropped off there?

Liz had never been to his parents' house in Durham. In fact, she had only met his parents once, nearly a year ago, because of her friendship with his younger sister, Savannah. She had invited Liz out to dinner with them after the political journalism colloquium Liz had orchestrated. That had been when Brady had been dating Erin, a talk show host out of Baltimore. Suffice it to say the dinner hadn't gone well.

Was she supposed to meet them now as Brady's girlfriend? They had been together again for only a few days and she was going to meet the whole family. She thought she'd been completely freaked out by the reporters stalking her class, but this momentarily paralyzed her.

She knew it was ridiculous in light of recent events, but she had a million girly thoughts run through her mind. Would his parents like her? Would they see her as the complication Heather did? How could she ever fit into such a close-knit family? Liz bit her lip and tried to hide her distress by looking out at the passing landscape.

These were normal things she should be able to handle. Parents loved her. They always had. Hayden had been certain for a while that his family liked her better than him. That just made her frown all over again. She had always felt so at home with Hayden's family. She had even been one of the few people at his sister, Jamie's, wedding. That relationship was heads-and-tails different from what she had with Brady. If only some part of this situation were normal, then maybe Liz wouldn't feel quite so queasy at the thought of what was to come.

The car rolled up in front of the Maxwell house shortly afterward, and Liz's eyes widened. She had been expecting a large house, but this was more like an estate or a compound. It was hidden from view from the main road by trees and an imposing fence. A sprawling lawn led up to the all-brick edifice with colonial-style columns and a double wraparound porch. The driver wove them along to the back of the house and into an enormous dark garage, and then ushered Liz inside through a side door.

Liz glanced around the small foyer in which she was deposited and wondered where the hell she was supposed to go and what the hell she was supposed to do.

Just as she was about to go wandering around, Savannah popped into the room. "Hey! Brady called and let me know you were on your way over," she said, giving Liz a quick hug.

"Well, that makes one of us, I guess." Liz was glad to see Savannah, but also anxious about the reunion. Savannah obviously knew that Liz was now dating her brother, but they hadn't had a chance to talk about it. "Um . . . do you know what I'm doing here?"

"Oh, Brady is leaving the office soon and figured it would be easier to just meet you here."

She really wanted to ask why Brady hadn't just told her that when they were on the phone, but she held it in. Their relationship was so new.

"Come on. I was just about to eat lunch," Savannah said, either not noticing Liz's frustration or choosing not to comment on it. "I skipped out of class early today after all the weird stares. My name wasn't even in the paper, but a lot of people know who I am at this point. Couldn't have been fun for you."

"Reporters staked out my advanced editing class."

Savannah nodded. "Yeah. I'm not all that surprised that's happening. It'll blow over."

"I wish it was already over."

"Isn't it weird being on this side of reporting?" Savannah asked. "I mean, I wasn't exactly in the spotlight most of my life, but I understood how media worked and how to avoid it. Now as a reporter, I see everything from a different perspective. You're probably experiencing the inverse of that."

"Yes. Weird would be one word that I would use to describe it." *Bullshit* would be the other.

"So . . . when were you going to tell me you were interested in my brother?" Savannah crinkled her nose and made a disgusted face.

Liz couldn't help but laugh. "Never?"

"Well, at least now I know what changed your mind about voting for him," she said, arching an eyebrow suggestively.

"Well, it was more that I just got to know him. He wasn't what he seemed to an outsider."

"How did he seem?" Savannah asked just as they walked into a massive kitchen.

Liz stopped to stare at the room, which was two or three times the size of the one at her parents' home in Tampa. Full granite countertops, double ovens built into the wall, French-door refrigerator, all stainless-steel appliances, an enormous island with bar stools to serve as an eat-in breakfast nook. A woman in her early forties had a number of things simmering in pots, and when they sat down, she placed a few gourmet sandwiches in front of her and Savannah. It took Liz a second to realize that they had a cook. She would have never even thought about something like that.

"Liz?" Savannah asked, waving her hand in front of her face.

"Sorry. What?"

"I asked how Brady seemed before you got to know him."

"Oh." Her cheeks colored and she turned her face to the sandwich in front of her. "Well, don't hate me, but he seemed spoiled, like he could get anything he wanted. Born and bred for the position. Out of touch with reality and in it for the money."

"Sounds accurate to me," someone said.

Liz glanced over and saw Clay striding into the room with a smirk on his face. His dimples were evident, blue eyes shining with barely contained humor, and his blond hair styled perfectly. Liz had met Brady's brother two years ago, when he had tried to convince her not to vote for Brady at a gala event. Ever since then he had been trying to get into her pants. It had almost worked last week in her moment of desperation, but she had ended up stealing his phone and calling Brady instead.

"What are you doing here?" Savannah asked in surprise. "Didn't you fly out yesterday?"

"State of emergency and all that. Supreme court can wait for family business," Clay said, sliding out the stool next to Liz and taking a seat.

"Clay," Savannah warned.

"I can't sit here?" he asked, already ignoring his sister. "Luisa, I'll take the same."

"Of course," the cook said, her cheeks coloring under Clay's gaze.

"Hey, Liz. It's been a couple days since I've seen you." He looked her up and down. "With this much clothes on."

Liz coughed at the statement and glanced over at Savannah. Her eyes were wide and disapproving. "Really not necessary," she mumbled.

"Clay, why do you have to do that?" Savannah asked.

"Do what?" he asked as if he had no clue. "Last time I saw her, she was in this tiny little dress." His eyes followed the image still in his mind. "And then . . ."

"Really, that's enough," Liz snapped, giving him an equally disapproving stare. "That might as well have been a lifetime ago."

"It was only Friday night," he said with the same cocky smile and a shrug.

"Do you have to do this? Can't you just be normal?" Savannah complained. "Especially after what Brady said. I would have thought that you'd learn. I guess getting thrown up against the wall like a rag doll by your older brother isn't enough to teach you."

Clay's face hardened. Liz could only guess what had happened between Brady and Clay after Brady had found out. She didn't see any visible bruises, so maybe there hadn't been any violence. She was just glad that she had missed it.

"You always come to his defense, Savi." He said the nickname like it was a slander.

"It's easy to come to his defense. He doesn't act like you."

"There's no one else like me," he said with a wink in Liz's direction.

"That's the truth," Savannah said.

Clay scooted his chair closer to Liz, completely ignoring his sister. "So," he said, leaning into Liz.

"Yes?" She leaned backward.

"Steal anyone else's phone lately?"

"Oh, honestly!" Liz cried. She stood up from her stool and looked down at him in frustration. She *had* brought his phone back, after all.

"Why don't you two just calm down?" Clay suggested, biting into his sandwich. "Savi here just likes to pick on me because I'm not her favorite."

"Pick on you?" Savannah asked incredulously. "*I* pick on *you*?"

"I guess it can't be helped. You need someone to pick on because Brady is too perfect for that."

"At least I'm not just jealous . . ."

"She loves me." Clay pointed his thumb at Savannah.

"I do," she grumbled. "Even when you're an ass."

"Have to live up to everyone's expectations. Someone has to be in the shadow of the sun. How does it feel?" he asked, staring meaningfully at Liz.

Was he saying that he was stuck in Brady's shadow or suggesting that . . . *she* was in Brady's shadow? Liz didn't have the energy for this. "Can't you harass someone else? I've had a hard enough day as it is."

"That's not the only thing that's hard," he said with a chuckle to himself.

"Not if I have anything to say about it," Brady said, walking formidably into the room.

Chapter 5

COMMUNICATION

Brady looked incredible in a tailored three-piece black suit, crisp blue shirt, and burgundy silk tie with a herringbone pattern. His brown eyes were cold when they looked at his brother, but melted into warmth when they were turned on her. Liz felt so much of the anxiety of the day dropping off her shoulders in just that one glance. How was he able to do that?

Brady cleared the distance between them in an instant and his mouth dropped onto her lips. The kiss was brief but fierce, possessive, and demanding. Passion sparked between them, and Liz felt like she could have stayed frozen in that moment forever.

Too soon he broke away and Liz was left with a void in his absence. She was pretty sure he was the most addicting thing in the world. When they were together, she felt like everything that had gone wrong in her life recently was going to be all right. At least she had him at her side. That was what helped get her through. Brady fixed everything.

Clay cleared his throat loudly. "Y'all need to get a room or something?" Liz took another step back from Brady, not even realizing they had just been staring into each other's eyes.

"No, and we don't need any of your snide comments either," Brady said, shooting Clay a meaningful look. "I don't want to have the same discussion we had on Sunday."

"We're calling it a discussion now? Could have fooled me." Clay leaned back on the island casually.

Savannah just huffed and swatted at him. "Can't you behave?"

"Can't you mind your own business?" he shot back.

"Savi," Brady said softly. She turned her attention to her older brother and shrugged like *he started it*. The whole exchange made Liz giggle.

Brady pulled Liz closer and fixed Clay with a hard stare. Liz knew that they didn't get along, but she hadn't realized quite how much until she was in the same room with them. Most of the negativity had come from Clay in the past, but there was obvious heat on Brady's end too.

"Aren't you supposed to be in D.C.?" Brady asked flatly.

"Aren't you?" Clay countered. "We had the same flight. You canceled yours. I thought it really must be dire to keep you in Chapel Hill two extra days."

"Why do I feel like you have ulterior motives?"

"Does it always have to be ulterior motives?" Clay asked. "Can't I just want to spend more time with my family?"

Savannah snorted. "No."

"Thanks for the vote of confidence, sis."

Liz shook her head.

"You manage to get through Yale Law School and get a job clerking for the Supreme Court, and yet you're still a terrible liar," Brady said.

"Sorry, I'm not a politician."

Clay and Brady glared at each other. Liz suspected she would need a machete to cut through the tension.

"No, you're a lawyer," Savannah quipped. "How much worse can you get?"

Clay smirked. "A reporter?"

Savannah stared daggers at Clay. Liz normally would have immediately defended her profession of choice, but considering reporters were the reason she was no longer on the paper, couldn't go to her last class, and had been chased across campus for information, well, she wasn't feeling that generous.

"Or maybe it's only bad when you're fucking the reporter," Clay offered with a wink.

Brady reached for Clay at the same time Liz put herself between them. She had known Brady's reaction even before Clay had finished his statement. She put her hands up on Brady's chest and pushed him backward gently. "He's antagonizing you! Just ignore him," she said.

"I don't care if it's about me, but you . . ." Brady said.

"I can take care of myself on this one," she said softly, meeting his gaze. "Come on. It's just Clay."

"Still standing here," Clay said.

Liz heard Savannah shush him. "Let's just get out of here. You have to leave today. I want to spend more time with you."

Brady straightened as if he just realized that he had been a little out of control and he slipped back into himself. "You're right. He's probably just upset that Andrea wants to marry him or hang out with him—or worse, sleep with him."

It was a low blow, but Liz couldn't keep from laughing. Clay was in some strange open relationship that Liz still didn't really understand. She was pretty sure he and his girlfriend hated each other more than they got along, and as far as she knew, they both slept around with other people.

Clay shuddered. "You used the *M* word."

"You are going to marry her eventually," Savannah said. "Why waste all of this time sleeping with other people all the time if you aren't going to end up with the woman who lets you do it without complaining?"

"You two are in rare form today," Clay said, addressing his siblings.

"And this is every day with you," Brady said.

"Come on," she whispered, tugging on Brady lightly. As much as she agreed with the things they were saying about Clay, she didn't like everyone ganging up on him. He might be an arrogant douche bag, but he was still family. He wasn't going to conveniently go away. No use burning bridges with people she had to see all the time.

Brady finally relented without much effort on her part and walked out of the kitchen. The whole experience of being around all three of them together was kind of strange. For so long, they had each been a separate part of her world. Her secret affair with Brady. Her friendship with Savannah. And her . . . antagonistic, maybe even flirtatious relationship with Clay. Now all three worlds were colliding.

Once they were sufficiently far enough away from Savannah and Clay, Liz grabbed Brady's hand. "Brady, hold on."

"Liz, we just . . ."

"Why did you have me brought here? What if I'd just run into your parents without you? That would have been awkward. And then you tell Savannah about me coming here because you're on your way over, but don't think to include me in that information? I know we're starting all over, but there is going to need to be some better communication."

"Liz," he said sharply, cutting off her long-winded ramble. "I would prefer to talk about these things in a more private setting."

Liz glanced around and saw that they were completely alone and then raised an eyebrow. "Can't you at least tell me what we're doing here?"

"I had to pick up some paperwork before I left the office." His voice lowered and his face softened as he drew her in closer. "You seemed so frazzled on the phone. I thought since this was closer for you and Savi was already here that it might be better than driving the forty minutes to see me, just to leave the office again."

"Well, I agree with that." Savannah had lightened her mood after all. "I just think you could have told me."

Brady nodded. "I admit that I'm used to being reticent with information."

"Part of your campaign mask."

"It's easier to control information if you don't give anything away."

"I get that, but I'm not the press anymore," she said. He slid his hand around her waist and hers wound around his neck. "I'm just Liz."

"I know that," he said, dipping his head so that his forehead rested on hers.

"Then act like it. Don't keep me out of the loop," she murmured. "You were the first person I called when the reporters followed me. I should be that for you too."

"My relationships have been rather cut-and-dried for as long as I can remember. What you're asking for is equality, and it's not something I've ever consciously given."

She stepped back. "Well, if we're not going to be equal in this relationship then why did you push for me to do this?"

"Hey," he breathed softly. "I didn't say I didn't want it. I said I wasn't accustomed to it. I want what's best for us to be together. A lot is changing in your life because of me. I can change for you too."

"Well, I'll make a deal with you," she said, reaching out and toying with his tie.

"Oh, no, what am I getting myself into?"

"You might like it." She couldn't keep the smirk from playing on her lips. He arched an eyebrow and waited for her to continue.

"If you work on this communication thing, then I'll let you take complete control . . . in the bedroom."

Brady laughed lightly and kissed her. "I already do."

"Not all the time."

"Maybe I like when you take control. I seem to remember a certain desk where you climbed on top . . ."

Liz blushed as she remembered the time they'd had sex on top of the desk in what had, at the time, been Hayden's office. It was now her desk . . . or she supposed after today it belonged to Massey. That sobered up her good mood. The stress of the day flooded her and she sagged a bit in Brady's embrace. It was still early and already she was exhausted.

Brady seemed to notice and started walking with her back to the garage. "Let's get you back to my place. We still have a lot to talk about, and I might take you up on that complete-control thing you were suggesting."

—

About an hour later, they arrived at Brady's house in the suburbs of Raleigh. Aside from last night, Liz had been there only once, after one of Brady's galas. It was also where he had defended their relationship to Heather and Elliott when they'd walked in and seen them together. It was the first time she had ever heard him say that he loved her—though admittedly he'd never said it directly to her.

It was also the place where everything had started to fall apart.

It was easy to see all that when she looked up at Brady's two-story brick house on a solid acre of land with a gorgeous view. But Liz was set on making new memories of them together. They certainly had last night.

Brady parked his Lexus in the garage and she followed him inside. The layout was open, with dark furniture and beautiful art-work. Liz was sure an interior designer had set foot in the house.

She wasn't sure how else he would have time to do this much work to the place. The best part, of course, was the expansive windows that showed the porch and the huge tract of land beyond them.

"So," she said, kicking her heels off and sinking into the couch.

Brady walked into the kitchen, popped open a bottle of wine, and brought two glasses out for them. "So."

Liz took a sip of her wine and leaned into his shoulder. "There's something different about this."

"What's that?" he asked.

"We've been back for ten whole minutes, and my act-first-and-talk-later boyfriend hasn't jumped my bones."

Brady reached for her wine and set it on the coffee table. "I could fix that," he said, nuzzling into her neck. He pressed her back into the sofa and soon they were kissing. So much of the tension fell away and she just enjoyed the feel of his lips against hers, the electricity that sparked between them, and the unending need to be closer to him.

After the trials of the last year, it felt like a miracle for them even to be sitting happily in the same room. It hadn't been that long ago when the tension—sexual and otherwise—had rolled off of them, when they hadn't been able to be around each other, when they had said cruel things just to keep their feelings at bay. Now having him here—Brady kissing her, smiling at her; enjoying each other's company—it felt as if all of those things had just been what they'd had to endure to get back to each other.

They had both made stupid decisions along the way. But since neither could deny what was happening, they had inevitably ended up here once more. She couldn't be without him. He couldn't be without her. She knew time would only tell the depth of the truth in that assessment, but she couldn't envision it any other way.

Brady tucked a lock of her hair behind her ear and gave her

another sweet kiss. "You've had a stressful day. Tell me how to make it better."

"I can think of a few ways," she murmured.

"We should talk about what happened."

"Not *exactly* what I had in mind." She gave him a sultry look, as if he didn't already know what she was talking about.

"All of this has happened really fast for you. I'm used to the spotlight. I want to make you more comfortable around it. It's not going away."

"I know," she said, conceding to the deeper topic. She ran a hand back through her hair.

"I have faith that you know how to handle reporters. You're a damn good reporter yourself." He had that proud look in his eyes that he got when talking about her accomplishments. She had seen it before, when he had found out that she was a Morehead scholar, the highest scholarship on UNC's campus, and when she had accepted the job at the *New York Times*.

"I understand reporters," she said with a shrug. "I was just bombarded today."

"Yeah. You weren't prepared for that, but you will be next time. I think that's half of the battle."

Liz sighed and nodded. She wanted Brady. This came with Brady. She would learn to deal with it.

"I wish you were going to be here all the time to figure this stuff out," she admitted. She didn't know why, but she felt really small and vulnerable divulging that. It went beyond needing her boyfriend nearby or even wanting to spend more time in the comfort of her new relationship. She was treading through dangerous waters without a guide and she had just learned how to swim.

Brady nodded. "I would like that too. I'm honestly not used to having someone else in my life that I want to see all the time."

She spared him a bright smile. "I seem to be a game changer."

"Understatement. You're more than the game changer. You're the game and the team and the league and the whole universe of sports wrapped up into one neat little package."

Another thought tickled the back of her mind. She had always needed answers, and just because she didn't work for the paper now didn't mean that had changed. "How often will I see you, though? I don't know how *this* works."

Brady actually managed to look uncomfortable for a split second. "Before you, I spent eighty percent of my time in Congress working. I came back to North Carolina as often as I could for things such as your colloquium, but my job is to take what the people want to Congress."

"How exactly can you do that without spending time *with* the people?" Liz asked dryly, not liking where this conversation was headed.

He gave her a pointed look. "I've lived here my entire life. I know the people. There's so much that goes into the job besides just sitting in meetings."

"I know," she said quickly. "I just want to see you."

"You will see me. I'll make sure of it. We have the weekends. If I can't make it here, then I'll fly you up to visit me. We'll make it work. I know we can't be together all the time, since you're still in school. Graduation should be your number one priority," he told her.

"School is the last thing I want to think about."

Brady leaned forward and kissed her. "You'll appreciate it more when you're done. And anyway, the sooner you graduate, the sooner I can have you around more. Summers in an election year are always a good time for me to be in Chapel Hill."

Liz swung her leg over Brady's so she was straddling him. "I think it's always a good time for you to be in Chapel Hill."

His hands ran up her dark jeans, grasped her hips firmly, and then slid to her ass. "I'm starting to agree with you."

"Just now?" she asked incredulously. Her lips hovered mere inches from his temptingly.

"Convince me," he commanded.

She brushed her lips against his, featherlight, always just out of his reach. "And here I thought you were the one who wanted complete control."

"I'm learning something about equality, baby," he growled before lifting her with his hands around her ass and throwing her back into the couch.

Their lips melded together with heat and intensity that could rarely be contained. Her fingers worked at the buttons on his shirt while he did all he could to work on the skinny jeans hugging her legs. Brady shrugged out of his shirt once she finished. He trailed kisses down her front and then tugged her jeans off of her body. Liz squirmed under him as he spent an interminable amount of time slipping each button of her shirt through its hole.

"Baby," he murmured against her bare skin. His fingers ran along the outline of her bra. He slipped under the material, causing her whole body to arch off of the couch in response. "You're the most beautiful thing I've ever seen."

She sighed and a smile touched her lips.

"I'll never know how I spent so long without you," Liz said.

He unhooked her bra and pulled her nipple into his mouth. She groaned at the feel of him sucking and gently biting it until it was erect.

"I want to be able to get my hands on this beautiful body whenever I can."

After spending equal attention on the other nipple, he dragged her underwear to the floor and placed a kiss on the sensitive skin.

"I want to be able to listen to your beautiful voice and have you tell me all of your genius thoughts." He kissed her once more. "I want you. Just you. All of you."

"Brady," she murmured. "Come here."

So he obeyed. His pants dropped to the floor and in an instant his body was covering hers. He pushed her legs open to accommodate him. Then he was inside of her and they were one.

All coherent thought left her mind. She was just with Brady and nothing else mattered. This was the way it was supposed to be. They were working through their problems, working for what they wanted, proving that they could be together despite all the obstacles in their path. The sex was amazing, incredible, unbelievable, but it wasn't all that encompassed their relationship. It had brought them together, but it wasn't what was going to keep them that way.

What held them together was the love they both felt to their very core, the knowledge that being apart had been soul crushing, and the willingness to push for what they wanted. And Liz had never wanted anything quite as she wanted Brady Maxwell.

Chapter 6

THE NEXT LEVEL

L et me take you to dinner," Brady said a few hours later.

Liz and Brady had been tangled up in his sheets all afternoon. While the thought of going out to dinner with him in public sounded wonderful, since their relationship had always been hidden, she didn't exactly want to give up their alone time either.

"Right now?" she murmured, trailing her fingers down his bare chest.

He seized her hand in his and drew her closer to him. "Yes. I'd like to take you somewhere where everyone can see how lucky I am."

Liz flushed at his comment. "I believe you're the catch. Aren't you North Carolina's most eligible bachelor?"

"Not anymore." He brought her hand to his mouth and kissed it softly.

And really, how could she deny him anything after that?

She changed back into the skinny jeans and button-down that she'd had on earlier. There wasn't a ton that she could do for her hair at this point. She finger-combed the knots out of the back and spritzed some water through it to help the natural wave. After sliding into her heels, she found Brady waiting in the foyer.

"Oh, casual Tuesday," Liz said with a giggle. "How did I get a sport coat out of this deal?"

"Must be your lucky day."

Liz wasn't so sure about that, but Brady looked damn good: khaki pants, a light blue shirt with a navy blue-and-white diagonal-striped tie, under a dark blue blazer. She didn't think she would ever get over how attractive he was, in and out of a suit. He took her breath away literally and figuratively.

Brady just shook his head at her stare and urged her into his Lexus. Almost as soon as they were out of the driveway she was fidgeting. He didn't say anything about it until they were almost into the city.

"All right, what are you nervous about?"

"How are you not?" she asked, looking out the window and avoiding his gaze.

"You do not need to be nervous to be seen with me." He reached for her hand and laced their fingers together.

"I know!" She bit down on her lip and tried to grope for what she really meant. "I'm not nervous about being seen with you. It's just new for me. I feel like there's an etiquette or protocol that I don't know."

Brady laughed lightly. "It shouldn't be any different with me than it was dating . . . anyone else."

The way he hesitated over that made Liz wince. She knew he was talking about Hayden, but that was the last person she wanted to think about right now. That relationship had gone up in a cloud of smoke because of what had happened with her and Brady. It wasn't exactly guilt that slammed into her, because she was still furious that Hayden had outed their relationship to the press. It just felt like a weight . . . a sadness that things had ended the way they had. She swallowed back the memories and returned to the matter at hand.

"And . . . it is kind of our first date," she said, peeking up at him.

"I believe I took you out for breakfast once and to a number of galas."

Liz rolled her eyes. "That breakfast was just us planning out our affair. We talked *terms*. You could hardly call it a date. And you didn't take me to either of the galas I attended. The first was for work."

"You did a lot of work," he said with a smirk. Both of them were clearly remembering the first time they'd had sex after the Jefferson-Jackson gala in Charlotte.

"The second gala, you took someone else."

"But I was with you," he reminded her. "And I flew you out to Hilton Head."

"Are you really going to bring up Hilton Head? Where you left me alone in a suite nearly the entire weekend?" she asked.

"Fine. This is our first date?" he asked cheerily.

"Yes."

The smile that crossed his face made her suspicious. He pulled out his phone a second later and jotted out a quick message before replacing it into his pocket.

"What was that?" she asked.

"Hmm?" he asked coyly. "Oh, nothing, baby. Just changing reservations."

"You made reservations?" She wanted him to take her to the nice places she had always envisioned herself being with him, but reservations meant fancy places, and she was hardly dressed for that.

"I always make reservations," he said. "Don't stress about it. I have it all covered."

"This is where communication comes in."

He winked at her. "Surprises are surprises. I'm allowed to keep secrets when it comes to that."

She couldn't even argue. She just needed to relax. Her day had been so hectic, between the reporters and the newspaper. But she had still gotten time with Brady, and that was what mattered. They would figure everything else out together. Right now she should let her boyfriend surprise her on their first date.

God, she was really going to have to get used to calling him her boyfriend. It sent a thrill through her every time she even thought it.

A short while later, Brady pulled his car up in front of a quaint restaurant with an impressive covered outdoor patio. She had never heard of the place before.

She took Brady's hand when he offered to help her out of the car. Brady handed the keys to a waiting valet and then escorted her into the room. She kept a soft smile on her face and her head held up.

The restaurant was small, with tables placed close together and lit only by candlelight. It seemed cozy, if a bit cluttered, but the food must have been great, because nearly every table was taken.

Their appearance garnered a few stares from the people seated nearby, and Liz followed Brady's lead. A waitress seated them at the only open table, in the far corner. Two gentlemen came up to them once they were seated and shook Brady's hand.

"I'm Jake Smith. Pleasure to meet you, Congressman," the first guy said. "I was really pulling for you in that race last year."

"Good to meet you too, Jake. I always appreciate meeting hard-working people out there who voted for me," Brady said. Brady turned to the second guy. "What's your name?"

"I'm Curt, Congressman. It's going to be a tough race this year," Curt said. His gaze shifted to Liz, and then back to Brady.

"Tough race every year," Brady said. "This is my girlfriend, Liz. I'm fortunate to have such a wonderful woman who will be there along the way."

They shook hands with Liz, who smiled, but said little. "Always good to have a strong woman behind you," Jake said.

"Only the best," Brady agreed.

"Well, we won't keep you," Curt said. "We just wanted to thank you for all that hard work you're doing. We knew your father when he was working for the Triangle area. Great man."

"I'll be sure to let him know you said that."

They all shook hands again and then were gone.

For the first time, Liz realized that maybe Brady's *entire* life really was one big campaign. He hadn't known those two men, but she was sure they would vote for him for life. She had wondered what it would be like to be on Brady's arm, and she knew this was only just the beginning, but that thought encouraged her.

"You seem . . . different," Brady said after water was brought to their table and he ordered a bottle of wine.

"Different good or different bad?"

"Neither. You seem more relaxed."

"It was kind of nice to see your interactions with everyday people. Do people always just come up to you like that?"

"It depends. I'm not always front-page news, so I get more privacy when I'm not. But I do run into a lot of people who want to talk to me. It's part of the job," he confirmed.

The waitress returned with their wine, and they ordered dinner. It was a tapas place and so they got a variety of items to share. The food was spectacular and the conversation was light. They knew so much about each other from when they had last been together, but it was a new experience dating without any of the red tape. Plus, so much time had passed since the last time they had been together that even though it seemed like they could pick up where they left off, there was much to talk about to return to that level of personal intimacy.

They ordered dessert and sat around talking about the most romantic things they had ever done.

Brady paid and then wrapped his arm around her waist as they walked toward the exit. "Stargazing in an open field?" he asked.

"Have you ever done it?"

"I've looked at the stars, but come on—Paris by candlelight, strolling an untouched beach at dusk, breakfast on a foggy morning in the mountains," he suggested.

"Those do sound very romantic," she conceded, smiling up at him. "I still like stargazing in an open field. I mean you're so in touch with the world. Just you and the person you're with in the quiet, in touch with your soul. It's indescribable."

They broke apart as Brady's Lexus showed up at the valet station. Just as they moved toward the car, a small woman appeared from around the corner. "Excuse me, Congressman Maxwell, do you have a minute?"

Brady turned and smiled at her. Liz noticed that the woman had a rather nice-looking camera around her neck, and without a second thought she looked for the recorder she found bulging the woman's pocket. Reporter.

"How can I help you?" Brady asked amicably.

"Could you comment on the state of your affair with Ms. Liz Dougherty?" she asked.

Liz's instinct was to snub the woman, tell her *no comment*, and walk away. But Brady just held his campaign mask in place. "Ms. Dougherty is my girlfriend," he said simply. "No affair. As you can tell we're out for dinner together before I return to D.C."

"Do you have any comment for the people who are saying that your relationship with Ms. Dougherty is a campaign ploy for more attention?"

Liz gritted her teeth even through her smile. She wanted to tell this woman where to shove it with her personal questions. The other part of her tried to tell her that she would have done the exact same thing if she were reporting on this case, but damn, it was hard when it was her own life.

"I can assure you that Ms. Dougherty is far from a campaign ploy."

"Ms. Dougherty, do you have any comment on the state of your relationship with Congressman Maxwell? It must be overwhelming dating such a high-ranking official after just ending your previous relationship," she said, staring Liz down.

Liz shot Brady a questioning look. She wasn't sure what she was supposed to say in this situation. No comment seemed best, but Brady was answering her. Maybe as long as she followed his lead and mimicked the way he handled the press it would be okay. He nodded softly and she took that to mean go ahead.

"The Congressman and I are very happy together. We're pleased to be able to share our relationship with the public," Liz said, holding her head high. It was strange to speak to a reporter the way people had always spoken to her.

The woman opened her mouth to ask something else, but Brady held up his hand. "We're running on a bit of a tight schedule for tonight. We really appreciate your questions, but we must be going."

"Just one photo?" the woman insisted.

Well, normally reporters just snapped photos whenever they could, so her actually asking for a picture was a real treat. He placed his hand back around her waist and they smiled for the camera. A flash went off once, twice, three times. The woman thanked them even though it was clear she wanted to ask more questions.

Liz sank into the passenger seat of Brady's Lexus and sighed. "Well, that wasn't so bad," she said after a moment.

"Baby, you're a natural." He found her hand again and squeezed it.

"It's easier when you're there."

"It'll get easier with time. Reporters, as I'm sure you're shocked to hear, are always going to be around."

"I know," she whispered. And she did. She knew how the job worked. She just had to get used to it from the other side.

Chapter 7
AVOIDING

Brady flew out of Raleigh late that night and he had a car drive Liz back to her house. She was relieved to see that reporters weren't waiting for her. She had let Victoria know earlier that she would be with Brady, and Victoria had responded that she was staying with Duke Fan in Durham. It did Liz some good to be alone. For now, her main priority needed to be catching back up in her schoolwork.

Already she was two days down this week. She couldn't risk endangering her scholarship in her last semester. Now that she didn't have the newspaper she would have plenty of time to make up the work. Thinking about the paper like that sent a pang through her chest.

In fact, without the newspaper, Liz found that she had a surprising amount of time to herself. She spent the next two weeks playing catch-up. Reporters still showed up on campus, but their numbers soon dwindled.

Brady had given her his weekends, but like her, he was playing catch-up with his responsibilities in D.C. She completely understood that he needed to make everything right and show his continued dedication to his career. This couldn't be a hiccup in the campaign.

Come Monday morning, she was feeling more put together and considerably caught up with her work. She had been avoiding talking to Professor Mires about what had happened since the news had spread. She wasn't sure if she would find disappointment on her mentor's face, and she preferred to see nothing at all.

Victoria had Duke Fan drop them off on campus right before their first class. It was still strange not to have to come in early or stay after for the paper, but Liz was trying to adjust. Victoria had tried to get her to go party with her this past weekend, but Liz had decided against it. While she had reporters still tailing her she thought it would be better to show herself as studious rather than a party animal. And anyway, she didn't really feel up to celebrating.

Victoria looked at Liz over the top of her Ray-Bans. "I think Daniel can pick us up after class if you want to meet here again. His class is canceled."

The girl was gorgeous and voluptuous in uber-tight, white-washed polka dot jeans, an insanely low-cut hot-pink sweater, and six-inch spiked brown boots. Liz didn't know how she managed in those clothes. She felt ordinary in a light black blouse with gold buttons, tucked into a burgundy high-waist skirt. She had on black tights and, surprisingly, gold flats instead of heels.

Victoria gave her the expression she had been giving her for nearly two weeks—a mix of concern and curiosity. Between Liz's losing the paper, having reporters follow her, and Brady being away in D.C., Victoria seemed to think there was a real risk that Liz would crack under the pressure.

"Stop looking at me like that," Liz said, bumping into her shoulder. "I'm fine."

"That's what people say when they're not fine."

"I have the man of my dreams. Why would I not be fine?"

"Don't give me that shit," Victoria said with an exaggerated eye roll. "For a girl who loves to be stuffed full, I know how hard it is to be happy with *everything* in a relationship."

"Oh my God, you did *not* just say that! Vickie, I can't unhear these things," Liz said, making a show of covering her ears.

"I'm just saying . . . I'm giving up threesomes in London and foursomes in Australia to be with Daniel."

"La la la," Liz singsonged.

"You're giving up the paper, which is kind of as hard."

"Did you just say that me getting kicked off of the paper is *almost* as bad as you giving up having sex with multiple men at once?" Liz asked in disbelief.

"Yeah?"

"Okay, just making sure I heard your crazy ass correctly."

Victoria rolled her eyes again. "It's not crazy. Once you've had . . ."

"No, stop right there."

"God, Liz, you wouldn't think you were fucking a congressman right now."

"I love you, but you're ridiculous." Liz shook her head. "Anyway I have to get to class. I'll meet you after!"

She watched Victoria traipse off across the quad and Liz could do nothing but just stare after her. She really was a force to be reckoned with.

Liz made it through her classes without an incident. She didn't see a single reporter. People had gone back to ignoring her.

Liz was stepping out of the journalism building when to her dismay she ran right into the teacher she had been avoiding.

"Liz," Professor Mires said in greeting.

"Hello, Professor Mires," she said. Liz had never gotten used to calling her Lynda.

"I'm glad I ran into you. Will you stay after class tomorrow? I'd love to talk to you about some recent work that has come up," she said with kind eyes and an easy smile.

"Oh, um, yes, ma'am."

"Perfect," she said cheerily. "See you then."

Liz watched Professor Mires walk through the doors and then retrieved her ringing phone from her purse. She glanced down at the number and saw that it was a D.C. area code.

"Hello?" Liz answered.

"Hello, I'm trying to reach Liz Dougherty, please," a man said. He didn't have a very distinctive voice and Liz couldn't place it.

"This is Liz. Who is speaking?"

"My name is Ted Cary with the *Washington Post*. I was wondering if you had just a few minutes to verify some facts."

Liz's heart rate shot through the roof. What the hell was the *Washington Post* doing calling her? The bigger newspapers had picked up her relationship with Brady, but nothing compared with what had been running in North Carolina. And she had thought the news would be winding down. What kind of questions would he ask her? Should she even comment on this?

She didn't know. The other reporters that she had spoken with had been in person, and after a few of the same responses she had blown them off. She was still in college, still had to graduate, and wanted to continue to have a life. She couldn't have reporters around all the time.

Curiosity won out in the end. She didn't know what they could want her to fact-check, but her reporter instincts told her that it was better to find out than to leave her wondering. She could always refuse to comment.

"What kind of facts can I help you with, Mr. Cary?" Liz asked diplomatically.

"Just a few simple questions."

"What kind of questions?"

"We're just checking out some simple matters before we move forward with our article about your relationship with Congressman Maxwell."

Liz felt a bit uneasy about that. It seemed every paper was writing about her and Brady right now. But she was sure that she could handle just a few questions, as she had done when she and Brady went to dinner. "I'm not sure I'll be able to answer your questions, but I'll do what I can."

"Very well," he said. "First, were you in charge of directing the UNC Political Journalism Colloquium in April of last year?"

Liz paused. "I assisted Professor Mires with the setup," she said. She wanted to clarify, but she knew better than to provide more information than was in question.

"So, you were at the event that day?" he probed.

"Yes."

"Did you see Congressman Maxwell at that event?"

"Yes." At least a hundred other people had been there and seen them together.

"Can you elaborate on where you saw him?"

"He was on a politician's panel that I attended." Still safe.

"Did you attend a dinner afterward with Congressman Maxwell's younger sister, Savannah?"

"I—" Liz cut herself off. Now, that *was* privy information. Hayden didn't even know that she had gone to that dinner. Savannah had wanted Liz to keep it secret because she didn't like to flaunt her family's status on campus. Liz had wanted to keep it secret because Hayden had thought there was some kind of connection between her and Brady. He hadn't known how right he was.

So, the question was: how did this reporter know about that dinner? Liz chose her next words carefully. "I ate dinner afterward, yes." There—she didn't exactly answer his question, and she hoped, but doubted, that he wouldn't notice.

"After that dinner, did you leave by yourself or did someone drive you home?" Mr. Cary asked.

Liz swallowed. Oh, God, what did he know? Or what did he think he knew?

"Where is all this going, Mr. Cary?" Liz asked. She tried to keep the tension and anger out of her voice, but wasn't sure how well she did.

"Just simple questions Ms. Dougherty. Fact-checking," he repeated. "You were at a dinner with Congressman Maxwell and left with him after the event, correct?"

"I can't confirm that," Liz said finally. Nothing had happened that night with Brady, but no one else had been there. "No comment."

He continued on, unperturbed by her reluctance to answer the last question. "Do you happen to know where you were the third weekend in October last year?"

October always triggered a bad response from Liz. October had been the month of her first fight with Hayden. It had been when she had called Brady and they had kissed. It had been the start of her self-torture with the guilt of feeling like she had cheated weighing down on her.

"That's rather specific. I'm not certain."

"Did you leave Chapel Hill in October at all?"

"I'm sure I did," she said.

"Did you leave North Carolina? Were you out of the state at the end of the month?"

"I was here for Halloween," she said in an unhelpful fashion.

"Did you see Congressman Maxwell at that time?"

"At Halloween? No."

She heard him sigh in frustration. She was purposely avoiding his questions and he knew it.

"Based on the Congressman's travel plans, he was in Chapel

Hill the weekend of the eighteenth of October. Can you verify that he was in fact there?"

"If you've already verified his travel plans, why would you ask me about it?" Liz asked.

"Can you comment at all on your contact with Congressman Maxwell since he has been in office?"

"Absolutely," she said cheerily. "We're very happy to be able to make our relationship official and tell the public."

Obviously not what he wanted to hear by his soft sigh. "Thank you, Ms. Dougherty. I'll be in touch if I have other questions. Is this an okay number?"

"Sure," she said, making a mental note to program his into her phone so she wouldn't answer his calls in the future.

"Wonderful. Thank you for your time."

Ted Cary hung up and Liz stared at her phone dumbfounded until a text came from Victoria asking her not too politely where she was. Liz jumped as if someone had just run into her, and started walking to their designated meeting spot.

Something didn't add up. Ted Cary knew too much personal information. That was rather obvious. But how much did he know, and why did it matter? She and Brady were together now. That was the story. What spin could he put on something like that?

There were a million scenarios, but she didn't know which one to even consider without first knowing where he would get that kind of information. She mulled it over on the drive home with Victoria, and as soon as she walked through the front door, she gasped like someone had just knocked the wind out of her.

She was dialing Brady's number before she even drew another breath. He answered almost immediately. "I thought I wasn't going to hear from you until later," Brady said.

"Erin."

Chapter 8
ONE STEP CLOSER

What?" Brady asked in confusion.

"Erin talked to a reporter," Liz told him. Erin was Brady's ex-girlfriend. They had broken up after he had visited Liz in October.

"What makes you think that? She's not the type to get involved with the press."

"She *is* the press," Liz reminded him. Erin worked as an anchor for *Baltimore Mornings*, though it was kind of a stretch in Liz's mind to call her press.

"So are you, and you're not eager to talk to anyone about our relationship. I highly doubt that Erin is either," Brady answered confidently.

"I received a call from the *Washington Post*," Liz explained.

That clearly got his attention. "About Erin?" he asked.

"No. Not exactly."

"Then why do you suspect her?"

Liz launched into everything that had happened between her and the *Post* reporter who had called her. She could almost hear the silence on his end growing heavier by the end of the conversation.

"When I suggested that you get more comfortable around reporters, I didn't mean that you should start confirming facts when we don't even know what the article is about," Brady said.

"I didn't confirm anything but what was public knowledge. I was at the colloquium, I was in charge of it, and you were there. Anything about us being together afterward or seeing you in October, I avoided. He wouldn't tell me what the article was about, just that he had simple questions for me."

She had felt so confident when she had dialed his number to tell him about what had happened. Now hearing his frustration made her feel unsure. Should she have just directed the man to Heather? Her first instinct had been to find out what he knew. It was the reporter in her.

"Liz, you can't just do what you want. Even if it might not seem like he was leading you into questions, he was. This is why I have a press team."

"I know," she said softly. "I still think it's Erin, though."

"There are a number of explanations," Brady said.

"But she was there at the dinner. I didn't tell anyone else I was there. Not even Hayden. You broke up with her right after your visit in October. It fits," Liz encouraged. She had to be right about this.

"I doubt Erin would do that," he said curtly.

"What? Why? If Hayden would do it . . ."

"Erin isn't Hayden," Brady said simply.

Liz ground her teeth together. "No, she's not," she said, trying to keep controlled, "but that doesn't mean she wouldn't say anything."

"Erin is one option. But we don't know for certain it was her. I'm going to have to get Heather on this right away, since the press is on this now."

Liz groaned. She did *not* want to talk to Heather. Liz wasn't a "Heather approved" choice for Brady. Heather was here for the long haul, and she wanted Brady to be with someone who would further his career. So far Liz was just a black mark on Brady's otherwise impeccable record.

"I'll be in touch about the *Post*," Brady said before saying goodbye and disconnecting.

Even though they talked every night when he got off work, she never felt as if there was enough time. She was ready to graduate so that they could be together more often. At least, until she moved to New York City. She sighed just thinking about her dream job at the *Times*.

About fifteen minutes after their call ended, just when she was getting into a TV show to try to numb her mind, her phone rang again.

"Hello?"

"Liz, this is Heather."

Well, that was fast.

"Hey, Heather."

"Brady told me I should handle a situation with the press. I feel like I've been hearing that a lot lately," Heather said coolly.

"Yeah . . ."

"Care to tell me what happened?"

"Didn't Brady tell you already?"

"He told me to handle the situation. I'm handling the situation. As far as I'm concerned *you're* the situation. One that keeps cropping up no matter how much I try to tamp it down," Heather said.

Liz wanted to give back a biting retort, but she really was in the wrong. At least partially. She hadn't meant to do any harm by talking to the reporter, but it seemed like everything she did could do wrong in Brady's world.

"I just . . . thought I could handle it. The questions didn't seem leading and then when I saw where he was going I got off the phone," Liz told her.

"I'm still just in shock over here. Why would you think it was a good idea to talk to a reporter *at all*? I don't know what your motives are in continually thwarting the system we have in place, but it stops today."

"Heather, I'm not thwarting the system! God, I just answered a few questions. I'm sorry."

"You spoke to a reporter and then you spoke to Brady about it. He doesn't need more things to deal with. That is why he has me. So next time you think about screwing everything up just give me a ring so I can remind you about how stupid it is. I'm here to take care of everything. Not you. Not him. Press go through me. End of the story."

"I understand that all press go through you, but I should still be able to call and talk to Brady about these things if I need to," Liz told her. Brady wasn't on a need-to-know basis with her. They had a relationship. She couldn't hold in everything that might bother him.

"This is why you're a problem," Heather spat.

"I'm not a problem!" Liz said. "I'm Brady's girlfriend."

"You think that just because Brady decided to give you a chance after your affair was outed that you're suddenly special? No, you're not. You have to follow the same routines as everyone else. You go through the right channels. You don't fuck this up, because every single thing that *you* do, God help us all, reflects back on him. He is important. He is special. We *need* him in office. You—" she said as if she couldn't even fathom why she was still talking to Liz, "you are just a sideline display. Nothing more than a phase. Just try not to screw up while you're still around."

Liz's heart stopped. *A sideline display. A phase. While you're still around.* Those words made her head spin.

Just the thought ate away at her. Could she just be a temporary thing for Brady? Could he be using her to try to cover up the bad publicity? Her gut instinct told her no, that she was crazy. But maybe it wasn't *that* crazy. She could never let Heather know that she secretly harbored these fears, though.

"I already apologized," Liz said gruffly. "I can't take back the conversation, but I *will* continue to talk to Brady as I please. Whether you choose to believe I'm here to stay or not is entirely up to you, but threatening me is only going to make me dig my feet in. So you should just get used to my being here."

"I've been around Brady since his very first run for office. Do you know how many girls have come and gone since then?"

Liz shook her head. She didn't want to think about that. "It really doesn't matter to me if it's one or a hundred. I'm here now, and you'll need more than empty threats to get rid of me. If you're upset because I spoke to the press, fine. I'll be more careful next time. If you're upset because I'm with Brady, then you'll just have to get over it."

"I'm *upset* because you're deteriorating everything we've worked toward. I don't care about your delusions. I care about doing my job, and I'm damn good at it. Next time a reporter calls you, get his name and number, and report directly to me what he wanted. Are we clear?"

Liz wanted to tell her to fuck off. She wanted to tell her that she wasn't an employee and couldn't be pushed around like this. But she couldn't. She knew that what Heather was doing was in Brady's best interest, even if she was a raving bitch when talking to Liz. She just hated that it seemed that everything Liz did brought another wave of disapproval.

"Fine."

"Thank you, Ms. Dougherty. It's always a pleasure," Heather snapped before hanging up.

Liz chucked her phone onto her bed in frustration.

Ambition. It was all just ambition. Ambition made the world go round. Brady, who used it to get into Congress at twenty-seven. Heather, who rode his coattails to push for her dream. Calleigh and Hayden, who used Liz to get ahead. Liz, who had spent her entire life doing everything she could to work as a reporter.

No one was exempt. Ambition did as much good as it did damage, delivered dreams as easily as it incinerated them. What was the price of it all? How far ahead could she get before she was pulled down? Liz thought about how perfect her life had felt last year—seemingly perfect boyfriend, highest scholarship in the school, editor at the newspaper, internship at the *New York Times*. It was exactly what she had argued with Hayden about back then. Already she didn't have the paper, and her new perfect boyfriend was kind of part of the problem.

She needed to get away so she could clear her head or else she was going to combust. Changing into workout clothes, she hopped into her car and drove over to the tennis courts. She hadn't been taking regular lessons for a while because she was so busy with the paper, but now that she wasn't on the paper she no longer had an excuse. She was ready to get her ass kicked to help her forget what was going on in her life.

She strode into the complex she had been going to for the past four years. Her regular instructor, Tana, was pretty hard-core, and Liz had even gotten used to Hank, a power tennis player who she'd had her differences with in the past. Either of them would probably laugh her off the court for how out of shape she was.

"Hello! How can I help you?" a cheery redhead asked Liz when she walked inside.

"Is Tana in?"

The girl checked her schedule and then shook her head. "She's already left for the day."

"Hank here by any chance?" Liz asked as her second-best option.

"Oh no, he's out all week on vacation."

Liz sighed. Great. Guess she would be serving to the net.

"But Easton is here." The girl's eyes got big and glassy when she said the name. "He just finished his last lesson of the day. I could ask him if you wanted." She was already out of her seat before Liz could respond.

"Um . . . who is Easton?"

"He's our newest instructor. He started in September, but he's *always* booked."

By Ginger's reaction, Liz could think of only one reason why. "Sure. Easton is fine."

The girl scurried through a closed door and a minute later she reappeared with a guy who Liz could only assume was Easton. He appeared to be college age, with perfectly tousled dark brown hair and light brown eyes. He was tall and trim and carried himself powerfully. His smile made the redhead receptionist swoon, but Liz just returned it with mild indifference. He was cute, but he wasn't Brady Maxwell.

"Can I help you?" he asked, leaning forward against the desk and twirling his tennis racquet.

"Tana and Hank are out today. Are you free for an hour?" Liz asked.

He straightened and smiled again. "Sure. Let's walk," he said, and then strode toward the courts. He opened the door for Liz and she followed him out. "You're playing with Tana and Hank, so you can't be too shabby. How experienced are you?" he asked.

"I've been playing my whole life. Very accomplished at hitting balls," she responded, straight-facedly.

Easton cracked a smile and nodded. "Where have they been hiding you?"

"I've been—" Liz cut herself off. She had been about to tell him she was the editor of the paper, but, well, she wasn't anymore. And anyway, he might not know what had happened with her. It would be nice to be around one person who didn't know that she'd had an affair with a politician. "I've been busy. Haven't been around as much."

"Well, let's get started. Need any pointers?" he asked. "I can show you some good footwork, the right swing, how to move your body."

Liz rolled her eyes. "Oh, please, no. I just need someone to beat."

"Then we should probably find you someone else," he said with a glint in his eyes.

After his first serve, Liz knew she was going to lose pretty handily. Her body protested with every swing, and the worst part was that it was clear that he was holding back to play with her.

"You're so good," she admitted when they took a short break. "How old are you?"

"Twenty-one, and thanks," he said, offering her a bottle of water. "You're really not bad."

"Ha! You make me look like a joke."

"You're just out of shape."

"Wow."

"No seriously. If you were out here every day, we'd be more evenly matched."

"I'm shocked you're not on the UNC team," she said.

"Well, I want to go to law school."

"Oh," she said flatly. Law school only made her think of Clay and how he was now clerking for the Supreme Court.

"Don't *oh* me. I want to be a politician."

"Oh!" Liz said, shaking her head. Damn, she could not escape her life. "Well, that's nice."

"You don't believe me."

"I really do. Let's just play."

And then they were back into the game. This was what she had come here for, after all. She put all of her energy into the athleticism of the sport. Focused on trying to crack through Easton's advanced passes. She was good, but not that good. Having the added pressure of wanting to beat him made her work twice as hard, and by the time they left the courts, she was breathing heavy and slick with sweat.

"I'm going to fit you into my schedule three times a week. We'll start off slow, but you should start running laps at least twice a week otherwise. Doctor's orders," Easton told her.

"I can't commit to a training regimen," she said. "I graduate this semester."

"I'm going to save some time anyway," he said as they walked into the air-conditioned lobby. He grabbed something from behind the counter and handed it to her. "Here's my card. Figure out your schedule and get back to me."

Liz slipped the card into her bag. Tennis had helped her forget her woes today. It might not hurt to start coming in more often. Maybe then she could think about something other than her failed attempts at living the life of a politician's girlfriend.

"I'll think about it," she said noncommittally. "Thanks for the lesson."

As soon as she got home, Liz hopped in the shower. She was toweling off her hair when she saw that she had missed Brady's call. Finishing with her hair, she slipped into sweats and then called him back. She was still frustrated about what had happened earlier, but tennis had improved her mood immensely.

"Hey."

"Hey," she said softly.

"I called Erin."

"Oh," she said, perking up. She hadn't thought that he would.

"You were right," he admitted.

"Damn." She hadn't really wanted to be. "What did she say?"

"To be honest, after she told me, there was a lot of crying, and then she hung up on me."

"She did!" Liz cried. "What for?"

"It wasn't a mutual breakup," he said stiffly. "She didn't tell me exactly what she told the paper, but I can only guess that it's negative from the way she was on the phone. She sounded like a mess."

Liz stood up and started pacing her room. "What does this mean for us, for you, for the campaign?"

Brady sighed and for the first time she really heard uncertainty crack through his confidence. "I guess we'll find out when the story hits, unless I get some information from Heather beforehand."

"I'm sorry. I shouldn't have said anything to that reporter," Liz said, feeling defeated.

"You were just trying to find out information. You didn't know what Erin had done or what kind of damage it could do. For all we know it could still be minimal."

"Or it could be disastrous."

Chapter 9
TWO WRONGS MAKE A RIGHT

Liz had gone through a million scenarios of what Erin's article could be about. All she really assumed was that it wasn't going to be pretty. Brady had broken up with the woman because of Liz. It wasn't a huge leap for Erin to guess that.

When Liz opened up the *Post* article in her email the next morning, it was clear that wasn't the only leap Erin had taken when speaking to the press.

As usual, it started out with the punch: Erin condemned Liz and Brady for sneaking around behind her back. They had worked so hard to portray their relationship as a positive aspect of his life that they were both so eager to share with the public, but now not only did they have the stigma of having hidden it, but Erin was making it seem as if the relationship had never stopped. She went as far as asserting that Brady had cheated on her on at least two occasions, but was *certain* it was more.

She claimed that when Brady had driven Liz home from the restaurant, the night that Liz had first met Erin, something had happened, and then again in October—both of the times the reporter had asked Liz about, and he'd included her own words stating she did see Brady the first time but had no comment on the relationship. It made Liz's heart heavy.

She couldn't stop herself from reading the rest of the article numbly. Erin spoke briefly about her relationship with Brady. She alluded to his always being distant and said that their time together was rocky. Not how Liz remembered it, but she had only met Erin once. She talked about how wronged she was by a man she had loved. That Brady had kept the breakup hush-hush. Again she asserted that was because he was still sneaking around with Liz at the time.

"God, I can't believe this," Liz grumbled, closing her computer and walking out into the living room.

"Hey!" Victoria said. "I was just coming to get you. You were gone yesterday, so I didn't get the chance to tell you— Wait, what's wrong?"

Liz had tears welling in her eyes. Had it really only been a couple weeks since all of this had started? It felt like a lifetime.

"Did something happen?" Victoria asked.

"Brady's ex-girlfriend spoke to the press saying he cheated on her with me while they were dating."

"Well . . . didn't you?"

"I mean, yeah, that one night in October, but we stopped. We didn't go farther, and nothing happened before that. And it all just looks *so* bad," Liz explained.

Victoria moved her to the couch and made her sit down. She plopped down in the seat next to her. "How badly does this set you back? Can't you just tell them to fuck off?"

Liz laughed bitterly. "I wish. I spoke to the press. I feel kind of like an idiot. I mean, what use is all my reporter knowledge that I've built up for years if I can't even handle the press in my own situation? I feel so shitty about it. I'm ruining everything."

"Okay, melodrama, calm down for a second. You're not ruining anything. People make mistakes. Brady isn't going to dump you for making one, and he's what matters here, right?"

"No, I mean, yes. He is what matters. And you're right: he isn't going to leave me because I spoke to the press. I just feel like I should be better," Liz tried to explain. "I feel like I mar his perfect reputation."

Victoria shrugged. "Would you rather deal with this bullshit and have Brady or be alone and not have to deal with any of this?"

Liz gave her a look. "I'm just saying it's difficult."

"Every relationship is difficult. And I respect your decision to blubber . . ."

"I don't blubber!" Liz cried. "You're so bad at this comforting thing!"

"Maybe, but you're not crying anymore," Victoria said, shooting her a wicked smirk. "I think you should come to terms with your relationship with Brady. As far as I see it, it's never going to be easy. You had to fight to get him and you're going to have to fight to keep him. The lowest lows bring the highest highs. And when you find someone who brings you both, that doesn't mean you should walk away; it means you have something special."

Liz smiled despite everything. "When did you become the bearer of wisdom?" Wherever it had come from, Liz liked it. It was clear from Victoria's face that she was happy and maybe even feeling similarly with Daniel.

"Happens to the best of us," Victoria said casually.

"Or the worst of us," Liz teased.

"Lowest lows and highest highs, bitch."

"Well, thanks for dealing with my lows lately."

Victoria beamed. "I have to listen to you so I don't feel guilty burdening you with my highest highs."

"Oh, God, I don't want to know if you and Daniel had a three-some," Liz said, pretending to cover her ears.

"Better!" Victoria squealed. "I got into three of the top genetics PhD programs in the country!"

"Victoria! That's amazing! Which ones?"

"MIT, Berkeley, and Johns Hopkins. I'm still waiting to hear back from a few others, but I would be perfectly content at any of them."

"I'm so proud of you," Liz said. "Did Daniel get into any of the same schools?"

Victoria brightened further. "Johns Hopkins for now. He didn't apply to Berkeley and MIT."

"Well . . . what are you two doing this weekend? I'm flying up to D.C. to go to some banquet. Have you been on the Johns Hop-kins campus yet?" Liz asked excitedly. "You could do a tour and finally meet Brady!"

"Oh, hell, yes, you know I'm in. I have to convince Daniel, but I can think of a few ways," she said mischievously.

"I don't even want to know!"

"Let me talk to him and I'll get back to you. It's kind of last minute, but I'm a last-minute kind of girl!"

❧

Liz's name appeared in the campus newspaper again later that week. Luckily it wasn't on the front page this time. She only saw it because a few people in class glanced over at her and snickered. She dug the newspaper out of the trash once they were gone and read a watered-down version of what the *Washington Post* had run. Wonderful.

She tossed it back into the trash and exited the room. She had never thought that newspapers were going to be the death of her. Only a few weeks dating Brady and she already despised reporters, media, and everything else in between.

She wasn't looking forward to her meeting with Professor Mires. She had put it off as long as she could, but she had to face her mentor. Professor Mires hadn't seemed upset when she had seen her yesterday, but Liz wasn't sure.

Walking into the journalism building, she pushed her shoulders back, took a deep breath, and straightened out the front of her skirt. *Here goes nothing.*

"Hello, Professor Mires," Liz said, walking into her office.

"Liz, we've been working together for nearly three years. You can call me Lynda."

"Yes, Professor Mires."

Her professor chuckled and shook her head. She was a pretty woman who tended to wear hippie clothing with long skirts. Liz found that hard to reconcile with the high-end reporter Professor Mires had been in her younger years. "Please take a seat. How have you been?"

Well, that was a loaded question if Liz had ever heard one. How *was* she doing exactly? Angry that she was in the paper again. Disappointed about getting kicked off the newspaper. Elated that she was back with Brady. Happy that graduation was looming closer so she could escape it all. But of course she didn't say any of those things.

"Fine," she answered.

"Of course you are. Now, I wanted to talk to you about your final term paper for the internship through your Morehead scholarship," Professor Mires said, jumping right in. "I'm going to need a rough draft before spring break so that we can get it cleaned up and out to the graduation department in time. How does that sound?"

Spring break. Well, that was coming up fast.

"Sounds fine."

"Perfect. Now let's discuss what you were doing . . ."

Professor Mires trailed off as Liz's phone blasted to life. She quickly apologized and silenced the ringer. She would deal with that after her meeting with Professor Mires.

After a thirty-minute conversation about her work for her internship and the avenues they had been working toward regarding her final paper, Liz was free to go.

When she stepped into the hall, she fished her phone back out of her purse and pulled up the missed call. The caller ID read NANCY—NEW YORK TIMES. She dialed the number and waited.

"Hello?"

"Hello, Nancy. How are you?"

"Hi, Liz. It's been an interesting afternoon to say the least. How have you been?" she asked.

"Just fine, ma'am. I've been keeping up with my classes and working on my internship term paper. I'm looking forward to seeing you and getting back to work at the *New York Times* over spring break."

Nancy cleared her throat. "That's actually what I want to speak with you about."

"About travel arrangements? I believe the university was going to have me leave on Monday," Liz told her.

"Unfortunately, Liz, the *New York Times* is going to have to terminate any further work with you," Nancy said.

Liz's breath caught in her throat.

"I'm sorry, ma'am," she managed to get out. "I don't . . . understand."

"After your relationship with Congressman Maxwell surfaced, we were willing to look the other way. In fact, I fought for you to stay on over the summer, because I believed things would blow over," Nancy said, and then sighed. "But everything didn't blow over. With your appearance in the *Post* today, I couldn't seem to justify keeping you on to my superiors. We can't have one of our own reporters continuing to surface in the news."

"So . . . so you're firing me?" she gasped.

"Officially, since no paperwork has been signed and we only had a verbal agreement, we're withdrawing our job offer," Nancy explained.

Same fucking thing.

"I see," she muttered.

"I do apologize for this, Liz. I was very excited to work with you all year and then again this summer, but my hands are tied." Her apology seemed sincere. She didn't sound cold, just resolute. At least Nancy was the one delivering the news and not some person Liz had never met.

"I understand," Liz said. "Is there anything I can do to change your mind . . . or your superior's mind?"

"I'm sorry. I think this is a final decision," Nancy said. "Good luck with all that you pursue. I know you'll find something else. You won't waste your talents."

What did she say to that? She mumbled something numbly and then got off the phone. She couldn't keep talking to Nancy about the job that she would never have again. Her dream job. Gone. Poof!

In a matter of weeks, everything that she had worked toward had completely fallen apart. No job. No internship. No paper. No prospects. How had she gone from complete and total success and control of her career path to this mess? And what was she going to do now? She had no path. The last four years had been wasted. If the *New York Times* wasn't going to hire her after they had already put the offer on the table, who would be willing to work with her?

She wanted to just go home and figure out how to fix everything. She wasn't crying as she had this morning only because she was in shock.

Professor Mires walked out of her office at that moment and paused with her hand on the door. "Oh, Liz, I thought you would already be gone."

"Sorry. I had a phone call," she said hollowly.

"Is everything all right?"

"Fine."

Professor Mires narrowed her eyes and pushed her door back open. "Take a seat, Liz. What is this all about?" She didn't sound unkind, just concerned.

Liz knew that she should have held it in, but she just couldn't do it; it all spilled out. She had to have a release somehow from all the pressure of carrying all of her troubles around. After she finished, Liz slumped back into her chair, exhausted.

"This is all . . . unfortunate," Professor Mires said, choosing her words carefully. "I'd heard about your relationship with the Congressman, but I didn't realize it had resulted in all of this."

"Well, no one else does either."

Professor Mires leaned forward on her desk, crossed her arms one over the other, and stared at Liz meaningfully over her glasses. "You are a very intelligent, charming, hardworking young woman. One of the very best that I have had the pleasure of working with. I cannot fathom that something like this would hold you back from achieving everything you set out to do. To be honest, I think it is an opportunity to see what *more* you can accomplish."

"What do you mean?" Liz asked cautiously.

"You want to be a reporter for a large newspaper. Well, one chance is gone. What are you going to do now? Every door that closes leaves another one open," Professor Mires said. "I'm not going to fail you just because you can't go to New York over spring break, or keep you from graduating with a degree in journalism just because you don't have a reporting job lined up. There is more to life than your job and your career. You never know. You might stumble into something else you like."

Liz knew this all sounded logical, but her heart was too heavy to put much stock into it.

"You took the GRE, correct?" Professor Mires asked.

"Yes," she said, nodding. She had taken the grad-school exam last semester at Professor Mires's request. She'd had no intention of attending graduate school at this point in her life, but the scores were valid for several years down the road and it might not be a bad thing to keep in the back of her mind.

"If you're interested, perhaps I could make a few calls and see if I could get you some late acceptances for graduate school programs. Would you be interested in using that as your plan B?"

Liz's mood brightened marginally. A plan. Oh, God, she hadn't realized until Professor Mires had said that how much she put into having a plan. Without one she had felt empty.

"Yes," Liz said, making a split-second decision. "If you don't mind making the calls, I would love the opportunity to apply to graduate school."

"Then it's settled," Professor Mires said.

Liz stood to go and then stopped and turned back toward her mentor. "Ma'am?"

"Yes, Liz?"

"Why do you do all of this for me? The colloquium, the internship, the *New York Times*, and now graduate school. I appreciate it, but I just don't get why you would help me so much."

Professor Mires pulled off her glasses. "Because you do it all for yourself. You go out of your way to be better and you do it exceptionally well. I'd like to clone you just for your work ethic. In truth, you go above and beyond and it makes me want to go above and beyond for you. Because someone like you, Liz, deserves more than taking a necessary temporary leave of absence and a job offer withdrawal."

Liz stared at her professor, slightly stunned. It was such a relief to hear someone truly believe in her and not judge her for her actions. It made the world feel like a better place, lighter, freer, worthwhile.

Before she made it out the door, she smiled back at her professor. "Thank you . . . Lynda."

A ghost of a smile crept onto her professor's face.

Chapter 10

LIKE A DREAM

Liz, Victoria, and Daniel flew to D.C. that Friday afternoon. They had received confirmation from Brady's secretary that someone would pick them up from Security and were told to just look for a sign.

She was glad that Victoria and Daniel had gotten approval to visit the Johns Hopkins campus so they could come with her. Victoria calmed Liz's jitters by cracking jokes the whole flight.

This was the first time she was going to be with Brady since he had agreed that they were going to be together. Sure, they'd had the few days after that, but he'd had a couple weeks to change his mind. Not that she thought he had. He would have been better off denying the allegations and letting their history fade into the wind than acknowledging her. It was just this nagging feeling. Maybe it was a result of Heather's condescension. Maybe it was more innate.

Either way it left her on edge. It didn't help that Brady wasn't picking them up. She had known from day one the demands of his career, but she still didn't want to take a backseat to it.

Their plane circled high above the Washington, D.C., metropolis. Lights shone bright from the city in the evening darkness. Brady was down there somewhere. She bounced lightly in her seat as they made their descent. She had been anticipating this trip all week, and she couldn't get out of her seat quickly enough once they landed at Reagan National Airport.

"Would you chill out?" Victoria complained. "We're not getting off of this thing any faster, and Brady isn't even waiting."

"Ouch, Vickie," Liz said. "No need to rub salt in the wound."

"Okay, *Lizzie*," Victoria jeered.

Liz stilled at that. She didn't like that Victoria used Hayden's nickname. She really should be more careful about calling her Vickie, but habits were hard to break.

She needed to get Hayden out of her head before she landed.

"Enough," Daniel said, wrapping an arm around Victoria's waist. "No catfights on the plane, Vickie."

"You always side with Liz. Why do I keep you around?"

He raised his eyebrows and smirked.

"I can get that anywhere," she snapped, but a smile played on her features.

"That's not what I remember you saying."

"Okay," Liz said, shaking her head. "My turn to say enough. I don't want you two to start a play-by-play on the airplane."

Victoria leaned into Daniel and giggled. Liz was sure they were whispering about what they were going to do to each other later, but she didn't care as long as she couldn't hear it.

Liz slung her bag over her head, hung her messenger bag on her shoulder, and exited the airplane. She waited impatiently for Victoria and Daniel to follow her through the airport, past Security, and out toward baggage claim.

She scanned the signs in front of her for the driver that was promised to collect them. No luck. She kept walking, hoping to catch a glimpse, but to no avail.

When her eyes reached the end of the line, she gasped and dropped her bags. Brady. He was here. He had come to pick her up. A million emotions hit her all at once. Her heart ached as it pounded fiercely in her chest. She had missed him so much. The weeks had stretched interminably long.

She caught his eyes and her stomach flopped.

Without a thought for Victoria, Daniel, or her discarded bags, she dashed across the airport. She felt as if she were in a movie as she rushed toward the man she loved. When she reached him, she threw herself into his arms. Her body thudded against his chest and she pressed her face into his shoulder. His arms pulled her flush against him and he hoisted her up so that her feet tucked up behind her. He smelled unbelievably masculine and delicious. The strength in the embrace grounded her, and everything felt right in the world.

"Hey baby," Brady whispered in her ear.

"You said you were sending a car."

"I have a car," he told her with a kiss on her temple.

He placed her lightly back on her feet. She could do nothing but stare up at him with a dopey grin.

"I got out early to come see your beautiful face," he said. She reached on her tiptoes and kissed him softly on the mouth once. She heard a flash behind her and turned just in time to see a few people stashing their phones and cameras.

"Should I not have done this?" she asked, concerned.

"No, Liz. I like you exactly how you are."

"What are people going to say?"

"Whatever they want," he said, taking her hand. "Try not to worry about it. You're with me now."

Somehow that *did* make so much of it better. Brady wouldn't have let her throw herself at him if he had been concerned about consequences. He wasn't one to forget himself in these kinds of situations.

"Oh, I dropped my stuff," Liz said, turning to see Victoria and Daniel walking toward them with her bags.

"I didn't think you'd want to lose this," Victoria said. She was shaking her head, but had a crooked smile on her face.

Liz reached out and took her bags. "Thanks. Sorry."

"No, you're not," Victoria said. "So you must be Brady." She eyed him up and down and then nudged Liz. "I see why you would say he's good in bed. He's really . . . tall."

Liz covered her face with her hand and shook her head. "Wow. Worst introduction ever." Brady was laughing softly. Liz had told him all about Victoria, but she didn't think she could ever adequately prepare someone for her best friend. "Brady, this is my insane roommate, Victoria, and her boyfriend, Daniel."

"Nice to meet you," Brady said, extending his hand and shaking with each of them.

"Daniel, huh?" Daniel asked. "I've upgraded from Duke Fan for the visit?"

"She didn't want to give you a reminder about how bad we beat you in basketball last week," Brady answered. "It was really a way of saving you some embarrassment."

"Geez, Liz, you've trained him already?" Daniel asked.

Liz couldn't hide her amusement. "Didn't have to. Brady played basketball at UNC."

"Another one," Daniel grumbled. "It's going to be a long weekend."

They all walked toward the baggage claim. Brady laced Liz's fingers together with his as they walked, and she realized he had that same dopey grin on his face she'd felt on her own earlier.

She couldn't believe how easily she had doubted on the plane. Now here she was in D.C., introducing Brady to her friends, holding his hand in public. She wouldn't truly believe it if they hadn't gone through hell and back to get to this point.

After collecting their luggage, they walked out of the airport and into the covered garage. The guys loaded the suitcases into the back of a shiny black Range Rover while Liz and Victoria got comfortable in the plush leather interior.

"This is top-of-the-line," Victoria whispered when she shut her door.

"Yeah," Liz said with a shrug.

"No. I mean, my dad was looking at these things and this has all the gadgets he wanted. I bet this is over a hundred thousand easily," Victoria said appreciatively.

Liz shrugged again. Money didn't matter. She had never really thought about it with Brady. She knew he had a house in Raleigh, a lake house, a Lexus, and that he had flown her to Hilton Head and put her up at a resort on a whim. She knew his parents had a mansion and a house in Hilton Head, Savannah drove a BMW, and Clay drove a Porsche. Yeah, she knew they were all wealthy, but she had never cared. She still didn't.

It was just Brady.

"All ready?" Brady asked once he sat in the driver's seat. He revved the engine and soon they were leaving the airport behind.

This trip to D.C. was already a sharp contrast to when she had come up here to visit Hayden. She had always enjoyed D.C. with him. It had been the first time he had admitted his feelings, the first time they had kissed, the weekend that had triggered Liz wanting more from Brady. Then there had been New Year's with Hayden, hanging with his sister, Jamie, and her husband, James, going to Jamie's art galleries.

So many memories washed over her at once. She hated thinking about them right now.

She glanced out the window as she collected herself. It was so
easy to remember everything that had happened with Hayden. It
hadn't been that long ago that they had been together and happy,
and then everything had spiraled out of control. She had no interest in going back to that, but it was so fresh, like an open wound.
She knew Hayden had been in the wrong by putting her relationship with Brady in the paper, and she didn't want to feel guilt about
cheating and jumping right to Brady, but it crept over her with all
the old memories.

"Liz?" Brady asked.

"Hmm?" she muttered, realizing she had been out of the conversation.

"We were just seeing if Italian was all right with you?"

Italian. Another Hayden memory hit her of going out to eat
after that very first press conference. God, she didn't need this right
now while she was with Brady. That was where her heart was . . .
where it had always been.

Time to make new memories.

"Sounds good to me."

Brady dropped Victoria and Daniel off at a hotel on the Johns Hopkins campus that the university had reserved for them for the weekend visit. They would be coming with Liz and Brady to the banquet
tomorrow night, but for now, she and Brady had the night free and
to themselves. And they both desperately needed some privacy.

The trip back into the city took longer than expected due to
traffic, and by the time they reached Brady's building the air was
thick with sexual tension. He parked in his designated space in an

underground garage and they took the elevator up to the top floor. The doors had barely closed before Brady had her pressed back into the wall and his mouth was on hers hot and heavy.

Three weeks had been too damn long without him. Now that she had him back she never wanted to go this long again. He brought her down to earth and reminded her with just one glance exactly why she was going through all of this . . . why it was all worth it. Because Brady was worth everything.

What had happened to her career—or lack thereof at this point—might have been the exact opposite of everything she had wanted, but after spending the week talking with Professor Mires, she felt a little better about losing her position at the *New York Times*. Now with Brady's lips on her, she was letting that get pushed further and further out of her mind.

His hands slid down her sides to grasp her hips and she squirmed suggestively against him. "God, I've missed you," he groaned against her lips. "Do you know how long I've been dreaming about these hips straddling me again?"

"How long, Mr. Congressman?" she teased.

"Years, baby."

"Is that all you've been dreaming about me doing?"

"You think my mind is that clean?" he growled, pulling her bottom lip into his mouth and sucking it in. She moaned and her eyes fluttered closed. "I've been dreaming about the noises you make when you come, the soft pants as I get you closer, the way your body flushes, the feel of your heated skin against mine."

The elevator dinged open and Liz was left panting just as he had said, as he stepped backward. "I'm thinking after that show, we should just stay in the elevator," Liz suggested.

A smirk appeared on his face and he stepped back inside the elevator. He slid a card into the slot at the top and pressed a button. The doors closed, but the elevator didn't move. Locked.

Liz's heart rate picked up, and she could feel her core pulse at the thought of what was going through his head right now. He just stared at her for a second, his eyes traveling from the top of her head down to her chest, over the curves of the navy dress, to her legs and then back to her face.

He crossed his arms and that damn smirk stayed in place. "Take off your panties."

"What?" she asked, even though she knew exactly what he was asking.

"Do it. Now."

Liz swallowed. Adrenaline kicked into high gear and she felt her whole body respond to being told what to do in a public place where they could so easily get caught. Without thinking more about it, Liz reached up and grasped the edge of the black lacy cheeksters she had worn specifically for him to see; then she dragged them down her legs. He watched with idle curiosity until she held them in her hand.

Brady stuffed them into his pocket, and then walked her until her back was pressed into the wall. His hand dipped beneath her dress until he found her most sensitive area hot, wet, and ready for him at the slightest of touches. He jerked her leg up around his hip and then started swirling his fingers through her wetness and then circling her clit until she was jerking in his grip.

"Brady," she groaned. "We . . . could get . . . caught."

"Just suggesting that makes your pussy clench," he whispered huskily into her ear. "I think you like it."

She really couldn't deny that, because the way he was working her with his fingers had her trembling and already close to coming. And he didn't let up, he kept his thumbs working circles around her clit all the while delving two fingers in and out of her until she dropped her head back and felt the first wave of her orgasm so close.

"Oh, God," she murmured.

"Come for me, baby. You're right there. I want to see you come," he encouraged.

How did he do that? Her whole body tightened at his command, because his fingers had stroked her into submission. And she could do nothing but release at his insistence.

"Most beautiful thing in the world," he whispered, kissing her on the lips as she tried to get her breathing under control.

Brady released her and then pressed another button on the elevator. Liz straightened her dress and ran her hands back through her hair. The sex had always been off the charts with Brady, but she thought it was incredible that every orgasm was better than the last with him. He took her to new levels with his fingers. She couldn't imagine where the night would lead them.

The doors dinged open again and she saw a couple walking to the elevator. "Hold the doors, please!" the woman called.

Brady held the door for them and then led Liz down the hallway, on shaky legs. They shared a secret smile, knowing how close they had come to getting caught. Just what he needed to get in the papers for his upcoming election: "Congressman Maxwell Performs Sexual Acts in Public Elevator. Can This Man Help Run the Country?" Seriously, she needed to stop thinking about life in terms of newspaper headlines.

Brady stopped at the last door in the hall. There weren't very many, which led her to believe that the apartments were huge. He swung the door open and she entered a modern chic bachelor pad.

"Penthouse," she whispered, taking in the expansive apartment. She guessed that the square footage on the place was more than on the two-bedroom house she rented with Victoria in Chapel Hill. It was huge, but surprisingly empty. It was clear he didn't spend much time here, but the decorations had been carefully crafted to entertain company.

"Yeah. I didn't want a house. Nothing up here compares to the real estate back in North Carolina."

"So you went as far opposite as you could get?" Liz asked.

His house in Chapel Hill was rather traditional, set in soft browns and blues with hardwood floors and dark wooden furniture. His penthouse in D.C. was set in a black, gray, and red palette with an L-shaped sofa and round chairs. The back wall was made entirely of glass overlooking the city, and was probably the best part of the house. The view was gorgeous.

"I don't spend a great deal of time here. Most of it I spend sleeping or on the phone with you," he said. He slipped out of his suit jacket and smiled at her expectantly.

Brady lived here. He slept here. He spent his time talking on the phone with her while he was here. She was part of his life, and he wanted her to be. It was just incredible and it made her light up to have it all come to her so suddenly.

"What's the smile for?" he asked.

"I'm in D.C. with you."

"You have been for a couple hours now."

Her smile brightened. "Sometimes it's hard to grasp that this is really real."

"Well, if it's a dream," he said, dipping his face down and kissing her, "don't wake me up."

Chapter 11

A BRIGHT FUTURE

An article appeared in the papers the next day with a picture of Liz and Brady kissing at the airport. Another featured him picking her up and holding her against him. Liz flipped through the article on Brady's iPad as she lounged in his bed.

She wasn't surprised to see her face there anymore. They had both anticipated that happening. Brady had let Heather know about the airport ahead of time, but she still wasn't pleased. Liz was certain that she could never do anything right in Heather's eyes. And at the moment, lying in bed next to her boyfriend in his penthouse . . . she really didn't give a fuck.

"I like that they're still toting that quote from Heather," Liz said absentmindedly to Brady.

He'd had Heather make a statement about Erin's accusations regarding their relationship. They had thought it would be better not to go on the defensive and just make it clear that nothing had happened. The statement read, "Congressman Maxwell never had illicit relations with Ms. Dougherty while dating Ms. Edwards. The details of their split were not made public to protect Ms. Edwards's privacy and for no other reason."

The papers had circulated it over and over again. It was still showing up a couple days later. People wanted to know more, but so far the campaign hadn't agreed to say anything else. Liz certainly wasn't going to spill.

Besides two kisses, she and Brady really hadn't done anything. They'd just agreed not to bring those kisses up. Since they hadn't gone anywhere it more or less was irrelevant. They wanted to keep it that way.

"Mmm," Brady said, tapping away on the MacBook in his lap. "Heather's good at her job."

"So are you."

Without taking his eyes off the screen, he moved his left hand over to her thigh and started working his way up her leg. "I have a job for you."

"Why do I have a feeling this is going to be sexual?" Liz asked.

"Would you deny me if it was?" Liz waited before answering. Brady turned to look at her with a raised eyebrow. "Well?"

"No," she conceded. She would give him whatever he wanted.

"I didn't think so." He placed his computer on the nightstand, grabbed her by the thighs, and slid her flat on the bed. Liz handed off the iPad and then wrapped her arms around Brady's neck. He kissed her deeply on the lips and she sighed into him. This was bliss.

"It's so good to have you here," he told her.

"I think I could get used to this."

They stayed like that for a while, lost in each other's kisses. She pressed her body firmly against his and let her hand trail down his six-pack. Every muscle was defined. Every inch smooth and beautiful. She reached the V that dipped down into navy blue boxers. He sucked in a breath as she fluttered her fingers against the skin.

"If you keep this up, we're not going to get anything done today."

"Who said I wanted to get anything done?" she asked, lowering her lashes and giving him a devious smirk.

"And I thought I was the demanding one." He kissed his way down her jaw. "Though I did have some surprises set up for you. If you want to lie in bed all day, far be it from me to deny you your wish."

His mouth had reached her collarbone and she felt his tongue flick out and caress her skin. She shivered.

Her brain didn't really comprehend what he was saying. Surprises. Something about surprises. Or lying in bed all day. Mmm . . . sex. His mouth hit her shoulder and his hand reached under her shirt to fondle her breast. She arched into his hand and forgot everything else he was saying.

He pinched her nipple hard enough for her to gasp. Expertly, he pulled her shirt over her head and brought the hardened nipple into his mouth. Her body came to life under his touch even after the marathon they'd had last night. Her lower half was sore from the exertion, but she didn't seem to care as he turned her on all over again. She didn't think she could ever get tired of this man.

He released her only to remove a pair of pink boy shorts she had slipped on last night. His boxers landed in the pile with her clothes on the floor and then he was hovering over her body, positioning himself between her legs. She lifted her hips to meet him and brought her legs to either side of his hips.

She urged him forward and then he filled her, sliding all the way into her with ease. "God, you're perfect," she groaned.

"Far from it, baby," he whispered, pushing her hair back from her face.

"Perfect for me."

And then they were moving together. In and out. Pushing forward. Taking their time and indulging in the feel of being perfectly in tune with another person. Nothing was rushed; every touch, every movement had meaning and purpose. They were pushing each other to new highs, gasping for breath and arching to get closer and closer to that complete oneness. It was like their two bodies had been made for each other, molded out of the same substance, born to lock together and go through this dance called life.

Liz's fingers dug into Brady's back leaving raw red marks as her nails scratched the surface. His hand wrapped around her middle and pulled her to a sitting position. Their lips locked all over again as he started bouncing her up and down on top of him. She felt him hit new depths, and she had to hold back her screams as he filled her over and over again.

The heat built between them. Sweat beaded their bodies. Brady grasped her hips and forced her down harder and harder. She felt the orgasm tear through her body all at once as he hit her in the exact right spot. She couldn't hold back and released the cries, yelling out his name to the city beyond the glass windows. Brady followed soon after and they both were left gasping for air, riding out the endorphin high.

They lay together in bed for a long time after that, snuggling in the tangled sheets, and listening to the sound of each other's heartbeat and the gentle hum of their breaths mingling.

Once they finally got out of bed, they took a long, hot shower and changed into fresh clothes. Liz was considering dragging him back to bed when he scooted her out of his place.

Frankly, she loved that they could go out together—even if there were reporters who wanted to photograph them together. She would put up with any of this to be with Brady.

He grasped her hand firmly in his as he backed his Range Rover out of the parking garage and started driving through the city.

"So, where are we headed?" Liz asked.

"Our new home," he answered immediately.

Liz choked and then started coughing and then laughing, trying to cover it up. She didn't think she did a good job, but what had he expected with that kind of statement. Their new *home*? Um . . . what the fuck was she supposed to say to that?

She still had to graduate. They had only been together a couple weeks. He was kind of getting ahead of himself.

Brady started laughing. "You should see your face."

Liz reached out and smacked him on the arm. "You're such a jerk!"

"I've been called worse," he said with a shrug. "By you, actually. What did you call me when we first met? Power hungry with my only interests in money?"

"And didn't you prove me wrong?" she murmured, squeezing his hand.

"Only with the best intentions. I believe I told you that you just needed to get to know me."

"I think I got to know every inch of you that night," Liz said, remembering the hotel after the Jefferson-Jackson gala they had attended.

"You abandoned your cheesecake for me. It's how I knew you were really into me."

"Maybe," she teased.

"Am I not convincing?" He brought her hand to his lips and gently kissed her hand, her palm, and then the inside of her wrist. She shivered.

"Yes, you're pretty damn convincing."

And it was completely true. As a politician, if he wasn't convincing, then Liz wasn't sure how he had gotten his job. And he had convinced her in more than just having sex with him—in falling for him, in loving him, in believing in him, in trusting him, in giving him her heart again.

Brady smirked and laced their fingers back together. He took a couple more turns and then pulled into a parking spot. "Here we are."

"Where is here?" she asked as she stepped out of the Range Rover and glanced around. Then her mouth dropped. "The White House?"

"I did say our new home."

Liz couldn't help it; she burst out laughing. "The White House is our new home? Still getting ahead of yourself, aren't you, Congressman Maxwell?"

"I like to plan ahead," he said as they started walking toward the White House. "It's all worked out so far."

"So it has," she said with a bright smile.

The only way to get access to a tour of the White House was through a member of Congress . . . and she sure had access to her Congressman's member.

She giggled to herself at the thought.

After showing identification at the gate, they were ushered through and Brady immediately started talking, giving her a full rundown of everything he knew about the building. It was like having her own personal tour guide. Apparently he had been in the White House dozens of times before he had ever been elected to Congress, since his father was a Senator and had been serving for nearly thirty years.

They entered the East Wing as the last of the regular tourists were being escorted out. Tours ended at one thirty in the afternoon, but since she was with Brady they were able to continue walking around. They passed through room after room. Blue Room, Green Room, Red Room, East Room, State Dining Room. Brady seemed to have more than his fair share of knowledge regarding the various rooms, and he was kind enough to indulge her in taking a picture with the portrait of George Washington.

Just when she thought it was over, he grabbed her hand and walked her toward the West Wing. Her heart fluttered. She knew it was silly to get this worked up, but she knew what was behind those doors. The President of the United States, the central point of the government, and, most important to her—the White House press offices.

Brady laughed when her eyes bugged out and he directed her down the hall. He opened the door to the press office. "Have a field day," he joked.

Liz walked in, mesmerized by the bustle. It was a weekend, so it was quieter than it would be on a weekday, but it was still abuzz with people working on articles, making phone calls, and speaking animatedly on the phone. She didn't dare interfere with anything that was happening, but just stared around her. This was her dream, the epicenter of all political journalism, and she was standing on holy ground.

"Thank you," she whispered to Brady when they exited a few minutes later. "That was . . . a dream."

"Good. I won't wake you up either." She smiled up at him, starry-eyed. "I have one more thing if you're interested."

Liz nodded. Brady walked farther down the West Colonnade, pointing out the famous Rose Garden that the Oval Office opened out to. Brady took her arm and directed her into the next room, and she stopped dead in her tracks.

"Are you serious?" she whispered.

She was standing in the Press Briefing Room, which was filled with only about fifty blue cushioned chairs facing a small podium in which the president gave speeches and addressed the press. If the press offices were holy ground, this was heaven for a reporter.

She ran her hands gingerly along the back of the first chair and imagined herself sitting there addressing the president. She wondered what they would be discussing, what topic he would bring forth to the public. She wondered if she would be addressed, what she would say, if her question would be answered, as it had been by Brady at her first press conference as a reporter.

And then she remembered: no paper and no job. She wasn't a reporter, not right now.

She whipped her hand back like she had been burned. She didn't belong here.

Her eyes shot over to where Brady was standing by, watching her with an adoring look on his face. He had done this for her. He had known what this would mean to her, and had wanted to make her happy.

It was with a heavy heart that she realized this pressroom might never be her future, because she was staring at what would be.

Chapter 12

MEANING

With a few hours left before the banquet, Brady and Liz had a small lunch and then drove back to his place to get ready for the event.

"So, I might have gone a little overboard knowing you were coming to visit," Brady said.

"Oh dear," she murmured. She didn't think overboard for Brady was like overboard for normal people. "How overboard?"

"I left you something on your pillow," he said with a smile.

He nodded his head toward the bedroom and she couldn't help herself; she rushed toward it. On the bed she found a small note. Her stomach did a somersault. Brady used to leave her messages like this. The first one she had ever found was at his lake house, which had instructed her on where to find the bathing suits in his closet.

Your present is in the closet.
Harder to remove than a bathing suit,

108

> *but I'll try not to destroy it.*
> *No promises.*
> *—B*

Liz shook her head and then walked into Brady's massive walk-in closet. A black floor-length garment bag hung facing the door with Versace written in big gold letters. Her eyes widened. *Versace?* He considered Versace a *little* overboard? She walked forward and unzipped the bag to reveal a red silk strapless gown. She checked the back and confirmed it was her size.

She might hyperventilate. It was so beautiful. She ran her fingers along the soft material and wondered how it would look hugging her body. As she moved to pull it off the hanger to inspect it further her foot nudged a box on the floor. She glanced down and saw the word Jimmy Choo written on the top. Who left a Jimmy Choo box *on the floor?* Blasphemy.

She opened the box to reveal black-and-silver peep-toe high heels with a delicate strap that buckled around her ankle. She tried to guess how much all of it cost. This was outright extravagant. Everything she had brought with her paled in comparison. Everything she *owned* paled in comparison.

With one more forlorn look at the expensive items, she walked back out to Brady.

His face fell. "You don't like it? Or it doesn't fit?"

"No, no, I love it. I haven't tried it on . . . any of it. I just . . . too much all at once," she admitted.

"Oh, is that all?" he asked good-naturedly. "No worries. It's on loan for tonight unless you like it and then, well . . . it's yours."

"On loan." She tried the word out for size. "Like what they do with celebrities."

He looked at her as if she was the most adorable thing he had ever seen. "I *am* kind of a celebrity, baby."

"Right. I forget. You're just . . . Brady to me."

He crossed the room and dropped a kiss on her mouth. "And that is why you're perfect for me."

Liz was relieved that the gown and shoes weren't here to stay, even though secretly she wouldn't mind having them in her closet. She and Brady had just started dating again. She wasn't sure she would have been able to accept such an expensive gift.

Liz returned to his room to start doing her hair and makeup. She pulled all her long blond hair into an elaborate low side bun with tendrils falling loosely, framing her face. When she finished, she delicately pulled on the soft gown. It fit her like a glove to the middle of her thighs and then bustled out in a mermaid design with a short train. The shoes added the extra inches she needed to keep the hem from dragging on the ground. She felt like a princess in a fairy tale, which was all too fitting when she walked out and saw Brady in a crisp black tuxedo with a black bow tie.

"Stunning," he murmured reverently.

She blushed and walked gingerly toward him. "Thank you. You look incredibly handsome."

"You look like I want to take you back into my bedroom and find out how fast I can remove a five-thousand-dollar dress."

Liz's mouth dropped. "Five thousand dollars? This is what five thousand dollars feels like?"

"And you look incredible in it. Almost perfect."

"Almost?" She arched an eyebrow.

"I think you just need one more thing," he said, pulling out a powder-blue box from his pocket.

"You weren't kidding about surprises this morning," she whispered.

He handed her the box and she took it in trembling hands. Tiffany's. What the hell was her life? She opened the box and found a pair of pear-shaped drop diamond earrings, each about a carat, set in platinum. They were simple, elegant, and positively exquisite.

"On loan?" she breathed.

His hand found her chin and brought her face up to meet his. "For you."

Wow. Brady had really outdone himself. But she felt rude rejecting the earrings after he had gone to all the trouble of picking them out for her, and they were beautiful. "Thank you," she finally said.

She removed the pearls she had been wearing and placed the diamonds into her ears. She took a look at them in the mirror and smiled. They did look amazing, and complemented the dress to perfection.

He kissed her on the mouth softly when he caught hold of her. "You're going to make it difficult to keep my hands to myself."

"I sure hope so," she murmured.

And then she kissed him. If they hadn't had somewhere to go, she wasn't sure he would have let her leave the apartment again.

They exited the building through the front lobby again and she noticed a shiny black stretch limo parked in front of the building. "Seriously?" she murmured.

"It's the only way to travel," Brady insisted.

The driver opened the door and Brady got in first, since Liz couldn't possibly slide over in that dress. They drove across town to pick up Victoria and Daniel, who were waiting for them outside their hotel.

Victoria screamed when she saw Liz's dress. "I feel underdressed," Victoria said. She was wearing a floor-length halter number that looked great on her curves, but it might have been the first time Victoria was right: she couldn't keep up with Versace.

"You look beautiful," Liz reassured her.

"Oh I know, but you look . . ." Victoria pondered the right word and then smiled. "You look like the fucking First Lady."

Liz blushed. "Can the First Lady wear strapless dresses?"

"You could. Right, Brady?" Victoria asked.

He smiled, that same adoring look in his eyes. "You can wear whatever you want."

They all piled into the limo and then drove back into the center of the city. The driver dropped them off in front of a convention center, where they were quickly escorted toward a banquet hall. Brady placed his hand on Liz's shoulder and pulled her aside.

"Mind if I talk to you before we go inside?" he asked.

"Oh, sure," Liz said hesitantly.

"Y'all can just head in and get drinks. We'll only be a minute," Brady told Victoria and Daniel.

"See you inside," Victoria said with a smile. Liz heard her say something about finding the bar.

"What's up?" she asked nervously.

"More surprises. I hope you're okay with this one." She arched her eyebrow and waited for him to elaborate. "Well, I don't mean to spring this on you, but my parents will be here tonight."

Liz swallowed nervously. "Your parents?"

"Yeah. Nothing formal. I just thought it would be nice to reintroduce y'all before we enter the banquet."

"Oh. Well, okay," she said, as if she had a choice.

"Don't worry." He kissed her forehead. "They're going to love you."

Liz nodded nervously and tried to straighten out her wrinkle-free dress. If they were going to pick a night to play meet the parents, at least she knew she looked fabulous.

Brady led her around a corner and into a smaller, nearly empty parlor. Her palms sweated, and she took a deep breath to try to calm herself. Brady squeezed her hand for reassurance and she plastered on a smile.

"Ah, there you are, sweetie," Brady's mother said, walking up and giving him a kiss on his cheek. "Your father was just wondering when you'd be in. Liz." She gave Liz a warm hug. "So nice to see you again."

"You too, Mrs. Maxwell," Liz said with a cheery smile.

"Oh, honey, please call me Marilyn."

"Of course."

"And I'm Jeff," Brady's father said, coming forward and extending his hand. Ever the politician. She shook his hand and felt herself relaxing. "We met at the restaurant in Chapel Hill, correct?"

"Yes, sir," she responded.

"I love that place," he said cordially. "We should all go back when we're home again."

"I think so too," Brady said, wrapping his arm loosely around Liz's waist.

"Then it's settled," Marilyn said. "We'll get together later this spring."

"Liz is graduating from UNC this May, so maybe around then," Brady suggested casually.

"Oh, that sounds lovely. I spent so many years there teaching chemistry. My first love," Marilyn said.

"Second," Jeff corrected, kissing his wife softly on the forehead.

"Well, of course, but I think I loved chemistry first." She shrugged unapologetically.

Liz just stared at them in awe. They were totally adorable and in love. She hoped that she would be like them one day.

"Let's not keep everyone waiting," Jeff said, ushering them to a side door.

They walked into the banquet hall and found it full of people dressed to the nines in formal wear. Tables were set up around the room for dinner, which was about to be served, and a dance floor took up a large portion of the front of the room.

"What's this for, anyway?" Liz asked.

Brady shrugged. "Just a state dinner. We have them all the time."

"Is the president going to show up?"

"Probably not. Usually the money goes to a charity. I believe this one is for children's literacy."

"A cause we can all get behind."

"Indeed," he said, motioning for her to follow his parents to a table. Victoria and Daniel were already seated at the designated spot.

Introductions were made and then everyone sat down for dinner. A couple appeared to fill the last two vacant spots and they seemed to be good friends of Brady's parents. Brady filled Liz in that the man was one of the senators from Massachusetts.

Dinner came and went with no problems or pauses in conversation. Brady's parents were expert conversationalists and kept the company entertained the whole night. At one point, Victoria insisted on switching spots with Liz so that she could speak to Marilyn about Johns Hopkins. She was working in genetics, but Marilyn had worked nearly thirty years in chemistry and knew faculty all over the country. Daniel weighed in at one point and soon the table was full of science speak that made Liz's eyes glaze over.

Once dessert was cleared and it was clear that they weren't going to pull Victoria and Daniel away from Brady's mother anytime soon, Brady stood and offered her his hand. "Dance?"

She glared at him. "You know I don't dance."

"I can make anyone look good."

"Yes, I know, but that was before anyone knew who I was."

Brady pushed his hand forward, telling her very clearly that he wasn't going to take no for an answer. "Liz, please."

Oh, and he asked nicely. She dropped her hand in his and let him help her up. "Only because you begged," she whispered cattily.

"I won't be the only one later tonight," he growled into her ear as he directed her to the dance floor.

She bit her lip. "I'll promise to act like I don't enjoy it."

"Sounds like someone needs a spanking to remember who is in charge."

Her cheeks felt warm as she moved into his arms on the dance floor. "You wouldn't."

"Don't tell me what I would and wouldn't do."

He twirled her around the floor and she focused on keeping up, but his eyes were gleaming with triumph at stumping her. "What if I enjoy it?" she finally asked him.

He smiled. "Then I'll spank harder."

"You should put your money where your mouth is."

"Oh, I will," he said, shifting her closer. "And my money is all over your body right now."

An image of Brady's mouth touching every inch of her body flew into her mind, and she licked her lips at the thought. Oh, yes, she wouldn't mind any of this one bit.

The song ended and Brady, knowing what was good for him, pulled her off of the dance floor. She smiled up at him, lost in their own world. Here she was in a red silk Versace dress, Jimmy Choos, and Tiffany earrings at a charity banquet with her boyfriend, a sitting congressman. She knew this was some kind of fairy tale, but she didn't mind living it for a night.

Then she turned around to go find refreshments, and came face-to-face with Erin Edwards.

"Oh," Liz whispered. She didn't know what else to say when confronted with the woman who had singlehandedly lost Liz her job at the *New York Times*.

"Hi," Erin said with an easy, casual smile that Liz immediately recognized as the woman's version of a campaign mask. She looked pretty with her dark hair in loose waves to her shoulders. She was wearing a soft blue floor-length dress with extensive beading that came up over one shoulder.

"Hello, Erin. I didn't know you would be in attendance tonight," Brady said formally, not taking his hand off of Liz's waist.

"I received tickets last minute."

Liz glanced around to see if anyone had noticed that they were all talking. The last thing she wanted was for it to end up in the paper that they'd had a confrontation with Erin.

"How have you been?" Brady asked, as if she hadn't sold them out to the press. But of course it made sense. They had to look like they played well with others. Over the course of his life Brady had acquired restraint in talking to people in public.

"Fine. Just fine." Erin took a step forward, lowering her voice. "How are you? Are you happy?"

This at least Brady could answer with ease. "Yes. Very."

Erin nodded and tried to hide the pain that crossed her face. It was then that Liz realized she had been looking at all of this wrong. Erin wasn't out to get them. She hadn't even been after her fifteen minutes of fame. She was a morning anchor, after all. She was on television every day. She was just a hurt woman still very much in love with Brady.

Liz knew that feeling. She knew what it felt like to be standing in Erin's shoes. Erin had probably thought that she and Brady would be a power couple, and when it had ended, she hadn't known what to do. Liz had wallowed for months after she and Brady separated, holding her secret to herself for over a year. Erin had gone straight to the press when she had put everything together, or so she thought. The other woman had done it because she was hurt, thinking that she had loved Brady for nothing even while they had been together.

Maybe Erin wasn't the bad guy after all. Staring at her looking so small in the banquet hall made Liz actually feel . . . sorry for her.

Losing Brady had been terrible. Liz could understand what she was going through.

"Well . . . well good," Erin said, forcing a smile back on her face. "I just wanted to check. I know things are . . . tense."

That was one word for it.

"But I just wanted to talk to you . . ." she continued, "to see how you were doing."

"We're doing just fine," Brady said, emphasizing the *we*. "I hope you're doing the same."

"Yes, of course," Erin said, stalling. "I should say that I'm sorry, Liz."

Liz fidgeted. She hadn't expected Erin to even address her. "Oh?"

"I'm sorry for making things worse than they are. I understand how the press can be."

Liz wasn't sure how sincere her apology was, since she had only just talked to the press this week. Maybe she had made a rash decision like Hayden had. A couple days after selling her out to the newspaper, Hayden had tried to apologize too. She wondered if Hayden had been feeling the same thing that Erin had—that he had made a mistake, he loved her, and wanted to make it all right. It was too little too late for both of them at this point.

"Thank you," Liz said. She didn't forgive the other woman, but she could accept her apology.

Erin seemed to realize that she couldn't say anything else to mediate the situation and gave them a half smile before departing.

"Well, that was fun," Liz said with a sigh.

"She was perfectly nice."

"She's still in love with you," she stated simply.

He shrugged. "That doesn't matter."

"Do you think she was really sorry?"

"As sorry as she'll ever be, I would guess."

That would have to be good enough.

They walked back over to his parents and saw that Daniel was talking quite animatedly with Marilyn. As they approached, Victoria stood and smiled radiantly at them. She threw her arms around Liz and whirled her in place.

"Thank you for bringing us. Marilyn is brilliant!" Victoria crooned.

Liz laughed and tried to steady herself. "I'm glad you're enjoying yourself."

"You seem tense."

"Erin was here."

"Brady's bitch ex?" Victoria said not too subtly.

Liz glanced around. "Yes. Keep it down."

"Oh right. Present company and all that. So, what happened?"

"She apologized."

"God, what is it with you and backstabbing assholes apologizing after they do something wrong? I bet these are the same people who slapped kids on the playground when they were little and then turned themselves in to the teacher," Victoria said dramatically.

"That does sound like Hayden," Liz confessed.

Victoria giggled. "It really does."

"Let's just forget about it. Things will work out."

"Oh, look at you, Ms. Optimism."

"Come on, bitch. Let's go dance!"

And they did. Despite the funny looks at the two of them together on the dance floor, giggling and cracking jokes, they had an all-around good time. Brady commandeered Liz at some point and Daniel scooped up Victoria. They spent the remainder of the night locked in each other's arms and making the most of their time together.

As the crowd dwindled, Brady's parents came by to say good night. Marilyn spoke briefly to Victoria and Daniel, offering them any help that they needed and saying to feel free to get hold of her with questions. Liz received a hug from both of them and then they were gone.

"We should get home," Brady said into her ear as they swayed back and forth to a slow song. "I'm thinking about all of the ways I'm going to make you beg."

He kissed her softly on the mouth and then gestured for them to leave. Victoria and Daniel followed them out. The limo ride was relatively quiet as they all basked in the afterglow of the party. They dropped the other couple off at Johns Hopkins and then returned to Brady's penthouse.

Brady closed the door and immediately reached for her. "How fast can I get you out of Versace?"

"It's just one zipper," she teased.

"Let me see." His hand slid down the side of the dress and tugged down on the zipper.

Liz sighed. She had been trying to push this thought out of her mind all weekend, but if the conversation waited until tomorrow then they wouldn't talk about it at all. She had wanted to tell him in person and here she was with her opportunity.

"Can we talk first?" she asked, biting her lip.

"What do we have to talk about?" he asked, nuzzling her neck. "I'm not usually a talk-first kind of guy."

Liz pressed her hands on the front of his tux. "I know, but I think we should."

"You've been teasing me all night and you'd rather talk?" he asked seriously.

"Rather talk? No. Need to talk? Yes."

He dropped his hands from her zipper and nodded. "All right. Are you okay? Did something happen?"

"Well, kind of. I just . . . wanted to tell you in person," she said, walking over to the couch and taking a seat. He sat next to her with a concerned look on his face. "I lost my job offer from the *New York Times*."

"What?" he asked. "When? How did that happen?"

"It happened Tuesday after the article ran about Erin."

"Tuesday," he said numbly.

"Yes. I, um . . . I really wanted to tell you," Liz tried to explain. "Nancy, my contact at the paper, called and said that they could have overlooked our relationship and they wanted to see if it would all blow over. But then when more and more information came out, she couldn't fight her superiors. They had to cut me loose."

Brady ran his hands back through his hair. "Cut you loose. They cut you loose because . . . of me."

"Well, because of Erin."

He gave her a pointed look. "Erin is because of me. I've ruined everything for you. You left me for my career to begin with, and now that we're together I've destroyed yours. You're not working for the UNC paper and you no longer have the *Times*. That's the equivalent of my losing the campaign." Even saying that seemed to pain him.

"Look, it's not your fault. I *chose* this, Brady. I chose you. We both knew what could happen."

"Yeah, but, Liz . . . your dreams of becoming a political journalist. I took you to the White House briefing room yesterday. If I'd known . . ."

"I still would have wanted you to take me." She took his hand in hers. "Dreams can change, anyway. My mentor is looking to get me into graduate programs' late admittance. I'm going to apply to some online columnist positions. I'll be okay."

"I know plenty of people who could help."

Liz cringed. "I was afraid you might say that."

"Why do you look like that's the worst thing I could say?"

"I know the business is who you know rather than what you know, but I want to make it on my own merit."

"Liz," he groaned. "I've destroyed your chance at the *New York Times*; you can at least oblige me the chance to help fix it."

"This is why I didn't tell you over the phone. I want to do this on my own, prove it to myself. Professor Mires encouraged me to take this in stride, and said that sometimes one closed door means another one opens. As much as I appreciate your help and know it's coming from a good place, I want to open my own door."

"Okay, but if doors remain closed, you'll let me help?" he pleaded. "At least promise me that. I *want* to help."

"All right. If nothing works out, then we'll try it your way."

She hoped that time would never come.

Chapter 13

MAKING AMENDS

Liz spent the next three weeks working away on her final term paper for her internship and managed to get it to Professor Mires on the Friday before spring break. She hoped it was everything that she expected of her, but turning in a first draft always made her anxious.

Professor Mires thumbed through the large document and nodded her head. "This looks great. I'll read through it over spring break and get it back to you on Tuesday during class."

"Sounds good. Thank you," Liz said with a smile. "Have you heard anything from your graduate school contacts?"

"Ah, yes," she said, standing and rifling through some paperwork. "Here are a list of places that you should apply. They'll be looking out for your application. I would recommend including the project that you presented at the colloquium last spring as your writing sample. It was superb."

Liz took the list and scanned it. Five places. Out of all the graduate programs she was down to five choices, and that was only if they accepted her late admittance. Missouri, Northwestern, Columbia, Maryland, and American University. At least two of them were in or near D.C.; that wasn't terrible odds.

Brady flew her to D.C. for the week of spring break, since she didn't have to be in New York City for her internship. As disappointed as she was about not working with the *New York Times*, it was a dream to spend an entire week with Brady. No interruptions. No rushed meetings. No secrets whatsoever. Just the two of them together every second they could be.

She got to see his office and meet the staff. Heather actually managed to act like a normal human being, even though it was clear that they were still on rocky ground. Elliott took her on a tour of the Rayburn building, where Brady's office was located. Liz and Elliott joked and laughed while they wandered down the plethora of corridors.

She and Brady had lunch on the steps of the Capitol building. He took her to fancy restaurants and dive bars and rooftop parties. He took her on a tour of old cemeteries. She insisted on peeking in at Hayden's sister, Jamie's, latest artwork and sighed in relief when she wasn't there. They snuggled in bed and watched bad movies over Chinese food. She fell asleep in his lap while he read on his iPad.

And they had sex. Lots of incredible sex. Nearly every morning and every night until her body was sore and satiated. If that was even possible with Brady Maxwell.

The next two months were a wonderful haze of Brady. They fell into an easy routine where every weekend he would fly down to Chapel Hill or she would fly up to D.C. Liz focused on her graduate school applications and the articles she was writing for fun on the side that she had submitted to a few online columns. She also started up regular tennis sessions with Easton. It made her feel better about having so much extra time and kept up her stamina, which she needed when it came to Brady.

Soon she was closing her booklet on her last final exam in her college career. She felt a little sentimental turning it in to her professor and walking out the doors. Campus was quiet. She had one of the last exams of the day, though there were still a few days left in the exam schedule.

This had been her home for the last four years, and it was surreal to think that she would be leaving it behind for . . . whatever was to come in the fall. She stared around at the brick buildings and beautiful landscapes with newfound appreciation. Everything was going to change.

She knew that before she left she had one more place she needed to go: the newspaper office. It was late enough in the afternoon that she hoped everyone would have cleared out by now.

Trekking across campus, she savored the short walk and then took the stairs up to the second floor of the Union. She glanced into the office and saw that it looked deserted. She breathed a sigh of relief and pushed the door open.

She wasn't sure what had brought her here. She hadn't set foot inside the office since clearing out her desk after Massey had requested her "temporary leave of absence." She had barely set foot in the Union for fear of running into anyone from the paper. The only person she still kept in contact with was Savannah and on occasion Tristan, but they had been her A-team from the beginning.

She ran her hands over the desks, most of which had been emptied for the summer, and then she walked to her old office. She and Brady had had sex in that office. She had spent a year of her life working as editor out of that office. It would always feel a bit like it belonged to her.

She toed the door open and took a step back. "Oh, sorry," Liz whispered, seeing Massey hunched over the desk on her laptop.

"Liz," Massey said softly, glancing around. "What are you doing here?"

"I was just leaving," she said, turning to go.

"Wait," Massey called. She jumped up from her desk and into the open doorway.

Liz stood still and took a deep breath before facing her again. "What's up?"

"I haven't seen you since . . . since you left."

"Left . . ."

"You know what I mean," Massey said. "How have you been?"

"Keeping myself busy. But I'm sure you guessed that with all the things popping up in papers," Liz said dismissively. She didn't want to have this rift in her friendship, and she knew it wasn't exactly Massey's fault that Liz had been forced out of the paper. Still, the argument hit too close to home.

Massey cringed at her statement. "Well, I'm glad you've been busy. When are you moving to New York?"

It was Liz's turn to cringe. "I was let go."

"Oh," Massey said. "That's awful. I'm so sorry."

"Yeah. It sucks," Liz found herself admitting.

"I can't believe they did that."

"Well, they did."

"What do you plan to do now?" Massey asked.

Liz shrugged. "Kind of an open game plan. Applying late to grad programs."

"Can you do that?"

"We'll see. Professor Mires thinks so."

"Oh right. She loves you," Massey said. "If I can get into UVA for the PhD program, then you're sure to get in anywhere . . . even late admittance."

"You got in!" Liz cried. "That's so great."

"Yeah. I was really excited. So much to do to get ready to go now, though."

Liz could feel the tension slowly draining out of her. She might be angry with Massey for what had happened, but she was angrier at the system that had made all of this the reality. Not any one person had ruined everything that she had worked toward. It wasn't fair to pin it all on Massey just because she was an easy target for Liz's animosity.

"I know what you mean. Victoria and her boyfriend are moving to D.C. over the summer. They both got into Johns Hopkins and are planning to live together when they go to school. Our house looks like a train wreck right now," Liz told her.

"Victoria and boyfriend in the same sentence is still weird to me."

"Join the club, but they're really serious now."

"Serious enough to move to D.C. together and get into the same PhD program," Massey said, shaking her head. "Who knew Victoria would be the first of us to settle down?"

Liz laughed. "No one! But I'm really happy for her. She needed someone like Daniel to keep her ass in line."

"And if any of us know her, we know he's probably keeping her *ass* in line a lot."

"Oh, God, you're as bad as she is," Liz cried, throwing her hands up.

Massey laughed. "So what about you? Are you happy with . . . everything?"

"I'm happy with Brady," she told her, and then glanced around.

"I'm not working," Massey said. "It's all off the record."

Liz sagged. She was so tired of reporters. She didn't like being on her guard all the time. "I spend every weekend with him and it's amazing. We just click. You know?"

Massey got a dreamy look in her eye. "I think I do."

"Are you dating someone?"

"Oh, no," she said, shaking her head. "But there is a guy I like. Knowing me, it won't go anywhere."

"You should go for it," Liz encouraged her.

"You're right. Maybe I will."

"Well, I should probably get out of here. I just wanted to look at the office one more time," Liz told her. "Probably sounds stupid."

"No, it doesn't. I know exactly what you mean."

Their eyes met and they both smiled. Everything wasn't suddenly better between them, but they at least had a chance that it would be. That was good enough for Liz. She was glad she had decided to come to the newspaper after all. Waving good-bye to Massey, she exited the newspaper building feeling just a little bit lighter.

Liz turned the corner to take the stairs and stopped dead in her tracks. She gasped. "Hayden?" She hadn't seen her ex-boyfriend since he had walked out of her house back in February.

"Hey, Liz," he said, walking the last few stairs to stand next to her. She took a few steps backward. "You look great."

"What are you doing here?" she asked numbly.

"I came to see you."

Liz just stared at him. "You drove all the way to Chapel Hill to see me?"

"It's not like it's the first time. I used to do it all the time," he said with that same stunning smile he'd always had.

Liz really took a look at him. The last time she had seen him he had been messed up from finding out about Brady, outing her to the paper, and then not hearing from her for the weekend. He had looked like a wreck. He didn't look like a wreck anymore. He was wearing pressed khaki shorts and a baby blue polo. His Ray-Bans were hanging from green Croakies and his hair was perfectly styled, a little shorter than normal. But something was different. It was almost like his hazel eyes seemed . . . sad.

"No, but that was before . . ." Liz mumbled.

"I know, but I just really wanted to talk to you. I haven't seen you in months."

"There's a reason for that," Liz said, crossing her arms.

"I know that, and I know you're . . . with him now." He didn't seem to be able to say Brady's name.

"Then why would you think to come here?"

"Because . . . I don't know, I just wanted to talk to you. I wanted to see you. I wanted to make sure you were okay," he said. "I want to make things better."

"How did you even know I'd be here?" she asked.

Hayden looked sheepish. "I checked the exam schedule for your classes, but I guess you finished early. I assumed you'd be at the paper. You live at the paper."

Liz laughed in his face and then covered her mouth. It was a symbol of how much had changed with her that she could even laugh at that fact. "I was forced out."

Hayden stared at her, stunned. "They kicked you off?"

"Suggested I take a temporary leave of absence," Liz said, rolling her eyes.

"Because of the article?"

"Yes."

"Wow, I'm sorry," he said. Liz could see the pain in his eyes for what he had done. An awkward silence ensued before he spoke up again. "What . . . what have you been doing in the meantime?"

"Basking in the greatness of my new relationship."

He cringed. "I deserve that."

"Yeah."

He took a deep breath, and if it was possible he looked sadder, like someone had just kicked his puppy.

"I think I should go. I'm meeting Savannah for lunch on Franklin. I was just passing through," she said, walking past him to the stairs. She heard him following her and sighed.

"Do you think I could walk you?" Hayden asked once they reached the bottom.

He wasn't going to make this easy, was he? "I think I know how to get to Franklin. It's like a five-minute walk."

He gave her a knowing look. "Please let me."

"Why are you pushing this?" she demanded.

"I have to make it right sometime. Might as well start today."

"You could have made it right by never reporting about what happened, but you didn't. You told Calleigh and you slapped your name on it. This is worse than that, Hayden."

"I shouldn't have done it," he said, holding his hands up. "I can't time-travel and change things, but you're happy now   with him What does it hurt for me to walk the five minutes with you to Franklin?"

"It had better not hurt a damn thing," she said. She walked to the exit and he kept up with her at an easy pace.

"You really do look nice today, Lizzie."

Liz shook her head at the nickname. Too many memories flashed before her mind all at once. Their first kiss in D.C., getting together on election night, lying near a waterfall in Hawaii, walking out of the newspaper together every day. They had spent so much time together, and that one nickname brought it all back fresh to her mind.

"Flattery is not accepted," she said, looking away from him.

"I guess I'm glad I went with nice then instead of gorgeous, because that really would have been flattery."

"Still not accepted." She didn't know how many times Hayden had called her gorgeous when they had dated. He needed to stop bringing up the past. The past was over. Things might be more complicated with Brady than they were with Hayden, but at least when she was with Brady she knew that she didn't want to be with anyone else. That hadn't been something she could say while dating Hayden.

He smiled faintly next to her and they started walking toward Franklin Street. It wasn't exactly uncomfortable. Things with Hayden had always been easy. Her romantic attachment to him had stemmed out of adoration for the way he ran the office, and his charismatic nature. It was only now that she was with Brady that she realized so much of her relationship with Hayden had been an extension of their friendship and less of the passion that came with romance.

That had been fine at the time, but knowing the alternative, it just seemed plain to her now.

"How was your spring break?" Hayden asked after a couple minutes.

"It was nice," she said. "I spent it in D.C."

"Ah," he said, understanding perfectly. "That makes sense. I finally got some time off to visit my parents, and Jamie said she saw you at a gallery exhibit."

"She did!" Liz gasped. "I didn't see her."

"I think she didn't know what to say."

"That would be a first," Liz said.

He smiled. "It would be."

"Well, maybe I'll look her up when I'm next in D.C. I don't want her to feel like she can't say hi," she said softly, even though she knew exactly what Jamie had been feeling.

"I think she'd like that."

They continued to Top O, where she was meeting Savannah, and then stood together for a couple seconds. Liz wasn't sure what to say. She didn't want any kind of relationship with Hayden, but it had been nice having a normal conversation. Things would never be how they were before. They couldn't just erase their relationship or its disastrous ending. Hayden looked as if he wanted to say something more, but he didn't.

Liz averted her gaze from his searching hazel eyes and finally spoke up. "Well, I should go on up and find Savannah."

"Yeah. Okay. It was great seeing you."

Liz bit her lip to keep from responding. It had kind of been nice to see him.

"Do you . . . think we could do this again?" Hayden asked tentatively.

"I don't know." Brady would *hate* for her to see Hayden. She knew how he felt about him. And she didn't really blame him.

"I'll be here on Thursday, because I'm covering graduation this weekend for the paper. Maybe we could get coffee or lunch?"

"I don't know," she repeated.

"Well, just think about it," he said, not pressing his luck. "I do want to make this right. And I'd like to see you."

"Maybe. I'll get back to you on that." She was going to have to tell Brady. She didn't know how much he was going to freak about this, but she hated holding grudges. She would never get over what Calleigh did, but Hayden was a different story. They had both made mistakes in that relationship.

"Giving me some hope. I'll let you get to Savannah," he said with a smile before departing.

Liz tried to clear her head as she jogged up to the stairs to Top of the Hill. Savannah was waiting for her at a table overlooking the street. She jumped up when Liz arrived and looked frantic.

"Oh my God, was that Hayden?" Savannah asked immediately.

"Yeah. It was . . . interesting."

"I can't believe he would come here to see you." She took her seat and Liz sat across from her.

"Me either. He said he wants to make amends and that he wants to see me again this week to try to . . . I don't even know," she said, struggling to explain. "Maybe apologize?"

"Sounds sneaky. Brady isn't going to like that."

Liz nodded. "No . . . he isn't."

Chapter 14
AN OKAY PLACE

Y ou did what?" Brady demanded, his tone harsh when she told him later that day that she had run into Hayden.

"He was on campus."

He paused before responding. "I don't want him anywhere near you."

She had been expecting this response. Even if she hadn't dated Hayden for a year and a half and he hadn't had sex with her after finding out about Brady, she knew that Brady would hate him. He had always been the jealous type. When she had kissed Hayden two summers ago and told Brady about it, he had freaked out. They were in a much better place than that now, but that didn't change how he felt about Hayden.

"I know you don't, but I couldn't really help it." She plopped back down on her bed and waited for his response.

"I don't care. You shouldn't have let him walk you anywhere."

"What did you want me to do?" she asked, getting irritated. "Push him down the stairs?"

"It would have been preferable."

"Maybe, but I mean . . . nothing happened. He just wanted to apologize and make things right."

Brady sighed. "Liz, that is guy code for he wants you back."

"No, it isn't," she said, sitting up straighter. "Plus, that's not even an option."

"Trust me. Him talking to you, stalking you to your class, showing up on campus, trying to apologize means he just wants you back. And frankly, he can't have you."

Liz shook her head. Yeah, Hayden had complimented her, but he couldn't honestly think that she would still be interested in him after what had happened between them. "You know my heart belongs to you."

"I just don't like the idea of him being able to get to you," Brady said. "I can't be there all the time. I'm not even getting in for graduation until Saturday morning."

"You don't have to protect me," Liz told him earnestly. "It's just Hayden."

"You're talking about the guy who raped you," Brady whispered.

Liz cringed. She hated that word. She still didn't relate to it or believe that it had happened. Yes, they'd had sex when she didn't want to, but she didn't tell him no or try to stop him. "That word, Brady."

"I'm just reminding you that he's not always had good intentions. I don't want him to hurt you, and the best way for that to happen is for you to just stay away from him."

"Well, he's going to be in town this weekend for graduation and wants to get coffee," she said, laying it out plainly.

"Absolutely not."

"I wasn't aware I was asking for permission," she spat.

"I'm telling you this is a horrible idea. You know it's a horrible idea. What good is going to come from it? You forgive him for the shit he put you through and suddenly you're friends again? The world doesn't work that way."

"I forgave *you* for the shit that you put me through!" she yelled back, standing and walking across her room in frustration. "And I never even said I was going to forgive him. I didn't say anything. I'm just willing to hear out what he has to say."

"Why? Why must you torture me with this? *Hearing out* your ex-boyfriend is the last thing that is good for us."

"You saw and talked to Erin," Liz pointed out.

"Erin didn't hurt you!" Brady cried. He was clearly pissed off at this point and it just made her more frustrated. She hadn't even wanted to see Hayden, but now this whole thing just irritated her.

"Erin made me lose my job! Erin pushed us back into the papers! You flaunted Erin in front of me for a year! She hurt me plenty."

"Hayden sold us out to the papers in the first place!"

"Just because *you* want to hurt him doesn't mean I can't see him."

"I do want to hurt him," Brady admitted. "I hate the guy. He's a douche bag. He's unstable. He's one more thing that kept you away from me. Can't you see that you shouldn't be around him?"

"Don't tell me who I should see. I can make decisions for myself."

"I'm not telling you! I'm asking you not to see him because it's fucking stupid, Liz."

"Glad to know my decisions are fucking stupid," she grumbled.

"It's not *your* decisions that are stupid. It's just anything that involves him. He's a parasite. He's feeding off of your good nature."

"My ex-boyfriend is a parasite?" Liz asked in disbelief. "You're really winning your cause."

"Fine. Go see him. Because that makes perfect sense."

"I didn't even want to see him! God!"

"Then why are you pushing this?" he asked, exasperated.

"Because you're making it seem like I can't see him if I want to. He didn't say he wants to get back with me. He said he wants to make things right. If he makes one move or says one thing about wanting to get back with me, I'll walk out of the building and let you tell me you told me so."

"I'd rather not have to tell you."

Liz sighed and tried to see Brady's side in this. They were finally together and now her ex-boyfriend, who for a long time Brady had thought she had left him for, was trying to come back into the picture. Not so crazy for him to be pissed about it.

"Look, I don't blame you for feeling like this, but I'm not one of your staffers. I'm your girlfriend."

"I know you are," he said with a sigh. "I'm not trying to dictate to you. I'm obviously poorly explaining my position. Let's hope I do better on the campaign this year. Tell me how to convince you this is a bad idea."

"Just trust me. If Erin came back to you, apologetic, begging to see you for coffee or lunch to make things right, what would *you* do? You would see her," Liz answered for him.

"What would you say if I went?" he asked.

"I'd be insanely jealous, but I'd know that you left her for me and that is what matters. That it's you and me."

"Can you and me not include . . . him?"

"It is just you and me, but . . ."

"But?" he prompted.

Liz sighed, trying to mull it over. "I don't know. If I decide to see him, I don't want you to be pissed at me."

Brady cursed under his breath. "You make this damn difficult, woman."

"Well, you're not the easiest person to live with either, Congressman."

"No one ever said I was. But if he hurts you now, I can't beat the shit out of him like he deserves," Brady said coldly.

"I'm telling you that Hayden doesn't want me back and he's not going to hurt me. If he does want me back, then *I'll* hurt him, okay? You have nothing to worry about."

"I'm not worried about us. I just . . ." Brady paused. "Hold on. Heather is calling."

"Okay."

Liz waited on the line for a few minutes, trying to dissect the conversation they'd just had. At first she had thought Brady felt threatened by Hayden, but even the idea of that was preposterous. Even while she had been with Hayden, she had been thinking about Brady.

"Hey, baby, I have to go. Can we continue this conversation tonight?" he asked.

"Sure," Liz said with a sigh. So much to think about. She wished they could have worked it all out before he had to get off the phone, but maybe it would be good for them to cool down before they got into another argument.

Liz tossed her phone back on her bed and ran her hand back through her hair. The whole conversation had spiraled so far out of control.

Trying to clear her head, she walked into the kitchen, popped open a bottle of red wine, and poured herself a glass. Victoria walked in just then and raised an eyebrow.

"Long day?"

"Exams are over," Liz said, raising her glass and taking a big gulp.

"I can't believe we're going to graduate in six days."

"I can't believe you're moving to D.C. right after that."

Victoria grabbed a glass and started pouring herself some wine. "You'll be up there all the time anyway with Brady."

"Yeah. It's just weird. We've lived together for four years."

"I'd totally go lesbian for you if that's what you're getting at," Victoria said with a wink.

Liz rolled her eyes and laughed. "Hardly."

"So, who were you on the phone with? I heard some raised voices."

"Brady," Liz said, taking another sip. "Hayden showed up on campus today and said he wanted to talk to me."

"God! Can't he just leave you alone and not interfere with your life?"

"I don't know. He just wants to try to make it better."

Victoria shook her head. "You know how I feel about Lane. I think you should let him suffer." Liz cringed and drank some more. "Seriously, you just don't like to see anyone hurting, do you?"

"Not really. I made up with Massey today."

"Massey is fine. Whatever. She didn't sell you out to the newspaper," Victoria said pointedly. "I know you. You're going to see him, aren't you?"

"I haven't decided, but Brady got all pissed off at me."

"Rightfully so, bitch! Think about it."

"I have!" she cried. "I'm not rushing into things. I didn't even really want to see him, but then talking to Brady, I kind of talked myself into it."

"If you ruin this thing with Brady because of Hayden . . ."

"No! No way. I'm not going there," Liz said vehemently. "Brady is everything. He's my past, present, and future. I just kind of want to close the lid on Hayden. It'll make it easier to stomach everything that happened knowing that we're in an okay place."

"He doesn't deserve an okay place," Victoria told her.

"Maybe not."

They stood together like that, going through a couple glasses of wine each. School was officially over and it was strange for both of them having nothing they had to do. They had spent the last four years working endlessly and now it was all coming to a close.

When they lapsed into silence, Liz turned to absentmindedly scroll through her phone. Her thoughts turned to her career and what she was going to do now that she was only days away from graduating without an acceptance letter to graduate school and no job on the horizon.

Then she remembered a lunch conversation with her friend Justin a year ago, when he had tried to convince her to come work for him. He had originally been part of Liz's scholarship program, but after he got a DUI, the university had stripped his scholarship. He'd dropped out of school and started his own company online that was just getting off the ground. He had tried to recruit Liz, but she had always been too busy. If he was interested, maybe she could use that as a starting point.

She jotted out a text to him.

Hey, do you have a free minute?

He responded almost immediately.

Sure. What's up?

She dialed his number and he answered on the first ring. She waved her phone at Victoria and then, on wobbly feet, took her wine into the living room.

"Hey," she warbled.

"What's up? You sound tipsy."

"Just a bit." She plopped down on the couch.

"Cool. What did you want to talk about?"

"Do you still need help with your blog?"

"Yeah. Why? You interested?" he asked.

"Um . . . yeah. What would you need me to do?" She had kind of called on a whim. All she knew was that Justin was running a company based around organizing YouTube videos and compiling them in a coherent categorical system.

"You'll just run the blog and keep the masses entertained. I can send you over the information. Just write your opinion."

"You know what? Sure. Let's do it."

"I knew you'd come around," Justin said cheerfully. "When can you start?"

Liz couldn't believe it was really that easy. "Now?"

"Awesome! I know you'll be perfect for this."

Liz laughed and then they got off the phone. She had just gotten herself a job! No strings attached. It felt good to know that her writing was still valued, even if it wasn't on the same level or even in the same discipline as she had been trained. Professor Mires had said one door closed, and another one opened.

Liz was starting to believe her.

Chapter 15

PRIORITIES

Thursday rolled around quicker than expected. Liz still had to decide what she was going to do about Hayden. Now that she'd had time to cool down after her argument with Brady, she had realized just how stupid the whole thing had been.

She and Brady hadn't talked about it since their argument Monday, but she knew him well enough to know that he was anxious about what she was going to do. And she didn't like that. Their relationship wasn't always going to be perfect. In fact, it had never really been perfect. But that didn't mean she couldn't work with him.

Liz crawled out of bed, took a quick shower, and then tidied up her room. Her parents would be in town tomorrow for graduation, so she had to get her house ready. She was afraid to look in the living room; with all the packing Victoria was doing, the place looked like a pigsty.

Liz was both excited and nervous for her parents to meet Brady. They weren't thrilled that their daughter was in the newspapers for having an affair with a congressman. No matter how much she told them that it wasn't like it was in the news, her father still had reservations.

Logging on to her computer, she opened her email to spend a few mindless minutes on the computer before her weekend was taken over by graduation. One email caught her eye. She opened it and just stared at the words.

"Accepted," she whispered.

Her article had been accepted. She had submitted a few pieces anonymously online to editorial columns. Nowhere too big or fancy. She knew that most would require her name to publish, but she had found some strictly online sites that allowed her to write without tipping off the editor that she'd had a stint or two in the papers herself.

The email went on to ask for her contact information and to discuss freelance payment for the column in question. She nearly jumped out of her seat she was so excited. It wasn't the *New York Times* or even *Raleigh News*, but her article on education policy reform had still been accepted and was going to be published in an online magazine. Her own ideas and words in print once more!

Liz grabbed her phone off of her nightstand to call Brady, and saw that she had a text message from Hayden.

Hey, when and where are we meeting today?

Oh yeah, she had never given him an answer. She bit her lip and jotted out a message back.

I don't think we should.

After a short pause, her phone dinged again.

Please let me try to make it up to you. I hate how everything ended.

No. I'm sorry. I can't.

She sighed, feeling bad, but she knew it was for the best. She had said Brady was her past, present, and future and she meant it.

A second later her phone started ringing. Hayden. This wasn't going to be fun.

"Hey," she mumbled.

"Hey. I thought we were going to get coffee," Hayden said.

"I said maybe, and now I'm saying no."

"Why?"

"It's not a good idea," Liz said. "You didn't like me seeing him when we were together. You should understand."

"Yeah, but you did it anyway, and I doubt you're going to kiss me. Unless I'm missing something."

Liz shook her head. "No, of course not."

"Then what's the big deal? I'm not asking for anything except coffee. I just want to make things right."

"You keep saying that, but I don't even know what that means," she told him. She was gripping the phone tightly in her hand.

"It means that I've felt terrible about what happened and how we ended. I want to know that we can salvage what happened even if we can't be together." He sighed heavily. "You meant . . . mean so much to me. I don't like the idea of us being on such bad terms, even if it is my fault."

"I understand what you're saying, Hayden, but it's over between us."

"I'm not trying to get back together with you!" Hayden said, exasperated.

"I believe you," she said. *Sort of.* "I'm just saying if you want things to be right between us then, fine. Things are right. But this is the end of the road for me."

"You really think everything can just be better like that? Just by saying they are?"

He sounded disbelieving, but she knew that she was making the right choice.

"I think the more you dwell on it, the more obsessed you're going to get with the notion that you have to make this up to me. You can't. You betrayed my trust," Liz told him flatly. "But I've moved on. I'm happy. And it's not worth potentially hurting him to make you feel better about the fact that you sold me out."

"So . . . I'm wasting my time here?"

"I guess. If you want to make things right, then just let it all go. I'm in a good place in my life. I know we have some good memories in our past and I'm thankful for them. They're just in the past, though. My new memories are going to be with Brady."

"What you're saying is he doesn't want you to see me," Hayden guessed with a biting tone.

"He doesn't and you can't blame him for that. But this is *my* decision. I told him he would have to accept whatever decision I make whether I see you or not. I decided not to."

"Nothing I can do to change your mind?"

"I'm sorry. No."

He blew out his breath heavily. "All right. Well . . . I hope he really is the one then."

Liz hung up the phone after that and sighed. She knew that she had done the right thing. Trust was hard earned once lost, but closure was as easy as shutting the door and being willing to move on.

She felt kind of drained, so she just jotted out a text to Brady letting him know about the article. He would get back to her later when he was out of his committee meeting.

Deciding that she would be better off with some exercise while she waited for Brady, Liz grabbed her racket and drove over to the tennis complex. Easton was just striding into the lobby drenched head to toe in sweat with a doe-eyed high school student when she arrived.

"Liz! I didn't know you'd be in today. You here for lessons?" he said, waggling his eyebrows up and down.

"Hardly. I'm here to kick your ass," she said.

"Have you *ever* beaten me before?"

"First time for everything."

"But not today, kid." He winked at her.

"I'm not a kid. I'm older than you. I'm graduating on Sunday."

"Oh, right! My cousin is graduating too. I'll be at the ceremony," he said, placing his racket on the counter and signing out the student he was with.

"Fun! You'll have to find me."

"Yes, because it's easy to locate one person in Kenan Stadium."

"Whatever. Are we going to play?" Her phone buzzed in her purse and, thinking it might be Brady, she pulled it out. Savannah.

Just saw Hayden on Franklin. Are you meeting him? Did you know Calleigh was with him?

Liz's mind buzzed. Calleigh, the redhead reporter who had sold them out to the press, and Hayden's ex-girlfriend. They worked together at the *Charlotte Times*.

He called me earlier and I told him I wasn't going to meet him, but he didn't tell me he was with Calleigh.

Good! Don't see him. Come have lunch with me. I'm so bored now that I'm done with finals. Just avoid Qdoba.

I'm at tennis. After?

Savannah agreed.

"Did you hear anything I just said?" Easton asked.

"What?" Liz questioned, looking up. "No. Sorry."

"I haven't eaten all day. I was about to get lunch. Can we do this later?"

"You want me to play tennis *after* I've eaten? If I vomit on you, it's your fault."

"Why don't we just get lunch together instead?" Easton suggested.

"I guess. Can my friend join us? She was just asking about lunch."

"Is she hot?" he asked.

Liz rolled her eyes. "Yes."

"Then definitely."

Liz shot Savannah a text message and then hopped into Easton's

Jeep. Parking was kind of limited downtown, especially with the graduation crowd already coming in, so they thought it would be better to take one car.

They met Savannah at Mediterranean Deli, as far away from Qdoba as possible on Franklin Street. It boasted the best Greek food in town.

"Liz!" Savannah called when they walked in. She waved at them from a table in the corner.

"Hey. This is my tennis instructor, Easton."

Savannah looked him up and down as if she were going to have him for dinner. Liz admitted he was hot, especially after working up a sweat on the courts, but she just didn't really get the appeal. She figured she was a little biased to Brady.

"Nice to meet you," he said, taking her hand in his and working his charm.

Liz left them to ogle each other and ordered some hummus and a gyro. Easton hopped up to go order the food when Liz returned, and Savannah's eyes had that same expression every other one of Easton's students had.

"Okay. Why haven't I met him before?" Savannah asked as soon as he was gone.

"You were dating someone?" Liz said.

"I dated a couple people. But come on, look at him. Wait, don't. You're dating my brother. It makes me look like a bad sister."

"He's a good-looking guy. Plus he's smart, wants to go to law school, become a politician."

Savannah wrinkled her nose. "You're losing me. I've had enough of law school and politicians."

"I thought you'd only been into motorcycles, tattoos, and drug dealers," Liz teased.

"Hey! Forrest was not a drug dealer. He just . . . was on drugs."

Liz arched an eyebrow. "Sounds like a winner."

"Why can't Easton be hot and into something that's not related to my family?"

"Beggars can't be choosers."

"I'm not begging," Savannah said stubbornly.

"You're a lot like your brother, you know?"

"Clay or Brady?"

"Both!"

"How insulting."

Easton returned at that moment and took the seat across from Savannah. They immediately took up a conversation as if they had known each other for years. Easton was an expert conversationalist. Liz had never felt a dull moment while around him. It made sense to her that he would want to be a politician.

They had just dug into their food when Liz's phone rang again. She glanced down at the screen. Still no Brady.

"I have to take this. It's Heather," Liz told them.

Savannah's brow furrowed. "That's strange. What does she want?"

"We're about to find out." She walked away from the table and found a seat on a bench outside. "Hello?"

"What did I say about staying out of the papers?" Heather asked icily.

"What are you talking about?"

"I said *anything* that might be suspicious, anything that might show up in the papers, anything that might make Brady look bad went through me," she all but growled. "I thought we were clear on this. We haven't had any negative incidents recently."

"Heather, I don't know what you're talking about." But she sure didn't like the sound of it.

"You were out gallivanting around with your ex-boyfriend? The one who, I don't know if you remember, wrote the article outing your relationship to the press!" Heather cried. "What made you think that was a good idea?"

Liz sat up straighter. How did Heather know that, and what did it have to do with the press? "Did Brady tell you that I saw him?"

"Brady knew about this?"

"I talked to him about it Monday. Why?"

"And neither of you thought to inform me of your catastrophic error? You allowed yourself to be photographed."

"Photographed?" Liz nearly shrieked.

"Yes, congratulations! Tomorrow your photo with your ex will be in the tabloids. I'm sure with some stupid slogan about cheating on Brady. Just what we need."

"No." Liz shook her head. "I did the right thing. I told him that I didn't want to see him. I told him Brady was more important."

"Well, none of that is going to show up in the tabloids," Heather said, giving her a reality check. "You became complacent. But you can't be complacent in this job. I don't care what you want to say about your relationship with Brady, but because he is in the public eye part of your relationship *is* a job."

"Heather!" Liz cried, her emotions all over the place. She couldn't believe how she was talking to her, but the worst part was that she was right in some ways. She had tried to treat her relationship with Brady like any other relationship and her life as it had been before showing up in the papers. Now she was about to be in them all over again because of it.

"I could have prevented this. Now we just have to deal with your poor choices," Heather said. "Be on the lookout for more information from me regarding the severity of the situation. In the meantime, hole up somewhere and try not to cause any more problems."

Click.

Liz stared down at her phone in disbelief. Heather had hung up on her again. She had done everything right in this situation except happening to walk for five minutes with Hayden and the whole thing backfired in her face.

Tears marred her vision and she tried to keep everything under control. She was simply too choked up. She glanced up and down the road that she was on and decided it wasn't safe. Heather was right: she should hole up. Now she would have her face in the papers two days before graduation. Just what she needed.

She stumbled back into the restaurant and over to Savannah and Easton. They were speaking animatedly when she approached, but their conversation cut off when they got a look at her.

"What happened?" Savannah asked. "Is Brady okay?"

"Yes, he's fine." Liz wiped at the tears in her eyes. Easton didn't really know anything about her life and she wanted to keep it that way for as long as she could. "Can you take me back to my house? I need to call Brady."

"Of course." Savannah grabbed her purse. "Sorry. Maybe we can meet up later?"

"Yeah, of course. Liz has my number," he said, and then turned to look at Liz. "Are you going to be okay?"

"Fine. Just fine." She turned away from him. The last thing she wanted was sympathy.

"Okay. Get home safe. Let me know if you need anything," Easton said.

Savannah and Liz quickly exited the restaurant, and Liz pulled her phone back out to call Brady.

"What happened?" Savannah asked.

"Pictures of me and Hayden together are going to show up in the tabloids tomorrow. Heather just got wind of it."

"Shit! Was she pissed?" Liz just stared at her. "Of course she was. Brady should really handle her. She's getting out of control. She shouldn't take this shit out on you."

"Shouldn't she? It's my fault. I should have thought about this. I let my guard down."

"Hey," Savannah said, grabbing her arm. "Listen to yourself. You are not the campaign. You're not running for office. You weren't born into this. It's okay to let your guard down. You're dating my brother, and that doesn't mean that you can't walk down the street with Hayden. Don't let her get to you."

"Okay," Liz said. She had no will to argue. She dialed Brady's number and he answered on the third ring.

"Hey, Heather just called and told me pictures of Hayden and me are going to show up in the paper tomorrow."

"Did you go see him?" Brady asked, clearly frustrated.

"No! I told him no," she told him. She wiped her eyes once more and sniffled. "I told him I didn't want to see him, that it wasn't worth it. These are from Monday when I first saw him."

"Shit! Where are you right now?"

"I'm with Savannah. We were out to lunch when Heather called," Liz said, leaning back in the seat of Savannah's BMW.

"All right. I'm going to deal with Heather. She shouldn't be calling you and sending you into tears. I can't have that," he growled. "I'm tired of her shit. You're with me. She needs to fucking get over it and treat you like you belong with me."

"She's only doing her job," she whispered. She had no idea why she was defending Heather's actions except that she felt like complete shit about what had occurred.

"Her job is on the line if she doesn't start treating you right and trying to make you happy."

Liz laughed lightly. "She's not going to like that."

"Well, if she doesn't like it, then she can find someone else to work for. She acts like she's irreplaceable. She's not. You are."

Chapter 16

GRADUATION

Liz couldn't stomach the pictures of her and Hayden together in the tabloids. Victoria had to read the attached article and give running commentary about what was said. By the end, Liz was doubled over in laughter from Victoria's ridiculousness. It didn't push aside the suggestions that, as Heather had predicted, she was cheating on Brady, or that she and Hayden had rekindled their romance.

Clearly none of it was true, but having it in print didn't look good for her, and it certainly didn't look good for Brady. Brady didn't say anything about his disapproval about the pictures. She knew he didn't like to see them, but most of his anger was directed at Heather.

Brady and Heather had gotten into a huge argument about how she had treated Liz. She figured Heather deserved to get chewed out for her actions, but Liz didn't like to see a rift in his campaign right before primary season.

Luckily, she didn't have much time to dwell on it, because her parents arrived that afternoon. They lived in Tampa, where her father worked as a calculus professor at the University of South Florida. Her mother was a third grade teacher at a local elementary school. Liz hadn't seen them since Christmas, and it was a reunion filled with tears, especially on her mother's part, about her baby girl growing up.

They ate dinner at a low-key restaurant and then stayed up to chat until late in the evening. Her parents seemed as anxious to meet Brady as Liz was for them to finally be introduced. It probably was never going to be easy to introduce a sitting congressman as her boyfriend.

Brady's flight was getting in early Saturday morning and, once he picked up his Lexus from his house, he met them for brunch. As Liz stepped inside the small diner, she was reminded of the first time they had come here together. They had agreed to continue their relationship on Brady's terms. She could have walked away at that point, but she hadn't. Maybe she never really could.

He was seated in the back of the restaurant when they arrived, and Liz directed her parents toward him. Her heart fluttered. He looked incredible in a blue button-down and khakis. Really casual for him.

He stood and gave her a quick hug. She folded into his arms and could have stayed there all day to avoid what was about to happen. Brady didn't even look fazed by this at all. She had been insanely nervous to meet his parents, sweaty palms and all. But he went on autopilot.

"Mr. and Mrs. Dougherty, it's so nice to meet you. I'm Brady Maxwell," he said, extending his hand to her parents.

"We've heard so much about you," her mother said, taking his hand. She gave him what Liz knew was her "social" smile. "Please call me Julie. This is my husband, Lewis."

Brady shook her father's hand too. "Lewis," he said cordially. Her father's lips were tight as he returned the handshake.

Brady gestured for everyone to take a seat. Liz breathed a sigh of relief when she sat down next to Brady and he laced their fingers together.

Liz was anxious to have everyone in the same place, even knowing that Brady was incredibly charming, because her father in particular still had reservations about Liz dating Brady. The fact that he was a congressman, that she had shown up in the papers because of him, the age difference, the drastic shift in her career trajectory all were strikes against him.

"How was the flight from Tampa?" Brady asked. He shot Liz a mischievous glance, and she couldn't hold back her smirk. Airplanes.

"Not too bad," Lewis said, frowning at them. "We were just happy to get into town early to spend more time with Liz."

"She's always so busy," Julie needlessly explained. She ran a hand back through her short brown hair. Liz had always thought she looked more like her mother, with her bright blue eyes and clear complexion, but she had her father's blond hair, even if it was graying at the temples now.

"I know," Liz said. "It's hard to find time to come home."

"Well, it's good that y'all are here now," Brady said. "I see my father all the time, but usually for work. I finally get to spend some quality time with them tomorrow night. Will you be joining us for dinner?"

"Oh, I'd been meaning to tell you about that," Liz said to her parents.

Her mother gave her a warm smile and then nodded. "That sounds lovely. We'd love to go," Julie said, nudging her husband. "Wouldn't we, Lewis?"

Her father nodded. "Yes. Unless we have other plans."

"I don't think we do?" Julie asked, turning to Liz.

"No. Plus, you'll love Brady's parents. They're really nice," Liz said.

"Meeting the boyfriend and his parents all in one weekend," her father said, flourishing his hand. "Trying to overload us?"

"Obviously," Liz said, shaking her head. She cracked a smile. "I'm overloading *you*."

"Don't tell us you were nervous," her mother said with the real smile that Liz knew and loved. "You've been telling us that everyone likes Brady all weekend."

"Oh, yes, we've heard it nonstop," Lewis said. He finally seemed to relax back into his chair.

"Convincing yourself or them?" Brady asked. He chuckled and squeezed her arm.

Liz threw her hands up and laughed. "Don't gang up on me. I can't take it."

Everyone broke into laughter, and seemed to dissipate the lingering tension. The way that Brady managed to fall rather easily into their joking attitude was good news. It meant her parents were starting to accept him.

By the end of brunch, it was clear that she had worried for absolutely nothing.

The day passed easily with her parents and Brady. They went back to her place and she changed into graduation attire so that her parents could take pictures. They walked around campus and her father played photographer with a giant SLR. He had been taking lessons in his spare time and was eager to showcase his newfound talent. They ended at the Old Well, where people were lined up to take pictures in front of the iconic symbol of the university.

When it was her turn, they snapped a few shots of her posing before her mother pushed Brady into the picture. He jogged over and grabbed her around the middle as he had in the airport and swung her around. Liz laughed when he placed her back on her feet and stared up into his face. He dropped a quick peck onto her mouth and she sighed.

Whatever papers were reporting about Hayden had clearly never seen her with Brady. There was no one else in her life.

———

Commencement began the next morning at nine thirty. Liz, Victoria, and their families were up bright and early doing last-minute touchups to hair and makeup, demanding an exorbitant amount of coffee, and looking bleary-eyed and excited.

Liz left her parents with Victoria's parents in the living room to answer the door when Brady showed up around eight thirty to walk with them to the stadium. He was in a light gray suit and Carolina blue tie with a silver UNC tie clip.

"How are you this put together this early?" Liz asked.

"It's my job," he said. He placed a kiss on her cheek.

"You probably haven't even had coffee," she grumbled.

"Guilty."

"So not fair."

Brady laughed. "Can we have a minute alone before we leave?"

Liz's eyes widened. "I don't think . . ."

"Not for that!" he said, scandalized. "Your parents are here."

"And I thought nothing stopped you," she said, walking him into her vacant bedroom.

"Almost nothing," he said, slapping her ass once he shut the door behind them. "I just wanted to give you a part of your graduation present alone."

"Graduation present?" she asked, arching her eyebrows.

"Nothing too big . . . yet."

"Oh, God. Please nothing bigger than the earrings," she said, flashing him the diamond drop earrings he had given her in D.C.

"I make no promises about that." He had a devilish smirk on his face when he reached into his suit pocket and pulled something out for her. "I know the necklace I got you wasn't anything extravagant, but it had . . . has special meaning to me. I like to see that you still wear it, and I thought I could add to it."

Liz bit her lip and pulled the necklace out from under her Carolina blue sundress.

"You're wearing it," he said, his eyes lighting up.

"I went over a year without it. I don't want to do it again."

"You won't have to," he assured her, then handed over a small pink box. "We have a whole hell of a lot more to look forward to than a necklace and a few charms."

Liz's smile widened and she took hold of the box. Inside was a small blue charm in the shape of a star. She looked up at him quizzically, wondering how this fit in with all of the other charms. An airplane for the very first time they had met and he associated her in a positive way to the feeling of flying he had always had as a child, the number 4 for the Fourth of July when he won her vote, a key for the time he gave her a key to his house at the gala, and a topaz gemstone to signify the end of November, when they were supposed to be together. Things hadn't worked out quite the way they were supposed to, but the two of them were here now.

"You can't guess?"

She shook her head. "What does it mean?"

He ran his hand down along her jawline and stared deeply into her eyes. "Your most romantic date is to lie in an open field and stare at the stars, but every day I'm with you is more romantic than the next. Romance had no meaning before you. So you must be my stars."

Liz held the little star in her hand with a newfound appreciation. Brady always picked the most thoughtful charms. Each one held its own meaning for their relationship. Holding this star reminded her that she was his universe.

She dropped the tiny star into her locket and sniffed. Tears had started forming in her eyes and she hadn't even realized it. "Oh, God."

"No crying," he said, wiping aside a tear that had escaped.

"I'm just so . . . happy. I never thought we would get here, and now we are. I love this so much, Brady," she told him. "Thank you."

"You're welcome." He kissed her deeply on the mouth and she felt her body swooning into him.

Brady pulled back and just stared at her for a second. A smile touched his lips. "Liz," he whispered. "I love you."

A gasp caught in her throat.

She had known. But he had never said those words. Not like that. Not to her.

"I love you too."

"I shouldn't have held that back from you for so long. I've known how I felt, but before it was timing and now . . . well now I don't have a reason. I love you, and I see nothing that could ever change that."

Liz threw her arms around Brady and he held her against him for a long time. Probably longer than they should have stayed cooped up in her bedroom with guests over. When they walked back into the living room, Victoria had finally ventured out of her room. Daniel walked out of the living room to see her. He had graduated yesterday from Duke and was now joining Victoria for her commencement.

Victoria was in a skintight blue-and-white dress and mile-high blue heels. Her dark hair was piled high on her head with tendrils escaping. She looked gorgeous. If Liz had attempted the same updo, she probably would have looked ridiculous, but Victoria pulled it off.

"Hey, bitch," Victoria said. "You look hot."

Liz shook her head. "My parents are in the living room."

"So are mine." Victoria shrugged, nonplussed. "Let's go graduate from this place. There is so much ahead of us."

"Not even a little bit nostalgic?"

"I haven't left yet. Where is the nostalgia?" she asked. "Don't get all sentimental on me."

"I'll try not to."

Victoria linked their arms together and paraded everyone to the front door. The walk wasn't that long, and there was so little parking on campus that it didn't make sense to drive. Their surrounding neighbors had the same idea and their group passed a ton of people in graduation caps and gowns.

Brady came up behind her and took her hand. Sometimes it was strange that she could still be out in public like this with him, but she wasn't complaining. At least if there were pictures today, it would show them together and happy.

They located Savannah at the entrance, and to Liz's surprise she was standing with Easton.

"Who's the guy?" Brady asked Liz.

"My tennis instructor."

"*That's* who you've been taking tennis lessons from?"

"Kind of hot, right?" He shot her a glare. "Joking. Savannah is totally into him. I guess I kind of set them up by accident."

"Well, he looks better than the last one. What was his name? It was something ridiculous."

"Forrest," Liz offered.

"Yeah. That's him."

"Well, Easton is nice. He's applying to law school and wants to be a politician. So be nice." She elbowed him in the ribs.

"*I'm* a politician, baby. I'm always nice. You should know that," he said, his voice dipping seductively.

"You can be nice like that later," she whispered.

"I fully intend to."

They reached Savannah at that point and Brady gave his little sister a hug. Easton puffed up a little until he got a good look at Brady.

"You're Congressman Maxwell," Easton said in awe.

"That I am," he said, sticking his hand out.

"Honor to meet you, sir."

Liz laughed and shook her head a little. "Easton, this is my boyfriend, Brady."

Easton shook Brady's hand and then dropped it as if he couldn't figure out exactly what Liz was saying. "I knew you were dating someone, but . . ."

"Yeah, you're not too observant," she said with a giggle.

"So that makes you . . ." He pointed at Savannah.

"His little sister," Savannah offered.

"I'm in the presence of political royalty."

Savannah just laughed. "I guess so."

"Well, it's really nice to meet you," he told Brady, "and put all the pieces together."

Victoria came up and nudged Liz along. "Show's over, folks. We'll see you after graduation!"

Brady gave Liz a kiss on the cheek before Victoria dragged her out on the football field. They found seats next to each other and started flipping through their commencement booklets. Soon the entire stadium was full of graduates and their friends and families.

The chancellor stood up and gave an introductory speech, and then it was an endless bout of speeches ending with the keynote speaker, a certain basketball player who had played at UNC during college and gone on to play professionally for the Chicago Bulls. Then students stood, diplomas were issued, tassels moved from one side to the other, a congratulatory response followed, and then they were free. Hats flew in the air all around Liz. She laughed and hugged Victoria, tears streaming down her friend's beautiful face.

"I thought you weren't nostalgic," Liz cried.

"We hadn't graduated then," Victoria told her. "I'm going to miss everything so much."

"Me too."

They hugged again. Four years together had officially come to a close and now they had to venture out into the real world. It was daunting, terrifying, and exhilarating all at the same time. Liz smiled at Victoria and threw her own hat up into the air.

———

The group from graduation arrived at Bin 54 to celebrate later that evening. Victoria's parents had left that night to get back to New Jersey, so she and Daniel had even joined them. The restaurant was a madhouse because of graduation. Luckily Brady's parents had reserved the cellar room well in advance, and there was enough room for everyone.

Savannah was walking up the stairs toward the bathroom when their group arrived. She grabbed Liz by the arm and whispered, "Do you have a minute?"

"I'm here with my parents. I have to make introductions and such," Liz offered apologetically.

"Everything okay?" Brady asked, looking between the girls.

"Fine," Savannah said immediately. "Just wanted to talk to Liz. Can you do introductions?"

"Sure, Savi. You sure you're okay?"

"I said I was." She straightened taller and gave her best impression of the Maxwell confidence.

Brady nodded. "All right. I'll see y'all in a minute."

Liz followed Savannah up the last few stairs and then stood at the top curiously. "What's this all about?"

"I invited Easton."

While that was surprising, since Savannah and Easton had only met this week, it wasn't completely unheard-of for Savannah. She had invited Liz in a similar fashion to one of these events last year. "So?"

"Lucas is here," she whispered, glancing over Liz's shoulder.

"Oh." Well, that made more sense. Savannah and Lucas had had an off-again, off-again relationship as far as Liz could tell. Savannah was head over heels for him, but he showed interest only when it was convenient for him.

"What should I do?"

"What do you mean, what should you do? You invited Easton, who is a great guy, to dinner with your parents after knowing him a week. You can't exactly kick him out now."

"I know," Savannah said, swatting her hand. "But what do I do about Lucas?"

"Do you still like him?"

The answer was written all over her face. "I mean . . . I guess." She shrugged.

"Right. Well, do you like Easton?"

"I just met him . . ." Savannah glanced away. "But yeah, I do. He's not like other guys at school."

"Then I think the best thing to do is to probably concentrate on Easton. If it doesn't work out then you've done nothing but make Lucas insanely jealous," Liz offered. She wasn't sure she was the best person to ask advice about what to do when you liked two guys. Her answer had always been Brady . . . even when it shouldn't have been.

Savannah laughed in an uninhibited manner, which really worked for her. So often she was reserved because of her upbringing. In moments like these, she was stunning.

"Okay. Thanks," Savannah said. She looked down and then back up at Liz. "You know how I once told you that I would never like my brother's girlfriends after Erin tried to act like my sister?"

"Yeah."

"Well, I guess I lied. You're one of my best friends, and I really wouldn't mind you as a sister," Savannah admitted.

Liz placed her hand on her heart and then hugged Savannah. "Thanks. Maybe a bit ahead of yourself, but thanks."

"Sorry to keep you from introducing your parents. God, I'm a wreck."

"You're fine. Don't worry about it. You probably saved me."

"Brady is great at introductions anyway." Savannah shrugged.

"True, but you can never be too sure," Liz said.

"All right. See you in a minute. I'll space out our entrances so it doesn't look like we were conspiring."

"Were we conspiring?"

"Just get down there," Savannah said, gently pushing Liz toward the stairs. Liz laughed and then jogged back down to the dining room.

She really was unprepared for the number of people who were in attendance for this dinner. It was more like a graduation party. At the head of the table sat Brady's parents. Her parents were seated across from them and then Daniel and Victoria, a blank seat for her, and then Brady. On the other side of the table sat Lucas's parents, whom she had met at this restaurant last year, their youngest daughter, Alice, then Savannah's open seat was wedged between Lucas and Easton. Surprisingly enough, seated next to Easton was Clay's girlfriend, Andrea, which could only mean one thing . . .

"Hey, beautiful," Clay said, wrapping Liz around the middle and pulling her into a hug.

Liz laughed, returning the hug lightly. She could feel Brady's eyes on them. "I didn't know you would be here."

"How could I miss your graduation?"

"I wasn't aware you knew I was graduating."

"Family outing and all that," he said, gesturing behind him. "You do remember Andrea, right?"

Liz glanced at his girlfriend, who was tall and slender, with too much makeup, bleached blond hair, and clothes that probably cost more than Liz's entire wardrobe. Andrea glanced up at them then and smiled at Clay.

"Yes, I remember. Nice to meet you again," Liz said.

She looked up at Liz as if she were an alien. "Have we met?" Andrea asked.

"Yes, at Jamie's art exhibit in D.C."

"Oh, Jamie!" Andrea crooned. Her entire face changed. She lit up like a lightbulb. "I love her work. She's so megatalented. She is selling her work at a fraction of what she should be selling them. Seriously like mega brillz. I want to keep her in my house and have her just paint for me so I can fill the house with her work."

"You already have," Clay teased her. Their eyes locked and a moment passed between them before Andrea scoffed at the attention.

"Don't make fun of her work. She's the fucking shit, Clay."

Clay raised his hands to fend her off. "Who am I to talk about the things you love in life?" he asked with a teasing smile.

Liz extracted herself and walked toward Brady just as Savannah entered the room.

"What was that all about?" Brady asked as she slid into her seat.

"Girl stuff."

"With Clay," he corrected.

"Probably wants to piss off his girlfriend," Liz offered.

"Or me."

"Not everything is about you." She glanced over at Clay and Andrea and saw them glaring at each other, but there was something about them that showed that they cared. Maybe it was the years that they had been together, or maybe she was just imagining it, but she was pretty sure she had seen something pass between Clay and Andrea that almost seemed like affection.

Savannah took her seat between Easton and Lucas and sent Liz a sly smile. Stuck between two guys, what a rough life.

Glancing around the table at her family, Brady's family, and all of their friends, Liz couldn't help but admire the entire group. Everyone she cared most about was sitting at this table right now, and they all looked completely comfortable. Well, aside from Savannah.

Liz's parents chatted easily with Brady's parents. Victoria was making somewhat pleasant, albeit inappropriate, conversation with Lucas. Daniel was leaning over the table to talk to Marilyn about his and Victoria's decision to go to Johns Hopkins. Brady was trying to get to know Easton, and Savannah had just said that she wouldn't mind Liz as a sister. It all felt so right.

A waiter came around and filled champagne flutes for everyone except Alice, who was only sixteen.

"Excuse me, everyone. I'd like to propose a toast," Brady said, sliding out of his chair. "To Ms. Liz Dougherty, for being the most beautiful, brilliant, strong-willed, caring, and gracious woman I have ever met in my life. Congratulations on completing your degree. You'll always look back on these days with fond remembrance, but this is most assuredly only the beginning of a very successful and prolific career." Brady raised his glass. "To Liz and Victoria."

Everyone raised their glass and toasted Liz's and Victoria's graduations.

Liz's smile couldn't have been bigger as she stared up at the man she loved. Seeing the adoration on his face made the rest of this day have even more meaning. He was right. She had felt it at the ceremony. This was just the start of her life.

Chapter 17
POSTGRAD STRESS

Liz's parents left the next day with all the reluctance that was to be expected, offering to help pay for things if she needed it, and encouraging her to continue to pursue her dreams. As if there were another option for her.

Her first article went live on the website that week. Liz had very low expectations for an article about education policy in an online magazine. She was just proud that she was published all on her own and received her first paycheck from it. Brady celebrated by taking her out for frozen yogurt and the most normal thing he could think of: they went and saw a movie.

He had to be back in D.C. for the week, and since she had no other plans at the moment, she agreed to go with him. When they were seated in first class, Liz pulled up her email and saw she had something from the website.

Dear Miss Dougherty:
Your recent article has been quoted in the Washington Post re-
garding the upcoming education policy bill that is in the House
of Representatives at the moment. Our traffic on the article has
quadrupled in a matter of hours. Would you be interested in
writing a follow-up article? We could post it next week.

Please respond to let us know if you are interested, as
this is a timely piece. Also, we would like permission to pub-
lish your name for the article so that you receive the credit
in the feature.

Sincerely,
Tom Vernon
Editor

Liz read and reread the short email until she thought she might burst. Her article had not only done well, but it had been quoted in the *Washington Post*. She went in search of the article and, after seeing her quote with a link to her article, she literally squealed.

Brady's eyes got big as he turned to look at her.

"Sorry," she said, lowering her voice. "Check this out."

She passed over the computer to him and he scanned the email. "You were quoted in the *Post*?" he asked.

"Yeah. Look." She showed him the article.

"Congratulations! This is your first article too."

"I know. I'm kind of freaking out," she said, bouncing up and down.

"They want you to publish with your name," he pointed out.

"Yeah. I'll deal with that, but, Brady . . . my paper is quoted in the *Washington Post*," she repeated.

"Baby, I'm happy for you, but you know you can't post your name."

"I know," she said softly.

And she did know. The press was already having a field day with their relationship, not to mention how it would look to the campaign. The media would probably think that she was just trying to feed the public Brady's agenda or something equally likely to make her look like a biased journalist. Plus, she liked the idea of having a little slice of something that she could control. Seeing her words in print again, even without her name attached to them, was exhilarating. It showed her that her work was still valued and not garnering attention just because of all the extra drama that seemed to be attached to her name lately.

"They seem to really want the follow-up," Brady said.

"I know. I can't wait to write it."

"I have no idea where you would get all this information about education policy," he joked. "It's not like you're dating the Congressman who is on the education committee proposing the bill."

"And you think the only reason I have information is because of *you*?" she asked, arching her eyebrows. If he thought that, then he was definitely mistaken. She had been invested in education policy long before she had ever known him.

"I don't think it hurts."

"I believe that *I* was the one to stump you at the press conference the first time we met," she reminded him. "*I* was the one who kept badgering you about education policy while we were dating. I don't need you to get information on education policy."

"Clearly," he said, gesturing to the computer. "You got into the *Post* without any help from me . . . just like you wanted."

Liz smiled. "I'm pretty much a badass. Got into the *Post* on my own, got my boyfriend to be on the education committee instead of the budget committee . . ."

"I believe I'm not on the budget committee because I represent the Research Triangle. Though it *was* nice to tell you I was on the education committee when I walked into your panel at the political journalism colloquium." He smirked down at her. "You should have seen your face."

Liz smacked him on the arm. "You did that on purpose!"

"Of course I did. I wanted to see you."

"You wanted to throw me off balance."

"Did it work?" he asked, lowering his face close to her mouth.

"It's working right now. What were we talking about?" she breathed.

Brady kissed her deeply. "I believe we were discussing what I was going to do to you once I got you back to my place," he whispered just loud enough for her to hear.

"Now I remember. Something about me laid out on your bed and your tongue all over my body."

"Is that a request, Ms. Dougherty?"

"Oh, yes."

His eyes slid down the front of her shirt and then back up to her eyes. "I might make a few requests myself."

"I'm always open to suggestions."

"I'll keep that in mind."

Just then the flight attendant started up the instructions and safety tips, and they began to taxi down the runway. Their banter tapered off and Liz was left aroused.

By the time they landed, she had drafted a letter to the editor accepting his offer to write a follow-up, but requesting to remain anonymous. She tried to argue that anonymity was important for her personal privacy. She hoped that would suffice.

The next few days were spent much the same as her spring break—more like a vacation than the end of her college career. She wasn't sure what she was supposed to feel like, but primarily she felt as if she was just floating. She didn't have anything really to do besides write the follow-up article for the online journal and write a few blog posts for Justin now that he had sent over the information for the blog. She wasn't sure how long it would take to get used to working for herself. Even as editor at the university paper, she had always had demanding deadlines, people reporting to her, and her reporting to the university. Now . . . it was just her.

The only downer came through rejection letters to graduate school that week. Professor Mires had said that she would hear by June 1 at the latest, and some had already trickled in. Not surprisingly, Columbia and Northwestern turned her down. She got into American University and was still waiting to hear from Missouri and Maryland. American was her backup school, but she was still holding out for Maryland, her number one choice.

On Thursday night when Brady returned from work, Liz was lounging in his living room with her computer on her lap and *Pride and Prejudice* on in the background. He started loosening his tie as he walked over to her. "Are you feeling like Elizabeth Bennet today?"

"Only if you are going to be as positively stubborn and arrogant as Mr. Darcy."

"Well, that sounds like me, but Darcy had his reasons for acting like that," Brady said.

"Are you defending him for snubbing her?"

"I'm defending him for getting a bad rep for what simply boils down to miscommunication," he said, picking up her laptop and moving it to the table.

"Darcy does *not* have a bad rep. Everyone loves him."

"Darcy and I are sounding more and more alike." Brady sat down next to her and scooted her into his lap. He started trailing kisses down her neck and she sighed.

"How do you do that?"

"What?" he murmured.

"Make me forget everything we were arguing about."

"Were we arguing?"

"Lovingly discussing the merits of Mr. Darcy," she said. Her hands gripped the front of his suit.

"I thought we were talking about the rest of your graduation present."

Liz pulled back to look at him. Her hand immediately went to the charm necklace she had been wearing nonstop. "The rest?"

"You can't think that a charm is all you're getting. I told you there was more."

"You don't have to get me anything, though, Brady."

"If you don't want it, then we don't *have* to go to New York City this weekend to visit Chris and his girlfriend," he said with a sly smile.

When he put it that way, there was no arguing. Of course she wanted to visit Chris, and it was as much a present for her as it was for him to go visit his best friend. She hadn't seen Chris since the gala she had attended with him the night that Brady had given her a key to his house.

They left early the next morning for New York. She was jittery when they landed, excited to be back in the city for the first time since she had been fired from her job with the *Times*.

Their luggage was carried out to a waiting town car that whisked them downtown. This was a far cry from the last time she had been in the city over Christmas break, but she wasn't complaining. Brady lived a certain lifestyle. He preferred first class to coach, a town car to a taxi, and designer suits to jeans and a T-shirt. It wasn't a life she was accustomed to, and it was strange to think that it was her life now.

The driver dropped them off in front of an apartment building in Chelsea and promised that he would be on call when they needed him next. They walked inside and had the receptionist call to let them up. Chris was on the fourteenth floor at the end of a narrow hallway.

Brady knocked on the door and Chris greeted them with a big smile.

"Hey, man," Brady said.

"About time you got here."

The guys reached out and hugged each other as if they hadn't seen each other in ages.

"Liz," Chris said, turning his attention to her. "I always knew you'd be back."

"That makes one of us," she joked. They hugged and then he let them inside.

The apartment was a decent-size two-bedroom. It had a really homey feel, with brown suede furniture, a wooden coffee table, and framed photographs everywhere. It fit Chris's personality. Where Brady was all politician charisma, Chris was totally laid-back. And when they were together, Brady seemed to feed off of Chris's eternal good mood. They had been friends their entire lives and loved each other liked brothers. She wished Chris were around more often.

"Y'all have good timing," Chris said. "I took a half day and just got back. Let's get out of here. We have to meet Mollie for her lunch break."

Brady sent a message out to the town car and it met them at the entrance when they got downstairs. Chris gave the driver their destination and then they were swept through the city. Liz stared out the tinted window at the skyscrapers they passed. Brady and Chris seemed to be discussing the finer merits of the NBA draft, which she promptly tuned out.

Soon enough the car stopped in front of a gray stone building. The building was decorated in rich reds and browns with low lighting and exquisite chandeliers. The bar took up a large portion of the room, but there were private dining spaces along the far wall and a second level to accommodate smaller private parties. The hostess took them to one of the upstairs tables, where a slender woman with straight shoulder-length brown hair sat by herself staring at the menu.

"Mols," Chris said, drawing her attention. She looked up from her menu with a soft smile.

"There you are. Did you get caught in traffic?"

"Some." Chris bent down and kissed her cheek. "As promised, Brady Maxwell and his girlfriend, Liz."

"Nice to meet you. I'm Mollie. Chris didn't tire you with his antics already, did he?"

"I was bored to tears," Brady joked. Chris sighed heavily as he plopped into the seat next to Mollie.

Liz slid into her seat. "He was just fine. Don't listen to Brady."

Chris slung an arm over the back of Mollie's chair. "No, really, don't listen to Mollie. She thinks I can talk your ear off."

"You can," she said.

"She just thinks I do it all the time."

"You do!"

Liz giggled just as the server arrived to fill drink orders. She perused the menu and her eyes bulged. Lobster as an appetizer. This place was classier than the sundress she had on. Oh well, Brady hadn't said anything, so she must be fine.

The waiter brought a bottle of wine for the table and poured out the glasses for everyone. Mollie held her glass out in front of Chris. "Do not let me drink more than one of these. I have to go back to work."

Chris winked at her. "I'd never encourage inebriation at work."

"Looks like Liz is going to have to be my advocate. Chris likes to get me drunk. Watch my back."

"Sure thing. Where do you work?" Liz asked her.

"At an advertising company. Right now I mostly focus on women's fashion."

"Chris tells me you work with some pretty high-end clientele," Brady chimed in.

"I do actually. Some of the outfits are beautiful and some are hideous, though. As with all fashion, I suppose. Either way, I love it. Plus it's how Chris and I met, actually. He came to my company's Christmas party and we totally hit it off."

"That's one way to tell the story," Chris said with a laugh. "I was there with someone else, but I left with Mollie."

"Isn't that obligatory at company Christmas parties?" Liz joked.

"I thought so," Chris said.

Mollie rolled her eyes and swatted at him. She redirected her attention to Liz. "What do you do?"

"I . . ." Liz paused. What exactly did she do? Before she would have said she was a reporter or a journalist. Now she didn't really have an occupation, so she went with the closest thing. "I'm a freelance writer."

"Ah," Mollie said, averting her eyes.

"She's very talented," Brady said, "and has been writing very sought-after pieces online."

"Oh really?" she asked. "Where?"

"The *Washington Post* recently quoted me regarding a piece I wrote on education policy," Liz said.

"Well, that's brilliant," Mollie said, seeming more enthusiastic at hearing the *Post* mentioned. "Doesn't Brady work in education policy? Wasn't that what you were telling me, Chris?"

"Oh, hmm?" Chris asked, oblivious. "Yeah . . . on some committee in Congress."

"The education committee," Brady offered.

"That's the one."

"You two complement each other," Mollie said. "That's good long-term." She placed her hand on Chris's arm.

Liz leaned into Brady with a sigh. At least she wasn't the only one who thought so.

Shortly afterward the waiter came to take their orders. The conversation shifted back to the guys' basketball addiction, since they had played in college. Mollie seemed to tune out as much as Liz did. Liz caught her eye and they both started laughing.

"What's so funny?" Brady asked, pinching her leg under the table.

"You two and basketball." Liz rolled her eyes. "You could talk all day about it."

"What would you prefer we talk about? Tennis?"

"Do you play tennis?" Mollie asked, her eyes wide.

"Yeah, I do," Liz said.

"That's exciting. I picked it up this year and I love it. So much fun and a great workout. I've been trying to convince Chris to play doubles with me, but he refuses."

"It's so boring," Chris complained.

"It is not!" Mollie and Liz said at the same time.

"You're probably just not good," Liz told him.

"Hey! I'm good!" Chris said. She had bruised his ego.

"Then it's set," Mollie said. "We'll play doubles tomorrow. I'm so excited."

"Brady and I will kick your ass. Guaranteed," Chris boasted.

Mollie put her head in her hand and sighed. "You don't even want to be my pair?"

"Guys versus girls, Mols. We'll show you how it's done."

"Oh, I'm sure. When was the last time you even picked up a racket?" she teased.

"It's like riding a bike."

"This should be interesting," Liz mused.

"Don't worry," Brady said, nudging her. "We'll go easy on you."

She narrowed her eyes. He knew that she played, but he had never seen her in action. He was in for a rude awakening. "Bring it, Maxwell."

All of those extra practice sessions with Easton were going to pay off. If she had done this before working out with him two or three times a week, she would have been winded after half a match. Now she could play for over an hour straight. These guys were going to need more than good luck on their side.

———

Chris quickly found out that playing tennis was *not* like riding a bike.

After having a few drinks last night, they had called it a night relatively early and gone back to Chris's house. Liz and Brady spent the night wrapped up together on the guest bedroom's queen-size bed. The next morning they had risen relatively early and taken the town car to the gym where Mollie worked out. They had indoor tennis courts, which really worked to Liz's favor, since she was used to playing outside in the North Carolina heat.

"How long have you been playing?" Mollie asked as she watched Liz warming up.

"Since I was seven," Liz told her.

"This is going to be great." A slow, ruthless smile spread across her face. "Let's crush them."

The guys let the girls have the first serve. Liz happily obliged them with an impressive serve that took Chris completely off guard. Her next serve Brady took and volleyed back to Mollie. Liz could tell that Brady had more experience than Chris, so he was her real opponent. Plus, he looked really hot in gym shorts, a Dri-Fit T-shirt, and tennis shoes.

Mollie's return serve showed Liz that she did have training, but nothing compared to Liz. Chris did start to get the hang of it again about halfway through the game, but by then the girls were already up by two sets. They volleyed back and forth for the next set, which went to the guys after Brady delivered a powerful stroke that neither of them could return.

He seemed triumphant about that, but strangely silent throughout the rest. She knew that Brady was incredibly competitive. He wouldn't be into politics if he weren't. But this was her sport. He could kick her ass at basketball and probably everything else, but not tennis. And she was going to prove it.

They played by official rules, where the winner needed to win six sets and beat the other team by at least two sets. Liz was playing on adrenaline and barely even noticed the time pass, but by the time they were down to the wire it was clear everyone was tiring. If they won the next point then that would be the game.

She could see the determination on Brady's face as they squared off. For a second it felt as if it were just the two of them. Their competitive natures wouldn't let them back off.

Liz raised her racket and served the ball across the net. Brady returned it where it was almost out of reach for her, but she got it last minute. It sailed over the net and hit the court once. Brady dove to get the brilliantly placed ball, but he was too slow by a fraction of an inch and it bounced out of court.

"Game!" Mollie cried. Her breath was coming heavily, but she was still jumping around victoriously.

Liz bent forward at the waist and took in a few deep breaths. Her heart was beating a million miles a minute. From across the court, she locked eyes with Brady and winked. She had beaten him. It didn't matter that it was at a game she had been playing nearly her entire life and it had been kind of close. She had still won and it felt amazing.

"Okay, you two," Mollie said, pointing across the court. "Since you lost, you have to take us to Schiller's for Pimm's."

Chris groaned. "Killing me, woman."

Mollie giggled. "It's only fair."

Liz walked across the court to shake hands with them, as was customary. Chris slapped her hand for a high five and then hobbled off the court mumbling to himself, "I knew there was a reason I didn't play this game."

"Hey, you," she said, walking up to Brady. "Good game."

"You were phenomenal," he told her.

"Didn't think a girl could beat you, huh?"

"You proved me wrong. It makes me want to take lessons. Is that guy Savannah is seeing available?" he asked.

"You can't steal Easton from me! Find your own instructor," she joked, batting at him.

Brady pulled Liz toward him.

"Ew. I'm all sweaty."

"You'd think I'd be used to it," he said with a smirk. "I have an idea. How about I ask my girlfriend to give me lessons?"

"Is she good at tennis?" Liz asked innocently.

"The very best. She's so good, in fact, that her boyfriend is going to have to remind her who's in charge the best way he knows how."

Liz's eyebrows shot up. "And how do you propose that?"

He dropped his mouth to her ear and nibbled on the earlobe. "Tonight when I have you all alone, I'm going to remind you exactly what happened the night you brought a Senator to his knees."

Chapter 18
PAY UP

As promised, that night the guys planned an evening for the girls that included Mollie's drink of choice. Liz went on a shopping excursion to acquire a cocktail dress. Brady tagged along and played *Pretty Woman* with the associate at Bergdorf Goodman. By the end of the encounter, Brady had insisted on a pair of Jimmy Choos and a dark magenta strapless dress that cinched at the waist to accentuate Liz's figure.

When they returned to Chris's apartment, Liz took over the bathroom. After a shower, she blew out her long blond hair until it fell loose past her shoulders. She spent extra time on smoky makeup to finish off the elegant ensemble. Chris greeted her with a whistle when she exited the bathroom. Brady just shook his head at his best friend and brought his girlfriend in closer.

"You look stunning," he told her. He kissed her once on her nose.

"You don't look too bad yourself," she said.

Actually he looked fucking unbelievable in a tailored black suit with a checked green tie that complemented her dress. And that smile . . . as bright as the fireworks on the Fourth of July, all for her. She could have melted right then and there.

"I think I could get used to taking you shopping if you look this radiant in everything I purchase," he said, assessing her.

"Am I not good enough for Brady Maxwell in a T-shirt and sweats?"

"No. Certainly not."

Liz arched an eyebrow. "I do hope you're joking."

"Someone as beautiful as you should be wearing designer clothes at all times. It suits you."

"Are you getting me designer sweats?" she asked.

"I'll put in an order."

"You're ridiculous."

"For you. Though you already know that I love you in whatever you're wearing. It's this brain of yours that I fell for."

"And here I thought it was my body," she purred.

He slid his hand down the curve of her waist. "Don't get me started. I have a promise to keep tonight."

"Time to head out," Chris called, interrupting the lustful glance between them. "We still have to pick up Mollie before the show."

Brady placed a kiss on her lips and then ushered her out the door. She followed Brady and Chris down to the lobby of the building. A black stretch Hummer limo greeted them at the curb.

When Liz had first gone home with Brady that night at the Jefferson-Jackson gala, she had been shocked by the luxury. Even though she had been in a limo since that night, it still made her heart jump. It fit them.

"After you," Brady said.

He took her hand and helped her slip into the dark interior. Expensive champagne chilled in a bucket, and soft music played in the background. She had to down two glasses of champagne that first night together to calm her nerves. She hadn't been sure about her decision to leave with him. Now she thought it was the best one of her life.

Brady and Chris slid in after her and immediately started pouring champagne for the ride. They toasted their good fortunes and good times and sipped the crisp champagne. Liz couldn't keep the smile from her face. A few months ago she would have never envisioned herself in a limo in New York City with Brady. Now she couldn't imagine her life any other way.

Sure, there were aspects that were far from desirable, but Brady seemed to overshadow them all. She wasn't one to define herself by a man, and even now in these moments she didn't feel as if she did that. Her career and independence were still crucial to her. It was why she couldn't accept help from him with her job. But her life felt more complete than it ever had before . . . even when everything had been going right. Now she had the man she loved, loving her back and encouraging her to pursue her dreams despite the obstacles. They had a fight for the election ahead, but she wanted to be there for him just as he was there for her.

She glanced over at Brady laughing at one of Chris's jokes and a smile touched her lips. She knew the future was uncertain, but she felt confident in him . . . in them. There were conversations that needed to be had about that future, but she didn't fear having them as she once had.

When they finally made it through traffic, the driver parked in front of a tall building. Chris hopped out to retrieve Mollie, leaving them all alone in the limo. Brady's hand immediately trailed down her inner thigh. Her legs were crossed, but that didn't seem to stop him, and really she wasn't planning to anyway. He pried her legs apart with ease.

"Don't move them," he growled in her ear.

Her body clenched at the command and she did her best not to squirm as his hand explored her thighs. She could feel her body warming up to his touch as it so easily did. His fingers brushed up against her sensitive skin and she couldn't help but jump.

He smirked at her. "No panties?"

"You like me better without," she whispered throatily.

His other hand closed around her wrist and brought it to rest on the front of his pants. She felt his dick lengthening in her hand and her eyes bulged.

"Do you see what you do to me?" he asked. She nodded and squeezed to emphasize her point. "Now let me see what I do to you."

He ran his fingers along the opening to her pussy gently at first and then probingly. Her wetness coated his fingers, betraying how turned on she was.

"Mmm," he sighed as he slipped up into her.

Her eyes fluttered closed and she dropped her head back on the headrest. She didn't know how much time they had and right now she simply didn't care. She had been craving him all day. She didn't care what he did to her as long as she got her release. And she felt it building beautifully, euphorically. Her whole world centered in on this moment, and her heavy breathing gave away how close she already was.

"Are you going to come for me, baby?" Brady whispered in her ear.

"Close," she groaned.

"How close?" His fingers slid in and out of her. His thumb circled her clit, drawing out the pleasure as long as he could.

Liz bit her lip, completely unable to answer him coherently. Her walls clamped around him, begging for what he was offering.

And then just like that he removed his hand, pushed her legs together, and straightened his suit to hide his erection. Her body protested the sudden movement. The climax hovering just at the brink was receding. Her eyes fluttered open and she began to protest, when the limo door flew open.

"Miss us?" Chris asked when his face appeared in the doorway.

Liz tried not to show how affected she was by what had just occurred. Chris's eyes flickered between the two of them and he laughed as if he knew what had just happened while he had been gone.

"Hey!" Mollie cried, pushing past Chris and sliding into the limo. She was wearing a slim black halter dress that flared out around her knees, and strappy black heels. "You ready for the show?"

"We're ready," Brady said. He dropped his hand over Liz's shoulders. "Aren't we?"

"Very," Liz responded. *Son of a bitch.*

"Awesome. I've seen this one, and it's my absolute favorite. You'll love it."

Chris dropped in beside her, the driver closed the door, and then they were off again. Mollie poured herself some champagne and refilled Liz's now-empty glass. Liz was going to need more than that to come down from her high.

They arrived at the theater and were directed to their own private box. Chris and Mollie stepped through the red curtain first, but Liz stopped Brady.

"Did you do all this?" she asked, gesturing around.

"If you mean taking my girlfriend out, then yes."

"I mean . . . all of it . . . the limo, champagne, box seats . . ."

"Well, Chris and I agreed, but it was my suggestion," he said with a shrug. "Do you not like it? You seemed to like it earlier in the limo."

"No, I like it! And I liked the limo . . . though I wished you would have given me one more thing," she said suggestively.

"What would that be?"

Liz ran her hands down the front of his suit. "I think you'll have to figure it out later when we're alone."

"Who says I have to wait until we're alone?" he asked, brushing his lips against her mouth.

"You just want us to get caught, don't you? Our faces all over the paper for indecent exposure."

Brady chuckled. "If it's news that I'm sleeping with my girlfriend then I'm doing something wrong here."

"Maybe if you're sleeping with her in the middle of a crowded Broadway show . . ."

"Who would even know?" he asked, backing her against the wall in the darkened corridor. The show was starting any second, all the lights were out, and they were in a private area where no one was around. The only people who would come by would be waiters asking them about drinks and their friends sitting at the front of the box.

"S-someone," she stuttered uncertainly.

He pressed his body firmly against her and she felt him through his suit pants. He wanted her. And, God, did she want him too. "No one will see us as long as no one hears us. Do you understand?"

Her whole body tensed. She loved this side of him. She loved how easily he commanded her presence and elicited these emotions from her. Her body was on fire from earlier, but just the demand in his voice made her hot all over again.

"Liz, do you understand?"

She nodded. "Yes."

"Are you two coming?" Mollie's voice called as she stepped into the hallway. "Oh, sorry, didn't mean to interrupt."

Brady smirked at Liz before backing away. "No interruption. We're coming."

Mollie quickly darted back into their private booth.

"We'd better be," Liz peeped as she passed Brady. He smacked her on the ass as she walked by and she bit her lip to keep from crying out.

"What did I say?" he growled.

"She didn't hear."

"Let's try this again," he said, swishing back the curtain to let her into the balcony. "No talking. No noise. Not a peep. Follow my directions and I'll let you come this time."

"*Let* me?" she asked as if his words didn't make her body tremble with desire.

"Yes," he growled, drawing her into him. He moved his mouth very close to her ear. "You know how I feel about begging, baby. I'm going to make your pussy beg for it."

It already was.

Brady took a seat at the back of the box and Liz moved to take the seat next to him. The lights flickered, the orchestra started up, silencing all conversation, and then the show began. As soon as the audience's full attention was on the show, Brady motioned for Liz to take a seat in his lap facing forward.

She did as she was told without a word, but glanced around, waiting for someone to notice that something was amiss. But no one could see into the box from this angle, and Mollie and Chris were dead set on the show. The skirt of her dress covered Brady's lap as he unbuttoned his pants and withdrew his cock. She felt the length brush against her thighs and she shivered all over. She couldn't believe they were doing this. Yet she had no intention of stopping him.

His hand slipped under her skirt and circled around her clit once more. She bit back her moan and just leaned into the pleasure. She had been so close earlier that it took nothing to wake her body up. They had been playing cat and mouse all day, and she was craving him so badly that she didn't even care how she got off at this point.

He slipped a digit inside of her and found she was slick and ready for him. Brady pushed her up to that point all over again before removing his hand and angling her body so he slid all the way in.

Liz's head lolled as he filled her. She fought for composure, but she had none. It took everything in her power not to groan right then and there and alert their friends to what they were doing in the back of the theater box.

Brady rearranged her skirt so that it completely covered his lap from view and then started rocking up into her. Her body tightened all around him, urging him on and demanding the release he had held back from her earlier. Her fingers dug deep into the rich material of the box seat at the same time his sank into her hips.

Her breath caught as a whirlwind of emotions hit her all at once. She wanted to cry out and scream and let the world know that she had the heart of this elusive man. She felt as if she was on top of the world despite everything else that had come crashing down around her. Her heart beat double time in her chest, her pulse quickening with every thrust, her skin superheating as adrenaline coursed through her body.

Brady pushed her down over and over again, and she was sure they were the only ones who could hear the soft sounds of their bodies meeting in rhythm. It was the privacy and intimacy of their joining amid the public atmosphere that pushed them toward climax. The orchestra played to their tempo. The actors sang their tune. The song hit a crescendo and Liz felt her own body come undone.

She collapsed onto herself as she came down from her own crescendo. Brady pushed up into her once more and she felt him finish, shuddering with his climax. They both sat there for a few minutes more until their breathing steadied out, before Liz excused herself for the restroom.

By the time she returned, Brady had righted himself and seemed completely engrossed in the show. He smiled a confident heart-stopping smile and motioned her over. She moved to take the seat next to him, but he pulled her into his lap once more.

"You were spectacular," he whispered, wrapping his arms around her waist and leaning her into him.

"You act as if I was part of the show."

"You were the whole show, love." He placed a kiss on her collarbone and traced his lips up to her neck.

Liz leaned forward and kissed Brady with every ounce of passion she had. There were no words to convey how she felt about him. There was only this moment.

When the show ended, they returned to the limo to go get drinks. Mollie gushed the entire time about the production and how she thought that it was even better than the last time she saw it with her girlfriends. Liz smiled and nodded at the appropriate times, but she hadn't really paid attention to much of what had happened.

Soon enough the limo reached their destination, and they all piled out into the chic bar. Liz thought she might feel overdressed, since she was used to the college scene, but everyone inside was in business suits and dressy attire. She received a few envious glances as she passed with Brady on her arm. She didn't know whether they were green over Brady or her dress. Maybe it was both. But she just raised her chin as if she belonged in high society.

Chris procured a booth in the back and a waiter came by to get their orders. Chris insisted on putting his card down, even after Brady tried to argue with him. But after a minute, Brady gave up and let Chris pay.

"I never thought I'd see the day," Liz said.

"What?" Mollie asked.

"Brady lost an argument and actually backed down."

"Oh very funny," Brady said. He pulled her close to him and planted a kiss on her cheek. "I didn't lose an argument."

"You're letting Chris pay. You never let anyone do anything you don't want."

"Then maybe I wanted to let Chris pay."

"No, you didn't," Chris said, shaking his head. "Don't let him fool you. He *hates* when people do things he can't control."

"Oh, no," Liz teased. "You hate me?"

Chris started laughing. "She's got you there, B."

"I don't want to control you," Brady said. "Chris has it all wrong."

"Now *that* sounds accurate," Mollie said.

"Wow. Thanks for the vote of confidence, Mols."

"Just call 'em like I see 'em," she crooned.

Their drinks appeared shortly and they all raised them to toast a night out with friends. Liz was so glad they had taken the time off to relax with Chris. She knew that it was the precursor to a very busy election season, and she was glad they at least got a bit of time alone before that happened.

"Brady's a control freak and I'm a know-nothing. Sounds like college, huh, Brady?" Chris joked.

"College is a bit of a blur," Brady confessed.

"Too much booze," Mollie said.

"Basketball," he corrected. "Takes over your life."

"That it does," Chris agreed. He raised his glass to Liz. "So, Graduate, now that you're out in the big world writing articles and getting quoted in the *Washington Post*, what are your big plans? You two lovebirds moving in together?"

"Uh . . ." Liz mumbled. Yeah . . . that was one of those conversations they hadn't had yet. They had only been officially together since February. Four whole months. Blissful months, but that was kind of fast.

Surprisingly the idea didn't bother her at all. This was Brady. She had known for two years that she wanted him, and now that she had him everything felt as if it was moving at a perfect speed.

Brady tapped his fingers on the table and leveled Chris with an *are you kidding me?* look.

"What?" Chris asked innocently. "Have y'all not talked about it? I thought that was a done deal. You only moped around about this girl a million years. What's the holdup now that you're together?"

"Chris, you're so tactful," Mollie said. She rolled her eyes and nudged him.

"I don't need tact with my buddy."

"I'd tell you to learn some," Brady said, "but after nearly thirty years of this, I should be the one to know better."

"Probably."

She wondered what exactly she was going to do about the living situation now that Victoria had moved out. It seemed sad to be in Chapel Hill by herself. Plus, after spending the week over spring break and the week after graduation with Brady, she found that she really liked being around him all the time. She liked being the person he came home to, spent his time with, got dinner with, talked about his job with. It made their relationship feel more complete. The phone could never do justice to that.

"I can't believe you haven't asked her," Chris said, pushing.

"Well, I was planning to talk about this in private after we go back, but Chris jumped the gun," Brady said, shaking his head. He turned to Liz and cupped her hand in his. "Will you move in with me?"

"I don't want you to feel pressured," she whispered, conscious of Chris and Mollie watching them.

"I've wanted you by my side since we got back together. Now that you're out of school there's no physical barrier between us and I don't want there to be ever again." His brown eyes were intense and sincere. "Please move in with me. I have the election ahead of me and I want my woman by my side."

"Are you sure?" she breathed emotionally.

"I've never been more sure. I don't want to control you or your decisions. If you don't want to move in with me yet, please tell me, but know that I want nothing more than to have you with me all the time," Brady said, his voice laced with power and seduction that came with a life built for politics.

"Okay," she whispered without another moment of hesitation. "I'll move in with you."

Chapter 19

ROAD TRIP

When they returned from New York City, Brady hired someone to move Liz up to D.C. A box of clothes and some toiletries were sent to his house in Raleigh for when they were in North Carolina, but otherwise her life now officially belonged with Brady.

He had wanted to have her car shipped up to D.C. for her, but she thought that was ridiculous. It was only a five-hour drive and she had done it before by herself. She badgered Brady enough about how stupid it was to ship her car no matter the cost that he finally gave up. It was a mini victory.

When the time came and she had the backseat full of stuff that she didn't trust the moving company with, she offered to drive Brady to the airport.

He gave her a reproachful look. "You think I'm letting you drive the five hours without me?"

Liz's mouth dropped open. "Do you drive anywhere?"

"I remember driving you to my lake house and back."

"That's different. This isn't necessary."

"Will I get to spend the five hours in the car with you?" he asked.

"Well, yeah . . ."

"Then it's necessary."

"Brady, you don't have time. Heather is going to flip. You have that rally to get ready for this weekend. It's the kickoff for the campaign. Aren't you supposed to be in meetings?" Liz asked.

She did *not* want to be blamed for this. Even if Liz hadn't heard from Heather since Brady bitched the other woman out, Liz could still feel her disapproval across state lines.

"What did I tell you about worrying about Heather? Leave her to me. You'll see enough of her once the campaign starts. No use worrying what she thinks now," Brady told her. "Now hand over the keys so we can get going."

"Ex-excuse me?" Liz stuttered, clutching the keys to her chest.

"I'm driving."

"Um . . . no."

Brady put his hand out. "I always drive."

"You always drive *your* cars. You'll have to take shotgun and be happy with it." She slid into the front seat without listening to another complaint from him.

She knew that she was pushing his buttons a little in the process, but when he sat in the passenger seat she felt immense satisfaction. He would comply if she were adamant enough. Not that she had any intention of getting rid of the dominant side of her boyfriend, but she didn't mind ordering him around a bit.

The drive to D.C. was all sorts of awesome for Liz, who found out that Brady actually liked late-nineties boy bands and Disney music, which came up randomly on her iPod.

"What? I have a younger sister," he argued.

Liz just giggled and sang along to the *NSYNC song that came on next.

He wasn't in the car long enough anymore to listen to audiobooks, he told her, but he used to listen to them all the time before he got into Congress. He said it was harder to concentrate on them when he was flying. She only had the last Harry Potter audiobook tucked away in her car, but she found no complaints from him when she switched over to that for the second half of the ride.

The only thing that interrupted their impromptu road trip was a call from Heather. Brady silenced the radio.

"Do you have to answer that?" Liz asked, glancing over at his cell phone in the car.

"She can't be that mad that I'm going to be three hours late, can she?"

"Are we talking about the same Heather?"

"It'll be fine. Just don't drive us off the road."

"If she asks, you make sure to tell her that I told you to fly," Liz told him.

Brady just laughed and answered the phone. "Hey."

"Hey! Hey?" Heather shrieked through the phone loud enough for Liz to hear. Brady shrugged and put it on speaker. "Hey is all you have to say?"

"How can I help you?" Liz snickered into her hand and Brady pressed a finger to his mouth.

"You were supposed to be here thirty minutes ago, Brady. We have the rally on Friday. Alex wants to talk strategy. There is a lot going on. More important things than moving your girlfriend when you've already hired a moving company. Where are you?" she demanded.

"I'm on my way to D.C."

"You're talking to me from the airplane?"

"Car actually."

Heather breathed out heavily. Liz could almost picture her closing her eyes and pinching her brows. "You're *driving* back to D.C.?"

"I'd consider myself more of a passenger. Liz is driving."

"I'm just glad you don't have to be in Congress today. You're acting like a teenager. Are you forgetting all of your responsibilities for this girl?"

Liz blushed at the statement. She felt ashamed at stealing so much of his time. She didn't want to take him away from everything that was important to him. But the venom in his eyes stilled her thoughts.

"That's enough, Heather. I am not a teenager; nor am I forgetting anything. Certainly not my duties to my country or my constituents. I am taking a short road trip through Virginia with my girlfriend and will be back in just under an hour and a half. Now, is there a reason for this call?"

Liz chewed on her lip as she waited for Heather's response. She hated being a constant source of conflict between Brady and Heather.

"Yes," Heather snapped. "I finally got some information about those pictures from graduation."

"What pictures?" Liz whispered.

"What did you find?" Brady prompted.

"I'm starting to see a trend here. Do you remember the lovely young woman Calleigh Hollingsworth?" Heather asked with her biting tone. "My sources tell me that she sold the picture of Liz and her ex to the tabloids. It reads like a setup to me. Ex happens to stroll into town. The girl he wrote the article with sells the photos."

Liz opened her mouth to protest. She didn't think Hayden would do that, but Brady shook his head. She really wanted to say something, but Heather didn't know she was listening in.

"I'm going to have a team keep tabs on her and see if anything else suspicious comes up. I don't want her to wreak any more havoc. I know we don't have a real threat for the primary, but I don't want to risk it. Any challenger is bad enough with what we've been through. I know Russell Kleeb has only done community activist work in Durham, but I think we should take it seriously. He'll latch on to anything that he can, and Lord knows what we're going to encounter come general election time."

"We'll make it through. Keep me posted of anything else. I'll be in the office soon," Brady told her.

"Loud and clear, Congressman," she said crisply. The line died in his hand.

"Does she *always* do that?" Liz demanded.

"What?" he asked.

"Hang up. She always hangs up on me. It's so annoying."

"Oh. That's just Heather. She is tight with her time," Brady told her.

"Huh. I just thought she hated me."

"She doesn't understand you," Brady admitted carefully. "Heather was interning for my father when I met her. I was about to graduate from college and had lofty plans to become president."

"I believe you still have those plans," Liz said. She was fascinated by the insight into his life and to find out more about Heather.

"I do." He winked at her. "My father said that she was the hardest-working person he had ever met, but not the easiest person to work with. I kind of took that as a challenge, and hired her on full-time to help with my first State Senate race. She proved invaluable. Though I do have to say that she has only gotten harder to work with. She's kind of rough around the edges, but she's earned the right to be."

"Rough around the edges is an understatement, but I guess I can get it. Politics is a hard world."

"Heather sees the world in black and white. If you're not good for the campaign, then you're useless. The woman has no clutter in her house at all. It's kind of terrifying."

"You don't have clutter," Liz said.

"I live at the office. There's clutter," he said.

"Not anymore!"

"Well, you can clutter up *our* place."

"I like the sound of that."

"Me too," he admitted. "I know Heather is coarse, but she just doesn't think you've proven to be useful. She doesn't see that you don't have to be of a certain mold to be an asset to the campaign. You're an asset to me. I love you. That's what matters in the end."

The rest of the drive to D.C. was left to the Harry Potter audiobook narrator. Liz had a lot to think about, but she wasn't sure how to bring it all up to Brady yet. She wanted to collect her thoughts first, and she was stuck on what Heather had said about the pictures of her and Hayden being a setup.

She didn't know how someone would act if they were setting someone up to take their picture, but she didn't think that had been Hayden. She would have assumed some nerves at the very least. Probably more likely would be excessive touchy-feely displays to try to make the pictures look worse than they actually were, but he hadn't done that. He had seemed too sincere in his apology to set her up like that even after everything that had happened between them.

Liz pulled into the parking garage to Brady's apartment sometime later. He had already procured the available spot next to his Range Rover for her car. Brady grabbed two boxes of clothes and Liz carried an antique jewelry box that had belonged to her mother.

They reached Brady's penthouse and she followed him to the front door. A smile touched her lips as she realized that this was now their place. Her stomach did a somersault as she crossed the threshold. Brady deposited her boxes in his walk-in closet. Liz followed him and placed the jewelry box on his dresser. She opened it and pulled out Brady's locket. She liked wearing it when he left so that she felt as if she had a piece of him close to her heart.

"What's that?" he asked, standing behind her.

"Your necklace."

"No. That." He reached inside and pulled out a small packet of charms. "Did you get new charms?"

Liz's cheeks turned rosy. "Uh, no."

He gave her a questioning look. "Care to explain?"

"Hayden got them for me when we were dating."

Brady's face turned murderous. "He got you charms for *my* necklace?"

"He didn't know it was your necklace, just that I used to wear it a lot. He thought I might want updated charms so I'd wear it again," she said softly.

"And?"

"What?" she asked confused.

"Did you wear them? Were you walking around with me dangling between your breasts?" he asked, fingering the locket where it was hanging. "With another man's charms inside them?"

"No," she told him, trying to remain calm. She knew that he wouldn't like that Hayden had given them to her. "I never wore them."

"Then I guess you don't need them, do you?" he asked, tossing them into the trash can and walking out of the bedroom.

Liz stood there in the wake of Brady's temper. Her hands were trembling slightly as she stared at the charms sitting at the bottom of the otherwise empty bin. She had no emotional attachment to the charms that Hayden had given her, but they were still hers to keep or throw away as she saw fit.

"Hey," she called, jogging into the living room. "You didn't have to do that."

"Did you want to keep them?" His arms were crossed over his chest and he looked as though his jealous streak had gotten the better of him.

"Not particularly, but it's my choice. Not yours. And you don't have to be angry with me about it."

"I shouldn't be angry that your ex-boyfriend gave you charms for my necklace?" he asked.

"They don't mean anything to me and I never wore them. What does it even matter?"

Brady eyed her suspiciously. "I don't like reminders that you were with him."

"I definitely do not think about Hayden like that. I've only ever wanted you. Now that I have you, I'm certainly not letting you go for anyone else."

"And yet you won't believe that he set you up for those pictures," he pointed out.

Liz's mouth dropped. "What? How did you—"

"I know you." He dropped his arms with a sigh. "I saw it on your face when Heather said it. Why won't you believe that he would do that after everything else he has done to hurt you?"

"It just doesn't seem like Hayden. He didn't act like that when I saw him. He was there to apologize."

Brady shook his head. "A hunch isn't good enough, Liz. I can't accept that from his past behavior."

"Well, then let me contact him," she blurted out. Brady gave her a sharp look. "I'll ask him about the pictures and see if he knew about them. I know him. I'd know if he was lying."

"No."

"Brady, seriously."

"I don't want you talking to him. We've been through this," he told her.

"What's the worst that could happen?" she asked.

"You tip him and Calleigh off and so she's more careful about who she sells information to," he growled.

Liz sighed. "What if I don't mention Calleigh?"

Brady grabbed her face between his strong hands and brought her close to him. "If you *must* talk to him, then fine. I don't like it.

I'll never like it, and I don't want this to become a routine thing. I don't want to have this argument again."

"I don't want it to be routine either. I just want to get to the truth," she said. Her eyes were locked on to his brown ones and she thought she was going to drown in that gaze.

"I trust you," he said, kissing her on the lips hard. "I'm going to have to tell Heather about this. So please report back as soon as your brief conversation is over."

"I will." He started walking toward the door, but she reached out for him. "I'm sorry that it's this way."

"Do I get you forever?" he asked, his words as smooth as silk.

The words caught her off guard. They had never talked about forever. They had never really talked about anything until he had asked her to move in with him.

"Yes," she murmured.

"Then it's worth it." He kissed her again before leaving. She was left to wade in the lingering ecstasy of his lips on hers and the whispered promise of forever.

With a sigh, Liz found her phone and hesitantly dialed Hayden's phone number.

"Hello?" he answered. He sounded both shocked and tentative, like he didn't know why she would be calling.

"Hey, Hayden."

"Is . . . something wrong?"

"No. Well, not exactly," she said softly.

The silence hung between them, thick with the breakdown of their failed relationship. She knew that she needed to say something, but she felt as if her tongue was stuck to the roof of her mouth.

"As much as I enjoy hearing from you, I am curious as to your reasoning," Hayden said. "I assume you have a motive?"

"Did you set me up?" Liz gasped out. "With the pictures."

"What?" he asked. "What do you mean?"

"I mean did you plant a photographer to get pictures of us in the paper?"

"Are you joking?" Hayden sputtered.

"You need to be honest with me here. If this is all true, then we're going to have serious issues. I don't know what your motive is, but it's not going to work. I just need you to tell me the truth."

"I've never lied to you before, Liz," he said. "I would never plant a photographer. I was there to apologize, not to try to break up your relationship. Guess my message was lost on you."

"I'm serious, Hayden!"

"So am I! I don't know who took those pictures. I'm sorry that they were in the paper, but I had absolutely nothing to do with that. Why are you asking me now anyway? That happened two weeks ago," Hayden demanded. "Wait . . . do you know who took the pictures? Is that why you're accusing me?"

Shit! He knew her too well.

"Should I even hazard a guess, since you've come to me to ask about it?" Hayden said dryly. "I hadn't thought about it at the time, but who had a personal vendetta against the subject and would know I was going to be in Chapel Hill?"

Liz held her breath. He was too smart for his own good. Not that it was doing any harm at the moment. He hadn't known that Calleigh was involved. It was clear in his voice. Crystal clear. And now he actually sounded pissed.

"Calleigh, huh?" Hayden guessed.

"I can neither confirm nor deny . . ."

"Oh, don't go all reporter on me now, Liz. I taught you everything you know."

"Not everything," she spat.

"Fine. Not everything," he said awkwardly. "Calleigh stalked me when she knew that I was coming to visit. I'd really like to know what she's up to."

"Wouldn't we all."

"It's probably good that I work on the inside then, huh?"

"What do you mean?" She didn't even know why she was continuing this conversation, but something had changed in Hayden when everything had snapped into place for him. He sounded more like himself—driven, ambitious, dedicated to the truth. She hadn't seen this person in a long time.

"She's taking this personally because I chose you, Liz," he said tenderly. "I just . . . think that maybe I could keep an eye on her."

"And why would you do that?" She wanted his intentions out in the open loud and clear.

"Partly because she's messing with people I care about, partly because she stalked me, and partly . . . because she got her promotion over me."

"The promotion for uncovering that I was Sandy Carmichael? God, she's such a bitch!"

Hayden laughed. "She sure has her moments."

"Every moment," she grumbled. "Well, I should probably go. I just . . . I guess I'm glad I called."

"Here to help. If I see anything strange, I'll just shoot you a text or something." He sighed as if he were contemplating saying more and then decided against it.

"Thanks, Hayden," she whispered, and then said good-bye before hanging up.

Knowing that Hayden wasn't involved in Calleigh's sinister plots made Liz feel as if a weight was lifted off her shoulders. Their conversation actually felt, if she dared to consider it, normal—or as normal as it was ever going to get with Hayden.

Chapter 20
THE KICKOFF

A few days later on the afternoon before Brady's kickoff rally for his reelection effort, Liz and Brady lounged around their apartment in D.C. She had started calling it their apartment after Brady had reminded her over and over that they shared it now and it didn't just belong to him. If she was living here, then it was theirs. That was all that mattered.

They would be flying out the next morning into Raleigh. Liz was nervous about her first official event at Brady's side. She had been to dozens of political events as a reporter. She had even been to a number with Brady in D.C., but the campaign trail was a whole different story.

She was worried about keeping up with her life while Brady was on the campaign trail. She had recently received her acceptance letter to Maryland for the fall term, which she was ecstatic about, since that was her top choice. Not to mention it was within the D.C. metro area, which kept her close to Brady while she focused on school. She had liked that they could be closer, but if he was gone through the November election she might still miss him a lot.

Plus she was concerned about keeping up with her writing. She had just turned in her follow-up piece to the online paper, and after glowing compliments from Justin, she had started posting more articles to his blog.

In fact, she had begun spending a lot of her free time on the computer, interacting with people who were now following what she considered her blog. Even if it was about YouTube movie ratings and other popular culture–related themes, she was the one writing the articles, and she liked talking to the people who enjoyed her pieces. It was a different level of personal involvement than she had ever had in journalism.

She was scrolling through the comments on the website as Brady practiced his speech for tomorrow. She had heard him reciting it to himself in the mirror the past couple of days. Actually, she could probably recite chunks of it back to him at this point.

"What do you think of that line?" Brady asked suddenly.

"Hmm?" Liz looked up from her computer. "Which one?"

"This one," he said. "'I personally believe that working for the people in Congress has been the most memorable experience of my life.'" He dropped the paper on the table. "Do you think that sounds too high school yearbook?"

Liz laughed. "No. I think that sounds fine as long as you deliver it with your normal charisma. But if you're asking my opinion, I think the stuff about Chris and staying to work in North Carolina is kind of repetitive, especially from last term."

"Yeah? I thought the consistency worked well."

She shut her laptop and snatched the speech from the coffee table. She skimmed the section she was talking about before continuing. "Okay. I see what you mean—it does have the consistency factor—but tomorrow is going to be people who know you and probably primarily people who have seen your stuff from two years ago. They support you no matter what, but you want to fire them up, right?"

A smile lit up Brady's face when she glanced up at him. "Right."

"What?" she asked.

"Just keep going," he encouraged.

"So, I think you're missing that. You talk about why you decided to work here and why the state is important to you, and used a personal example to drive it home. It's a clever trick to get people to empathize with you."

"I didn't realize you had dissected my speeches so completely." Brady walked around the table and took the seat next to her. He crossed one leg over the other and draped an arm across the back. He managed to look completely engrossed in what she was saying and totally laid-back. She swore they taught politicians how to do this.

"I've seen all of your speeches. When I did research on you two summers ago, I watched the ones from your State Senate races. Your father basically invented the formula. It works. Very effective. But I think you're missing your pull here. You're not convincing these people to vote for you. They already will. You're convincing them to essentially work for you, whether through time or money."

"All right. I see your point. What would you suggest?" he asked, leaning forward and brushing a loose lock of hair from her face. He ran his hand down her jawline and stared at her so intensely that she found it hard to get out her next comment.

She was actually directing one of his speeches. A speech that he'd had a professional speechwriter work on for him. Someone who knew him and had likely been on staff for years. Oh, well, she couldn't back down now.

"I'd focus on what keeps people motivated, not what motivated you to begin with. What continues to keep you motivated? Your work in the education committee, fulfilling your commitment to the Research Triangle, bringing back money to support education. I'd focus on that from a fulfillment aspect, not an issue aspect, and then bring it home with a personal example . . . perhaps a political colloquium you attended while in office." She laughed softly, though she thought it might be a good idea, since the colloquium had been a way to show his dedication to the people and the university system that was so important to his district. "There are other examples that you could use; that was just my suggestion."

"You know, you're pretty brilliant, baby." He dropped his mouth onto hers and she forgot everything they had been talking about. They moved in perfect unison, his hands tangling in her hair, their tongues volleying for position. Everything slowed to that moment and she reveled in the feel of her handsome, successful boyfriend finding *her* to be the brilliant one.

They arrived in a town car to the side entrance of the rally point. The event wasn't nearly as big as the Fourth of July event she had attended two summers ago, but it still boasted a relatively large stage, with a crowd pressing in. Liz could see the flashes of the press anxious to nab a picture of Brady . . . maybe even to a get a picture of her.

Their relationship was hardly a secret, but they had an unwritten rule to avoid press as much as they could. On the campaign trail, there would be no avoiding them. The worst of their relationship woes had passed, but they were still a story, especially now that Brady was running for reelection. D.C. was the Hollywood of politics, and Brady was their fresh young star.

Liz had already read articles recently about their moving in together. They hadn't been secretive about that, but still, it was strange to see it online. She had wanted to claw her eyes out when she read the comments. Slut, whore, gold digger, and home wrecker were the nicest things she was called. Apparently they were also rushing into things because she was pregnant, and she and Brady were going to have a shotgun wedding in a few weeks to try to cover it up. Not to mention Brady felt bad for her and was using their relationship to hide his other rampant affairs. The Internet was a really pleasant place.

She had confessed to Brady about it when he found her upset over the comments one afternoon.

"You cannot let people make you feel like this. Are any of those things true?" he had asked.

"No," she had whispered.

"Then don't even bother yourself with them. There is a certain level of discretion you have to learn. When you're in the public eye, you have to actively choose to ignore and avoid things like this. Nothing good comes from it."

So she had stopped looking. She didn't think that she was strong enough to build up a complete resistance to it, but it was a start. Her journalism background made her naturally curious, which wasn't helpful in this situation.

Their car came to a stop and Brady exited first. She followed him into the sea of reporters. His hand reaching out for her and guiding her through the crowd was the only thing keeping her steady. She didn't duck her head and hide from the cameras as she would have four months ago, but it still unnerved her.

When they reached the roped-off area where she and Brady would wait along with much of his staff, Liz let out a sigh of relief. It was still strange that reporters made her so uneasy when she had always wanted to be one. She tried to brush off the encounter and focus on what was going on around her.

Heather was speaking swiftly to the reporters on the other side of the roped-in area. Liz had seen these conversations before, usually to talk about interviews, spotlight segments, Q&A time, and more. Elliott was on his phone, talking animatedly to whoever had his attention. Alex, Brady's campaign manager, was sitting at a nearby table lost to his computer. He was all strategy and planning and not usually the person in the field.

And then there was Brady, her Brady, going over last-minute details of his speech with the speechwriter. Liz had rewritten some of Brady's speech to show him more what she was talking about. To her surprise he had taken it to his speechwriter and they had agreed to keep it. Her own words in one of Brady's speeches! She had felt a tingle shoot through her at the prospect of him reciting her words to his captivated audience.

She could feel a buzz of excitement running through everyone in the vicinity. This was the big leagues. This was what it was all about. The start of everything Brady was working toward. She peered out at the crowd and was staggered to see that the tent that was erected for the event was full of people.

Then she heard it. *Max-well. Max-well. Max-well.*

Her breath caught as the cheer started off quiet and then slowly began to rise as more and more people picked up the chant. Soon the sound of Brady's name was deafening, taking over the rally space.

She glanced over at him and he was smiling brightly. She saw it for what it was. He lived for this. Born and bred to be the magnificent person he was, to crave the spotlight and people cheering his name, to mold the country for the people. And he was hers.

"All right," Heather snapped, walking back over to them. "Are you ready?"

"Born ready," Brady said confidently.

"Of course you were. Now let this crescendo and then make your entrance. Afterward I've arranged a few interviews, then a quick meeting with some donors, and a dinner with Chelsea about that fracking thing she keeps shoving down your throat."

"Chelsea, really?" he asked. "Can't that wait?"

"They're sending a *ton* of money our way trying to sway your vote on that. You have to meet with her."

"Who is Chelsea?" Liz interrupted.

Heather barely gave her a passing glance. "After that you're free for the night, but tomorrow morning we have a photo op with the mayor."

"Sounds good, Heather," he said in a dismissive tone. Heather gave him a pointed look and then walked over to stand by Elliott. Brady turned back to face Liz. "Chelsea works for an environmental lobbying firm that's trying to get me to make a statement about fracking in the North Carolina Mountains. They're huge supporters, so I can't ignore them. So we have dinner plans."

"*We?*" Liz asked, surprised.

"Of course. You're part of my life. You'll entertain at my side." He swept her up in his arms and kissed her briefly on the mouth. "Now I have to charm the crowd as much as I did you."

"Let's hope you use different tactics," she said breathlessly.

He popped one more kiss on her mouth and smirked. His campaign mask slid easily into place, all charm and charisma with an underlying arrogance that no one could ignore, and just a touch of something that inherently drew people to him. Brady had it all.

"Good luck," she whispered.

"Don't need it, baby. I've got you."

With that Brady turned and sauntered up the small set of stairs and onto the stage as though he owned it. The chant turned into uproarious applause as his followers extolled his very presence. She moved next to Heather on the side of the stage to watch him deliver the speech he had been working on all week.

Heather stood with her arms crossed and her mouth set in a straight line. Liz wondered what it must be like for her—always worrying about every minute detail related to Brady and the campaign and never having a moment to truly enjoy it. She and Heather were on bad terms, but that didn't mean that Liz didn't understand where Heather was coming from, especially after Brady had told her more about how they had started working together.

Liz was jarred from her thoughts as Brady's smooth voice filled the speakers. "Welcome!" he cheered.

The crowd went crazy, screaming, clapping, and throwing Maxwell banners into the air.

"It's good to be back home, Raleigh. Good to be back with the good people of North Carolina and every single one of my supporters here!"

Liz felt herself relaxing into his speech. She had heard it dozens of times this week and almost knew it by heart. She would never be comfortable enough to give a speech in front of dozens of people, but Brady was a natural. He commanded attention. Each time his eyes were cast out on the crowd it was as if he were speaking directly to every individual in the audience.

She even saw Heather nodding along with Brady's speech. It was nice knowing that she wasn't immune to his onstage demeanor. Though it shouldn't have surprised her. Heather was a professional, but believed in Brady and what he stood for. She wanted to further her own career through him, but she trusted him.

Liz trusted him too. Hearing him speak about his love for the people and his desire to continue to enact change only reminded her all over again why she had fallen for him and how he had won her vote. She had thought that he was just in it for the fame and fortune. Lining his pockets with ill intentions while fooling everyone with a pretty face and good pedigree. He couldn't have proven her more wrong.

She held her breath as he got to the next part of the speech, the part that she had helped him work on. His audience was captivated as he started in.

"When I was elected to serve as the member of Congress for the Fourth District of North Carolina, you conferred on me your support and your trust. You believed me when I said that I was going to take your beliefs and ideas to D.C. with me and look out for your benefit," Brady said, pacing the stage. "Over the past two years, I've done exactly that. Whether I was spending my time on the education committee trying to enact better legislation for our future leaders, helping to get more appropriations for the research community we have invested in, or just spending countless days working among you, listening to you, and taking into account your concerns.

"I was in Chapel Hill just this last year for a special political journalism colloquium hosted by the university. At that event, I, along with several of my colleagues, spoke about the future of our country. We reached out to students, faculty, as well as any other citizen who chose to attend the function. We wanted to hear you and we wanted you to hear us. We're here for you. No matter where you come from or what you're doing right now, this is your country."

Liz smiled as she heard her words spoken into the crowd. It was magical, almost like a fairy tale, to hear someone so compelling deliver her words. It almost gave her the same amazing feeling as when she read her words in print and when she saw other people reading them too. But this time it was Brady, and he was swallowing the room whole with them.

The next part was what Brady added, and it made her blush every time.

"A particularly precocious young woman spoke during this colloquium regarding education policy. I asked her one question—what important factor from her research should I take back to D.C.

regarding education? Her response stuck with me to this day. She said to treat students as individuals and not as numbers on paper. I could never agree more. I never want to treat any of you as a number, but rather as individuals. And the only way I can do that is to win another term in the Congress."

The crowd cheered uproariously at the mention of him seeking another term. Brady waited until the crowd died down and then finished the remainder of the speech that his speechwriter had put together. It was brilliant. He was brilliant. He had the crowd at attention and she knew just by hearing the chants and seeing their enraptured faces that they were with him through and through.

Brady barreled down the stairs and scooped Liz up. He planted a kiss on her lips before releasing her. "You were incredible," she told him.

"They loved your words, baby."

"They love you!"

"We're a team," he whispered. She shivered at the way he said that and couldn't keep from inwardly jumping up and down. That was nothing short of what she wanted with Brady.

"That was fantastic," Heather told him. "Now let's move on to the interview and soon enough you'll be on your way to dinner."

The rest of the afternoon passed quickly. Brady answered question after question regarding his reelection efforts. He smiled and stood for photos. On occasion she would even stand with him when interviewers asked if their photo could be taken together. Heather scowled every time it happened, but she could hardly deny them when Brady himself seemed eager for her to be standing there.

Liz excused herself from the donor meeting that Brady had to be in attendance for to work on her next article. Since her previous columns were still getting some good press, the editor had offered her a feature piece. He still tried to get her to use her real name, but after she had explained to him that she had no desire for it to show up in papers, he had stopped bothering her. He had started jokingly titling her papers Dear Congress, as a play on the advice columnist Dear Abby, and the name had stuck.

This was the first article that she had written where the idea had manifested from a conversation with Brady. It had taken hold while she was helping him write the speech he had just delivered, where the emphasis was on the individual rather than the masses. She hoped that it didn't align too closely with his speech, and she might even have him take a look at it just to be sure. In the meantime she just needed to get something down. She couldn't fix a blank page.

"Knock-knock," Brady said, appearing in the open doorway.

"Hey," she said with a smile.

"You ready to get out of here?"

"Dinner?"

He nodded. "I wish we were going straight home."

"To bed?" She closed her laptop and stood.

"That works."

"Do we have time for me to change?" She had been in this blue cotton shirtdress all day and she wouldn't mind a change in appearance before they met with a lobbyist.

"Not much time."

Liz sidled up to him and he wrapped an arm around her waist. "I'll be quick."

He leaned over and whispered in her ear. "Only when we're in a crowded theater."

"Tease," she purred.

"No. If I was teasing," he said, turning and pressing her back into the wall. His hand slid up her thigh and pulled it up around his hip. "I would tell you about how much I want to fuck you just like this."

A moan escaped her lips and all she wanted to do was tug him closer.

"But I'm not a tease," he said before stepping away from her.

Liz dropped her leg and stuck her bottom lip out. "Not nice."

"Come on, baby. If you want to change out of that dress before dinner, we need to leave now."

She threaded his tie through her hands and tugged him closer. "Two can play at this game, Congressman Maxwell."

"I look forward to it, Miss Dougherty."

They took the town car out to his house so Liz could change. She latched on to his arm when they pulled into the driveway. "Come with me?" she whispered.

He gave her a searching look. "We don't have time."

"Please?" she pleaded.

"Begging," he groaned. She loved using his weaknesses against him.

Brady followed her out of the car and spoke briefly to the driver before following her inside and up into his bedroom. She plucked a green strapless dress out of the closet and a pair of nude pumps.

"You requested my presence?" he asked, walking toward her.

"Stand right there and don't move." She must have sounded convincing enough, because Brady stopped and did as she told. "You can look but not touch."

He arched an eyebrow, but made a big show of stuffing his hands into his pockets. If he could slam her into walls and turn her on then she could certainly do the same to him.

Ever so slowly, Liz started turning in a circle so that he could feast his eyes on her body. Her hands went to the buttons on her dress and from top to bottom she plucked each one open. By the time she reached the last one, Brady had taken two steps closer to her. She could see the desire on his face.

She turned her back on him, shaking out her blond curls, and then dropped the dress over her shoulders. It pooled at her feet, leaving her nearly naked from the behind save for her baby-pink bra and matching silk thong. She heard Brady suck in a breath behind her and she couldn't help but smirk.

Her hands reached behind her and undid the hook and eye that released her breasts from the bra. She tossed it to the ground behind her at Brady's feet and then slowly turned back to face him. He had moved forward another few feet. This time his expression didn't just hold desire; it was outright need. He looked ready to pounce on her, but she held her hand up.

"Uh-uh. Look. No touch," she cooed.

His breathing was increasingly ragged as she continued to boss him around. She plucked the side of her thong like a guitar string. His hands twitched in his pockets as if he wanted to be the one doing that. Then she dragged the underwear down her thighs to the floor. She was left before him in nothing but her black heels.

"What do you think?" she asked, twirling.

"I think that you've teased long enough."

"Ah-ah!" she said, stepping out of his grasp. "We have an important dinner to attend. I need to get dressed."

"You make this impossible."

Liz giggled and walked over to her dress. She pulled it off the hanger and began unzipping the back. She felt Brady's hands slide around her. "I love you," he whispered.

She smiled. "I love you too."

"Get dressed and we'll fix this problem when we get home." His hand slid between her bare legs and she shook all over. Brady sighed. "All right. Let me just text Chelsea and tell her we're going to be late."

Liz nodded and walked back into the closet to change. She pulled the dress on and started fixing her hair in the mirror, when he returned.

"Take that off," he commanded.

"What?"

"Off. Now."

"What about dinner?"

"Dinner is canceled. Chelsea asked to reschedule, because she's not feeling well. She asked if we could just talk at the Jefferson-Jackson gala next weekend."

"Is that already coming up?" she asked.

"Later than last year," he said with a shrug. "Now back to business at hand. That dress belongs on the floor."

Chapter 21
JEFFERSON-JACKSON GALA

Three weeks later, Liz stepped out of Brady's limo in a floor-length teal off-the-shoulder gown. She and Victoria had gone shopping earlier that week for the dress, and the silky material fit like a glove. Her hair was swept into an elaborate updo, with a braided section pulled back into an intricate bun. She brushed her bangs to the side, to conform to the natural wave of her hair, which she tucked loosely behind her ear. She wore dangly diamond earrings and a thin diamond necklace that brushed her collarbones.

She remembered how two years ago she had shown up in a simple black knee-length gown. She had caught Brady's eye then, and now she was on his arm. Not for the first or last time, she felt as though she were living a dream.

Brady stepped out behind her in a tailored black tuxedo. He was all sharp lines and perfectly angular features. His brown eyes were intense and formidable, but his campaign mask slid into place just as quickly. The charm returned with more confidence than most people carried in a lifetime. He offered her his arm, and she slid her hand into the crook of his elbow.

They walked gallantly into the event. The last time she had attended the Jefferson-Jackson Gala was the first time she and Brady had slept together. Their chemistry had been electric, and after only one dance, she hadn't ever envisioned herself saying no to him. Of course she had, and they had been separated for a time, but that was their past. The five months prior had been some of the best moments of her life, and all she saw when she looked at Brady was her future.

They drew eyes around the room at their entrance. Some still whispered about the way they had gotten together and vague details that Erin had given the papers, which had died away with time. Some looked on with judgment in their eyes. But others did seem to be coming around to the fact that they were always together. The sooner they looked less like a spectacle and more like a couple the better.

"This way," Brady said.

He guided her over to a front-row table that was already full. Each table sat ten people and there were at least fifty tables throughout the massive room decorated in the classic red, white, and blue.

Brady introduced her to the people seated at her table. Three of the men had worked with Brady when he had been a State Senator and each of them were accompanied by their wife. The only other person at their table was a small woman and her date.

"Liz, may I introduce you to Chelsea Young, lead lobbyist at EMi."

"Nice to meet you," Liz said, sticking out her hand. Chelsea was shorter than Liz by nearly a handbreadth, with almond-shaped brown eyes and blond highlighted shoulder-length hair. She wore a lavender hi-lo spaghetti-strap dress and pale pink lipstick.

"The pleasure is all mine," Chelsea said. "And this is my date, Ben."

They all shook hands again before taking a seat with Liz to Brady's right and Chelsea to his left.

The room quieted as a figure walked out onstage—Brady's father. He had been the introductory speaker two years ago when she had been here.

Brady's father took the microphone in his hand and smiled that Maxwell politician smile. "Hello and welcome to the fifty-fifth annual Jefferson-Jackson gala." Everyone applauded and Jeff waited for the cheers to die down before continuing.

"It's always a pleasure to stand before you at this annual bipartisan event that brings us together as a reminder of the mutual goals we are all looking toward—bettering this great nation. Two years ago I stood before you as your opening speaker, and the Jefferson-Jackson committee has once again honored me by asking me to speak before our esteemed keynote speaker."

Liz saw Chelsea lean into Brady and whisper, "Your father seems to get better and better at this every year."

Brady smiled politely and nodded. "All the practice."

"Are we going to be able to have a word after dinner?" she asked.

"As promised," he agreed.

"Perfect." Chelsea retreated from Brady and crossed her hands over each other in her lap.

With the hustle and bustle of the last three weeks on the campaign trail, Liz had forgotten about the dinner meeting with Chelsea that had been canceled. She had been relieved at the time that she got to continue with her little striptease, but was back to being curious about the lobbyist's role in the political side of the campaign.

If Brady took the money from the company, how obligated was he to work with their interests? She knew that lobbying companies held a lot of influence. They swayed politicians one way or another with tactics from expensive dinners to just being downright annoying.

Brady's father finished his speech to the sound of applause and then dinner was served. Brady ordered drinks from a passing waiter, and a glass of red wine was placed in front of Liz shortly afterward.

"So, Brady," the man to her right said. "How is life in Congress?"

"Exceptional. We're fighting the good fight."

"And that education bill you've been working on—do you think that will come to the floor?" another man asked.

Brady had been working pretty extensively on a bill in the education committee that did a number of things, including lowering student loan interest rates for college students and removing fees for underprivileged students to apply to college and take standardized tests. Liz knew that ideally Brady wanted to include something that scaled back some of the mandates on teachers that put all the emphasis on test taking and less on applied learning, but he wasn't sure if he could get that through Congress.

"We're working on it right now," Brady said vaguely.

"Getting stalled in the Rules Committee?" the first guy asked.

"Just waiting to get it on the calendar. I don't think we'll have too much trouble once it's there." Brady's confidence about his projects oozed from every pore. She knew that when he was alone he had his doubts, but everyone was entitled to them. Brady just couldn't allow his to show in public.

"Well, I think education reform is essential," the wife of the second speaker spoke up. She was in her early fifties and strikingly beautiful, with short brown hair and long earrings that dangled to her shoulders. "Have you seen some of the things on the news right now? They say we have the highest test scores and grade point averages for incoming classes, and yet retention rates are down. I think this starts in the primary schools, and once professors get ahold of these students it's almost beyond their repair."

Liz smiled brightly. It was almost as if she were hearing her own words being spoken back to her. Her feature piece had been on this very subject, and it was encouraging to hear that someone else had similar ideas. "I completely agree," she said, speaking up. "How do you expect professors to teach students critical thinking when they've only been taught memorization and how to take the test? You can't. We need to be treating these students as more than just machines. They should be learning and experiencing subject matter, not plodding away, only able to recall what they had learned for their last exam. My father is a professor, and he always attempted to explain to me how the subject matter had a practical application, which assisted in cognitive reasoning skills. Seems pretty straightforward to me."

"This is exactly the kind of forward thinking we need," the woman's husband said, tapping the table enthusiastically.

Brady found her hand under the table and squeezed gently. She smiled back at him softly just as dinner arrived. Brady had prime rib. Liz had decided on a braised chicken. She saw that Chelsea had just ordered a salad and was barely picking at it. They resumed the conversation as people began to eat their meals.

"You know, I recently started following this columnist and I think you would love him," the woman said, pulling her phone out of her purse.

"Oh, really?" Liz asked enthusiastically. She was always looking for new people to follow.

"Yes! He hasn't written much, but his pieces really strike a chord in the current debate. I was lucky that I caught his first piece quoted in the *Post*."

Liz's heart leaped into her throat. No . . . that was just a coincidence. Tons of people were quoted in the *Post*.

"Here we are. Oh, well he doesn't list his name now that I'm looking for it, but he goes by Dear Congress."

All of the air whooshed out of Liz's lungs at once. She felt Brady's hold on her tighten. He knew about her secret identity and she was sure he was listening very closely now. Neither of them wanted to be found out just yet. It was taxing knowing that she couldn't reveal herself as this mysterious person, but at the same time exhilarating that her words were making a difference, they were being heard, and she had a voice once again.

"Dear Congress," Brady said with a chuckle. "Sounds like someone I should start paying closer attention to."

"You really should. He might help you with that bill you're working on."

"I'll brush up on him—or her—when I get home, Barbara."

Liz bit her lip and tried to keep from giggling. She knew that she shouldn't think it funny, but it still was to her. If she was penetrating the reading circles of elite politicians, then it could only mean good things.

The conversation turned to lighter subjects and soon dinner was cleared away. The keynote speaker was a prominent North Carolina activist named Harold Carmine, who gave a charming speech centered around the bipartisan nature of the occasion and advocating compromise in the current divided times.

Carmine finished up his speech, the lights dimmed, and music started playing through the speakers. This was the beginning of the real party, where everyone could mingle and dance. Last time Liz had made it as far as the dessert table for Oreo cheesecake when Brady had swept her into a dance. This time she was looking forward to that dance, even if she still wasn't that great a dancer.

Brady placed his hand on the small of her back and leaned into her when they stood. "I have to meet with Chelsea for a bit. Will you go with Barbara? She likes you."

Liz laughed and nodded. "All right. Save me a dance."

He arched an eyebrow. "You want to dance with me?"

"I think I do every night," she whispered.

"That is a very different kind of dancing."

"And I'm much better at it."

"I'll have you prove that to me later," he said, squeezing her arm and then following Chelsea over to a now-empty table.

Liz followed Barbara over to another group of women and listened to them chatter among themselves. It was clear that they had all known one another for some time. Liz was introduced to several of the women and then conversation resumed. After a few pleasantries, the women started talking about some event they had all attended. Since Liz obviously hadn't been there she found herself tuning the conversation out and just smiling and nodding at the right points.

Her eyes found Brady across the room. He and Chelsea's postures were incredibly comfortable. She was leaning forward as she spoke animatedly about what Liz could only assume was the environmental policy. Brady had his leg crossed at his ankle and the man managed to make it look damn sexy in a tux. Brady shook his head at whatever she had been saying and splayed his hands out in front of him. She could see him stiffen, as if he were trying to get her to see his point and she was resisting.

There was something about Chelsea that Liz couldn't put her finger on. Despite the physical differences between the women, Liz thought that Chelsea was a lot like Heather: always working, headstrong, and ambitious. Chelsea might be short, thin, and have a sort of reserved elegance in her features, but she still seemed just as hard and calculated as Heather.

Liz shook her head and turned her attention back to the conversation at hand. The women were discussing charity work, which she had always had an interest in.

"What charity are you heading for the upcoming season?" Barbara asked Liz.

Everyone turned expectant eyes toward her.

Charity. What charity she was heading. She had been to enough events to know that many of the women in attendance didn't work and instead just helped plan fund-raising parties for charity. A few of them would even take a position on a board. Liz hadn't been in the political arena long enough to have investigated anything like that. She already had a range of charitable organizations that she agreed with, but she had never had time or funding while she had been in school to do much about it. Now that she had the means it only made sense to help however she could.

"A children's literacy and education charity," Liz said quickly.

It was a politician's truth. She was absolutely interested and invested in education policy. She just hadn't taken that a step further, but she would talk to Brady about it later and they would figure something out. It complemented the work that he had been doing in Congress anyway.

"That's lovely," one woman said with a smile.

Liz was about to reply when she felt someone brush her elbow. "Mind if I interrupt?" Brady asked smoothly.

Her eyes glanced up into his and then over to the table he had been sitting at with Chelsea. The woman was gone.

"Of course."

"You owe me a dance." Brady took her hand in his and nodded at the women. "You'll have to excuse us."

They preened and relented as Brady escorted Liz out onto the dance floor. He could charm anyone, even people who were immune to the charisma within the political arena.

"That was a quick meeting," she said once she was in his arms again.

"Chelsea has some very different ideas about how to get me to agree to her position than what I can accommodate," he told her.

"What does that mean exactly?"

"She likes to make demands and her company likes to throw money, but I'm not a man to be bought. You were the one who thought I was in it for the money, and apparently she also believes that."

Liz sighed. She had inferred that from one meeting with Brady, but knowing him now she knew it wasn't the truth. Brady actually believed wholeheartedly in everything he worked on. "Well, do you not agree with her position?"

He seemed to ponder this as he twirled her around the ballroom dance floor. "I agree with her underlying policies, but not with her methods. Also, I don't think that what EMi is asking for is feasible in Congress. It's hard enough getting education policy reform in the climate right now. It's all well and good that we're at a bipartisan event, but the world works in partisan ideologies that frequently clash. She wants something more extreme than I can promise would go through."

"So, do you think it's better not to introduce anything at all?" Liz asked. She could gauge his feeling on the matter, but she wanted to know exactly where his head was.

"I could introduce an anti-fracking bill knowing it would fail, but it does feel unethical. If she's going to fund my campaign, then I want her to know why she's doing it."

Liz leaned into Brady as they danced. Here was the man she had accused of entering politics for profit, talking about turning aside money for ethical reasons.

"You know, you're really nothing like I thought you were when we first met. I'm so glad I got to know the man underneath the mask."

"And I'm glad I finally found someone worth sharing it with," he whispered.

Chapter 22
FOURTH OF JULY

Liz and Brady's town car rolled up to the Fourth of July festivities three weeks later. Brady's family, Clay's girlfriend, Andrea, as well the rest of Brady's team were in the cars following behind them. The park where the event was held was filled with families excited about the fireworks later on that evening. Kids wearing red, white, and blue outfits were chasing one another, grills were set up around the perimeter, and all around people were enjoying the outdoors after the parade that had gone through the park earlier.

When Liz had been at this event two years ago, Calleigh Hollingsworth had actually given her a press pass so Liz could be backstage for questions. She had just come to see Brady's speech, the very speech that had won her vote. She fingered the locket around her neck that had the number four in it and smiled at the memories.

As soon as they reached their destination, people crowded in on all sides. Liz looked over at Brady with her eyes wide. "What's going on?"

"They're just here to see us. We had a crowd the past two years too," he said, drawing her closer for a kiss.

The driver came around and opened the door for them. Liz stepped outside, but people didn't part for them. They just crowded in more. She froze, unsure how to proceed. Brady stepped out behind her and urged her forward, but people weren't moving. They weren't getting out of their way. She knew that reporters hassled people and followed them. She had been exposed to that herself, but she had never felt more claustrophobic than that moment.

Just then a large man dressed in all black appeared through the crowd. "Sorry, Congressman Maxwell. This way," he said and then started walking them toward the stage.

Liz steeled herself and then followed the man through the crowd of reporters. Flashes were going off on all sides and Liz smiled as she walked. Then she heard someone call out over the crowd.

Home wrecker.

Liz had looked out into the crowd and realized that the person was talking about *her*. Then someone else chimed in.

Whore. Slut.

Her mouth dropped open at the familiar accusation and she bristled all over. How dare people say that about her! She and Brady had been dating since February. She knew that people wanted a story and could see them wanting to provoke her, but what the hell?

She didn't have time to process it. She had to follow their escort, and with Brady's soothing hand on her back she pushed forward, trying to ignore the insults.

Once they had been shepherded through the group and landed safely in their closed-off area, Liz turned to Brady with questions in her eyes. His family and staff appeared a second later. It seemed that the crowd had no interest in them . . . just her.

"What the hell was that?" Liz asked Brady.

But Heather was the one to speak up. "There are still rumors flying that you broke up Brady and Erin. It's been circulating again in the tabloids."

"It'll blow over," Brady said confidently.

"When? When will it blow over? It's been five months. You and Erin broke up in October."

"Yes, but I never announced that publicly."

"So now it looks like I'm the home wrecker," Liz said.

She hadn't been looking in the papers after that first breakdown. She hadn't wanted to know what people were saying about her. But now she knew that was her grave mistake. She wasn't prepared for this.

"Are they still saying I'm pregnant?" She touched the stomach of her loose, flowing red-and-white dress. It wasn't the best choice if she wanted people to think that she wasn't carrying Brady Maxwell IV at the present moment.

"We know you're not."

"But they still think I am?"

"Yes," Heather answered.

"Don't you think that's important for me to know?" Liz gestured down. "A skintight dress might deter some of that reasoning."

"Then they'd just say that you'd had an abortion or faked it," Heather said callously.

"Why don't you just shut the fuck up!" Liz screeched at her.

Heather glared at her, but Brady shot her a warning look. He put his hand on Liz's shoulder and she immediately sagged into him. God, she was wound up. "It's okay. It doesn't matter." He stroked his hand back through her hair soothingly. "We know the truth, baby."

"It doesn't matter if we know the truth," Liz whispered. "People are going to think what they want to think, and that's going to negatively affect the campaign, isn't it?" She looked up at Brady expectantly.

His jaw was set and he just nodded.

"I did say this from the beginning," Heather said.

"Oh, because 'I told you so' is really going to help anything right now," Liz snapped.

Heather looked as if she was ready to yell at Liz when Clay stepped in. "You know, Heather, you have a lot of pent-up anger. I think I could help with that." He winked at her and she turned her glare on him. "Just a helpful suggestion."

"Aren't you full of them," Brady said, shaking his head.

"You were the ones raising your voice in public. Now, you know I prefer that we're actually acting like humans rather than robots, but dare I say . . . you're bit of an embarrassment, Big Brother." Clay had his devil-may-care smirk on his face as the words tumbled out of his mouth. He looked as if he had been waiting to say that his entire life.

"He's testing my patience, isn't he?" Brady asked, directing the question at Liz.

And she couldn't help it. She laughed. "Yes, he is. Don't worry; you're not really an embarrassment . . . I am."

"She should have picked me," Clay said with another wink.

"As if there were even a choice," Liz said.

"Ouch." He covered his heart as though he was wounded.

"Clay," Andrea snapped, grabbing his arm. "Why are you being an asshole again?"

"It's in my blood, babe," he said, retreating to his girlfriend's side.

"That's the damn truth," she muttered.

Heather took a deep breath as if she was trying to calm herself down. "Maybe you should make a statement, Brady."

"I already did, when we first got together. Nothing else needs to be said," he said.

"Maybe if they heard you refute the rumors then they would lie low for a while. We have to get through the primary still."

"I'm making a statement every day just by being with her. I don't need to say anything. The rumors will go away," he said sharply. "Addressing them makes them seem like they matter, and they don't."

Heather looked as if she wanted to say more, but even she knew a losing battle when she saw one. "Well, just get ready for your speech then, and I'll talk to the press, and to the police about clearing the area."

She walked off and left Brady and Liz alone. Liz didn't know what to say. A part of her agreed that they shouldn't say anything about it and just let it blow over, but the other part of her wanted to scream at the media to stop following them around. She had only been with Brady for five months, and already the entire political process exhausted her.

"Try not to worry about the press, okay, baby? Things are going to blow over. We'll always be in the spotlight, but there's not a whole lot we can do about everyone else. As long as we're good then that's what matters. And we are good, right?"

"Of course," she told him.

"Good." He leaned down and kissed her. "I can't wait to get you to Hilton Head and really be able to be with you."

"Me either." She wanted to replace the memories of when Brady had flown her out to Hilton Head. This time he wasn't going to ignore her. There wouldn't be another woman as his date—only be the two of them together with his family for a whole weekend on a much-needed vacation.

"Well, I should run through the speech before going up there. You know, I love that we work together and that part of the speech is part of you."

Liz smiled at the compliment. He had started practicing his speeches in front of her and asking her to point out anything she would change. It had become a fun routine between them and always ensured that she heard his speech a million times before he walked up to that podium to deliver it.

Almost as soon as Brady walked away, Savannah took his place. "How are you holding up? I heard what those people were saying." Her brown eyes were large and concerned.

"I'm all right. Just frustrated."

"I don't think most people actually believe the media."

"Someone has to or they wouldn't latch on to it," Liz said.

"They'll find something else to talk about soon. You and Brady are the real deal. I've never seen him happier," Savannah said, glancing at her brother. "Others will see that too."

"I hope so. What about you? Are you and Easton still hanging out?"

Savannah tried to hide her own smile. "Yeah. We've been together all summer. He's really great."

"But?" Liz prompted.

"I didn't say but."

"Yeah, but I know you."

Savannah sighed. "I invited him to Hilton Head with us."

"And?" Liz had a feeling she knew where this was going.

"Lucas is going to be there."

"Do you think something will happen between you and Lucas?"

Savannah shrugged. "I don't know. No. He's been home all summer and we've been hanging out again. I just get mixed signals from him. Nothing has happened since Fourth of July two years ago, but it's just weird between us. Or maybe it's weird how normal it is. I can't keep it straight."

"It'll work itself out, just like this media bullshit," Liz said. "You really don't need a guy who hasn't made a move in two years. I made that mistake. Hayden was only interested in me once Brady and I had already started dating. I swear, it's like a beacon for guys."

Savannah laughed. "An 'unavailable' beacon. It screams, 'I'm dating someone else, so come hit on me.'"

Both girls started laughing. There was really nothing else to do at that point. No matter what happened in life there were always going to be problems. It was finding out how to deal with them that determined character.

Brady was walking up to the podium to give his Fourth of July speech with his father. Liz moved over to the side of the podium so that she could watch him. Marilyn strode over a moment later, just as Jeff began speaking.

"You know, dear," Marilyn said, not taking her eyes from her husband, "love blooms in the most unlikely of places. It flourishes in the most difficult circumstances. And it lasts despite all reasons it shouldn't."

Liz felt tears prick the corners of her eyes. That one piece of advice grounded her. She and Brady hadn't said that it would be without difficulty. They had said it was worth it. And it was.

"Thank you," Liz whispered.

"I have been in your shoes. It's not without its moments of hardship. When I met Jeff, he was in business school at Chapel Hill while I was in college. I had no idea what I was getting into, knowing that he wanted to be a politician like his father. I've not regretted a moment. Sometimes you have to fight through the bad times to get to the best moments of your life."

Marilyn reached out and grasped Liz's hand.

"Yours are before you. Of that I'm sure," Marilyn assured her.

They stood like that together with the weight of mutual understanding between them as they watched the men they loved deliver speeches. It might have been only a handful of times for Liz, but it had been a lifetime of speeches for Marilyn. And she still gazed up at her husband with utter admiration for the work he was doing and the man that he had remained during their marriage.

"Thank you so much for having me out today. Looking forward

to another two years. Happy Fourth of July!" Brady called from the stage at the close of his speech.

The crowd applauded, and then father and son descended the stairs. Jeff clapped his hands together. He had a big smile on his face that showed how much he was looking forward to this trip. "Couple minutes with the press and then get out of here?" he asked.

Brady agreed and they wandered off to the media area. Liz and Marilyn trailed behind them to listen in on what was going on and to smile for the cameras. Two years ago Liz had stolen Brady away for five minutes to tell him how he had won her vote. They had ended up in an argument and then he had skipped the first day of his vacation to stay home with her. She was glad that this year they were able to vacation together.

Liz immediately noticed the flaming red hair in the crowd of reporters. Calleigh Hollingsworth. And she was walking right toward Brady. The bitch had nerve, continuing to badger Brady. She must think that since he was the story that got her the promotion she was craving, that he might be able to provide her with more juice to go even further, or maybe to another paper.

At the same time, it felt personal. If she was looking for another promotion, then why would she put so much effort into taking pictures of Liz and Hayden and then selling them to the tabloids without attaching her name to the photos? She was up to something. Liz wasn't sure what it was, but she sure wanted to find out.

Without thinking twice, she excused herself from Marilyn's company and walked right up to Calleigh. "Miss Hollingsworth, what a pleasure," Liz said, her voice sweet as molasses.

Calleigh turned to Liz, and Liz wanted to do a little dance when she saw the surprise on her face. She quickly recovered, but it was clear that she hadn't expected Liz to ever talk to her again.

"Miss Dougherty, how are you?" Calleigh said, trying for similar pleasantries.

"Amazing. I've never been better, really."

"Even without your *New York Times* reporting position?" she asked smoothly.

"I think I've finally found the right career move for me, but I don't think I would ever really be happy without the man I love. I couldn't imagine going through life pining over someone who doesn't want me."

Calleigh's jaw clenched at the jab. "What is this new career exactly? Following around your boyfriend to campaign events and mooching off of his money?"

Liz took a deep breath. Calleigh was baiting her because she was pissed that Liz had made a stab at the fact that Hayden didn't want her. She needed to keep a level head. "That's so nice of you to say. How is your boyfriend?"

"I'm not currently dating anyone," she said flatly.

"Then perhaps you shouldn't judge mine. We're perfectly happy," Liz said with a smile. "Write about that."

Brady came to her side a few seconds later. "Miss Hollingsworth," he said cordially. "What were we talking about over here?"

"How perfectly happy we are," Liz said, wrapping her arm around his waist.

"That we are. You'll have to excuse us. We have prior engagements to attend to."

"Always great talking to you two. You're so very . . . insightful," Calleigh said.

Liz followed Brady back to his family, who all seemed ready to head back to the line of cars waiting for them. Heather had worked her magic and police had cleared an area for them to walk through. A minute later she and Brady were cloistered in a town car bound for the airport.

"Did you really *have* to go talk to her?" Brady asked with a resigned sigh.

"She's up to something."

"And you thought goading her was going to get her to stop?"

Liz turned her head to face him. "I was just talking to her. She started goading me by making fun of me losing my job and then saying I was mooching off of you! I even ignored those statements when I could have been a bitch back, but I wasn't. She should know that I'm not afraid of her."

"She's an annoyance. Nothing more. Just ignore her from now on."

"She feeds off of that," Liz insisted.

Brady's phone buzzed and he pulled it out to check it. "You feed off of goading her."

"I'm not goading her! The woman just deserves to be put in her place."

He typed out a reply, then tossed the phone back into his suit pocket. He looked really irritated. "She does, but not by you."

"Is everything all right? You're not really mad at me, are you?" She hadn't meant to upset him.

"No, baby, it's not you," he said, lacing their fingers together. "Chelsea won't stop badgering me about this fracking issue, as if it's the only thing on the agenda."

"She's texting you about that?"

"Yeah. She's insistent."

Liz chewed on her bottom lip. "Isn't that kind of unprofessional?"

"A bit, but it's not the first time. You'd be surprised what people will do to get what they want."

Would she? Glancing up at Brady, Liz really didn't think that she would.

They arrived on Hilton Head Island later that afternoon. They had a car waiting for them, which drove them to Brady's parents' beach house. Liz had dreamed about coming out here and being welcomed by his family when she had been here two years ago. Now she was actually doing all of this.

The Maxwells' beach home was a massive three-story construction on a secluded piece of land. A butler came forward and began to unload their luggage as Brady whisked her through the front door and began to tour her through the house. It had seven bedrooms, a kitchen the size of Liz's entire house back in Chapel Hill, and a projection screen that took up a whole wall in the living room. The back door led out to a clear blue resort-size pool with lounge chairs and cabanas. She smirked when the memory of having sex with Brady on a cabana in Hilton Head came back to her, and Brady seemed to guess and shared the memory by planting a deep kiss on her lips.

Beyond the pool was a small beach and the Atlantic Ocean as far as the eye could see.

"It's beautiful," she whispered.

"My great-grandfather had the house built in the thirties and we've maintained it ever since."

He led her back into the house to change into bathing suits, and then they spent the rest of the afternoon doing the most amazing thing she could think of—lounging around lazily by the pool, taking periodic dips to cool off from the blazing South Carolina sun, and walking hand in hand down the beach.

The next day Brady gave her a tour of the town. They rented bicycles and went on a several-mile-long nature ride. When they returned to the beach house, sticky from sweat, they raced each other through the house, stripping down to their bathing suits, and then doing cannonballs into the pool. Andrea screamed at them for getting her wet, but they were lost in the euphoria of being together.

They knew that when they returned to reality there would be so many more demands on their time. They wanted to cherish each moment that they had now.

Later that night, they were wrapped up in each other's arms in bed and Brady was stroking her hair back and kissing her forehead. "You're so beautiful."

She sighed and nuzzled closer to him. "You're not so bad-looking yourself."

"Well, glad that I meet your approval," he joked.

"Always."

"That's how I feel about you."

"That I always meet your approval?"

"No," he whispered. "You're my always."

Liz's breath caught at the word. Always. Forever. Brady was making promises with those words, and he always kept his promises.

"Hey, come with me," he said, pulling the sheet off of their naked bodies and straightening.

"Why? We were so comfortable." Her eyes dropped to his dick, already lengthening at the sight of her silhouetted in the light from the moon.

"It's three in the morning. Everyone's asleep." His hands slid down her hips and roughly dragged her toward him. He bent at the waist and started trailing kisses down her stomach. She groaned deep in her throat. "Just come . . . with me."

"You've convinced me," she said breathily.

He laughed and continued his way down until he was buried between her legs. Her fingers dug into the sheets as she felt his tongue lap and swirl and tease her most sensitive area. He pushed her legs farther apart for him and then slid a finger inside of her.

"More," she groaned.

He obliged her and pushed a second finger up into her. Her back arched off of the bed as he started sliding his fingers in and out. She felt as if at any moment she might combust. He knew every inch of her body and how to extract the maximum amount of pleasure from each stroke. And just when she thought she couldn't handle any more, she came with an intensity that made her see stars.

As she came down from her release, Brady pulled on some swim trunks and found a bathing suit for Liz. She stood on wobbly legs and managed to get into her suit with only a little assistance from Brady.

He grabbed her hand and started directing her down the two flights of stairs, through the kitchen, and out onto the back patio. There was only one light on near the cabana overlooking the stairs that led down to the ocean. Otherwise everything was pitch-black and silent.

"Where are we going?" she whispered into the stillness.

"I want to take you in the pool . . . I mean take you to the pool."

Liz glanced back up to the quiet house. All of the lights were out in all of the windows, but that didn't mean that no one would look down and see what they were doing.

"Everyone's asleep," he repeated. He started guiding her out into the clear blue water. Even with the superheated temperatures, the pool was still cool to the touch, and it took Liz a minute to get used to the water.

Brady turned so that he was walking backward. His hands were on her waist, pulling her deeper into the water. When he was shoulder deep, he scooped her up into his arms and paddled them over to a secluded step on the other side of the pool.

She took a seat on the lowest step and then scooted up to the highest step so her body was in only a few inches of water. She leaned her head back on the top step and sighed. "This is a dream, right? Everything is too surreal, too amazing, too all-consuming, Brady."

"I want it to always be like that," he said, running his hands up and down her bare thighs.

"I never thought life could be this good until you."

"I thought that life was just work before you."

"Even when you were with other people?"

His eyes found hers in the darkness. "Everyone else worked around my work, but I don't do that with you. I still have my work priorities, but you're part of that. I'd rather drive the five hours to D.C. with you than get back an hour early to sit in a meeting. I'd rather have you help me with my speeches and have your beautiful face to return to when I'm finished than anything else. I want you to be happy and have your own life, but I want it to coincide with mine."

"It will," she said.

His hands found the strings on her bikini bottoms and untied them. "It was hard to see before that the campaign, the politics, all the work was worthwhile only if I had someone to share it with."

Liz ran her fingers back through his hair and then pulled him forward for a kiss. Their bodies melded as the words filled her heart with joy at finally finding its match. Brady kept their lips pressed tight together and undid his trunks to release himself from the confines of his shorts.

He pushed himself up into her in one swift motion. She was already so warmed up from what had occurred earlier that her body tightened around him instantly. She wanted this. All of this. Everything he would give her.

His body. His heart. His soul.

As they got closer, Brady thrust harder and harder inside of her. She felt the steps dig into her skin, but she lost all sense. The pain didn't matter, the tangled mess of her hair didn't matter, the water lapping around her body didn't matter. It was just the here and now.

They finished together in a wave of emotion. Her body ached all over from every jolt against the steps, but at the same time she felt euphoric. She and Brady were completely in sync. All was right with the world.

And then they heard voices.

Brady yanked Liz off of the step and farther into the darkness. She worked quickly to tie her suit back in place and she felt Brady straightening himself out behind her. They remained completely still as they waited to see who was coming up from the beach at this hour. If they had been caught having sex, it would have been pretty embarrassing.

Liz recognized Savannah first, and then saw Lucas appear. Brady moved behind her, but she put her hand out to stop him. She put a finger to her lips and shook her head. Brady looked at her curiously but stayed hidden. Liz was pretty sure that Brady didn't know the extent of what had happened between Savannah and Lucas, and she didn't want them to think anyone had seen them.

Lucas stopped on the last step and grabbed her arm. They spoke for a few minutes and Savannah continually grew angrier with him. A second later he grabbed her around the waist and placed a rough kiss on her lips.

Savannah pushed Lucas back forcefully. A loud crack rang out into the night air as she slapped him across the face. Liz gasped softly just as Savannah stomped away from him. Lucas followed close at her heels, but the rest of their interaction was lost to Liz and Brady.

"I'm going to beat the shit out of him," Brady said, shaking his head.

Liz laughed. "I don't think that's probably the best thing for Savannah."

"You knew about this?" he accused.

"I knew that she liked him, and was torn about bringing Easton."

"Correction. I should call Chris, get him down here, and then we can *both* beat the shit out of him."

"We were in their position not too long ago, Congressman Maxwell," she joked, poking him in the ribs. "They'll figure it out themselves without big-brother interference."

"I'm glad she trusts you with this stuff." He grabbed her and pulled her in close again.

"She was one of my closest friends before we became a couple."

"It's just nice knowing how much my family likes you," he said, trailing kisses down to her ear, "because I'm never letting you go."

Chapter 23

BONFIRE

The first weekend in August, Liz was invited to Charlottesville for Justin's bonfire birthday party. After spending the past two months doing nothing but writing articles as Dear Congress, posts for Justin's blog, and following Brady around the campaign as though it were her job, she was excited to spend the weekend with her friends.

"What are you doing?" Brady asked. He had just walked into the bedroom and she had an empty suitcase sitting on the bed. They were back in D.C. for the week, but she knew that he always had weekend plans now that the campaign was in full swing.

"I'm going to Charlottesville for Justin's birthday, remember?"

"I thought that was next weekend."

"Nope. His birthday is the first."

"Hmm . . ." he said, taking a seat on the bed.

"Hmm?"

"Well, that changes things."

"And what does that change?" She rearranged the pile of clothes sitting next to her suitcase. She was only going for two days but she had no idea what to pack.

"My plans for the weekend," he said simply.

Liz dropped the shorts she had just picked up and looked up at him. "What?"

"I'm coming with you."

"Where?"

"Liz . . ."

"You want to come to Justin's kegger?" she asked incredulously.

"You act like I'm above a kegger. I went to one or two when I was in college. I still remember what they're like. I doubt they've changed much in seven years."

Liz shrugged. "I just don't see my suit and tie at a kegger with a guy who was in a frat and was more or less kicked out of school for a DUI."

"I think I'm more than just a suit and tie," he said sternly.

"You know what I mean."

Brady walked around the bed to face her. "You wanted me to go with you before, when I thought I was busy. If it were next weekend then it would have been impossible, since it's the gala, but I can go with you this weekend."

Liz reached up on her tiptoes and planted a kiss on his lips. Brady's kiss was deep and passionate this time. And he seemed to have no real desire to let her go. He pressed her knees back into the bed and she leaned back onto her clothes. Liz giggled against his lips and came up for breath.

"Clean clothes!"

"Priorities," he said with a headshake.

"My priorities are making sure both of us are packed and in my car in the next hour so we can drive to Charlottesville."

"Oh, so now you're letting me go with you?" he teased.

"It's not that I didn't want you to come to Justin's. I just didn't think that you'd be interested or have time."

"Well, I want to come. I always want to come."

"Mind, meet gutter," she joked. "We only have an hour before I need to leave."

"Who said I needed an hour? No suits or ties needed this weekend. I'll just throw some stuff in a duffel and we'll have the other fifty-eight minutes to ourselves."

"Whoa, there, Casanova. It might take you two minutes, but you know women take a bit longer."

"I always focus on you," he growled. His hand ran up her bare inner thigh.

"I'll be as quick as I can," she insisted, skipping around him. He sighed as she scurried back into the closet.

She was quicker than she expected and as soon as her suitcase was snapped shut she was lost in Brady's arms once more. They never seemed to be able to get enough of each other. She hoped that they never would.

———

About two hours later Brady pulled into the outskirts of Charlottesville. He had insisted on driving his Range Rover, since he had ridden in her car for the five-hour road trip and claimed to have feared for his life. Once he had started talking about getting her a new car, she had relented to having him drive just to get him to shut up. She knew he had been joking, but she loved her car.

The navigation system directed them through the town and to a brick town house with a line of cars as far as the eye could see. So clearly this party wasn't going to be a small affair.

Brady looked around incredulously. "You sure you want to crash here tonight? I could get us a hotel."

"Then we couldn't get wasted," she said, slinging her purse over her shoulder.

"I could drive."

"You missed the key word *we*."

"Then I'd call a cab," he said as if it didn't matter which option they chose.

"Just slum it with me, Maxwell." She walked around to the trunk and extracted her suitcase.

He immediately retrieved it from her and hoisted his duffel onto his shoulder. He looked really hot in khaki shorts and a fitted Brooks Brothers T-shirt.

"It's never slumming with you, baby."

They walked up the stairs and through the front doors. A half-dozen people sat in the living room, Liz could hear voices down the hallway, and at least another dozen were out on the back porch. Just then Justin came jogging down the hallway and barreled into her. He lifted her off her feet and swung her around.

"Hey, my favorite employee," he said casually.

Liz laughed and stepped out of his reach. "You're so ridiculous. Justin, this is Brady. Hope you have room for one extra."

"The more the merrier," he said and then stuck his hand out. The guys shook, sizing each other up for a second, and then released.

"Nice to meet you," Brady said cordially.

"You too. I'm just used to seeing you as a floating head on TV."

"Good to know I have a body attached," he said.

"Sure is. You want a beer, man?" Justin asked, falling easily into the frat-boy host.

"Lead the way."

Liz followed the guys back into the kitchen. She waved at a few people she recognized before exiting onto the patio, where the keg was set up. Justin poured them each a drink in a red Solo cup. Just as she went to take her first sip, a blond girl rushed up the stairs.

"Justin didn't tell me that you were coming!" Massey screeched in excitement. She rushed over to Liz and threw her arms around her as if the last time that they had seen each other hadn't been awkward at all. She was already really drunk.

"Surprise, sugar," Justin said, grabbing Massey possessively around the waist and planting a sloppy kiss on her cheek.

Liz's brow furrowed as she took in what she was seeing. "I'm sorry . . . are you two . . . together?" She knew that they had made out at her birthday party last year, but that had been over a year ago. No way they had been together that long.

"Well, yeah," Massey said with a shrug. She tossed her shoulder-length blond hair to one side and her brown eyes went wide. "I start grad school in like two weeks, but I moved up here right after graduation."

"Oh right, you're going to UVA," Liz said, the pieces falling into place.

"Yep. Justin and I kept in touch after your birthday party. Then once I moved here, one thing led to another . . ."

"And now you're together."

"Yeah. God, I'm so glad you're here. I was so fucked up at school about all that newspaper stuff. I should have never kicked you off," Massey drunkenly rambled.

"It's really okay," Liz said awkwardly.

"Wait, she was the one who kicked you off?" Brady asked. He looked mystified by the drunk girl standing in front of him.

"Oh. My. God! You're Brady Maxwell," Massey cried.

"Yes, I am."

"Well, fuck me sideways. Y'all really *are* dating."

Liz shook her head. "I'm not sure how I could have made that more clear. And how much have you had to drink?"

Massey shrugged. "We started with whiskey and then mixed it with tequila. And then I've been washing it down with beer."

Liz's stomach protested at the thought.

"Brady, this is Massey," Liz said as an introduction. It was strange having Brady meet the rest of her friends.

Brady politely stuck out his hand and Massey shook it. "You know, you're way hotter in person."

"Thank you," he said, all signs pointing to the fact that he was trying not to laugh at her.

"I see why she fucked you on the side."

Liz cursed. "Okay, lush, you've had one too many and need to start in on the water."

"God, do you remember your birthday, when you thought that shit tasted like Kool-Aid? You were so fucking adamant about it," Massey reminded her.

"I bet it would taste like Kool-Aid to you right now."

"No way. I'll never be as far gone as you were that night."

Justin kept her from stumbling and laughed. "Chill your hot ass. I don't want you passing out before we get the bonfire going."

"I'm not going to pass out!"

"You did last time."

"Whatever. It's not my fault. We were smoking too. You know that messes me up."

Justin just squeezed her tighter. Something seemed to catch his eye and he stood up straighter. "Well, look what the cat dragged in."

"The life of the fucking party. Obviously," Victoria said, strutting out on the patio in a silver minidress that barely covered her ass, and black high heels. Daniel followed on her heels in a checkered button-down and black shorts. He had black-rimmed glasses on, and they worked for him.

"Vickie!" Liz cried. "If I'd known you were driving down from D.C., then we could have ridden together."

"Last-minute change of plans. We didn't think we'd be here," she said.

"Hey, man," Brady said, shaking hands with Daniel.

"'Sup. How's the campaign?" Daniel asked. He ran a hand back through his hair, then stuffed his hands back into his pockets.

"Smooth sailing so far. How was the summer lab work?"

Liz stared between them, dumbfounded.

"What are you guys, like, buddy-buddy now?" she asked when she got closer to Brady.

"Daniel is a good guy. My mother introduced him to a colleague he worked for this summer. We kept in touch."

"Networking really is your thing, isn't it," she said.

"It's not what you know but who. That's why I wanted to help you find a journalism position earlier this year, but I should have known you could do it all on your own." He kissed the top of her head and drew her in closer.

"I am a bit stubborn."

He raised his eyebrows. "A bit? You make a filibuster look like compromise."

"Oh, ha-ha. I'm not that bad. I don't need sixty senators to get me to change my mind."

Brady tried to hold in his laughter, but he wasn't able to and it erupted out of him. "I'm hoping you're only going to need one."

"You're not a Senator yet, Representative Maxwell."

"Give me a few years."

"You're as strong-willed as I am."

"Just as ambitious."

Liz shook her head. "No one is ambitious as you."

"That's why I always win."

Liz smiled and hoped that remained a fact. She didn't want to be the reason he lost; that was for sure. She would do everything in her power to ensure that didn't happen.

Justin started crowding everyone down to the fire pit. They spent an exorbitant amount of time building it to extreme heights. It reached a full inferno just as the sun fell over the horizon. By then even Brady seemed to have reached a tipsy point, which rarely happened.

"I can't believe we're having a bonfire when it's a hundred degrees outside," Victoria complained.

"Well, it's a good thing you're not wearing any clothing then, or else you might be hot," Justin joked.

"Hilarious, asshole."

"It is ridiculously hot," Liz agreed. "Aren't you glad you're not in a suit?"

Brady glanced up from his phone. "I would be sweltering in a suit."

"Are you working?"

"Just Chelsea."

Liz crinkled her nose. "Why does she always text you? Just tell her to schedule a meeting or something," Liz said, the alcohol making her haughtier than she normally would have been.

"All right," he said with a laugh. "I'll turn it off. No work this weekend."

"Heather is going to *love* that."

Brady tucked the phone back into his pocket. "Who cares?"

As the night wore on, the numbers around the bonfire started dwindling. A lot of the people who had been there were locals, so they just headed home. There were only a few other people from out of town. As expected, Massey was completely passed out in Justin's lap while he smoked a cigarette. He passed one to one of his frat brothers who had driven up for the party, and he lit up.

"So Liz, what are you doing up in D.C. besides working for me? You just hanging out doing charity work for starving puppies or whatever the other Stepford Wives do up there?" Justin asked, blowing out smoke.

"Justin, you're such a twat," Victoria spat. She adjusted her tiny dress and rolled her eyes. "Liz could never be a Stepford Wife."

"She really couldn't," Brady chimed in. "She's too strong-willed and independent."

"Well, we all know that I wasn't a GDI," Justin said, laughing to himself.

"You're reminding me *why* I'm a goddamn independent and not Greek."

"Don't hate the player, hate the game, babe." Everyone groaned.

"Anyway I've mostly been writing for you and following Brady to campaign events before grad school starts," Liz said.

"Give yourself some credit." Brady nudged her. "You've practically been writing my speeches all summer. If you weren't already set on journalism, then I might suggest speech communications. You're better than my speechwriter."

Liz beamed at his compliment. "Thank you." She had never considered speech communications or even speech writing before Brady, but she did enjoy it.

"You're at Maryland, right?" Justin asked. "How much is that going to interfere with the site?"

"I'll make time. I like the blog."

"That's what I like to hear." Justin turned his attention back to his cigarette.

Liz glanced over at Brady. "It completely slipped my mind until Justin just mentioned it, but when we were at the JJ gala I was asked what charity I'm heading."

"You're not heading a charity."

"Well, yes. I know that. But I told them I was working with underprivileged children and education. I figured it was a politician's truth."

He tilted his head to look at her. "You mean you want to do the work?"

"I don't want to head any charity," she quickly amended, "but you know how passionate I am about education, especially reform in primary education. I thought it would be an easy thing to move into and I thought . . . you know . . . since, well . . . you know people."

Brady eyed her curiously. "Are you asking for my help?"

"I thought it might be good to have something to stand behind while I stand beside you."

"Are you sure you want to add more work to your plate?"

"It isn't work," she insisted. "It's doing something I believe in and helping people less fortunate. The same thing that you're doing in Congress, just on a different scale."

"I'm going to keep you," he whispered into her hair.

"I sure hope so."

"I'll get you in contact with the right person. Thank you for letting me help you."

She closed her eyes and breathed in the late-night air mingling with the smoke from the bonfire. She let her mind drift away as she lay snuggled in Brady's arms, content in the company of good friends and the love of her life.

Chapter 24
A REDO

Liz tugged anxiously on the black-lace sheath that hugged her figure like a glove. It had detailed cap sleeves and a lace V neckline. Her hair hung loose to the middle of her back in delicate finger waves, and light, smoky makeup had been carefully applied. This was her big debut at Brady's biggest fund-raising gala of the year.

Two years ago Brady had brought someone else to the event, but had ended up confessing that he loved Liz later that night. It had all been so confusing at the time, and some of that old anxiety materialized inside of her once more.

"Would you relax? You're going to be fine," Brady assured her. He placed his hands on her shoulders and slowly kneaded the tense muscles.

"I know. I know."

"Then would you lose some of the tension? You've been to gala events with me before."

"I know, but never one *for* you, where I'll have to parade around and pose for pictures with you all night," she said softly.

"You're not just arm candy. You're the woman I love. I want people to get used to seeing you with me. Where you belong."

Liz sighed softly and turned to look up into his brown eyes. "Do you always say the right thing?"

"It's my job."

"Okay. Let's go then. I can't be any more ready than I am right now."

"You'll do fine. Don't worry. The limo is waiting," he said as he walked toward the door. "Can you grab my phone?"

"Sure." Liz snatched her gold beaded clutch up off of the table. Brady's phone was sitting next to it. She grabbed that too, stashing it into her purse as she followed him out the door.

The driver opened the door for them and they both slid into the darkened interior. Brady wrapped an arm around her waist and planted soft kisses down her neck and over her shoulder.

They pulled up to the front entrance of the convention center a few minutes later. Heather was waiting outside with a photographer and a woman who Brady told Liz was the event planner. The photographer snapped shots of each of them stepping out of the limo. Brady placed his hand on the small of her back and more photos were taken. Liz smiled until her jaw hurt and then smiled some more. The photographer finally stopped and the event planner rushed over.

She walked Brady through the last-minute details as Liz stood a short distance from Heather, waiting to go inside.

"Are you happy that the primary is so close?" Liz asked Heather, trying to strike up conversation.

"Sooner it's over the sooner we can work on the real race," she said, barely glancing at Liz.

"Crazy how much has changed in two years. This was the night you first found out about me and Brady."

"Perhaps you shouldn't just say everything that's on your mind tonight. No one needs to know you were here before," Heather said harshly.

"Look, I know you hate me, but do you mind toning down the condescending-bitch voice for two seconds? I was just carrying on a perfectly normal conversation with you, and every time I try, you snap at me. I'm not here to mess up Brady's chance at reelection. In fact, I've done nothing but support him. I've even been writing Brady's speeches. Good speeches! I've done everything exactly how I've been told."

Well, aside from the Dear Congress articles, but she wasn't about to bring them up.

"He loves me. He told you two years ago, and it still hasn't changed. I'm going to be around for a while. I'd appreciate if you started treating me like a human being."

Heather didn't say anything for a moment, and then she turned to look at Liz. "You're right."

"What?" Liz gasped.

"Would you prefer I disagree with you?"

"No. I just . . . was expecting you to."

"You're a liability. That much is very certain, Liz. I've stood by that from day one."

"Yeah. I remember."

"But . . ." she said, cutting Liz off. "He is happier."

Liz beamed. She made Brady happier. She wasn't sure Heather could have said anything that would have made her feel better in that moment.

"He's not happier with me, mind you. And even I can objectively admit that your speeches are good. I read the draft you gave him of his acceptance speech for the primary." Heather cut her eyes back to Liz. "It's solid."

"Thank you," Liz said, a little shocked.

"The only problem with that is that you can't fuck up now."

"I didn't plan on it," she said stiffly.

"If you hurt him, if you break him, if you make him forget what is important, then you've ruined a brilliant and driven man. Just remember that."

Well, it seemed the old Heather still existed.

"I'd never do that."

"Intentionally. Now don't do it unintentionally either. Prove to me that you're not going anywhere," she said before turning and walking to the event planner.

"How pleasant," Liz muttered under her breath.

"Ready to go, baby?" Brady asked. He extended his arm and she placed her hand on his elbow.

"Ready as I'll ever be."

They walked through the double doors into the massive ballroom decorated in black and gold. A group of people waited at the entrance to greet them. And then came the almost endless number of pictures. Liz was introduced to person after person she was sure to never remember. Only a few faces were familiar from previous events, and even then she wasn't sure she remembered all of their names.

Barbara, whom she had met at the Jefferson-Jackson gala, was there and hugged her as if they were old friends. Liz promised to find her later to talk about the education for underprivileged children that they had discussed earlier in the summer. Apparently Barbara had thought it a great idea and wanted to help. Liz was a bit floored by it, but Brady just whispered how important and charming Liz was and then they moved on.

Finally at the end of the entrance line was Brady's family, with Clay noticeably absent. Marilyn gave her a firm hug. "You're doing great," she said discreetly, then pulled back to observe her for the cameras. "You look lovely, dear."

"Thank you," Liz said graciously.

Savannah was in a strapless gold number in a silky material that hung on her frame as if she were a runway model. They hugged and Liz realized how much she had missed her. They hadn't been around each other much since Hilton Head. Liz had never had a chance to ask her about what had happened with Lucas, and she wasn't sure she wanted to admit to having even witnessed it.

"We should hang out more," Savannah said with a laugh.

"I know. I feel like we've been together but apart all summer."

"Agreed."

"Is Easton here?" Liz asked, glancing around.

"No. He went home for the summer after he left Hilton Head."

"That sucks." Or maybe it didn't. Liz spotted Lucas standing near Chris and his girlfriend, Mollie.

Savannah followed her gaze and her face darkened. "Well . . . *that* doesn't suck," she said pointedly, nodding her head at Lucas.

Savannah sighed. "If you say so."

Liz didn't get to say anything more, because Brady touched her arm to motion her for another picture. Liz stood among his family as if she belonged there. The flash went off several times and then they were free of the first crowd. Now they had to mingle with the other guests for pictures.

After a seemingly endless number of people she didn't know, though Brady somehow remembered every single person's name, they found a familiar face.

"Chelsea," Brady said in welcome. "You remember Liz?"

"Yes, of course. We met at the JJ gala," Chelsea said. Her hair was tied in a stylish French twist and her makeup accented her almond-shaped eyes. She had on a stunning blue beaded halter gown.

"Nice to see you again," Liz said politely. Liz wasn't sure how happy she really was to see Chelsea. The woman had been aggravating Brady all summer about that damn environmental bill.

Just then Clay materialized at Chelsea's side. "Hey, babe. It's been a while since I've seen you," he said, putting an arm around her waist.

Chelsea rolled her eyes as Liz herself had done a number of times. "Hello, Clay."

Brady fumed at the sight of his brother. "Clay," he said warningly.

Clay put his hands up as if he were innocent. "I was just talking to our old friend. I didn't realize she was even going to be here. God, it's been what, like two years, Chels?"

"I'm typically around during election time," she said dismissively. "It's kind of my job."

"I bet," Clay said with a wink.

"Picture?" the photographer asked, rearranging them so Brady was between Liz and Chelsea, and then snapped the photo.

Brady leaned forward toward Clay, but Liz could hear what he whispered to him in a dangerously low voice: "Try to stay out of trouble for once in your life."

"High on my priority list," Clay said sarcastically.

Liz placed her hand on Brady's arm. "Just leave him."

Brady nodded and walked away with her after he excused himself from Chelsea. "He is the only person who gets under my skin."

"Other than me?" she joked.

"You're different."

"Just imagine what it's like living in your shadow. He graduated from the best law school in the country and is clerking for the Supreme Court and you're still the golden boy. That can't be easy."

"Why are you defending him?"

"Because you're as blind to the good in Clay as he is to the good in you," she told him plainly.

"If there was ever good in Clay, then he lost it a long time ago," Brady said, as if he were unable to reconcile the image he'd had of his brother for so long with the one Liz was presenting.

"You should just give him a chance. You're more alike than you realize, which is where I think some of the tension stems from."

"I'm nothing like him."

"Well, you're both stubborn," she pointed out. He shot her a warning look. "This won't be resolved tonight, but maybe you should consider resolving it in the future."

He thought a moment before responding. "I'll consider it."

Well, that was as good as it was going to get.

They finished their circuit of the room and ended up where Lucas, Chris, and Mollie were standing. She and Mollie hugged as Chris and Brady shook hands. Liz watched Brady out of the corner of her eye. She knew he wouldn't do anything tonight, but this was the first time they had seen Lucas since Hilton Head, and she knew Brady was still pissed about what had happened.

Champagne was passed out to the guests as Brady walked up to the stage to deliver his speech. Liz felt her phone buzz twice as she walked over to the podium to stand with Chris, Mollie, and Lucas. She wanted to pull it out, but felt as though she should be paying attention.

Brady tapped the microphone once and waited for his audience to become silent. The crowd hushed and Liz felt another buzz from her purse. *God, so annoying.*

"Hello and welcome!" Brady called into the microphone. "It's my pleasure to be here tonight and have each and every one of you in this room supporting me. Winning my seat in the House of Representatives would not have been possible without you all in this building right now, and it won't be possible for me to remain there working for you if I don't have your continued support."

Liz felt her phone buzz at least three more times while Brady gave the opening to his speech. Jesus, someone must really need to get a hold of her. Maybe her parents were calling. Maybe it was an emergency.

With a sigh, she opened her clutch and saw Brady's phone light up. She had completely forgotten it was in there when they had left. Her eyes scanned the first message to make sure it wasn't an emergency.

I'd rather you were fucking me than giving this speech.

Chelsea. Liz's stomach dropped out of her body. Her mouth went dry and she felt all the blood drain out of her face. She tried to swallow, but found she couldn't. Her heart was racing in her chest as she stared at the message. Another one came in.

I miss Hilton Head. Ditch the girlfriend and take me instead.

Her hands shook and she was afraid that she might drop the phone. No. No way. This . . . this wasn't even possible. She tried to rationalize. Brady wouldn't do this to her. He loved her. She was his world. He'd said forever and always. Those were promises.

Make up an excuse and meet me in the back room. It'll be worth it.

She couldn't read any more. Liz dropped the phone back into her purse and tried to collect herself. Her breathing was heavy and she placed her hand on her chest. She needed to get out of there. She needed to clear her head and think and figure this out. She couldn't keep listening to Brady's speech, the speech she had helped him with, with Chelsea's words in her head.

She stumbled sideways into Chris and he placed a hand on her arm. "Excuse me for a second," she mumbled and then walked purposefully away from the stage. She could feel Brady's eyes on her as she left, but she didn't turn back to look for him.

She knew where the side exit was to the restroom. She had used it two years ago in this very room to meet with Brady about him bringing another woman to the gala. Was history repeating itself and now she was the other woman?

Liz heard footsteps behind her and just as she made it through the door, Chris caught up with her. "What's going on?" he asked. "Are you sick?"

"Sick," she scoffed. "That's one word for it."

"Are you going to throw up? Do you need anything?" he asked, concerned.

"How long have you known, Chris?"

"Known what?"

"About Chelsea."

Chris looked uncomfortable and scratched the back of his head. "I mean . . . like forever. They were on-again, off-again in college."

"Since college," she gasped. "Wait . . . environmental lobbyist." Her head spun as the pieces all fit together. Brady had brought a date to the event he had held at Hilton Head two years ago when he had flown her down there and had said that it was an environmental lobbyist he had known since college. Chelsea fit the bill. Chelsea must have been that date. He had said that nothing was going on then, but that had clearly changed. "She went to Hilton Head with him."

"Um . . . a couple times. Why?"

"Why?" she demanded. Liz pulled Brady's phone out, lit up the screen, and handed it back to Chris. "I would think my boyfriend cheating on me would be reason enough."

"What? Brady would never . . ." He trailed off when he started reading through the texts that were visible on the home screen.

"Tell me again what Brady would never do."

"I'm sure there's an explanation for this," Chris said.

"There's always an explanation," she said, shaking her head. "Take that back to Brady. I need to disappear for a little while."

"Liz," he said, grabbing her arm.

"What would you do if you saw those texts on Mollie's phone?"

He sighed, seeing he was caught, and then released her. "I'll take it to him, but he's going to come after you."

"Looking forward to it," she said sarcastically, and then turned to walk down the hallway.

When Chris left, she paced, trying to clear her head. All it seemed to do was make things worse. Brady was irritable every time

Chelsea messaged him. That was exactly how he had been with Liz. Brady had turned his phone off at Justin's birthday party after Chelsea had texted him. He had done the same thing when Liz had been at Hilton Head. And it seemed as if he had been messaging with her all summer and she had been at events for him under the pretenses of working for EMi. Hadn't Liz done the same thing as a reporter?

It all fit so closely together that she almost felt stupid for not having seen it for what it was sooner.

Chapter 25
ONE AND THE SAME THING

Liz heard the door open behind her. She sighed, resigned to speaking to Brady about this. She would rather hide out in the bathroom, but that wouldn't help anything. Her emotions were running high, though. She wished she had more time to try to rationalize this before hashing it out.

Expecting Brady, Liz turned around and found Clay instead.

"Hey, sexy," he said with that insufferable smirk.

"Do you need something, Clay?" She was already irritated, and Clay never seemed to help that.

"I just saw you dart off looking pale and sick."

"And you decided to be nosy?"

"I decided to come check on you. Something happen with Brady? I saw you scrolling through your phone."

"What, are you stalking me?" How was she always so transparent to Clay?

"I just know the signs. So what happened?"

"Like I'm going to give you more ammo to hate Brady." She was defending him even now, when he had majorly fucked up.

"Do you have ammo? I thought he was perfect."

"Oh. Ha-ha. You're hilarious. I don't need any of your shit tonight," she said, turning away from him.

"Whoa. He must have really fucked up if you're being a bitch to me."

Liz spun around. "Do you walk around calling all women bitches? Or am I just lucky tonight?" She glared at him and crossed her arms. "Mind finding someone else to harass for a change? I don't know why I defend you to him anyway."

"I don't need defending. I'm fine with everything exactly how it is. But you're just picking a fight with me because you're mad at him."

She looked away from his probing gaze. He was right. She was mad at Brady. And Clay was just trying to make sure she was okay.

She looked back up at him and he gave her a small nod, as if he had read her mind. She sighed heavily. "What do you know about Chelsea?" Liz asked.

"Ah," Clay said, his dimples showing.

"What does that mean?"

"You'd think that when he has someone like you and went through all the trouble to keep you . . . that he would let the past rest."

A knot formed in the pit of her stomach at Clay's words. This wasn't encouraging. "Chris said they were together in college," she offered.

"I'm sure he meant that they've been fucking since college," Clay said casually, as if it didn't make Liz feel as if she had been slapped across the face.

"No. I just . . . can't believe he would do this," she whispered.

His eyes roamed her face and he shook his head. "God, you're so innocent. Do you think that you were the first he ever hid? You were the one he got caught with. He's like a kid with his hand in the cookie jar. He would have eaten the cookies if he hadn't got caught, but he never would have fessed up to it."

"You're such an ass," she said hoarsely.

"I'm a realist, and I know my brother."

"Just . . . leave me alone. I thought for a second you might be here for some semblance of comfort. Instead you just brought salt to rub in the wounds," she said. Her hands were fisted at her sides. "Go back to your arranged marriage and leave my life out of your scheming."

"Fine. Just remember this feeling when he tries to change your mind," Clay said with a shrug before turning to leave.

Liz really wished that she had something that she could throw at that moment. Clay's departure only pissed her off more, and she wouldn't have minded aiming something heavy at the back of his head.

She sagged with the weight of her anger. She couldn't just stand here. Liz stormed around the corner to the bathroom that she and Brady had had a confrontation in two years ago. She had thought that she liked getting to redo so much of their relationship, but she didn't want to ever relive this feeling.

Liz walked into the bathroom and bolted the door. She leaned forward heavily on the sink and blew out all the air in her lungs. Her face was pale, but her eyes didn't hold the sick feeling that went through the rest of her body. Her eyes looked livid. And she realized that she wasn't actually sad or disappointed or sick . . . she was pissed.

How could he do this to her? She had given up *everything* for him. She had given up the *New York Times*, the UNC paper, her credibility, her privacy. God, she had moved in with him and spent her whole summer on the campaign with him. She didn't even know when he would find time for this, but then again, he had found time for her.

She wanted to think that she was jumping to conclusions, but Chris's and Clay's remarks made her think that she wasn't. She was clearly losing her touch as a reporter if she couldn't even put together the most in-your-face details like this.

A knock at the door pulled her out of her thoughts. "Occupied," she called back even though she was pretty sure she knew who was on the other side.

"Liz, open the door," Brady said brusquely.

Liz took a deep breath and then unlocked the door. Brady was inside the bathroom in a split second with the door closed, holding up his cell phone. "*This* is not what it looks like," he said immediately.

"Really? It looks like Chelsea wants you to meet her in a back room, take her to Hilton Head, and fuck her. As far as I've gathered . . . those are all things you've done before," she said coldly.

He cringed. Brady Maxwell actually cringed. "They are, but that's long in the past."

"Long in the past like two years ago, when she was your date that time you flew me to Hilton Head?"

"She was my date, but if you remember correctly, I told you that she wasn't much of a date and that nothing was going on between us. Because nothing is going on between us, Liz. Absolutely nothing," he told her.

She wanted to believe him. She really did. But she wasn't sure she could trust his words at this moment. "Then how do you explain those messages? That doesn't read like absolutely nothing."

"Those texts were completely out of line. Chelsea and I had a sort of relationship for a while. It wasn't serious."

"It wasn't public? It was on your terms? You had her when you wanted her?" Liz asked harshly.

"No. Please listen to me," he said, his voice softening. "She is nothing like you. She can't even compare to you."

"Then why is she sending you messages asking you to fuck her?" she yelled in his face.

Brady remained resolute. "I don't know. Probably because she's drunk. She messaged me at the start of the summer insinuating that she wanted to start something up again, and I told her no, that you and I were serious."

"What about all the text messages? What about turning your phone off when she messaged you at Justin's? What about you acting exactly the way you did when you and I were hiding something?" she demanded, crossing her arms.

"I can say it a million times if you want me to. There's nothing going on with Chelsea and me. I wasn't trying to hide anything. She was messaging me about work. Insistently, really, and it was annoying," he said with a sigh. "If I was trying to hide her would I keep telling you that she was calling and have her show up at events and give you my cell phone?"

"Oh, yeah, because it's great to know that if you really wanted to hide something from me you would be better at it."

"I'm not saying that! God, this is all coming out wrong," he said, reaching forward and grasping her shoulders gently. "I'm saying that I love you. I love you with all of my heart. I love you so much that when I look at you I feel completely right . . . like I've both found myself and lost myself in the depths of your blue eyes. I could never cheat on you, because the thought of being with another woman repulses me. You intrigued me from day one, and each day it only gets better. Don't you remember? *I'll always be your airplane.*"

Liz closed her eyes as she soaked in Brady's words. Airplanes. Damn airplanes always did her in.

Why did he have to be equal parts charming and persuasive? Couldn't she have fallen for someone whose career didn't depend on being able to convince thousands of people to like him? And the hardest part was that she didn't like him . . . she loved him wholeheartedly. She wanted to succumb to his easy words, throw herself into his arms, and forget that any of this had happened. But the ache in her chest held her.

"Why didn't you tell me about Chelsea? I was around her this whole time. She was probably laughing in my oblivious face. You spend all of this time hating on Hayden and being jealous of a relationship that's dead, but you don't think that I have the right to know that I'm going to be around an ex of yours?" she asked. Her eyes fluttered open and she met his gaze head-on.

"To be honest, it didn't cross my mind. After I told her that I no longer saw her that way, I assumed she would just move on and act professionally by never bringing it up again. I was clearly wrong."

"How does it feel to admit that?" she asked with a harsh laugh.

"It doesn't happen often, but I do make mistakes." One hand slid to the small of her back and the other up into her hair. "Like letting you walk out the door two years ago and not following you . . . demanding you see reason . . . offering you the world."

He dropped his mouth down onto hers, but she pulled back after a second with a sigh. She shook her head and walked away from Brady. Her head was still spinning with everything she'd heard tonight. All she wanted was to forget that this had all happened, but it *had* happened. So now she had to deal with it.

"You still don't believe me?" Brady asked.

"I want to. I really do," she said earnestly.

"Do you want me to get down on my knees? Do you want me to beg forgiveness for not telling you about Chelsea sooner? Do you want me to plead with you to reconsider? I'll do it. Whatever you want me to do. I'll do it," he insisted. "You mean everything to me. I don't want this to ruin the best thing in my life."

"Then why didn't you tell me? If it meant nothing and it was no big deal, why didn't you tell me?" she demanded, searching his eyes for the explanation. "You should have told me."

Brady hung his head for a second to collect his thoughts and then seemed to relent. "You're right. I should have. You deserved to know, even if it meant nothing. And it means nothing."

"Not good enough," she said, backing away. "When Hayden came up to me at school because he wanted to see me again, I called you and told you as soon as I got home. I didn't hide anything from you. Not even for a day."

"I wasn't purposely hiding it from you. When it happened, you were already dismantling your life and stressed about graduation, being in the paper, and then moving in with me. I didn't want to lay more stress at your feet."

She had been insanely stressed out at the start of the summer. Everything seemed to be piling on top of her head, but still she would have wanted to know what was going on. "What about after that, when I met her? No heads-up?" she asked.

"It was over by then. The only contact I had with her the rest of the summer was completely professional and you were there every time. These texts came out of nowhere, and I'm going to ask to work with someone else from EMi from this point forward," he told her. "I assume they assigned her to work with me because I've known her a long time. But I'm cutting off contact. I don't need *this* to interfere with the love of my life or my career."

"Aren't they the same thing?" she whispered harshly.

"Liz, please just think about this for a minute," he said, closing the distance between them once more and backing her up against the wall. He placed his hands on her hips and then rested his forehead on hers. "I love you. You *are* the love of my life. Please . . . please," he said hoarsely, "don't let this ruin us."

She sighed. Blind trust. That's what he was asking for. Did she trust him? Did she trust him not to play her like that? That nagging feeling crept through her, but then she let his words wash over the anger. This was Brady, the man who wouldn't even tell her he loved her when he knew he did because he couldn't promise her a relationship. Now he was promising her everything that she'd ever wanted, and she couldn't stop thinking that it was all too good to be true.

But Brady wouldn't give her those things if he didn't want to. He wouldn't have gone public, had her move in, travel around the campaign, use her speeches, or tell her he loved her if he didn't mean it. He had made all of that clear from the get-go. But he was doing those things, and it made her reevaluate her reaction to this.

Maybe it was one-sided. Maybe Chelsea just wanted what she couldn't have anymore. Maybe he wasn't playing her. Maybe.

"You love me?" she whispered.

"So much."

His lips found hers again, soft and tender, with every ounce of that love pouring between them. It was as sweet as honey and intoxicating as the hardest liquor. She couldn't let a few text messages ruin their relationship. It hurt to even think about letting this go. She wanted it . . . she wanted Brady more than anything else in her existence.

They stayed like that for a few minutes, lost in each other's embrace, forgetting that an entire gala went on behind them. There was only Liz and Brady, the taste of his kiss, the feel of his lips, the ecstasy of being completely wrapped up in him.

After another minute passed, they broke apart simultaneously. "We should get back," she whispered.

"Are we okay?"

Liz nibbled on her bottom lip and then nodded. "Yeah."

She might be hurting emotionally, but who was she kidding? She was never walking away from Brady Maxwell again.

Chapter 26

THE PRIMARY

Two years ago today, Liz had walked out on Brady. She had given him the campaign and his career free of worry about a relationship that he couldn't commit to. She had chosen his happiness over her own and inevitably had just made them both pretty miserable. Now they were back in the same spot and yet . . . not in the same place at all.

Standing backstage at the election results party where Brady would give his acceptance speech, Liz paced the small conference room. Brady kept shooting her a look that said calm down, but there were no reporters, so she was able to feel the jitters that she would have to hold back in a minute when they exited.

Heather grabbed her arm. "You're making me anxious. Go out in the hallway if you're going to pace."

"Sorry," she said, running her hands down the white-eyelet dress.

"If you're like this now, how are you going to handle the general?" she probed.

"I'll be fine." Liz's eyes drifted to Brady and a smile crept on her face. "I'm just excited to be here for him."

"You'll do more good if you appear composed and resolute," Heather said, dropping her voice as she issued the advice. "He needs someone strong. Be strong for him."

Liz opened her mouth to say that she was strong and composed, but knowing Heather she would have snapped at her that actions spoke louder than words. So she just closed her mouth, stilled her feet, and found an empty seat.

They had spent the last week working nonstop on the primary campaign. Brady met with constituents, spoke at even the smallest of events, and Liz watched as more and more Maxwell for Congress signs went up around the Triangle. Most nights she fell into bed exhausted from a long day working, then got up early the next morning to start it all over again.

She knew that if the information about her and Brady hadn't come out earlier that year, this would have been an easy primary election for them. Brady's opponent could hardly be considered competition, yet he was garnering support from people who were influenced by the negative reports they had gotten about Brady's character.

It made Liz want to work twice as hard to help Brady before she started graduate school in a couple weeks. She was everywhere at once, and Brady continually told her how appreciative he was to have her there at his side. Part of that was the aftereffect of the Chelsea text messages.

Brady had spoken with EMi the next day requesting a new representative, and within a day he had a meeting with a lanky man in a cheap suit named Gary who looked and acted nothing like an ex-girlfriend.

"So, what happened to Chelsea then?" Liz had asked after they met Gary.

Brady had shrugged. "I never asked. I'd assume if she still has a job that she was transferred out of the state."

That put Liz at ease. It did make her feel bad that she had potentially gotten the woman fired, but then she had to remind herself that Chelsea was the one who had acted unprofessional. It had been the wrong circumstances. In the end, Liz could only think about herself and Brady, and it was better for them not to have her around.

It made Liz see their relationship with new eyes. Their relationship wasn't damaged or hurt from what she had discovered. In fact, they were stronger than ever. If anything it was Liz's hurt feelings that had clouded her mind when she had first found out about it. She hadn't wanted to believe that he would do this, but her insecurities bloomed and she couldn't see past it to the man who loved her. She had no such problem right now.

Brady's eyes flickered to her once again as his campaign manager walked away to talk to some other people in the room. "You want to take a walk?"

She nodded. "That sounds nice."

They exited the conference room and walked to the waiting area that led to the stage where Brady would be giving his speech. His family was standing there in a small circle, along with Andrea, Easton, and Chris. Liz peeked a look at the audience from their vantage point and gasped.

"What?" Brady asked, concerned.

"There are so many people."

He smiled, bright and brilliant. "More than there were two years ago."

"Yes," she agreed. "I mean, there were a lot of people for you then, but now . . . it's packed."

Two years ago they had nearly filled up a convention ballroom in Raleigh. This time Brady had chosen one twice as big as that on the UNC campus and it was filled to the brim with supporters and press. She could see the press line along the center of the room set up to film and photograph the events that were taking place. But the most beautiful thing of all was the sheer number of everyday citizens here to celebrate their own Congressman. Brady inspired people to take action, and it showed today.

"All here to hear *your* speech," he said with a wink.

"No one is even going to know that I wrote it," she insisted.

"Maybe."

"They're here for you, Congressman Maxwell. Not for your scandalous girlfriend."

"I'm sure someone out there is here for the scandal," he joked.

Liz rolled her eyes. "Yes, those people seem to be everywhere."

Liz had managed to avoid the news as much as she could, but Heather was sending sporadic updates when Liz showed up in the papers. The rumors were vicious, and even though Brady insisted that the people were just jealous and looking for a story, she still didn't like it.

Luckily she was swamped and didn't have a ton of time to dwell on it. The only thing that she had managed to do in the small moments of spare time she had was to write another article for her Dear Congress column about the environmental fracking legislation that was going around right now. Funny to think that Chelsea had given her the idea.

The editor had turned her column into a biweekly thing, and she didn't want to miss a post amid her hectic schedule. She had even put the blog with Justin on hold for the time being. She told him she would start up again once the primary was over. It was getting harder and harder to do everything that she had on her plate, but she was trying to keep up.

Chris appeared at their side while Liz was still peering out to Brady's captivated audience. "Hey. Y'all ready?"

"Of course," Brady answered immediately. "Good to have you here this year."

"And you?" he asked Liz with his ever-present goofy grin.

"I'm not the one giving the speech."

"Still, your first election and you look a little jittery."

"Gah, am I that obvious?" The guys just shrugged. "What? Are y'all born with the ability to hold your nerves in during the election?"

"Just a lot of practice," Brady told her, rubbing her back comfortingly.

"Well, where's Mollie? This is her first election. She should be here nervous with me," Liz said.

Chris glanced away and grit his teeth. "We, uh . . . broke up."

"What?" she and Brady asked at the same time.

"You didn't tell me," Brady said.

"I know; you're in the middle of an election."

"What happened?" Liz asked.

Chris shrugged, looking uncomfortable. "It actually happened after the fund-raising gala. Well, you know she left early for work stuff. That wasn't the first time that happened. I was fed up with always coming behind work. She didn't take it very well. It's been kind of a rough week."

That sucked. She liked Mollie, but Chris deserved someone who would put him first.

Brady glanced at her and she could see he was thinking the same thing. She was glad that they were on the same wavelength.

"Well, I just wanted to check on y'all. I'm not still in your speeches, am I?" Chris joked, trying to lighten the mood.

"I got a new speechwriter," he said, placing his arm around Liz's shoulders. "And she insisted that I take you out of them."

"Thank God. The man needed new material. I was tired of hearing my sad story replayed over and over again," he said, nudging Brady. Then he turned to Liz. "So, you're writing his speeches now, huh? Busy girl. Speeches, grad school, and those articles you're writing."

"I have to keep up with my boyfriend," she joked.

Brady kissed her on the top of her head. "You're the only one who can."

Chris laughed softly. "I'm glad that Brady manned up and went after you. You two belong together."

Brady's team emerged from the back conference room and Chris took that as his cue to leave. Heather and Elliott led the group with Alex trailing, permanently attached to his iPad.

"We just received word that results will be in in a matter of minutes," Heather told him.

All eyes turned to the mounted television screen, where muted broadcasts of the primary results were taking up the local news channel.

"Do you hear before they announce on television?" Liz asked.

"The results come to us first and then they're reported out," Elliott informed her.

Liz realized she was wringing her hands and quickly hid them behind her back. Composed. Resolute. Strong. She repeated the words that Heather had uttered like a chant in her head. It helped her get through the next few agonizing minutes.

"Just got it," Alex said. Brady's campaign manager walked forward. "Here we go. Final numbers read fifty-nine to forty-one percent to Congressman Maxwell."

A cheer rose up from the people backstage with Brady. Liz turned and threw her arms around him. She didn't know why she had been so freaked out. She knew the likelihood of his losing was small, but this was her first election. She felt compelled to hold on to her nerves for the unknown. Maybe one day this would all seem like a piece of cake, but right now it was fresh and new and exhilarating.

"Congratulations," she whispered in his ear.

"Thanks, baby." He squeezed her and then placed her back on her feet.

Everyone backstage seemed to want to come over and congratulate him too. Liz took a step back as Brady shook hands with the team that stood behind him the whole time and then his family. Just as Brady bent down to give his mother a hug, uproarious applause broke out in the convention center.

"They've just heard the news," Heather explained.

It was so strange sometimes to see all of this from the other side. To get the election results before the news media, before she would have gotten them as a reporter.

And then she heard one of her favorite sounds. A cheer rose up from the crowd. *Max-well. Max-well. Max-well.*

"That's our cue," Heather said with a huge smile on her face. Liz had never seen Heather smile so brightly. "Congratulations, Brady."

"Y'all act as if you were worried," he joked, but it was clear all the tension had left his body. He had an entire general election to contend with, but at least one obstacle was out of his way.

Heather strode out onto stage, a total natural before the audience. She stepped up to the microphone, with a smile. "Ladies and gentlemen, we're pleased to have you here tonight at the celebration for Congressman Brady Maxwell III."

The crowd cheered at the mention of Brady's name.

"With the announcement that he has won the nomination for the Fourth District, I'm happy to introduce you to the man who you entrusted two years ago and who you continue to believe in today. Congressman Maxwell!"

Brady's campaign mask slipped easily into place as he walked with confidence and power onto the stage as if he owned it. He was bred for this. It was what he was best at. He could wow a crowd, and tonight was his moment.

The crowd started up their chant again and the applause hit a record high. Bulbs flashed as people took pictures from all areas of the room. Red, white, and blue MAXWELL FOR CONGRESS banners hung everywhere. People were holding the signs above their heads and waving American flags in the air. It was a madhouse; Brady couldn't even speak because the enthusiasm was all-consuming.

He laughed softly into the microphone. "Thank you. Thank you."

It proceeded like that for nearly five minutes before Brady was finally able to speak. And then he delivered the acceptance speech that she had written for him.

She could hardly listen to her own speech without tears welling in her eyes. Brady had worked on it with her to tailor it to his cadence, and still she felt emotional. It mirrored the speech he had given at his last acceptance in some ways and spoke of the people he had met along the campaign. Liz had met many of the people that she referenced. An older woman who always donated to candidates she believed in each race, even though she didn't have much money to spare. A young man who organized his high school to try to get all of the eighteen-year-old students registered and voting, and he was now actively working for the campaign.

There were so many stories. She couldn't ever hope to capture them all. But she just wanted to focus on the things that were important to Brady—dedication, ambition, trust, hope, and working for the good of the community.

And when he finished, the cheers were even louder than they had been before.

Heather leaned over toward Liz and spoke low. "You did a really good job with that speech."

Liz just stared at her, stunned. She was still not used to Heather acting normal, but ever since Liz had confronted her at the gala she seemed to be trying harder. "Thank you."

Brady came offstage and scooped her up into his arms. "Brilliant. So brilliant. Like nothing else I've ever experienced," he muttered against her skin.

Liz breathed in for what felt like the first time. She had survived her first election, and not just survived—Brady had won!

Chapter 27
MINE

The celebrations seemed to last forever.

Brady spent hours talking to reporters and answering questions about his victory. Then he spent even more time with the constituents who had come out tonight to see him. He was a star—smiling for pictures, shaking hands, kissing babies—the politician's agenda. The room had an energy about it that seemed unstoppable.

It was certainly infectious. Every second that she felt as if she was getting tired, her feet were hurting her, or she couldn't keep a smile on her face, she saw the people who greeted Brady. They were the reason they were even here today, the reason Brady had won.

After the primary party, they moved to another celebration for his high-end donors. Most of them had been at the fund-raising gala last weekend. They had been seated at the primary party, but Brady liked to thank them in additional ways. It was good to keep donors happy.

Liz sipped champagne and smiled at the faces that she had seen over and over this summer. She wondered what each of them wanted in return for their donation. How many of them had agendas they wanted to press on Brady, as Chelsea had?

She forced those thoughts out of her head and just enjoyed a night of celebration. Brady had the rest of the week off before delving into the general election, and she looked forward to those precious moments alone with him before school started. Between school and the campaign she wasn't sure either of them would have much time together. Her chest ached at the thought of not being there to help with every speech as she had over the summer, but she had to sacrifice some of that for the greater good—her own independence.

She loved Brady like mad, but she needed a life beyond him. Liz was ready to begin anew. The more she thought about it, the more excited she got about her work in the PhD program. The thought of working in journalism, creating original research in the field, to maybe one day become a professor like her mentor was all too intriguing.

Marilyn approached her near the end of the evening and pulled Liz into a hug. "It is really wonderful to have you here, dear."

"Thank you," she said. Her voice was always thick with emotion whenever she spoke with Brady's parents.

Marilyn pulled back to look at Liz with her hands still on Liz's shoulders. "Don't be a stranger when you start school. We've enjoyed having you around this summer."

"I'll be back on the campaign every chance I get."

"We know you will," she said with an easy smile. "Good night."

Jeff said good night as well and then they departed. Clay and Savannah had never made it to this event and Chris had retired about an hour ago. The numbers were dwindling and only a few older drunk couples remained dancing in the center of the room.

Brady returned to her side after escorting his parents out. "Are you about ready?"

"Dying to get out of these heels," she admitted.

"I'll have someone pull the car around."

Brady said a final farewell to the remaining guests and then they exited the party. It was just past three o'clock in the morning when they finally sat down in the back of the town car. Liz sighed heavily and leaned into Brady's arm that he had wrapped around her shoulder.

"This was an amazing night," she breathed.

"I loved sharing it with you." He kissed her temple and she just sighed louder.

Liz had a feeling that she was going to fall asleep on the drive back to Raleigh. Her mind was exhausted as much as her body was. She couldn't wait to sink into the soft mattress and wake up to five full days with Brady lounging around the house.

A second later, Brady was shaking her awake and she realized that she must have passed out. She fluttered her eyes open and yawned wide as she came to. "Are we home already?"

"No, baby, just a short detour," he said. The door opened and Brady helped Liz out of the car.

She glanced around her, trying to figure out where they were. It was pitch-black. The car headlights and the light of the moon offered the only illumination of where she was. There were no buildings and it appeared that they were at the end of a paved road. Everything before them was gravel.

"You brought me to the woods?" she asked, confused.

Brady didn't have a chance to respond before the driver handed him a few things and then with a nod returned to the car. Brady passed her a jacket, which she took, though she was utterly confused. Next he handed her a flashlight.

"Ready?"

She stared down at her heels. "What is going on? And do you expect me to walk through the woods in these?"

Brady laughed. "It's a short walk, and not through the woods. There's a path."

"Okay," she said apprehensively.

Liz slid the jacket on over her party dress. It was mid-August so it wasn't exactly cold outside, but the wind whipped up around her, causing her to shiver. She flicked the flashlight on and walked with Brady across the street to the concrete path that led down the dirt road.

She felt a bit as if she were at the beginning of a horror movie. Walking around in high heels at night in the middle of the woods with nothing to defend herself and only a flashlight that was probably going to break in a matter of seconds. She had so many questions, but Brady didn't seem as if he was going to answer any of them, so she just kept pace next to him and listened to the crickets chirping in the woods surrounding them.

True to his word, they stopped after only a few minutes when they reached the end of the sidewalk. Before them stretched nothing but a cleared grassy knoll that led down to a glistening uninhabited lake.

He kissed her softly before she could say anything and then gestured for her to walk a short distance down the hill. Brady unrolled the bundle that the driver had handed him. It appeared to be a relatively large quilt, which he spread out before her.

"Take a seat," he said, and then took his own advice.

Liz gratefully kicked off her high heels and then sank down onto the quilt. She was terribly confused, but too tired to fight him. Plus she was curious as to what they were doing here.

"Are you going to explain yourself?" she finally asked when he remained silent for another moment.

"I took a girl out to dinner once," he said. "She had been uncertain about the election for longer than she had been uncertain about me. We'd been apart for a long time, and I wanted to prove to her that my feelings were genuine."

Liz smiled. "Me? I'm that girl."

"You are. I took her out to dinner. I wanted to be seen with her. I wanted to claim her. I wanted to claim *you*."

"Well, I'm yours."

"And that night you said that the most romantic thing was sitting in an open field looking up at the stars." He gestured around him. "I give you the stars. I already have mine."

Liz's mouth fell open. The stars. He was giving her the stars. She glanced up and realized exactly what was going on. They had driven out of town to a secluded park with no lights for distraction simply to stare up into the night sky, as she had said six months earlier to him on a whim while they were out to dinner.

"I love you," she whispered. "You . . . you seem to understand me unlike anyone else."

"I feel the same way. We're a matched set."

"Brady, you gave me the stars."

"I'd like to give you a lot more than that," he said.

Then as Liz stared at him, stunned by his words, Brady shifted to one knee and pulled a small blue box out of his pocket. Liz's eyes widened and her hand flew to her mouth.

"They say the measure of a man is what he does with his power. I've come to find that I have no power without you. So, I want to share it with you for the rest of my days." He opened the box, and a glittering princess-cut diamond with matching diamonds to either side shone bright in the moonlight reflecting off of the lake. "There is no other option for me. It's just you. I don't need to wait any longer to see if that's true. I lost you this day two years ago, and I never want to live without you again. This time you're mine, and I plan to do right by you."

Liz felt tears prick her eyes at his words and she wasn't sure if she was breathing.

"Will you, Elizabeth Anne Dougherty, do me the honor of marrying me?"

A million thoughts flew through her mind all at once. Was she ready for this? They had been together six months. In the grand scheme of things it wasn't that long, but it had already felt like a lifetime.

He had told her once before that he could never be cajoled into marrying. That he could date, but marriage wasn't on his horizon for a long time. But he loved her, and wanted this life with her.

She felt a tear run down her cheek as she nodded. "Yes. Yes, of course I'll marry you."

A smile broke out across his face. He plucked the ring out of the box and slid it gingerly onto her finger. It fit so perfectly that it was as if it were always meant to be there.

And then Brady was kissing her. Their lips melded together. His hands tangled in her hair and hers grabbed on to his waist, trying to get him as close as she could. She had never seen this moment coming. Even in her wildest fantasies she hadn't pictured this happening until years down the road, but here and now couldn't have been more perfect.

Brady was right. There was no need to wait. They had already been through hell and back. They had already realized they couldn't live without each other. They lived together and worked together and traveled together. There weren't any obstacles holding them back from this. And she wanted it.

She wanted to be with him. She had always wanted it. Life without Brady had always been like walking out of Technicolor into black and white: drab and lifeless.

They stayed like that until they both broke apart gasping. Brady wiped the tears from her cheeks with his thumbs. Tears of joy and happiness and contentment.

After a moment, Brady laid them back on the quilt, cradling her body against his. They lay there staring up at the stars, lost in the euphoria of their engagement.

Chapter 28
RIGHT DIRECTION

Liz and Brady spent his five days of vacation celebrating their engagement. The day after the primary, they had lunch with his family to tell them the news. The welcome she received brought tears to her eyes. Marilyn and Jeff both hugged her and told her that they were happy to have such a wonderful future daughter-in-law. Savannah was jumping-up-and-down excited. Even Clay smiled at the news. Though it did seem to make Andrea more pouty and bitchy than normal.

Clay had hugged her when they were leaving and whispered in her ear, "I guess the golden boy is still perfect, huh?"

Liz had smiled as she drew back. "Don't worry. No one will take your black-sheep title."

He had laughed and shaken his head. "I was never worried about that."

"You should be worried about Andrea, though. She looks like she's ready to be married off."

Clay had just shrugged. "She'll survive." He had looked pensive for a moment before deciding that he could continue. "I want what y'all have."

Liz hadn't been sure that she had even heard him right, and then he was gone. Sometimes that man confused the hell out of her.

That weekend Brady had flown them down to Tampa. She had wanted to see her family before school started; now she had the excuse—to tell them about her engagement.

Her parents were, as Liz had expected, shocked. She and Brady had only been dating for six months and that seemed fast to them. But she explained that she couldn't think of her life without him and she was insanely happy about the decision. After that they seemed to relax. She didn't blame them for having an *is this man taking advantage of my baby?* feeling, but that was so far from the truth that it was easy to dispel it.

As soon as the apprehension left their faces, her mother immediately launched into preparations and they didn't stop until the minute they were getting back on the plane. What kind of dress do you want? You look lovely in white, dear. Will Victoria be the maid of honor? I loved the Trenton wedding last year, and she had champagne and rose as the color palette. Are you thinking something like that? I wonder what floral arrangements we should look into. Orchids or lilies? Spring or fall? Tampa or D.C. or Chapel Hill?

The questions went on and on and Liz just listened, answering as best she could. The only thing that she knew for certain was that they wouldn't have any time to plan until after the election. November 3 was Election Day and then after that . . . they would have the rest of their lives.

Liz's first day of school at Maryland in the journalism program was on Monday. She met with her advisor that morning for the first time. She took a seat in an oak chair facing his desk.

"Welcome, Liz. We're pleased to have you in Maryland's Journalism Department."

"It's a pleasure to be here, sir."

"Feel free to call me Terry. We're colleagues now," he said with a warm smile. "Lynda spoke wonderfully of you when I spoke to her. She said you were hardworking, and we're always glad to have students like that here."

Liz smiled and imagined the conversation between Terry and Professor Mires.

"I went ahead and got together your class schedule as well as your teaching assignment for the semester. We put you with Dr. Mary Whitley's Tuesday/Thursday ten a.m. section and you'll have a breakout Thursday afternoons at two."

"That sounds great," she said, relieved. She didn't want to have any Friday classes so that she could be with Brady during the campaign as much as possible.

"I placed you in the four prerequisite classes as you can see here," he said, passing her a sheet of paper. Four classes starting at three thirty in the afternoon Monday through Wednesday and Friday. Her stomach dropped. She knew that she would have a heavy load, but she hadn't anticipated a Monday *and* Friday class.

"Sir . . ."

"Terry, please."

"Terry," she corrected herself. "Is there any way that I can take the Friday editing class next semester? As you might be aware, my fiancé is running for Congress in Chapel Hill."

He nodded. "Yes, I think I heard that. Maxwell?"

"Yes. Well, if it doesn't disrupt my entire schedule, I'd like to be able to be helping on the campaign as much as possible."

Terry looked through his notes and started reading a piece of paper. "Ah. You do have an interest in political journalism. Well, I'll check with the head of department to verify that we can make an exception, but I don't see why not. We like to tailor curriculum to our students."

"Thank you, sir."

Terry smiled again and laughed. "Please call me Terry."

With her schedule arranged and everything seemingly in order, Liz moved easily back into the academic setting. Her classes were small and the classwork rigorous, but she found that, as she always had, she enjoyed the work. It kept her focused and motivated. It did make juggling her Dear Congress articles and Justin's blog, which she'd resumed writing after the convention, much more difficult.

Sometimes as she was writing a new article, she found that she actually wished that she could be interacting on the blog. It was a strange new dynamic. Her journalism work still had followers, but it was hardly as interactive as Justin's blog. She worked more or less as a moderator for the social media rating platform, which was Pinterest meets Goodreads for movie and YouTube addicts. She would start topics and write posts based on her conversations with others on the site. It was . . . fun. A good hobby that paid well without the stress of her career.

But she was determined to be dedicated to both as best she could without stretching herself too thin with the campaign, the engagement, graduate school, and her charity work with Barbara. Her nerves were shot just thinking about it. And two weeks after school started, when she was overwhelmed with a pile of work, Brady dragged her away.

"Come with me to New York this weekend."

"What?" she asked, glancing back at her work.

"Just for Saturday. We're shooting the commercial and I'd like to celebrate the engagement with Chris. Better yet, bring Victoria. Then we'll have the maid of honor and the best man all in one place."

"Brady . . . I have so much work."

He stroked a hand back through her hair. "You'll get it all done, but stressing about it every second of every day isn't productive."

"Kind of like you and the campaign."

"The campaign has an expiration date."

"A new one every two years," she teased.

"You're frazzled. There's so much you want to do and not enough hours to do it all. It's making you be *less* productive. Take a day off. Come with me," he pleaded. "I want my fiancé at my side."

God, the way he said that word. Fiancé. It rolled off the tip of his tongue, circled around her, and drew her toward him. She just wanted to sink herself into the word.

———

Brady, Liz, and Victoria arrived in New York City at an ungodly early hour on Saturday morning. Liz had dozed on the plane, but Brady, as usual, was unable to relax for much of the flight. A town car carried them across town to Chris's apartment. He slid into the car with them with a yawn as a greeting.

The car pulled away from the curb and started driving them toward the studio where Brady was filming his campaign spot today.

"So, you're finally getting hitched," Chris said.

"One of us had to," Brady said. He was rubbing circles into Liz's hand, which he held in his lap.

"Well, if you knew Liz then you wouldn't be surprised," Victoria said. "She's a long-term-commitment kind of person."

"Am I?" she asked, arching an eyebrow.

"You are."

"I'm glad for that," Brady said.

"My bestie is a keeper," Victoria said, patting her arm. "She didn't do any of the wild and crazy things I did. Though she did fuck a senator once."

Everyone in the car started laughing.

"More than once, I've heard," Chris said.

"Oh, don't y'all know the gossip? I'm a slutty home wrecker who caught the guy by getting pregnant." She placed her hand on her stomach. "I'm at least six months now and not even showing. Such a mystery."

"Well, obviously you got rid of it once you trapped him. That's a thing," Victoria said dismissively.

"That's how I trapped him, after all," Chris said, fluttering his eyelashes.

"Getting you pregnant was the most awkward experience of my life," Brady joked.

"If only the reporters could hear you now," Liz said.

"Let's thank God that they cannot."

They arrived at the building just on time. Brady was rushed away by the hair and makeup team. Chris teased him incessantly about it until the door closed behind him. They were given a brief tour of the studio Brady was using, which wasn't much more than a few workrooms, a changing area, wardrobe, and then the main set with a green screen and very expensive camera equipment. Their escort left them to sit on a couch where they could see what was being filmed, but not interfere. Plus, there were doughnuts!

Thirty minutes later, Brady appeared from makeup. He looked like himself and not. An even more perfect version of himself.

"His flawless face has to withstand the high-definition lighting and camera work," a man explained when Chris started to make fun of him again.

"You look great," she encouraged.

"I would kiss you right now, if it didn't mean I would have to spend another thirty minutes in makeup." He looked weary of the chore, and it made her giggle. Served men right to see what women had to go through on a regular basis.

Liz had heard Brady memorizing lines for the commercial earlier this week. She hadn't had time to work with him on what he was saying, but she knew that he would be brilliant. Also, in film there were dozens of takes, so they could get it perfect.

Brady thumbed through a stack of note cards and turned the phrases over in his mouth before the director walked him over to the comfortable brown chair. They had a couple different furniture pieces, from the chair to a podium to a large presidential-looking desk. They wanted to see which one suited him best with the lines delivered. The backdrop would be chosen from a computer screen, likely an American flag or a cozy study.

And so they began. The first thirty minutes it was interesting to watch the new experience. Brady had done ad spots before, so he knew the drill, but Liz had never seen any of this. Victoria, however, got bored very easily and ended up spending much of the time texting with Daniel on her phone.

"You know," she said, "we should have dropped him off and went and looked at wedding dresses."

"You're probably right."

"How much longer do we have? We could still go," she offered, looking up.

"I have no idea. I wouldn't even know where to begin with dresses, though. Plus, you know I'm not really getting started with that stuff until after the campaign."

Victoria sighed heavily and sank back into her seat. "I know. Have you decided anything, though? Fill me in! I miss you! I'm stuck in school all damn day and I need something lavish and entertaining to fill my travel-deprived mind."

Liz laughed lightly at her dramatic friend, but told her everything they had decided in the three weeks since Brady had proposed. "Brady wants to do a Biltmore wedding in Asheville."

"Holy fuck! How much is that going to cost?"

"Do you think I'm going to ask that?" Liz's gaze shot to Brady. "His parents were married there and it's gorgeous. I'm really excited to visit and see the gardens."

"Fuck. I can't wait. What else? What groomsmen do I have to choose from?" she asked with a wink.

"Aren't you bringing Duke Fan?" Liz asked with a hesitant smile. She never really knew with Victoria.

"Oh yeah. Of course, but maybe he'll be up for playing."

"I don't even want to know."

"Probably not," she conceded.

"Back on topic. I'm thinking just you and Savannah for bridesmaids. That means Brady will have Chris and Clay."

"He's actually going to take that arrogant brother of his?" Victoria asked, surprised.

Liz had wondered the same thing. She had been happily surprised when Brady had said he wanted Clay in the wedding. Clay . . . the man who had tried to sleep with her and hated everything about Brady's career. "I think deep down he loves him."

Liz hadn't even realized that Chris had slipped away until he returned, looking frazzled. "What's wrong?" she asked immediately.

"I need to speak with Brady," he said, averting his gaze.

"You can't. If you interrupt him with your news then he'll never finish his commercial. At the very least, he'll never reach the same level of composure," she told him. "Not the way you look right now."

"Just spill," Victoria said, standing between them.

"I had a call from Mollie."

"About what? I thought y'all were broken up," Liz said gently.

"We are." He took a deep breath. "I'm sorry, Liz."

"Sorry about what?" she asked cautiously. Instinctively she braced herself for what was coming.

"Mollie was freaking out. She was talking with one of her friends who works for CNN." Liz didn't like where this was going. "They were out to lunch and her friend mentioned that they were writing an article on the real identity of Dear Congress."

Liz placed her hand on the table to steady herself. "Okay. So CNN is writing an article about *me*?"

He splayed his hands out in front of him. "I'm so sorry."

"Did she say who told CNN that it was me?" Liz asked, trying to remain calm.

He shook his head. "I don't know. Her friend was just gossiping, I guess, and didn't think it would matter. Mollie pretended to use the restroom to tell me, she was so frantic."

"So, what's going to happen?" Victoria asked. "Who even cares about some stupid articles Liz wrote? She's not running for office. Brady is. And they weren't even controversial articles."

Chris shrugged again. "I don't know their spin on the issue. I just know that Brady should know so that he can get Heather to find out."

Liz knew he was right. She looked over at Brady smiling casually for the camera as he delivered his lines effortlessly. He finished that run-through and caught her staring at him. He must have realized something was wrong, because he stood, spoke to the director, and then walked over to them.

"What is it?"

Chris and Liz exchanged a glance and she nodded. Chris dove into the story he had just told Liz. Brady's face grew darker and darker.

"Great," he said, blowing out a breath. "I'll get on the phone with Heather immediately."

"I should probably get a hold of my editor to talk about damage control," Liz said. "How do you think they'll spin it?"

"How would you spin it?"

Liz slowed her mind enough to think about it from a reporting side. "Congressman Maxwell's girlfriend is spinning articles on policy to promote his platform. Or maybe Congressman's girlfriend hiding behind another pseudonym—what else are they hiding?"

Everyone stared at her and she clenched her jaw. "I only think of the worst because it was my job."

"I'll go call Heather."

"Just when she was starting to like me," Liz whispered.

"It'll be okay," he insisted before pulling out his phone and making the call.

Liz wasn't so sure. She had a decision to make. She had had something like this blow up in her face before, and she had no intention of it happening again. Before she had sat idly by as the media displayed her life how they saw fit. She had an opportunity to take control and she was going to need to seize it now before anything destroyed all that she and Brady had worked toward.

She opened up her email and wasn't all that surprised to already see one waiting for her from the editor, Tom Vernon. So, he already knew, and he wanted to speak with her on the phone. He had listed his number.

Tom answered on the second ring. "Hello?"

"Tom, this is Liz Dougherty. How are you today?"

"Miss Dougherty, what a pleasure to finally speak to the person behind Dear Congress."

"Thank you, sir. You are headquartered in New York City, correct?"

"What? Oh yes."

"As this is a difficult situation, would you mind if we met today to discuss it in person? I'm in the city until late this evening."

After a brief pause, he responded. "I believe that can be arranged."

———

Tom Vernon's office was cluttered with old cups of coffee, empty 5-hour Energy shots, and piles and piles of paper. The sight of the office probably explained why it took so long for him to get back to her most days.

"Miss Dougherty, so nice to finally meet you."

"You too," she said politely.

"I trust you found the office just fine."

"Yes, I did." Liz crossed her legs and sat up straighter. "Do you mind if we get to the point of this matter? It's clearly out to the public that I'm Dear Congress."

Tom straightened his tie at her curt demeanor. "Well, yes, of course. I was the one who contacted CNN about it."

Liz's mouth fell open slightly. "You did what?"

"It's an election year, Ms. Dougherty, and we're always trying to garner more readers. So I made a discreet call to a source at CNN. With your celebrity status we could be *huge*!"

"You outed me to the press for more media coverage?" she asked, shocked.

"Look, we love your work here as Dear Congress and we'd like to keep you on. You generate buzz. You're popular. People are interested in reading what you have to say, and they were interested in it before finding out who you are. Do you know what it will be like come Monday when it appears on CNN? Through the roof."

His eyes were shifty, his smile too big; his entire body language was overly enthusiastic. All she saw when she looked at him was desperation oozing out of every pore. He wanted her to stay and he wanted it badly. He liked the controversy. He liked the promise of increased readership to the online column that the scandal could deliver. He would probably pay her double or triple what he had been paying her. All because her name was attached to it.

"Thank you for the offer, Mr. Vernon, but I have to decline," she said, standing.

"What? I don't understand."

"Besides the fact that you outed me to the press without my consent? When we had a deal to keep my work anonymous?"

"But it's going to generate huge numbers for you!"

She wished that she knew how to explain it to him in a way that would make sense. When she had written her first article for him it had been because she didn't have any other options. She had wanted to prove to herself as much as to everyone else that she could still write articles and be successful on her own. She had *needed* these articles.

Now what did she have? Brady, school, her charity, and Justin's blog, which she loved. The world was at her feet. The need that she'd had before was gone. She had already proven to herself that she was good enough. Plus, so much of the fun of being the Dear Congress persona had been the anonymity and knowing that no one else really knew who she was. Without it, the idea lost some of its intrigue.

So, Liz raised her chin and gave him the best answer that she knew how. "No amount of notoriety would be worth it, Mr. Vernon. Furthering my career off of my relationship with Brady wouldn't be right. If that means leaving the articles behind, then so be it," she said. "I quit!"

She wasn't a pawn in someone else's game. She wouldn't let the media or Tom Vernon or anyone else dictate how she was going to live from now on.

Chapter 29
FIANCÉ

So you got fired again?" Justin asked over the phone later that day.

"I wasn't fired. I quit," Liz insisted.

"You hold down jobs worse than I do."

"You started your own business and seem to be doing okay with that."

Justin snorted. "Only because I'm the boss."

"Well, whatever. I decided that I was with the company only because I had been desperate after graduation. It filled a void and now I don't really need it anymore."

"Wait, wait, wait," he said, his casual demeanor momentarily disappearing. "You're not calling to break up with me, are you?"

Liz rolled her eyes. "If you're asking if I'm leaving the site, then no. Not unless you don't want any more drama behind my name. I just thought you would like to know the nonsense your employee is getting into."

"Oh. You know I don't give a fuck," he said, sounding relieved. "I just thought you'd want to leave, since you're going to be Mrs. Maxwell and all."

Mrs. Maxwell. Her whole body tingled. Holy shit! She was really going to marry Brady. She sighed pleasantly at the thought.

"Just because I'm getting married doesn't suddenly change who I am. I'm still getting my PhD, working with a children's education charity organization, writing political speeches, and running a movie blog for a certain someone. I'm more than the man that I'm in love with, and I enjoy the work. It's fun to interact with the people on the blog. It's nice to have a hobby." Though she did miss tennis. She had no idea when she would fit *that* in with everything else.

"Good. Then you're not getting out of it. I'm going to hire a lawyer or something and make you fill out a contract that says you'll stick with me."

Liz laughed. "I have a team of lawyers here who will be happy to look that over for you."

"I'll make sure they don't find the loopholes."

"You're ridiculous."

Justin murmured something under his breath and then sighed softly. "Thanks for sticking with me. It means a lot."

Oh, wow. He sounded . . . sincere. "Of course, I really do like it."

Brady tapped her on her shoulder. She was in Chris's guest bedroom and hadn't realized that he was behind her. "Need to talk to you," he whispered.

"Hey, Justin. I have to go. Tell Massey I said hey."

"Will do. See ya."

Liz stuffed the phone back into her pocket and turned to face Brady. She had informed him about quitting Dear Congress as soon as she had returned. "What's going on now?"

"Just spoke to Heather again. CNN announced the news."

"And what does that mean for us?" Liz asked. She hated that this was all happening, but they were trying to stay on top of it, control it. That had always been the strategy. The only problem was that Brady didn't want to address the rumors; he didn't want to tell people that the media were all liars and to ignore what was in the news. The media twisted stories and he thought addressing it would only make it worse.

"I think I'm going to have to speak to the press. Heather thinks it's a good idea. I guess we'll be announcing our engagement a little bit early," he said, wrapping his arms around her middle and dropping his lips onto hers. She eased into him, letting the tension wash off of her.

"I'm excited," she told him. "Do you know what you're going to say?"

He seemed to consider for a second, and then a smile spread across his face. "Yes."

⟞⟝

The pile of paperwork that she'd had to work on earlier in the week had come with her to Raleigh, where Brady was getting ready to address the press. As suspected, her Dear Congress articles were already being warped by Brady's opponent as some kind of ill-conceived attempt to make Brady's policies seem more influential. Liz didn't think it really made sense. Her articles weren't all related to what Brady was working on in Congress, and she had never once mentioned him.

But anything that happened on campaign was an issue. Just as she had been a liability two years ago, because she could have been used by his opponent to negatively impact Brady. She just hoped that this conference would dull the blade that his opponent was driving in with the news of her articles.

She heard a knock on the door and turned from her work to see Savannah walking into the room. "Hey!" Liz said, jumping up and hugging her.

"Two weeks into school and you're already causing trouble?" she asked.

"All in a day's work. What about you? How is the Washington division?" Savannah had been made head of the division, which Liz and Massey had run the two years prior on the campus paper. She was setting herself up to be editor-in-chief next year. Liz couldn't believe that Savannah was already a junior. Time passed so quickly.

"It's all right. I'm glad Josh replaced Massey, though. She could never replace you, and the paper was kind of shit all spring semester," Savannah admitted.

They hadn't really talked about her leaving, because it had hurt Liz too much at the time to think about it. Now she was just glad that Savannah was happy again on the paper. Liz knew that they were both in the right places in their lives.

"Well, that's good. Josh will do a good job. I worked with him some before Massey took over," Liz told her. "You and Easton still together?"

"Yep. We actually have dinner plans tonight, so make this press conference quick." She snapped her fingers twice.

Liz laughed. "I'll do what I can. So what ever happened with Lucas?"

"Lucas who?" Savannah asked coyly. "No, I just gave up on waiting around for things to change with him. It was never going to happen, and Easton is so great."

"Good! I'm so glad for you," Liz said enthusiastically. "You know you're going to make a beautiful bridesmaid."

"Oh my God, I can't believe we're going to be sisters," Savannah gushed. "I never wanted a sister, but I couldn't imagine one better."

"Thanks. Let's go watch your brother tell the world."

Liz smiled at Savannah. She felt really lucky—as if she had the world on her shoulders. Now they just needed to get through the campaign.

The girls walked to the waiting room, where Brady was talking animatedly with Heather. He glanced up at her when she walked in and immediately stopped talking. "Everything all right?" she asked when she reached him.

"Fine. We were just disagreeing about methods for this press conference."

"Isn't Heather the best?" Liz asked.

"Yes. I just want to do things my way on this one."

Liz completely trusted him, but he didn't normally go against Heather's suggestions. She wondered what he was going to do. Not that she thought he would do anything to harm his career, but she couldn't help but worry for him.

"Don't let them bait you when they get to the Q&A," Liz warned him.

He gave her that gorgeous smile wrapped in his campaign mask as he backed up toward the entrance. "As if I could be baited."

Liz arched an eyebrow. "Airplanes, baby."

He laughed heartily. "Touché."

And then he was gone. Liz followed his staff to a position where they could watch him address the media. She had done this dozens of times and still she wasn't used to being on this end of things. She wondered what it would feel like now to have her voice recorder in her hand, pushing through the crowds, and vying for a chance to get the Congressman's attention.

She was almost certain that it wouldn't feel the same as it once had. Reporting had lost some of its flair when she had lived life on the other side.

With a smile that radiated confidence and energy, Brady walked up to the microphone. He had such an incredible presence about him that was hard to ignore. Even when Liz had openly disagreed with his policy positions, he had still captivated her.

"Ladies and gentlemen, thank you so much for coming out today on such short notice. I don't intend to take up much of your time. I simply came here to address some of the accusations that are being thrown around about me and my fiancé."

The quiet room filled with buzz. Liz heard the word spoken over and over again. *Fiancé.* What an entrance. If the audience hadn't been taken in by his confidence and tenacity, they were all listening now.

"Ever since our relationship was made public, rumors have flown around about *why* we're together. As if I need a reason to be with the woman that I love. As if I need a reason to pick *her*. As if in some realm of this universe, she isn't good enough for me, a sitting congressman. The names that I have seen and heard hurled at her, at us, have been disgraceful. It would be nothing short of traumatizing for a woman walking into a public relationship, if that woman were anyone other than Liz Dougherty, who is without a doubt one of the strongest people I have ever encountered."

Liz felt her face flush. He was refuting everything those people had said about her even though he hadn't thought that it would do any good. She saw it on his face then. He didn't care. He just wanted to defend her. He didn't want to see her cry ever again or have to deal with the backlash of another failed attempt at a journalism career. He wanted to take the pain away.

"So, let me stand here right now and set the record straight. Liz Dougherty and I started a relationship two years ago. We broke up and then got back together in February of this year. At no time was I with anyone else while Liz and I were together. She's not a home wrecker. She's not pregnant. And she's certainly not doing anything to try to get me to stay with her other than being the amazing woman she is."

Brady paused to let the words sink in. "As for her work as a journalist, yes, she is Dear Congress, as the media made known yesterday afternoon. The articles she wrote were not in collusion with me. They were an outlet for her after graduation. They were fun. A hobby that received mass acclaim from little-known media outlets such as the *Washington Post*, the *New York Times*, and CNN. Yesterday she quit of her own volition after the editor requested that she continue writing these articles. She didn't quit because of me; she quit because she is getting her PhD and needed more time for her career than for her hobby.

"I implore you to see our relationship for what it is, and not what it is being twisted to mean. Judging someone is easy. Accepting the truth that Liz and I are happy together seems to be much more difficult. So just for the record, Liz Dougherty is the best thing that has ever happened to me, and it is my pleasure to announce that we will be getting married next year." Brady raised his hand to the audience as a signal to them. "Thank you and have a nice day."

The room exploded as everyone seemed to speak at once. But all Liz saw was Brady. She couldn't believe what he had just done, and now she understood why Heather had been arguing with him. She probably hadn't wanted him to be so . . . brash and condescending, but it sent a very clear message. He loved her. They were getting married. Whatever the media hurled at them didn't matter, and he wouldn't tolerate it any longer.

Brady went on to the Q&A section, but Liz didn't need to hear the questions. She took a step away from the entrance with a pleased sigh.

Her phone buzzed in her pocket and she slid it out to check the message.

Are you at the conference?

Hayden. Well, damn. She hadn't heard from him since the start of the summer, when she had accused him of conspiring with Calleigh against her and Brady.

Yeah, I'm here.

She received a reply almost instantly.

Can we meet up?

Yeah, that wasn't going to happen. How would it look to have Brady confess his love for her and that they were getting married, only for her to go meet her ex-boyfriend? Not smart.

I can't. Why?

I have a lead on C.

C. Calleigh. She had almost forgotten that Hayden had agreed to keep his eye on Calleigh and tell her if anything was amiss.

How bad?

There was a pause as she waited.

Nothing concrete yet, but I've overheard a couple times that something is being planned. I'm trying to figure it all out. I only have strong suspicions that I thought I'd tip you off to now. Then y'all could investigate. I'd rather do it in person, though.

Liz chewed on her bottom lip. *I can't meet. If you can, send me what you think now and I'll pass it along.*

Okay.

Liz started to put her phone away, thinking that was the end of the conversation, when it buzzed one more time.

Congratulations on your engagement.

She cringed and got rid of her phone. She knew that he was only being nice, but she could feel his pain in those four words. Hayden had wanted that with her, but it hadn't been in the cards. And he'd had to stand there in the audience while Brady announced their engagement to the world and talked about how much he loved her. She didn't feel bad that Hayden knew, just that it hurt him.

With a heavy sigh, she returned to the opening and stood next to Heather. "How is he doing?" she asked.

"Great. The reporters seemed surprised by his brashness, so they're feeding off of it. I'm going to wrap it up here soon, though."

Liz turned her attention to Brady and the reporter who pushed her way through the crowd to speak. Calleigh Hollingsworth.

"Congressman Maxwell, you refute the claim that Miss Dougherty is the reason for your breakup with Miss Edwards. Yet, you *are* the reason that Miss Dougherty left her boyfriend, are you not?"

"Miss Dougherty was not on good terms with her boyfriend and they broke up as a result of miscommunication."

"I see," Calleigh said. "Miscommunication over the extent of your relationship?"

"Over a past relationship that had no bearing on who she was dating at the time. As much as that relationship has no bearing on the current now," he said curtly.

"And you don't think that she turned to you simply because her previous relationship failed? Or that she is using you . . ."

Brady cut her off with a swift slap to the podium. He still looked calm, but Liz knew him well enough to know that he was actually pissed.

"For the record, I am very much in love with Liz Dougherty. I plan to spend the rest of my life with her. You can keep asking me questions about how we got together and what effect that has if you want, but I don't see how they're pertinent. What matters is that we are together and will remain so."

He shot Calleigh a biting look.

"I just hope if you find yourself in a similar situation, someone doesn't judge you for falling in love."

Chapter 30
SWIFT BOAT

I *have some evidence.*

The text came from Hayden six weeks after the press conference where Brady confessed his love for Liz and told the whole world of their engagement. Since then it had been nonstop action. Between her classes and teaching Monday through Thursday and helping Brady on the campaign Friday through Sunday, Liz was about spent. She enjoyed both aspects of her life, but she felt a bit like a head case.

She was thankful she had Brady, who never showed how overworked he was on the campaign, but she saw his private moments of weariness. If even he was tired from the work, then she was definitely allowed to be.

You're not going to like it.

Great. Liz wasn't looking forward to this conversation. She had been hoping that whatever Hayden had been talking about all those weeks ago had just blown over. She had hoped that Calleigh

Hollingsworth had just gotten over herself and she and Brady could move on with their lives. Apparently not.

Is it serious?

She didn't really want to see Hayden or have him waste her time. But if she thought that whatever Hayden knew would hurt Brady with only two and a half weeks left in the campaign, then she would do whatever it took to make sure that it didn't.

Worse than I thought.

Liz sighed and closed her computer. She wasn't going to get any work done now with all of this swirling around in her head. She was already planning to meet Brady in Durham tomorrow for the Delta Rae show that night. The band was from the area and had come out in support of his campaign. It was going to be really fun, but now she was going to be spending some of that time dealing with this shit.

I'll be in NC tomorrow. There's a show in Durham. That would be the easiest time to meet.

Liz jotted out the information to him and then called Brady to let him know what was going on.

"How do you even know he actually has information?" Brady asked.

"I don't," she said with a sigh. "But do you want to risk it?"

"I'm going to be there when this happens."

"What? No. You know he won't talk if you're around," Liz insisted.

"The guy doesn't even deserve to see your beautiful face, let alone get to talk to you after what happened. I haven't forgotten, and I don't trust him. I need to be there."

Not that she blamed Brady for how he was feeling, but having him around to get vital information from Hayden probably wasn't a good idea. Hayden had enough reason to dislike Brady, just as Brady had reason to dislike Hayden. She would rather avoid the awkward moment of bringing them together. "Shouldn't you be working?" she implored.

"In the middle of the concert?" he asked, exasperated. "I'll be a figurehead at the beginning and end, but they're the main show. It's just my event."

"You're not going to budge on this, are you?"

"No."

Liz sighed. "Okay. Just . . . tell Heather, and figure out a way for Hayden not to be seen coming in and out of the building. We don't need another problem."

⌒

Liz arrived with Brady to the theater later that evening. Brady left Liz in a back room, where the majority of the noise was muffled.

"I have my opening speech and then Heather will bring Hayden backstage to discuss the *supposed* evidence."

Supposed evidence. She knew how much Brady hated this, and he was trying to make light of the situation. Hayden had better have something concrete or she was never going to live this down. Liz had a sinking suspicion that he did, though. He wouldn't have contacted her out of the blue for nothing. Or at least she hoped not.

The wait felt like an eternity, but soon enough she heard the band start their first song. She hadn't realized that she'd been wringing her hands in anticipation. With a deep breath, she tried to calm her nerves and release the tension.

Brady returned to her side. After planting a kiss on her forehead, he leaned back against the wall and crossed his arms. He seemed as though he wanted to be ready in case Hayden tried anything, which she thought was unlikely even if Brady wasn't in the room.

Heather walked in a second later with Hayden on her heels. She firmly closed the door behind them. Liz caught Hayden's eye and saw him assess the situation with a reporter's eye. He shifted from Liz to Brady to Heather and back in a millisecond and his smile dropped.

"Quite a party to do business," Hayden said.

Brady nodded at Heather, who shrugged and left. She would hear the whole thing later. If it made him more comfortable with one less body in the room, then by all means.

Hayden's eyes were trained on Liz. "Is he staying?"

"Yes."

"I see."

"Is there a problem with that?" Brady asked.

"Brady," she murmured softly. "Just leave it."

Hayden just shrugged. "No problem. I guess I shouldn't be surprised."

"What kind of evidence do you have on Calleigh?" Brady asked without further ado.

Liz rolled her eyes to the ceiling with a sigh. "Thank you for agreeing to meet with me today. I don't know what you have, but I'm sure it wasn't an easy decision to decide to let us know."

"It was quite simple," Hayden said, tossing a manila envelope onto the table. "Calleigh ruined everything, and you don't deserve the way she's been treating you. It's personal, not professional. She's getting sloppy, because she's treating it like it's a vendetta rather than an actual reason to attack y'all."

"Well, still . . . thank you." She could feel her cheeks burning under his gaze. She held no lingering feelings for Hayden, but it was clear that he still cared for her. And he was doing this because of that.

"Don't thank me yet. We have to stop her first."

"What exactly are we stopping her from doing?" Brady asked, pushing off of the wall and leaning over the desk.

"The specifics I don't have. I only know what I heard and have gathered from this," he said, pointing at that paperwork. "I overheard Calleigh on the phone a couple times in the past few weeks talking about an ad spot, and Brady's name came up. It was never anything solid, and over the past couple weeks I debated messaging you again to let you know that she was planning something. But you said I needed evidence, and I got you some."

He slid the manila envelope across the table to Liz and Brady. She opened it and saw that there was a small stack of Calleigh's emails. Liz's eyes widened. "How did you get these?"

"Calleigh had a computer glitch one day and came into my office freaking out. She asked me to look at it. When I didn't immediately fix the issue she got irritated and said she was going to see if anyone from IT was back from lunch. I tinkered with the computer a few minutes and got it running again. When everything came back up that email was on the screen. I'd heard Calleigh mention the name Ted before, and I saw that it matched the email address. So, I just printed the whole conversation and hoped that was enough." Hayden sighed. "I've read it all. It doesn't detail exactly what the ad spot is for, but they're filming something negative. And she has a meeting with this Ted person tomorrow in Greensboro."

"Hmmm . . . I have an idea." Both guys looked at her skeptically. "You're not going to like it."

⟶

Liz stood in front of a large gray building, staring up at the small gold plaque that announced it was a production studio. Strange place for a meeting, but a perfect place to film an ad spot. She hoped that she was making the right decision.

Her hair was slicked back into a ponytail and she was wearing dark jeans and a blazer. Her voice recorder was tucked into her front pocket—conveniently hidden from sight. She switched it on before walking inside and felt the familiar flutter of butterflies at what she was about to do.

She squared her shoulders and hoped she looked confident and professional. Then she pulled open the heavy door and walked inside. A receptionist was on hand. Her face was buried in her computer, and from what Liz could gather she was playing a computer game rather than working. Perfect.

"Excuse me," Liz said, drawing the woman's attention.

"Yes. Sorry. How can I help you?"

Liz took a deep breath. "I'm here to see Ted. I have an appointment with Miss Hollingsworth."

The woman checked her computer and seemed to confirm that both Ted and Calleigh were supposed to be here today. "Oh, you're right on time. Ted is already in the studio." The woman stood, waved her card across the door, and opened it for her. "All the way to the back."

Liz thanked her and then quickly passed through the door before the woman could reconsider. She made her way down the hallway. The door was closed, but there was a window that Liz could peek through. There was a guy sitting in a chair who she assumed was Ted, a few cameramen, and a handful of women off to the side. One woman was standing in front of the camera. No one looked familiar. No Calleigh.

As quickly as she could, she pulled out her phone and snapped a few pictures of the room, zooming in on the faces of the people standing around, and then the sign next to the room. It read CT AD SPOT and underneath it LEAD: CALLEIGH HOLLINGSWORTH. CT . . . hmm. Probably *Charlotte Times*. Did the paper know what she was doing or had Calleigh just used their name?

Liz pocketed her phone again and backtracked down the hallway. She peeked into some of the rooms. Most were empty. Few people used a production company on a Sunday afternoon. Where was Calleigh?

She heard the door opening behind her and swiveled. Calleigh stormed through the front entrance, all flowing red hair and tight black clothing. She stopped dead in her tracks when she saw Liz.

"What the fuck are you doing here?" Calleigh demanded.

A smile spread on Liz's face. "We need to talk."

Calleigh glanced uneasily down the hallway to the production studio. "How the hell did you know I would be here? Are you stalking me?"

"No. I just came here to talk to you. Can we have a minute or do you have to be in production?" Liz asked casually.

"What do you know about the production?" she asked, narrowing her eyes.

"Perhaps that's something we could talk about." Liz gestured to a few of the empty rooms.

Calleigh seemed to be deciding whether or not it was worth it to ignore her. "Fine," she muttered, and walked into the nearest room. She plopped down into a chair and Liz took the one opposite her. "So, what is all this about?"

"I could ask you the same thing. You do realize what you're getting yourself involved in, right?" Liz asked.

"I'm not getting involved in anything," Calleigh said, crossing her arms.

"Sure. You know, when this blows up, it's blowing up in your face. You're going to take the fall. Your name is on that door." Liz pointed back out to the hallway.

Calleigh threw her chair back as she stood. "And what do you think, you're some saint coming to warn me?"

"I'm trying to make you see reason. I know you don't care about me or Brady. I know that you'd like nothing more than to see us crash and burn. But I thought maybe by appealing to your sense of self-preservation, you would reconsider your schemes for one moment.

Because I assure you that if you go through with what you're planning . . . you'll crash and burn just as we will."

"At least we'll go down together," Calleigh said mercilessly.

Liz shook her head in disgust. What kind of life was it to live with such desperation for revenge that Liz didn't even deserve? "You want Brady to lose the election."

"Obviously," Calleigh said, rolling her eyes. "He doesn't deserve to be in Congress and you don't deserve to be at his side."

"Don't you think that's up to the people to decide?" Liz asked.

It was Calleigh's turn to crinkle her nose in disgust. "No."

And then Liz remembered the conversation she'd had with Calleigh over two years ago. They had been discussing whether Brady would win, and when Liz had said that she just wanted people to vote, Calleigh had said she would prefer only the educated be allowed, a high school diploma at the minimum, a college degree preferred. She really didn't believe that the people should decide. She was an elitist who thought that the highly educated should be making decisions. Liz thought it was very shortsighted.

"So, you think that by releasing this fabricated ad spot, you're doing the people a favor? All because Hayden wanted me and not you?" Liz asked in shock.

"Don't even bring him into this," Calleigh growled.

"That's what it is. Isn't it? Hayden left you, he and I dated, and then even after we broke up he *still* doesn't want you. So, you're taking it out on me. You should be happy. I'm the one who got you that promotion!" Liz said, laying into her.

"Oh yeah, thanks for being a whore and letting me write about it," Calleigh said cruelly. She walked across the room and got up into Liz's face. "I love how you think everything just revolves around you! You think you're so special. You're not the only one Brady hid. And once I tell the rest of the world, I hope your perfect little world really *does* come crashing down. Then maybe you'll remember who you're messing with."

Liz took a step back, astonished. "That's who those girls are in the production room? Brady's old . . . conquests?"

Calleigh looked hesitant for a moment. She opened her mouth to speak and then closed it, as if she had realized that Liz had baited her into telling her what the ad was about.

"You're getting women to say that he slept with them like me. You're going to make a joke out of our relationship, tarnish his entire reputation, have him lose the election all because of some stupid vendetta. You're sick," Liz whispered.

"He did sleep with these women. The world deserves to know what kind of family man he really is. Do you know how many he has been with since you've been together?" Calleigh asked.

"Yes," Liz answered without a doubt.

"Well, soon the world will too."

"The answer is *zero*."

"Keep telling yourself that."

"You're going to put up an ad with a bunch of women who are going to lie about sleeping with Brady in the last nine months? Because you and I both know that none of those women were with Brady."

Calleigh pushed past Liz to the door. She turned back once more to look at her. "Sometimes the truth doesn't matter," she said, and then exited.

As soon as she was out of the door, Liz palmed her voice recorder and switched it off. "Sometimes the truth will set you free."

Chapter 31
CHANGE

Cease and desist.

Those had never been words that Liz thought she would be happy to hear. But after she had brought the voice recorder and pictures of the production studio back to Brady, Heather, and Elliott, coupled with the emails and Hayden's testimony, they had a pretty solid case. Heather had been pissed to hear what Liz had done, but after listening to the voice recording even she had reluctantly agreed that she was glad that Liz had gone.

The paperwork went out to Calleigh and the *Charlotte Times.* They'd had plausible reason to believe that CT on the door had stood for the paper, and since Calleigh was an employee of the paper, a recognizable name, and she represented them, the campaign wanted to cover their bases. As an unbiased news source, who relied on advertisement money from both sides of the aisle, Liz was sure they weren't going to be happy to hear what had happened.

"Well, I suppose you did the right thing," Brady begrudgingly admitted.

"You seriously doubted me."

"I never want to send you in the line of fire. So many things could have gone wrong."

"Hey, I'm a good reporter. I might have given it up, but I still know the tricks."

He drew her into his arms. "You did good."

"What do you think will happen to her?" she asked after a moment.

"She'll be demoted, but more likely fired."

Calleigh was getting what she deserved. She had even admitted to trying to tear them down for no other reason than because Liz had once had something that she wanted. Even after getting her promotion she hadn't been satisfied. Maybe she would never be satisfied.

Feeling Brady's arms around her, Liz knew that she would never have that problem.

Liz had gotten one of the other teaching assistants to cover her classes and informed her instructors that she would be absent the week before the election. She spent her days walking through neighborhoods, knocking on doors, making phone calls with volunteers, and handing out Vote for Maxwell fliers wherever she could. The poll numbers coming in had everyone on edge. Some numbers showed him down by a percentage point and then up by a percentage point, but either way the win-lose ratio was negligible. It was a perfect toss-up.

Volunteers pushed forward with renewed energy in the last leg of the race, encouraging people to vote down ticket for Brady after they voted for their presidential choice. There was always a tailcoat effect when it came to presidential elections. In a toss-up race, it generally helped the candidate who was of the same political party as the president. But the presidential race seemed to be just as close as the congressional race, so Liz wasn't sure how much impact it would have. She hoped they both came out on top.

Clay and Andrea showed up Thursday afternoon to go canvassing, and asked for clipboards. Liz stared at them. As far as she knew Andrea didn't do anything that involved walking or getting hot, unless you counted hot yoga. And Clay had never supported his brother in anything.

"What's the catch?" she asked as she passed them clipboards.

"No catch," Clay said.

"Do you even know how to canvass?" she asked him.

"Babe, I've been canvassing longer than you've been alive."

"So . . . why are you doing it again?"

He shrugged it off. "It's just what you do."

"Even though you don't agree with your brother?" Liz pushed.

"Just drop it. It's no big deal." He handed Andrea another clipboard and then they left.

Liz was dumbfounded. There were so many sides to Clay Maxwell that she couldn't tell up from down when he was around.

"You know Clay is out canvassing for you?" Liz said when Brady showed up later.

"Yeah."

"I don't get it with you two."

"Campaigning is in our blood. We've been doing it all our lives. He wants to be attorney general one day," Brady said, calm and unconcerned, as if Clay always came around to helping before elections. But maybe it wasn't that he always did it, rather that it was expected of him. Another Maxwell trait.

Savannah showed up every afternoon to help out despite her rigorous coursework and the school paper. Some days Easton would come with her to help, and he joked with Liz about how she needed to come back to tennis lessons. She missed them, but she didn't even have time to plan her own wedding. Tennis was a little farther down the list.

The Saturday before Election Day, Brady addressed an outdoor Halloween festival. Hundreds of people showed up to hear him speak right before the election. Alex always stressed the importance of face-to-face contact. It was the old shaking-hands-and-kissing-babies branding, but it worked. He spent half the day doing just that—speaking to the people. Each contact brought him that much closer to winning the election; each person was one more vote.

When the event was nearing a close, Brady finally returned to her side. He wrapped her in his arms and kissed the top of her head. "Don't tell anyone I'm exhausted."

"I wouldn't dare."

"I still have to talk to the press. Come with me?"

"Of course," she said, taking his hand.

They walked over to the reporters and questions immediately started flying for Brady. He answered them all with his campaign mask firmly in place. No traces of his exhaustion were present. In fact he looked as vibrant and confident as ever.

Heather came to stand at Liz's side as she stood idly by, more as a source of comfort than anything.

"I can't believe it's almost over," Liz mused softly to Heather.

"It'll be back before you know it."

Liz wasn't sure if that was meant as encouragement or not but she let it slide off of her. There were only two more days until Election Day.

"You know," Heather said, "you should go stand up there with him. I bet there are more than a few reporters who wouldn't mind asking you a question or two."

Liz's head whipped so quickly to the side that she got a twinge in her neck. She cringed and massaged the aching spot. What the hell was Heather getting at? "You . . . want me to talk to . . . report-ers?" she stammered, certain she had heard her wrong.

"Do you think that you're not capable?"

"No. Oh no, I do. I just . . . I'm confused."

Heather sighed and then did something miraculous. She smiled at Liz. A real smile. "I believe you've earned that position at his side. I might not always approve of your methods, but they are effective. You stopped a potentially election-threatening scheme from unfurl-ing. You have been with him every step of the way, even when it fatigues you considerably. You help him with his speeches and give him strength when he seems to be flagging. Though no one would know that but you or I. He loves you. The media will learn to love you. Go show them why."

Liz stumbled over a thank-you, too shocked to know whether Heather understood what she was saying. She hadn't thought she would earn Heather's approval for years to come. She had been pre-pared to fight for it. And somehow she had earned it before the end of the election.

She took the few meager steps to stand at Brady's side. The temperature had gradually dropped since they had arrived, and she was glad that she had the blue scarf knotted around her neck and the white peacoat to keep her warm. Raising her chin and pushing her shoulders back, she let Brady's confidence flood through her, warm her, and then she smiled.

He glanced at her with tenderness in his eyes. He didn't have to ask to know that Heather had sent her up here. One nod from him was all she needed to know that she was doing the right thing.

Reporters looked hesitant for a moment, unsure of whether she was taking questions. Brady started talking to the woman standing beside him. Liz waited patiently, not sure whether she should offer first. She had never done this before. Then one reporter stepped for-ward through the throng and stuck his microphone out toward her.

"Miss Dougherty, how did you and the Congressman meet?"

Liz sighed. That was an easy question. She could do this.

"At a press conference. I asked him a particularly troubling question. I don't think he liked me very much," she said with a wink.

The reporter laughed. A few others did too when they realized it was a joke. "Did you start a relationship that night?"

"Oh, no. It wouldn't start until many weeks later. I wasn't interested in getting involved with a state senator, but eventually he changed my mind."

A particularly brave reporter stepped forward. "Was it simply a sexual relationship?"

Liz tried to keep from blushing, but wasn't sure how well she succeeded. She glanced over at Brady and he seemed ready to jump in whenever he was needed. "No," she barely whispered. Then louder. "No. Where my fiancé is concerned it was never purely physical. Next question, please."

The questions turned from their relationship to who she was, what she enjoyed, what she was studying, her dreams and aspirations, and on and on. She was sure details about her life would show up in newspapers all over the country this week. Who was the mysterious Liz Dougherty?

She had once told Brady that the only secret she had was him, and now everyone knew that one. But she was strangely okay with it. Her place was at Brady's side, and she wanted to see him to the White House. *Their* home, as Brady had jokingly called it.

Brady stepped away to do a video interview with a reporter, which Liz suspected would air in clips on the evening news. Her questions kept coming and she was surprised to find how exhausting it was. She had never considered how much work it was just to stand around and answer the incessant questions hurled at her. People were polite, but she couldn't keep from feeling tired. But this was her life now, and she wanted to do her part. After Tuesday, she would return to D.C. to finish the semester and start planning her wedding to marry Brady. The thought strengthened her, and she kept going.

Numbers lessened and it looked as if they were about to close down the Halloween festival when one last reporter started asking Liz questions.

"How do you feel about the accusations of being called a slut, a whore, and a home wrecker?" she asked impassively.

Liz swallowed. She hated those names. They were so false and hurtful. "I'd encourage people to stop using those terms. Brady and I have been together for nine months now. It's quite clear that those things aren't true."

"Nine months," the woman said disapprovingly. "So, then you didn't have his child? Or did you cover it up and have it hidden somewhere?"

Liz sputtered and then tried to collect herself. "No. We don't have a child. I was never pregnant."

"Why do you think that you can direct people as to what they think of you? And do you think it's fair to tell them to stop calling you true names? You did rip apart the Congressman's relationship with Miss Edwards."

"People may think whatever they want, but I did not separate Erin and Brady. They broke up on their own terms months before we ever got back together."

"Do you feel like a sham of a reporter standing here answering questions for your fake relationship?" the woman pushed.

Liz's mouth dropped open. What the hell? How did she even respond to that? Maybe she shouldn't. Maybe she should just say no comment and retreat. The woman was trying to get a reaction out of her. It was tactless.

Before she could speak up, she felt a presence at her side. She was immediately grateful that Brady had returned, but looked up and found Clay. "I'm sorry for interrupting, but I couldn't help overhearing the wonderful conversation you were having. I thought I would answer some of these questions for Liz."

Liz's eyes widened. Oh fuck! That was not a good idea. She shook her head slightly to try to tell him to stop. But he just smiled that wicked grin, a dimple appearing.

"I've had the opportunity to witness Congressman Maxwell's relationship with Liz since the beginning. Or at least almost the beginning," he said with that same arrogant smile for Liz. Then he turned to face the reporter. "And if we're evaluating reporter tactics, maybe you should reevaluate your own professionalism. My brother loves this woman very much. There was no adultery, no home wrecking, nothing distasteful about it at all. They *only* problem was that they fell in love at the wrong time. It's a model relationship. One of commitment, dedication, honesty, and loyalty. Perhaps you should start bothering someone else with these kinds of questions, because there is nothing else to be found on my brother."

Liz openly gaped at him. Where the hell had that come from?

"Thank you. We'll take no more questions," Clay said with a curt wave. He tucked Liz's hand under his arm and then walked her away from the reporters.

When they were out of earshot, Liz finally found her voice. "What was that?"

"I believe I just defended your relationship with Brady to a particularly troubling reporter," he answered.

"Yes. Thank you, but . . . what the hell was that, Clay?"

Clay shrugged and smiled down at her. He still had that uncanny amusement in his expression, but she saw that he was serious too. "What? I'm not completely heartless."

"No. But you don't agree with our relationship, and you certainly don't believe in your brother."

They stopped and Clay turned her to face him. He brushed a strand of hair out of her face and a strange looked passed over his face. "Maybe someone proved me wrong."

"Me?" she whispered.

"No someone else," he said sarcastically. "Of course you. You've changed him. He loves you. There's an . . . energy between you that is hard to explain, but it's there. It's obvious to everyone who knows him. And maybe . . . just maybe it makes me see what you had been telling me all along. Maybe he's actually in this for the right reasons." He paused and glanced off into the distance. "And not just because our father wanted it for him and not me."

Liz felt for an instant as though she finally understood Clay. She could see his life stretched out before him. The second brother with Brady the prodigal son, the golden boy always one step ahead. Maybe he had even once wanted to become a politician. Maybe he had wanted to become president, but his father had encouraged Brady. And Clay's love for both politics and Brady had hardened with time. What would become of the man now that it was finally thawing?

Clay kissed her forehead softly at her clear astonishment. "Be good to him. He needs you."

And then he walked away.

"What was that about?" Brady asked when he appeared at her side a minute later.

"Nothing. Clay just told a reporter off for degrading our relationship and basically endorsed you for Congress."

It was Brady's turn to look startled. "Are we talking about my brother still?"

Liz smiled and nodded. "He loves you. He just doesn't know how to show it."

Brady seemed to ponder this for a moment. "Well . . . I suppose at least we have that in common."

"You have a lot more in common than I think you'll ever realize."

"Well, I'm thankful I have you to realize that for me."

"I'm always going to be here," she told him.

"I sure hope so, or else I'm going to need my ring back," he joked.

Liz slapped her hand over the ring. "You can't have it."

He grabbed her firmly around the middle and kissed her lips feverishly. "Good. You're mine?"

"Always."

He brushed his nose against hers. "It's worth it?"

"You're worth everything," she whispered.

Chapter 32

BRADY

Every Election Day morning growing up, Brady would wake up super early with his family. He would dress with care in what his mother had put out for him the night before. She would make sure he looked presentable, and then the whole family would pile into his father's Mercedes and he would drive them to the polls.

As a child, Brady remembered liking it more than Christmas, even without the presents. The months of anticipation leading up to this one big momentous day for his entire family brought them all closer than they ever were. And every other year, when his dad came home victorious once more, they celebrated—just the four of them, and then when Savannah was born all five of them—before his father went to all the necessary parties.

When Brady got older, he thought that the ritual might diminish—that he would enjoy Election Day less, since it really was so much work, but the small moments with just his family were unlike anything else. As time passed, Clay helped and participated only begrudgingly, and as they grew further and further apart so did Clay's love of the election. Clay saw it as a duty, whereas it remained to Brady a gesture of love and devotion.

Brady remembered the first time that he walked into the voting booth after his eighteenth birthday. He cast his ballot for his father and knew as he had known his whole life that there was nothing else for him. Politics was what he loved more than anything—his greatest joy from his childhood and his deepest ambition as an adult.

All of that had changed with the entrance of Liz into his life. He had never thought that anything could replace his dreams of becoming president. When he had fallen for her, he had fought tooth and nail to keep his life exactly how it was. But he couldn't do that with Liz. Without even meaning to, politics slid down a spot, and she became his number one priority.

Liz was still sleeping when he woke up on Election Day. Her bare chest was pressed firmly against him and her head nuzzled his shoulder. An ache throbbed in his groin at the sight of her nearly naked in his bed. Exactly where she belonged.

He was seeing the spark of a new Election Day tradition.

"Baby," he growled into her ear. He ran his hand demandingly down her side, under the covers, and onto her thigh. She roused softly and he felt himself harden further as her body moved against him.

"Brady," she whispered.

His hand slipped in between her thighs and brushed lightly against the black lace boy shorts she had worn to bed. He preferred when she slept naked, but he couldn't keep himself from wanting to fuck her all night. The panties didn't help all that much, though. He had ruined a few pairs.

"Mornin'," he muttered. He rolled her onto her back and brought his lips down hard on hers. She responded with the fervor that always exploded from their kisses. He couldn't get enough.

"Someone is in a good mood." Her blue eyes were alight and he could see the need evident in them.

He bent down and nipped at her neck. The moan that escaped her lips urged him on. "I love your body." And he let his hands worship the soft, smooth skin of her breasts, down her flat stomach, to her hips.

His thumbs hooked around the boy shorts and he eagerly dragged them to her feet. She squirmed under his scrutiny, but held his gaze, ignoring any self-consciousness. He had forced that out of her. Or maybe he had just opened her up to what was already lying dormant inside of her.

"Make love to me," she whispered.

Fuck! The way she said that. The way she pleaded with her big blue eyes. Begging was a particular weakness for him. And some days he just wanted to fuck her senseless when she opened her mouth and asked for it. But he could make love to her. He wanted to. God, he loved her.

Love sliced through him. It held on tenaciously, never giving up even when he had wanted to give up. It didn't care about the past, present, or future. And every day that he held on to that searing emotion, he felt as though he was finally living.

He kissed up her thighs and she whimpered at the tender caresses. He would take his time with her, savor every inch of skin, her eager pants of pleasure, her body as it responded so perfectly to his commands.

He spread her wide and slowly slid his fingers into her. She was already wet and needing him, tightening around him, trying to fill that ache. He slid in and out and in and out until her eyes rolled back and her body struggled for release. Then, when he felt her dying for it, he leaned forward and flicked his tongue against her clit. Another groan left her mouth, encouraging him, and he feasted on her body until she came apart at the insistence of his mouth.

Then he discarded his boxers and readied himself before her opening. Her eyes fluttered back open when he pushed her legs even farther.

"God, yes," she said in the same breathy voice she got right after orgasm. "Take me."

So he did. He slid his cock all the way into her, grasping her hips in his hands and pushing just a little bit farther.

"Fuck," she cried.

"You feel so fucking good, baby."

He leaned forward over her, brushed her hair out of her face, and brought his lips down to her. They kissed tenderly as he started up an easy sensual motion. He could do this all day. Who needed the election? He had his prize already.

She broke away with a gasp, her body arching back as she tried to get him deeper. "I take it back," she whispered. "Fuck me."

He nipped at her earlobe and thrust once fiercely into her. "I'm sorry. I didn't hear you."

"Please. Please fuck me," she pleaded. She already knew that was what he wanted from her. "God, I want you."

"Like this?" he crooned, starting up a quick pace. Their bodies slammed together. All he could hear was her encouraging pants, and the smacks of skin on skin.

She bit out one word. "Harder."

Well, he could fucking oblige her.

He grabbed her leg, threw it onto his shoulder, and then pushed into her deeper. The feel of her so tight around him nearly made him lose it, but he wasn't going to finish without her. She was so damn close. He thought she might come at any moment, and he loved to get her at least twice.

"I love you," she said, reaching out and digging her nails into his shoulders.

"I love you too, baby."

He felt the tension burst out of her as she pulsed around him. He had no control in that moment. She sucked the life right out of him. He grunted, collapsing over on top of her as he emptied himself within her beautiful body.

They lay like that together until it was clear that their busy schedule was going to interfere with Brady's request for round two. After a quick shower, Brady put on a fresh suit with his favorite blue tie. Liz appeared out of the bathroom like a vision. Her wavy hair had been straightened, her blue eyes were bright, and the white dress she had chosen was modest but fit her perfectly. He knew what was lying underneath it and he couldn't wait to get his hands back on it.

He pulled her toward him. "Your mother was right. You look great in white." She blushed at the compliment. "I can't wait to see you walking down the aisle toward me on our wedding day."

"You're just excited about the lingerie afterward."

"I'm excited for you to become my wife and take my name," he said, running his finger around the diamond ring on her hand. "We have the rest of our lives for everything else."

He kissed her tenderly before they exited the house together. He wouldn't have minded taking the town car to the polling location, but following tradition, they got into his Lexus and drove into town.

A camera crew greeted them when they arrived. Brady had warned Liz that one would likely be there to ask a few questions after he cast his ballot. Standard protocol.

"So," he whispered as they got into line behind a little old woman with a cane. "Who do you plan to vote for?"

Liz giggled and shook her head. "You're silly."

He raised an eyebrow.

"You, of course," she said, shaking her head.

"Oh good. I need every vote."

Liz laughed and walked in front of him to cast her ballot. Brady took his own card from the poll worker and walked into the voting booth. He stared down at his name with a sigh. He hoped he never got used to the feeling of seeing his name there. It should never be commonplace to have the people vote for him. He wanted to win, but it was a privilege earned, not a right.

He filled out the card, punching his name last, and then exited the voting booth. A woman handed him an *I'm a North Carolina voter* sticker with a toothy grin. He slapped it proudly on his suit and then walked outside.

Liz was waiting for him. She looked giddy from the experience. "I just did my civic duty," she told him triumphantly, pointing at her own sticker.

He leaned forward and whispered in her ear. "And here I thought you did that this morning."

She blushed and smacked him lightly on the shoulder. "Brady Maxwell."

"At your service."

"Congressman Maxwell," a reporter called, interrupting them. "Mind if we have a word with you?"

"Of course not," he said amicably.

He walked over to where the reporters were standing and answered their questions. It felt good to be free. He had cast his ballot, and he had done everything that he could to ensure his victory. There were volunteers out right now trying to get people to the polls, and there would be people doing that until the polls closed.

He had a busy day ahead of him to get out the vote, but he did it cheerfully. If he couldn't be out there with his supporters to get the word out, why would they bother?

The day passed in an exuberant blur. Everyone was in an incredible mood. The city was alight with the buzz of Election Day. Whether it was volunteers eager to help where they could or just the everyday citizen happy that the campaign signs would come down, their voice mails would stop being filled with chatter, and the television would be free of advertisements, there was something in the air that day.

It was nearly poll close when Brady and Liz retreated to head-quarters to wait out the reports. Liz was exceptionally quiet and lost in thought as information came back to them from the field confirming his victory or loss of a particular precinct.

"So . . . where do we stand?" Liz finally asked. He realized that she looked nervous.

"We're down," he told her. He had seen the look in Alex's eyes without even tallying what had come in.

"It'll be a toss-up," Alex corrected. "It'll come down to the wire again. Hopefully we have the votes. You two should get ready for the party tonight."

Brady nodded and Liz just chewed on her bottom lip. "What's going on in that pretty head of yours?"

She turned her head from him and seemed lost in thought. "If you lose, it's my fault," she whispered.

"Is that what you're worried about?" he asked with a laugh. He grasped her chin and forced her to look at him. "If I lose, it's because the people of North Carolina in the Fourth District didn't want me to represent them. That's the only reason. Nothing you or I could do would change that. All right?"

"But . . ."

"No. I'm not going to let you take the blame. If I lose, it's on me," he told her earnestly. "But I haven't lost yet."

"I know. But . . ."

"Let's wait until the final results are tallied and then start talk-ing blame."

"Sorry," she said, shaking her head. "I guess I'm just worried."

His hand brushed back into her hair and then he kissed away every worry in her head. She had become his rock, his strength. He could give her some of what she always gave him when he got stressed out.

When he pulled back, she was unsteady on her feet, her lips slightly swollen, and a blush crept onto her face. "How do you do that?" she whispered.

"What?"

"Make me lose myself so completely with you."

"Only giving you a taste of your own medicine."

She smiled up at him and he was lost all over again. He wasn't sure how he had ever thought that he could live without that smile. He knew that tonight was a big night for them. They had come out to the public about their relationship in February, knowing the consequences that might await him in November. Tonight they would find out if those consequences materialized.

———

Brady changed into a fresh black suit and knotted a navy tie with tiny red-and-white polka dots around his neck. He hadn't thought it would be possible for him to be more nervous about getting the results in the second time he ran for Congress than the first. He had been in such an overwhelming state of depression when he had won two years ago that even though he had been nervous, his thoughts had automatically turned toward Liz. Wondering if he should have gone after her, wondering what she was doing, wondering if he had made the right decision.

Now he was on the precipice at the end of his first term, and similar questions plagued him. He was glad he had finally gone after her, and he knew that he had made the right decision. He just hoped that hadn't cost him his job. Not that he would change a damn thing if he could do it over. She was worth it all.

Liz appeared in the entryway in a knee-length purple pleated dress he'd ordered for her from New York, and her Jimmy Choos.

Around her neck hung the necklace he had gotten her so long ago. Diamond drops in her ears and a massive diamond ring on her finger told that she was all his. She would always be his.

"Are you ready?" she asked, her nerves from earlier already dissipated. She looked like strength, wearing what she called his campaign mask as if she had invented it.

He had always said that politics was a perfect balance of openness and restraint. It was what he loved so much about Liz. She had restraint in spades, but when she let go, it shook his world. She did everything with such unbridled tenacity, and went after the things she wanted headfirst, with a self-assurance that he had seen in few people.

"Very," he replied.

"We should go. Everyone is probably waiting."

"I'm so honored to have you at my side," he told her.

"Honored?" she asked, raising an eyebrow.

"Yes. You are the most amazing woman I've ever met," he said, closing the distance between them. "It's an honor to have you there with me."

"Well . . . I'm honored to be there."

"I've been thinking a lot about how we started." He fingered the necklace dangling between her breasts. She narrowed her eyes. "I know that it wasn't the best of scenarios, but it brought you into my life. We might be unconventional, but who needs convention? I fell in love with you. You stole me away, and I'm glad that you didn't give me back."

"Never," she insisted.

"Good. Now let's go win an election." He kissed her lips and then they exited the house together.

A town car drove them to the grand hotel downtown, where Brady's election party would be in full swing in one of their massive ballrooms. His friends and family were congregated in a small reception room, where they would receive the news. Everyone he cared about was in attendance, just the way it had always been. Liz had even included Victoria and Daniel in the festivities. Chris was there with his family. Brady kept a close eye on Lucas, whom he still didn't trust near his sister. Luckily, Savannah had brought her boyfriend, Easton. The guy seemed all right. Had a good head on his shoulders.

His mother and father greeted them when they walked into the room. His father wouldn't be up for reelection until next term, and it was nice to have his constant presence here for him during the hardest two elections of Brady's career.

Heather and Elliott appeared next, as serious and reserved as ever. But he knew them well enough to know that they were nervous but excited. They wanted him to win. They had staked their careers on it. They were two of his closest friends.

In just a few minutes he would find out if it had all been worth it.

Liz wandered off to talk to Victoria and Savannah. They fawned over her dress and giggled about nonsensical things. He was glad they were there for her. He knew that she was as stressed and nervous about the outcome as he was.

Heather looked as though she wanted to say something, but he just smiled. "Excuse me for a minute."

She nodded and returned to her conversation with Elliott. There was something he probably should have done a long time ago, but the election had gotten in the way.

He approached his brother, who was sitting there seemingly bored by whatever his girlfriend was going on about. Clay turned his gaze to meet Brady's and his brother scowled.

"Andrea, do you think you could give us a minute?" Brady asked.

"Uh . . . sure. Whatever," she said, grabbing her cocktail and walking away.

"Did you need something?" Clay asked. He already looked bored again.

Brady stuck his hand out. "I wanted to thank you for helping me."

Clay stared down at his outstretched hand as if it might attack him. "Is this some kind of joke?"

"No. Thank you for your time and especially for what you did for Liz. I really appreciate it."

Clay tentatively put his hand into Brady's and they shook. "Well, she needed the help."

"I know. Usually she doesn't."

"That's the truth," Clay agreed.

They dropped their hands and Clay stood awkwardly, as if he was waiting for Brady to lay into him for something.

"You know, this morning I was thinking about when we were younger and how Election Day used to be like Christmas."

"Are we going to go into one of your stories?" Clay jeered.

Brady ignored him. It was just Clay's usual sidestep. "We'd wake up early and go to the polls with our parents even before Savannah was born. We'd get ice cream at the victory after-party. As we got older something changed between us. I know it might not be salvageable, but hope that one day we can change that."

Clay stared at him blankly for a few seconds. Brady thought that he might laugh in his face and tell him to fuck off. Typical Clay. But after a minute he nodded. "I think I'd like that."

They shook hands again, and a bond that Brady hadn't felt since they were kids flowed between them. He hadn't realized until that moment how much he had missed Clay.

He turned to return to Liz's side. "What was that about?" she asked. She never missed a thing.

"Making amends like I should have done years ago."

A bright smile broke out onto her face, and she was about to say something when the doors to the reception room opened.

Everyone turned to face the front as Alex walked inside. His nose was buried in his iPad like always.

When he looked back up at his audience, Brady felt as if all of the air had been sucked out of the room in anticipation. Then Alex's eyes sought his in the crowd and he smiled. "Congratulations, Congressman! You're in for another term."

Brady scooped Liz into his arms and swung her around as a cheer rose up from the room. Everyone was hugging, applauding, and cheering his victory. He had done it. Against all odds, he had won a second term.

"Congratulations," Liz whispered into his ear. "How do you feel?"

"Like I'm on top of the world," he admitted. "How do *you* feel?"

"Like I'm on the top of the world with you."

"Every day for the rest of our lives."

Epilogue

TWELVE YEARS LATER

Jefferson, if you do not stop tormenting your sister I won't let you have ice cream after the conference," Liz snapped at her nine-year-old son. He was the spitting image of his father, but had the devilish tendencies of his uncle.

"I wasn't doing anything," he said. He put his hands behind his suit as if he were innocent.

Liz bent down and wiped the tears from her daughter's face. "It's all right, Jacqueline. Jefferson will apologize. He didn't mean it."

"He did mean it! He *hates* me," the five-year-old girl cried dramatically. Her blond hair fell in curls past her shoulders and seemed to be perpetually knotted, but her big blue eyes kept Brady wrapped around her little finger.

"He doesn't hate you. Do you?" Liz asked. She looked warningly at her son. "Jefferson?"

"I don't hate you, Jackie," he said, rolling his eyes to the ceiling. Well, that would have to do.

"All better?" she asked her daughter.

She sniffled twice and then nodded. "Do I still get ice cream?"

"Yes. Of course you do. Now, are you ready to join your father? It's a big day," Liz said with a bright smile for both of them.

Liz straightened and ran her hands down the front of her cream-and-navy dress. Her hair was twisted back into a conservative bun. She took a deep breath and then urged the kids forward. Big day indeed.

"Jeff, will you hold my hand?" Jacqueline asked, widening her blue eyes.

"Girls are gross."

"I'm a sister, though."

Liz was about to intervene, but Jefferson sighed and stretched his hand out. "Fine."

They walked hand in hand into the conference center. Staff were milling around with their heads buried in computers, signaling to one another, and otherwise looking frantic. A representative ushered them across the room. Liz's eyes locked with Heather's when she spotted her and she smiled.

Heather shuffled through the crowd with ease and dismissed the other representative with a flick of her wrist. "Liz, so glad you're here." She bent down, ruffled Jefferson's hair, and gave little Jacqueline a quick hug.

"How is he?" Liz asked.

"Oh, you know. The same," Heather said with a shrug. "Excited to see you and the kids."

"We would have been here sooner, but I had that symposium," Liz told her, which wasn't really necessary since Heather knew Liz's schedule as well as Brady's by now. She had graduated with her doctorate from the University of Maryland and accepted a position in the Journalism School at UNC Chapel Hill. She had spent the last seven years working with her mentor, Professor Mires, at the university.

"Of course. Well, he's waiting for you," she said and then started leading Liz back to Brady's room.

Heather knocked twice and then entered. "I brought you something."

Brady's head popped up from the cards he was reading and he broke out into a smile. "Nothing better in the world."

"Daddy!" the kids screamed, launching themselves across the room.

Brady hoisted them into his arms and planted firm kisses on both of their cheeks. "I've missed you two like crazy."

"We missed you too," Jefferson said.

"Yeah, Daddy," Jacqueline said. "Mom promised us ice cream, though."

Brady glanced up at Liz and her body melted at the sight. He arched an eyebrow. "Bribes, baby?"

"Ice cream is tradition. You know that."

"Of course. What flavor do you want?" Brady placed Jefferson on his feet and planted Jacqueline in his lap. "Huh, pretty girl?"

"Chocolate!" she cried.

"Chocolate it is!" Brady said. "Jefferson?"

"Cookie dough."

"My favorite," Liz said, walking up behind him and straightening out his hair back in place.

Liz's and Brady's eyes met, and she felt herself relax all over again. The past twelve years had been good to them. Though their two beautiful children, Brady Jefferson IV and Jacqueline Marilyn, would always be their greatest accomplishment in life, they had so much to be thankful for. Brady had spent two more terms in the House of Representatives before serving two four-year terms as governor of North Carolina. The commute between Chapel Hill and Raleigh had been much easier on them than to and from D.C.

"How long will we have after this?" she asked him while the kids debated ice cream flavor choices.

"I negotiated the rest of the week. I thought we could take the kids to the lake house."

"They'd like that."

"Should we bring a babysitter?" he asked with a wink.

She laughed softly. "Might not be a bad idea, knowing you."

"And I'm the only one?"

She couldn't keep a coy smile from her face. "Of course not."

"I love you," he said, leaning forward and kissing her lips.

"I love you too." She reached out and straightened his blue tie. "You're going to be wonderful."

"With you at my side."

Heather walked back into the room at that moment. "Brady, it's time."

"Come on, kids," Liz said, ushering them behind their father.

They reached the entrance to the stage and Liz saw the massive crowd that had come out that day to hear Brady speak. Tears welled in her eyes and she tried to push them down. This was a happy day. They had been looking forward to this for a long time.

Liz already knew the drill after so many years of being a politician's wife. Press conferences and rallies had become second nature. She felt the time approaching and gave Brady a big hug.

"Wish me luck," he whispered.

"You don't need it."

"You're the best thing that ever happened to me."

"I know. I'm so proud of you," she said, laughing lightly. "I'll always be your airplane."

He kissed her cheek. "That's right. Airplanes, baby."

She swallowed the lump in her throat and then pulled back from her husband. She gave him an encouraging smile and then she heard it.

"Governor Brady Maxwell!"

The crowd roared all around them and Brady stepped out onto the stage. Liz followed close behind with the kids holding her hands. They stood on the stage to the left of Brady, who immediately launched into his prepared speech.

Liz let her eyes drift over the crowd. It was filled to the brim. She would never get tired of the cheers that ran through the crowd. *Max-well. Max-well. Max-well.* It was a chant that never failed to bring a smile to her face. A chant that she had once associated with her husband's success now she associated with *their* success. She was a Maxwell too, after all.

Brady was coming to the close of his speech and he gestured to her. She smiled and walked forward with the kids. Brady took her hand in his and smiled down at their children.

A lifetime of politics leading up to this one moment.

Brady's strong voice carried through the speakers. Liz sighed when she finally heard him utter the words she had been waiting for since she had met him all those years ago.

"I am Governor Brady Maxwell, and I'm running for President of the United States."

ACKNOWLEDGMENTS

From the beginning, I've thought about these books as three parts—Part I, the Campaign, Part II, Postcampaign, and Part III, Reelection. As a campaign worker myself, I've experienced all three of these parts of life and tried to interject the feelings inherent in each of these sections into the books. The Campaign is a whirlwind of energy and excitement. Postcampaign elicits what we jokingly refer to as PCSD, Postcampaign Stress Disorder. After living for months with one objective in mind, you find yourself lost, stressed, and inactive. Reelection comes around and you get the itch to go back and work on a campaign, to feel that vibe all over again.

In a way, I feel as if this encompasses Brady and Liz's relationship in the same way that it is significant to someone who works on campaign. So, I must thank all the people who kept me alive to live through all three parts of this experience, and to inevitably use those experiences to write the Record series. Thank you—Meera, Gregg, Alex, Hannah, Daniel, Kiran, Susan, and so many more!

Without a number of people in the industry this book would have never existed. I'd like to thank my agent, Jane Dystel, for finding me a happy home with Montlake Romance, and my editor, JoVon Sotak, for believing in the story and working with me.

To early readers who helped me get through this book—you are my rock stars! Jessica, Bridget, Trish, and Rebecca—you were all there when I needed you most. <3 you guys!

And of course, my fiancé, Joel, who put up with me while I was writing and watched our puppies.

Most of all—to my readers! Thank you for loving Brady Maxwell and wanting more of his story with Liz. I hope you enjoyed their happy ending and are picturing them blissful on their journey to the White House!

ABOUT THE AUTHOR

K.A. Linde grew up a military brat traveling the United States and Australia. While studying political science and philosophy at the University of Georgia, she founded the Georgia Dance Team, which she still coaches. Postgraduation, she served as campus campaign director for the 2012 presidential campaign at UNC Chapel Hill. She is the author of ten novels, including five in the Avoiding series and three in the Record series. An avid traveler, reader, and bargain hunter, K.A. lives in Athens, Georgia, with her fiancé and two puppies, Riker and Lucy.